Gregor Weichbrodt
I Don't Know

Frohmann Verlag / 0x0a

Gregor Weichbrodt is part of the writers' collective 0x0a.
More info at www.ggor.de and www.0x0a.li

This is a Frohmann Verlag and 0x0a project, released in 2016.
http://frohmann.orbanism.com

© 2016 by Gregor Weichbrodt and Frohmann Verlag, Christiane Frohmann

Sources: Wikipedia, "Articles for deletion", 2006/12/16 – 2016/09/14.
Cover design and layout: Gregor Weichbrodt

ISBN Paperback: 978-3-3944-195-60-5

Das Werk, einschließlich seiner Teile, ist urheberrechtlich geschützt. Jede Verwertung ist ohne Zustimmung des Verlages und des Autors unzulässig. Dies gilt insbesondere für die elektronische oder sonstige Vervielfältigung, Übersetzung, Verbreitung und öffentliche Zugänglichmachung.

Die Deutsche Nationalbibliothek verzeichnet diese Publikation in der Deutschen Nationalbibliografie; detaillierte bibliografische Daten sind im Internet über http://dnb.d-nb.de abrufbar.

Contents

I Don't Know 5

About this book 248

I Don't Know

I'm not well-versed in Literature. Sensibility – what is that? What in God's name is An Afterword? I haven't the faintest idea.
And concerning Book design, I am fully ignorant. What is 'A Slipcase' supposed to mean again, and what the heck is Boriswood? The Canons of page construction – I don't know what that is. I haven't got a clue. How am I supposed to make sense of Traditional Chinese bookbinding, and what the hell is an Initial?
Containers are a mystery to me. And what about A Post box, and what on earth is The Hollow Nickel Case? An Ammunition box – dunno. Couldn't tell you.
I'm not well-versed in Postal systems. And I don't know what Bulk mail is or what is supposed to be special about A Catcher pouch.
I don't know what people mean by 'Bags'. What's the deal with The Arhuaca mochila, and what is the mystery about A Bin bag? Am I supposed to be familiar with A Carpet bag? How should I know? Cradleboard? Come again? Never heard of it. I have no idea. A Changing bag – never heard of it.
I've never heard of Carriages. A Dogcart – what does that mean? A Ralli car? Doesn't ring a bell. I have absolutely no idea. And what the hell is Tandem, and what is the deal with the Mail coach?
I don't know the first thing about Postal system of the United Kingdom. Please don't talk to me about The Postcode Address File.
I also don't know about Postcodes in the United Kingdom. And I have never been to The London postal district.
I definitely don't know anything about Post towns in postcode areas covering London. Do people even go to London?
I'm also not conversant with Arthurian locations. Camelot – how should I know what that is?
Mythological kingdoms, empires, and countries are unfamiliar to me. Shambhala – doesn't ring a bell. Kingdom of Saguenay – I don't know how to begin. I haven't the foggiest idea. Shangri-La, is that even a thing?

I'm not familiar with Life extension. Sierra Sciences – I don't understand that. What in the world is Cryonics? Wouldn't know. I'm completely ignorant of Privately held companies based in Nevada. I don't have any idea what Cashflow Technologies is. Where is Barton's Club 93? I just don't know about that. I also have no clue what 3G Studios is.

I haven't kept up on Video game companies of the United States. ESim Games – I don't understand this. What, in the name of all that is holy, is Reaxion, and what is Industrial Toys anyway? Damned if I know. I also have no idea what UFO Interactive Games is.

I also couldn't tell you what Companies based in Sunnyvale, California are about. I couldn't tell you about SearchFox.

I don't know any Software companies of the United States. Brandlive – not my area of expertise.

And I'm not hip to Companies based in Portland, Oregon. What's up with CD Baby? And what is Glass Alchemy? I don't have any idea. Stumptown Coffee Roasters – don't know.

Don't ask me about Articles created via the Article Wizard. Don't ask me what The Ryerson Index is. I'm also certain that I've never heard of Shaista Khan Mosque or what the deal with The Speckled Chub is. I haven't the remotest idea. I don't have any idea who Martin Heydt is. Concerning Australian websites, I am fully ignorant. Oneflare – I don't know what that is. And what is Blackle? What the hell?

I'm not well-versed in Energy conservation. I don't know what Energy-Efficient Ethernet is or how I'm supposed to know something about A Low-energy house.

I don't know what people mean by 'A Building'. Builders' rites – not my field. Earthbag construction – I don't even know where to start. No idea.

I also know nothing about Construction trades workers. I'm sorry, did you say 'A Plasterer'?

Crafts are a mystery to me. The American Craft Council – never heard of it. A Craft – dunno. I can't tell you that.

And I don't know the first thing about Educational organizations based in the United States. Czechoslovak Society of Arts and Sciences? Doesn't ring a bell.

I surely don't know anything about Slovak-American history. The Greek Catholic Union of the USA – I don't know how to begin. I've never heard of Rusyn-American history. What the fuck is Rusyn American, and what is The American Carpatho-Russian Orthodox Diocese supposed to be? Can you tell me how to get to Byzantine Catholic Eparchy of Phoenix, St. Michael the Archangel Ukrainian Catholic Church or Saint Anne Byzantine Catholic Church? Doesn't sound remotely familiar.

Ukrainian-American culture in Maryland is unfamiliar to me. The History of the Ukrainians in Baltimore? How should I know? I don't know about Ukrainian-Jewish culture in the United States. And I have no clue where The Alliance Colony was. I have no idea where Woodbine Brotherhood Synagogue or Young Men's and Young Women's Hebrew Association Building is. I have no clue.

And I haven't the foggiest notion what Properties of religious function on the National Register of Historic Places in New Jersey are about. Evangelical Lutheran Church of Saddle River and Ramapough Building, Richwood Methodist Church, Mays Landing Presbyterian Church or Rockaway Valley Methodist Church, is that even a real place?

I'm not familiar with Hamilton Township, Atlantic County, New Jersey. The Atlantic County Institute of Technology – I don't understand that.

I haven't kept up on Public high schools in Atlantic County, New Jersey. What the shit is Hammonton High School?

I'm also completely ignorant of Hammonton, New Jersey. What is 'Plagido's Winery' supposed to mean, and what is the idea with The Early November?

I'm not conversant with American emo musical groups. I have no clue what Alesana is or what on earth The Hated was or what people say about it. What in God's name is From First to Last, and what's Mortimer Nova got to do with it? I just don't know. Please don't talk to me about Tickle Me Pink.

I'm not hip to Musical quintets. Burning the Masses – what is that? What's the deal with Datarock, and what in tarnation is Hinder? Search me. I have no idea what The Trinity Band is or what in tarnation Iwrestledabearonce is or if the whole concept makes sense to me.

I couldn't tell you what Death metal musical groups from California are about. Deeds of Flesh – doesn't ring a bell.

Concerning Computers and the environment, I am fully ignorant. Green computing – I don't understand this. The Climate Savers Computing Initiative – not my area of xpertise. Couldn't say. Power management – don't know.

I'm also not well-versed in Sustainable technologies. What is 'Energy technology' supposed to mean again, and what is A Windpump? Am I supposed to be familiar with A Geothermal heat pump? Come on. Don't ask me what A Laddermill is. Ask someone who knows something. Environmentally friendly? Come again? Never heard of it. And don't ask me about Heat pumps. Applications of the Stirling engine – I don't know what that is. I don't know what The Vortex tube is or what the hell it has to do with A Heat pump. Don't ask me. The Stoddard engine – what's that supposed to mean? I'm clueless about that. Entropy production – not my field.

I don't know any Hot air engines. What about The Crookes radiometer?

I also don't know the first thing about External combustion engines. The Minto wheel – never heard of it. A Stirling engine – what does that mean? Not a clue.

I certainly know nothing about Articles containing video clips. I don't have any idea what Gertie the Dinosaur is or what The White-legged Damselfly is about. I couldn't tell you about Lonchaeidae. I just don't know.

I definitely don't know what people mean by 'Black-and-white films'. And I'm certain that I've never heard of The Wedding Guest.

I surely don't know anything about American drama films. What the hell is Johnny Comes Flying Home, and what the heck is Woman Trap? A Rich Man's Plaything – how should I know what that is? I just don't know that. The Altar Stairs? Doesn't ring a bell. I have no idea. How am I supposed to make sense of Broadway Lady?

I've never heard of American silent feature films. What in the world is Bolshevism on Trial, and what the hell was Nice People? What's up with The Face in the Fog, and what on earth is The Corbett-Fitzsimmons Fight? I haven't the slightest idea. I'm sorry, did you say 'The Cinema Murder'?

Lost films are a mystery to me. What, in the name of all that is holy, is Moby Dick—Rehearsed?

Films based on plays are unfamiliar to me. What is Boudu Saved from Drowning?

And I'm not familiar with Films directed by Jean Renoir. What the fuck is The Amazing Mrs. Holliday, and what is the mystery about The Woman on the Beach?

I don't know about RKO Pictures films. Rachel and the Stranger, is that even a thing?

I also haven't kept up on Films based on short fiction. Johanna Enlists – I don't understand that. Holiday Affair – I don't know how to begin. I have absolutely no idea. I have no clue what The Gay Falcon is or what the current state of research is on The Cathedral or if it's good to know. I haven't the foggiest idea. Dawn on the Great Divide – doesn't ring a bell.

And I'm not hip to American crime thriller films. Murder in New Hampshire: The Pamela Wojas Smart Story – I don't understand this. One False Move – dunno. I just don't know about that. What the shit is A History of Violence?

I haven't the foggiest notion what New Line Cinema films are about. Hall Pass – not my area of expertise. Living Out Loud – I don't even know where to start. I haven't the faintest idea. I also have no idea what Short Cuts is.

I'm not conversant with Films directed by the Farrelly brothers. What in God's name is Dumb and Dumber?

I'm completely ignorant of Films set in Colorado. Please don't talk to me about City Slickers. 5 Card Stud – what is that? How should I know? What is 'Beerfest' supposed to mean again, and what is Christo's Valley Curtain about?

I couldn't tell you what Films featuring a Best Supporting Actor Academy Award winning performance are about. Django Unchained – don't know. I don't know what The Fighter is or why people are so interested in Goodfellas. I definitely don't have any idea.

I don't know any Films about Italian-American organized crime.
Am I supposed to be familiar with The Last Don? And what is 'The Godfather' supposed to mean, and what is The Big Heist again? Wouldn't know.
And concerning Screenplays by Mario Puzo, I am fully ignorant.
What about Superman II, and what is the deal with Superman II: The Richard Donner Cut?
I don't know the first thing about Superman films. What's the deal with Return of Mr. Superman?
Don't ask me about Indian films. Bhool Bhulaiyaa – never heard of it. What the hell is Nee Thodu Kavali? Couldn't tell you.
I also know nothing about Indian film remakes. Biwi No.1 – what does that mean? Namma Preethiya Ramu? Come again? Never heard of it. I can't tell you that.
I've never heard of Films about disability in India. How am I supposed to make sense of Vaada Raha?
I'm not well-versed in Hindi-language films. Sheikh Chilli – how should I know what that is?
I don't know anything about People from Derby. Terrashima? How should I know? Who is this Tony Hateley guy? What the hell? And do I need to know who Thomas Roe, 1st Baron Roe, Patricia Greene or Bhavesh Patel is?
I'm not familiar with Birmingham City F.C. players. And who on earth was George Getgood? Who the shit is Trevor Hockey? I haven't the remotest idea. I have no clue who Keith Bannister or Arthur Samson is.
I also don't know about Southampton F.C. players. I've never heard of a person called Djamel Belmadi or Paul Baker.
Algerian expatriates in Qatar are unfamiliar to me. Who is Messaoud Berkous?
Algerian handball players are a mystery to me. And who the fuck is Fatiha Iberaken, Souhila Benaicha or Souhila Abdelkader?
I certainly haven't kept up on Living people. And who the hell is Michaël Cordier, Avishay Braverman, Chiaki Kyan or Neal Kedzie?
I'm not conversant with Israeli Labor Party politicians. Is Baruch Kamin famous or something? I also don't know who Baruch Osnia

was. No idea. Are Hagai Meirom, Haneh Hadad or Zvi Nir famous or something?
I'm not hip to Israeli educators. Amos Bar – who was that? I have no idea who Eliyahu Moyal was. Damned if I know. What's up with Akram Hasson, Nawaf Massalha or Yaron Ezrahi?
I frankly couldn't tell you what Moroccan Jews are about. And I don't have any idea who Moshe Ivgy is.
I don't know any Israeli people of Moroccan descent. I also don't know anything about Maor Asor, Guy Tzarfati, Moshe Abutbul, Avital Abergel or Asaf Ben-Muha.
I also haven't the foggiest notion what F.C. Ashdod players are about. And who is this Murad Abu Anza, Assi Tubi, Amir Ben-Shimon, Gaëtan Varenne or Yaniv Ben-Nissan guy?
I'm completely ignorant of Jewish footballers. Dror Kashtan – doesn't ring a bell. Who the shit is Árpád Orbán? I just don't know.
And don't ask me about Hapoel Petah Tikva F.C. managers. Am I supposed to know Freddy David?
I also don't know what people mean by 'Israeli footballers'. I have no clue who Alon Buzorgi or Salim Tuama is.
I also know nothing about Hapoel Haifa F.C. players. I've never heard of a person called Muayan Halaili.
And concerning Israeli Premier League players, I am fully ignorant. Tamir Ben Ami, Hen Dilmoni, Udo Fortune, Schwenck or Almog Cohen – who are they?
People from Nuremberg are a mystery to me. And I have no clue who Matthias Kessler or Hans Dürer is.
And don't ask me about German expatriates in Poland. I also have no idea who Christian Hefenbrock, Uwe Schneider or Mordecai Mokiach is.
And I'm not hip to Germany under-21 international footballers. Who on earth is Bernd Korzynietz or Patrick Herrmann?
Germany B international footballers are unfamiliar to me. Christian Gentner – doesn't ring a bell.
I've never heard of German footballers. Is Willi Kund famous or something? I don't know who Markus Reiter or Marco Weißhaupt is. Not a clue.

I don't know anything about SpVgg Greuther Fürth players. Do I need to know who Sven Boy, Borut Mavrič, Thomas Pledl, Christian Eigler or Eduardo Gonçalves de Oliveira is?
I haven't the foggiest notion what Brazilian expatriates in South Korea are about. Are Rafael Costa, André Luís Alves Santos, Rodrigo Fernandes Valete, Eduardo Francisco de Silva Neto or Renato Medeiros famous or something?
I know nothing about Seongnam FC players. I've also never heard of a person called Oh Seung-Bum.
I definitely don't know about K League players. Who the shit is Joo Jae-Duk, Lee Lim-saeng, Hong Chul, Jasmin Agić or Lee Ji-nam?
And I'm not familiar with Dankook University alumni. Who is Danny Ahn, Jeon Sang-Wook, Lee Yo-won, Oh Seung-hwan or Park Seok-jin?
I also don't know what people mean by 'South Korean female models'. Who the hell is Na Ree, Shin Hyun-bin, Yoo In-young or Heo Ga-yoon?
Concerning Miss Korea winners, I am fully ignorant. I don't have any idea who Kim Joo-ri, Lee Seong-hye, Oh Hyun-kyung or Kim Joo-hee is.
I'm not conversant with People from Seoul. Sook-Ja Oh – who is that?
I haven't kept up on South Korean composers. Who is this Lee Ha-na or Bahnus guy?
I don't know any South Korean film actresses. Who the fuck is Kim Young-ae, Lee Se-young, Park Ye-jin, Kim Ji-mee or Kim Hyo-jin?
I don't know the first thing about South Korean television actresses. What's up with Kang Hye-jung, Lee Mi-sook, Jo Bo-ah, Kim Yoo-jung or Seo Young-hee?
I couldn't tell you what South Korean stage actors are about. Am I supposed to know Song Ok-sook, Byun Hee-bong, Lee Young-ah or Ra Mi-ran?
Chung-Ang University alumni are a mystery to me. I have no idea who Park Geun-hyung is.
And I'm not hip to South Korean film actors. Lee Dong-wook, Cha Seung-won, Sung Dong-il, Lee Chun-hee or Yeom Jeong-ah – who are they?
I'm also completely ignorant of South Korean Roman Catholics. Who

on earth is Han Duck-soo, Lee Wan, Moon Jae-in, Kim Hyun-joo or Park Jin-young?
South Korean singer-songwriters are unfamiliar to me. I have no clue who G-Dragon is. And don't ask me what Humming Urban Stereo is. I'm clueless about that.
I obviously don't know anything about English-language singers of South Korea. And what in the world is TVXQ? And what is Blady? Don't ask me.
And I'm not well-versed in Grand Prize Golden Disk Award recipients. I don't have any idea what SG Wannabe is.
And don't ask me about K-pop music groups. What is Sistar, and what is the idea with 2NE1? What, in the name of all that is holy, is Donghae & Eunhyuk? Come on.
I also know nothing about Super Junior. What the fuck is Super Junior Full House?
I've never heard of South Korean reality television series. Explorers of the Human Body – I don't know what that is. What in God's name is The Voice of Korea, and what is Jessica&Krystal anyway? I have absolutely no idea. What the shit is I Am a Singer?
I don't know what people mean by 'Korean-language television programming'. The Wedding Scheme? Doesn't ring a bell. The Great Merchant – I don't understand that. I just don't know that. I couldn't tell you about Two Women's Room.
Concerning Television series set in Joseon Dynasty, I am fully ignorant. Dae Jang Geum – I don't know how to begin.
I haven't the foggiest notion what South Korean historical television series is about. Iljimae – what is that? Am I supposed to be familiar with Emperor of the Sea? I haven't the slightest idea.
I don't know about South Korean romance television series. Assorted Gems – what's that supposed to mean?
I surely haven't kept up on Munhwa Broadcasting Corporation television dramas. 7th Grade Civil Servant – I don't understand this.
I'm not familiar with Pegah Gilan players. Pejman Nouri or Sirous Dinmohammadi – doesn't ring a bell.
And I don't know what people mean by 'Montenegrin emigrants to the United States'. Nero Wolfe, Ekrem Jevrić or Afërdita Dreshaj –

doesn't ring a bell.
I'm also not well-versed in Internet memes. Nikki and John Pranksters in Love, is that even a thing? What is 'My Girlfriend's a Geek' supposed to mean? Wouldn't know.
And I couldn't tell you what Japanese films are about. What about Hana no Ko Lunlun?
Concerning Toei Animation, I am fully ignorant. And what is 'Sarutobi Ecchan' supposed to mean again, and what is Dragon Ball: Episode of Bardock supposed to be?
I don't know anything about Comedy anime and manga. Strawberry Marshmallow – dunno. I'm also certain that I've never heard of Happy Lesson. What the hell?
I've never heard of Tokyopop titles. I'm sorry, did you say 'Girl Got Game', and what's World Embryo got to do with it?
I also haven't the foggiest notion what Seinen manga is about. What the hell is Little Fluffy Gigolo Pelu, and what in tarnation is Amagami? Mahoromatic – not my area of expertise. How should I know?
And don't ask me about Japan-exclusive video games. Iron Commando: Koutetsu no Senshi – I don't even know where to start. What's the deal with Subarashiki Hibi, and what the hell is Ayakashi Ninden Kunoichiban? Damned if I know. Holy Umbrella: Dondera no Mubo? Come again? Never heard of it. I haven't the remotest idea. Koro Koro Puzzle Happy Panechu! – don't know.
I don't know about Platform games. Qwak? How should I know? Psybadek – how should I know what that is? No idea. And please don't talk to me about Chip 'n Dale Rescue Rangers 2. I have no clue. I don't know what Magical Tree is or what the mystery about Bionic Commando: Elite Forces is.
I haven't kept up on Fictional cyborgs. I also have no idea who Machinesmith or Misty Knight is.
I'm completely ignorant of Fictional roboticists. What in the world is Iron Man?
And I don't know the first thing about Fictional engineers. Don't ask me what The Unorthodox Engineers were.
I'm not hip to Science fiction short story collections. I don't have any

idea what Stardrift and Other Fantastic Flotsam is or what the hell Toast: And Other Rusted Futures is.
Short stories by Charles Stross are unfamiliar to me. How am I supposed to make sense of The Jennifer Morgue?
I'm not conversant with Spy novels. What is The Spiraling Worm?
And I know nothing about Cthulhu Mythos novels. At the Mountains of Madness – never heard of it.
I don't know any American horror novels. And what the fuck is The Devil's Labyrinth, and what the heck is Murder in Amityville? I also have no idea what Mistral's Kiss is or what is supposed to be special about Goosebumps. I haven't the foggiest idea. What, in the name of all that is holy, is The Historian?
I also don't know what people mean by 'The Amityville Horror'. What in God's name is Amityville: The Final Chapter, and what is The Amityville Horror Part II? Amityville: The Horror Returns – I don't understand that. Doesn't sound remotely familiar.
I obviously couldn't tell you what Horror novels are about. One Door Away from Heaven – not my field. That Cursed House in Amityville? Doesn't ring a bell. I just don't know. The White Body of Evening – what does that mean? Search me. What the Night Knows – what's that supposed to mean?
And I'm not well-versed in Novels by Dean Koontz. Am I supposed to be familiar with The Door to December? I couldn't tell you about Twilight Eyes. Ask someone who knows something.
Concerning Works published under a pseudonym, I am fully ignorant. The Crystal Horde – I don't know what that is. And what the shit is The Scarlet Slipper Mystery, and what on earth is Imre: A Memorandum? Not a clue. The Adventures of Tintin: Breaking Free – dunno. Couldn't say. What's up with The Blood Doctor?
I also don't know anything about Novels set in Budapest. What about The Paul Street Boys?
I also haven't the foggiest notion what Hungarian novels are about. The End of a Family Story – I don't understand this. Eclipse of the Crescent Moon – doesn't ring a bell. Don't ask me. Parallel Stories, is that even a thing?
Don't ask me about Novels set in Hungary. Garden, Ashes – what

is that? What is 'The Romanian: Story of an Obsession' supposed to mean again, and what is Brigitta about? I just don't know that. I also have no clue what Under the Frog is or what The Angel Makers is or what to make of it.

I've never heard of Novels set in Romania. What the hell is The Passport, and what is Cel mai iubit dintre pământeni again? What is 'The Land of Green Plums' supposed to mean, and what is the deal with Craii de Curtea-Veche? Couldn't tell you. Windmills of the Gods – I don't know how to begin.

I'm not familiar with Transylvania in fiction. Dracula? How should I know? I'm certain that I've never heard of The Hunger Angel or how I'm supposed to know something about The Carpathian Castle or what it actually means. I'm clueless about that. What's the deal with The Pied Piper of Hamelin?

I also haven't kept up on Gothic novels. I don't know what Gothic Hospital is or what on earth A Sicilian Romance is or how to make sense of it. Melmoth the Wanderer – I don't even know where to start. I have absolutely no idea.

I'm also completely ignorant of Demons in popular culture. I don't know the first thing about The Stand or what in tarnation The Legend of Zelda: Twilight Princess is. Un-Go – don't know. Come on. Please don't talk to me about InuYasha. I just don't know about that. I don't have any idea what Georgina Kincaid is.

And I'm not hip to Anime and manga based on novels. Genji Monogatari Sennenki – how should I know what that is? Brave Story? Come again? Never heard of it. I haven't got a clue. I have no idea what Denpa Onna to Seishun Otoko is.

I definitely don't know about Dengeki Bunko. What is Black Bullet? And what is Pita-Ten? I just don't know. Don't ask me what Please Teacher! is.

Science fiction anime and manga is unfamiliar to me. I'm sorry, did you say 'The Five Star Stories'?

ADV Films are a mystery to me. What, in the name of all that is holy, is The Super Milk Chan, and what is the idea with Megami Paradise? Kaleido Star – not my field. I don't have any idea.

I know nothing about Comedy-drama anime and manga. How am I

supposed to make sense of Bakuman?

I'm not conversant with Slice of life anime and manga. Meganebu! – not my area of expertise. Solanin – what's that supposed to mean? I have no idea. Anohana: The Flower We Saw That Day? Doesn't ring a bell. How should I know? The Cosmopolitan Prayers – I don't know what that is. Chitose Get You!! – I don't understand this.

And I don't know what people mean by 'Mecha anime and manga'. Shirogane no Ishi Argevollen – dunno. I couldn't tell you about Immortal Grand Prix or what the hell it has to do with Baldr Force or what it is all about. Wouldn't know. GoShogun – never heard of it. I haven't the faintest idea. What in the world is GR: Giant Robo? I'm not well-versed in Anime featured in the Super Robot Wars series. Linebarrels of Iron – I don't understand that. Gun Sword – I don't know how to begin. Damned if I know. Macross Zero – doesn't ring a bell. I have no clue. NG Knight Ramune & 40 – what does that mean? I've never heard of Mobile Suit Gundam Wing.

I also haven't the foggiest notion what Real Robots was about. I'm certain that I've never heard of The Gundam or what the heck Cyber Troopers Virtual-On Oratorio Tangram is or whether I should care. Concerning Bandai Visual, I am fully ignorant. Gunbuster – don't know. Am I supposed to be familiar with Shigofumi: Letters from the Departed? I haven't the remotest idea.

I couldn't tell you what Anime with original screenplays are about. What in God's name is Sisters of Wellber, and what is the mystery about Cluster Edge? Please don't talk to me about Valvrave the Liberator. I can't tell you that. What the fuck is Vandread?

I don't know anything about Fantasy anime and manga. I don't know what Tokyo Babylon is or what Kirby: Right Back at Ya! is about.

I haven't kept up on Occult detective anime and manga. Dream Hunter Rem – I don't even know where to start. I have no clue what Mystery of the Necronomicon is or why people are so interested in Descendants of Darkness. No idea. And don't ask me what Neuro: Supernatural Detective is. I haven't the slightest idea. Witch Hunter Robin – not my area of expertise.

I don't know any Light novels. I also don't have any idea what GJ Club is.

Don't ask me about Gagaga Bunko. What the shit is Rideback, and what is Sasami-san@Ganbaranai anyway? Aura: Maryūinkōga Saigo no Tatakai – what is that? Doesn't sound remotely familiar.

I'm also not hip to Anime and manga based on light novels. What's up with Sunday Without God, and what is The Ambition of Oda Nobuna supposed to be? Oreimo, is that even a thing? What the hell? What is 'Amagi Brilliant Park' supposed to mean again, and what's If Her Flag Breaks got to do with it?

I certainly don't know about GA Bunko. Light Novel no Tanoshii Kakikata – what's that supposed to mean? I don't know the first thing about No-Rin or what the current state of research is on Maid Deka or if it's worth knowing. Ask someone who knows something. I have no idea what Shinkyoku Sōkai Polyphonica is or what the deal with Inō-Battle wa Nichijō-kei no Naka de is or what people say about it.

I'm not familiar with PlayStation 2 games. Romance of the Three Kingdoms IX? Doesn't ring a bell. Viewtiful Joe – not my field. I just don't know. And what is 'Kao the Kangaroo Round 2' supposed to mean, and what the heck is SpongeBob SquarePants: Creature from the Krusty Krab? Couldn't say. Kingdom Hearts II – I don't know what that is.

Video games developed in the United Kingdom are unfamiliar to me. What's the deal with MotoGP '07, and what the hell is Incoming? What about Kingsley's Adventure? I definitely don't know that.

I'm completely ignorant of Windows games. Tony Hawk's Underground Pro – I don't understand that. And what the hell is Tiger Woods PGA Tour 07? I haven't the foggiest idea.

I'm not conversant with Xbox 360 games. Mistborn: Birthright – how should I know what that is? And I'm sorry, did you say 'Sonic's Ultimate Genesis Collection', and what is Call of Juarez: Gunslinger? Don't ask me. I couldn't tell you about Front Mission Evolved or what is supposed to be special about Zeno Clash II or what to think about it.

I don't know what people mean by 'Video game compilations'. Metal Slug Anthology? How should I know? Gradius III and IV – I don't understand this. I have absolutely no idea. How am I supposed to make sense of Intellivision Lives!?

I'm not well-versed in Crave Entertainment games. Mojo! – I don't

know how to begin.
Video game cleanup is a mystery to me. World Basketball Manager? Come again? Never heard of it. And what is NHLPA Hockey '93? Search me.
I've also never heard of Sports management video games. Kevin Keegan's Player Manager – doesn't ring a bell. Please don't talk to me about Championship Manager 5. Couldn't tell you. And I'm certain that I've never heard of Championship Manager: Season 02/03 or what Out of the Park Baseball is.
I couldn't tell you what Linux games are about. Shadowrun Online – never heard of it. I definitely don't know what Cortex Command is or what the mystery about RE: Alistair is or if it's good to know. Not a clue.
I also don't know anything about Ouya games. What in the world is Sonic the Hedgehog 4: Episode II, and what in tarnation is Sine Mora? What in God's name is Pier Solar and the Great Architects, and what is Rose and Time again? I haven't got a clue.
I haven't the foggiest notion what Video games featuring anthropomorphic characters are about. And what the fuck is Lugaru, and what on earth is Blinx 2: Masters of Time and Space? I also have no clue what Mad Dash Racing is or how I'm supposed to know something about UmJammer Lammy. I just don't know.
I also haven't kept up on Time travel video games. Shadow of Memories – dunno. Command & Conquer: Red Alert – don't know. I don't have any idea. Am I supposed to be familiar with Command & Conquer: Yuri's Revenge? I have no idea. Ginga Fukei Densetsu Sapphire – what's that supposed to mean? Killer Instinct 2 – I don't even know where to start.
Concerning Video games set in Antarctica, I am fully ignorant. What the shit is Endless Ocean 2: Adventures of the Deep? And what is Global Operations? I haven't the faintest idea. What's up with QuackShot, and what is Road Riot 4WD about?
I also know nothing about THQ games. And I don't have any idea what Brunswick Circuit Pro Bowling is or what on earth Super Star Wars: Return of the Jedi is or if the whole concept makes sense to me. I don't know the first thing about Zoo Tycoon DS or what the hell it

has to do with Worms: Open Warfare 2. Come on.

I really don't know any Super Nintendo Entertainment System games. Final Fantasy V – what is that? What, in the name of all that is holy, is Tuff E Nuff, and what is the idea with Powermonger? I just don't know about that.

And I'm not familiar with Virtual Console games. I have no idea what R-Type III: The Third Lightning is or what the heck League Bowling is or what it actually means. Fatal Fury 3: Road to the Final Victory – what does that mean? I haven't the remotest idea. Double Dungeons – not my field.

Don't ask me about Cancelled Atari Jaguar games. Arena Football '95 – I don't understand that. Thea Realm Fighters, is that even a thing? How should I know?

Video games with digitized sprites are unfamiliar to me. What is 'Doom II: Hell on Earth' supposed to mean again, and what is the mystery about The Need for Speed?

I'm not hip to Multiplayer null modem games. What about Dungeon Keeper 2, and what is the deal with Null modem?

I'm also completely ignorant of Out-of-band management. What the hell is NC-SI, and what's Dataprobe got to do with it?

I don't know about Privately held companies based in New Jersey. Jackson Hewitt? Doesn't ring a bell. What is 'Acsis' supposed to mean, and what is MediaNow supposed to be? I can't tell you that. Flavor Unit Entertainment – how should I know what that is?

Companies based in Morris County, New Jersey are a mystery to me. Coldwell Banker? How should I know? Quest Diagnostics? Come again? Never heard of it. No idea. Don't ask me what Century 21 Real Estate is. I'm clueless about that. I couldn't tell you about Avis Rent a Car System.

I'm not well-versed in Parsippany-Troy Hills, New Jersey. What's the deal with Actavis?

I frankly couldn't tell you what Companies listed on the New York Stock Exchange are about. And what in the world is DAQO, and what the heck is Cardinal Health? What in God's name is The Hanover Insurance, and what the hell is MSC Industrial Direct? I haven't the slightest idea. Unum – I don't know what that is.

I've never heard of Insurance companies of the United States. Please don't talk to me about Insurance Services of America. What the fuck is California Casualty? Damned if I know.
And I'm not conversant with Hospitality services. A Hotel reservation system – not my area of expertise. I'm certain that I've never heard of EZTABLE or what Roomorama is about. I just don't know. Am I supposed to be familiar with Knowland Group? Wouldn't know. Coffee service – I don't understand this.
I haven't the foggiest notion what Websites about food and drink are about. I'm sorry, did you say 'OpenRice', and what in tarnation is LocalEats?
And concerning Multilingual websites, I am fully ignorant. I have no clue what Wikiversity is or why people are so interested in Gramble. Wikipedia – never heard of it. What the hell? I don't know what Presseurop was.
I also know nothing about Virtual communities. What the shit is APBRmetrics, and what was ICity? WinCustomize – doesn't ring a bell. I just don't know that. What's up with ATHEMOO?
I haven't kept up on Computing websites. And what is WinPenPack, and what is Ars Technica anyway?
I don't know anything about Free software distributions. The OpenDisc – I don't know how to begin.
Concerning Belgian people of Serbian descent, I am fully ignorant. And do I need to know who Aleksandar Mutavdžić or Bratislav Ristić is?
I don't know the first thing about People from Niš. Am I supposed to know Slobodan Antić or Želimir Žilnik?
I also don't know the first thing about Irish people of Italian descent. I don't have any idea who Margaret Mazzantini is. Nicholas Lumbard – what does that mean? Doesn't sound remotely familiar. Is Freddie Scappaticci famous or something?
I also haven't kept up on Republicans imprisoned during the Northern Ireland conflict. I don't know who Seán Mac Stíofáin was. Who the fuck is Billy McMillen? Not a clue. Do I need to know who Ian Milne, Michael McVerry or Rose Dugdale is?
I'm completely ignorant of People from Belfast. And who the shit is

Ernie Graham? Who the hell is Stephen Nolan? I have no idea. BBC Radio 5 Live presenters are unfamiliar to me. Who is Sally Bundock?
Don't ask me about BBC World News. Declan Curry – doesn't ring a bell.
I'm not hip to British business and financial journalists. And who on earth is David Goodhart, Mickey Clark, Andrew Verity, Dan Atkinson or Dominic Laurie?
And I don't know about German people of Turkish descent. I've never heard of a person called Tarık Çamdal. I also have no clue who Erdal Çelik, Necat Aygün or Koray Günter is. I just don't know.
Olympic medalists in football are unfamiliar to me. Who on earth is Julio César Enciso, Uwe Kamps, Tomasz Łapiński, Clément Beaud or Kate Markgraf?
I surely couldn't tell you what Olympic silver medalists for the United States are about. And I have no idea who James Butts, Larry Black, Kelly Kretschman or Hanna Thompson is.
And I don't know the first thing about UCLA Bruins men's track and field athletes. Am I supposed to know Brandon Estrada or David Bunevacz?
And I'm completely ignorant of People from Torrance, California. Kenneth Bae, Jared Sidney Torrance or Harry E. Sloan – who are they?
I'm also not well-versed in Metro-Goldwyn-Mayer executives. Is Lee Rich famous or something? I have no clue who James Thomas Aubrey, Jr. was. Search me. Who the shit is Mary Parent, Dan Kolsrud or Giancarlo Parretti?
And don't ask me about Burials at Westwood Village Memorial Park Cemetery. Jane Greer – who was that?
I know nothing about Cancer deaths in California. I've also never heard of a person called Linda Laurie.
I definitely don't know any Singers from New York City. I don't have any idea who Imelda Marcos, Ruth Gerson, Alice Smith, Patti Austin or Élan Luz Rivera is.
I also don't know about American pop singers. Who the fuck is Curt Boettcher? Who the hell is Oskar Saville or Will Oakland? I haven't got a clue.

I'm not familiar with 10,000 Maniacs members. John & Mary – I don't even know where to start. What's up with Dennis Drew or John Lombardo? I'm clueless about that.
American folk guitarists are a mystery to me. Are Jay Mankita, Sean Rowe, Joshua Radin, Beck or Steven R. Smith famous or something? I've never heard of People from Troy, New York. And do I need to know who John E. Sweeney is? John R. Fellows – doesn't ring a bell. I definitely don't have any idea. Who is this Samuel Wilson, George Fisher Baker or Maureen Stapleton guy?
I'm not conversant with American financiers. Who on earth is Alfred Lee Loomis or Mohnish Pabrai?
I'm not hip to American people of Indian descent. I have no idea who Anil Nerode, Amar Mehta or Shihab Rattansi is.
I haven't the foggiest notion what University of Chicago alumni are about. Who was Erving Goffman? I surely don't know who Grant Cornwell, Warren Kozak, Annie Marion MacLean or Guenter B. Risse is. No idea.
And concerning Social psychologists, I am fully ignorant. I don't know anything about Christina Maslach.
And I haven't kept up on Scientists from California. Mary Main, Willis Linn Jepson, Barbara Tversky, William Gambel or Michael T. Ullman – who are they?
I don't know what people mean by 'Attachment theory'. How am I supposed to make sense of Theraplay, and what is Attachment in adults again? Is Sue Gerhardt famous or something? Damned if I know. An Affectional bond, is that even a thing? I frankly haven't the slightest idea. What is 'Attachment disorder' supposed to mean again? And I couldn't tell you what Child development is about. What the hell is Child and Youth Worker, and what on earth is Thriving? What, in the name of all that is holy, is Learning to Live Together: Preventing Hatred and Violence in Child and Adolescent Development? I haven't the remotest idea.
I'm also not well-versed in The University of California. Don't ask me where The College of California was!
History of Oakland, California is unfamiliar to me. What about The Key System, and what was Moore Dry Dock Company about? I

definitely don't have any idea what The Key Route Inn was. I just don't know. Am I supposed to know The Oikos University shooting? How should I know? What is 'The Oakland Long Wharf' supposed to mean?

I know nothing about Public transportation in San Francisco, California. And I have no idea what The San Francisco Bay Ferry is or what in tarnation AC Transit is. SamTrans – what's that supposed to mean? Wouldn't know. Muni Metro – how should I know what that is?

I also don't know about Public transportation in Alameda County, California. Bay Area Rapid Transit? How should I know? The Berkeley Branch Railroad – don't know. Don't ask me. What in the world is San Leandro LINKS? I can't tell you that. And what is The Altamont Corridor Express?

I don't know the first thing about California railroads. The Yreka Western Railroad? Come again? Never heard of it. Amtrak – I don't understand that. I just don't know that. The Western Pacific Railroad Museum – dunno. I have no clue. I couldn't tell you about The Arizona and California Railroad.

I'm not familiar with Utah railroads. Don't ask me what The Deseret Power Railroad is. And what in God's name is The Utah Railway, and what is the idea with The FrontRunner? What the hell?

I've never heard of Transportation in Weber County, Utah. I don't know where Ogden-Hinckley Airport is. The Bagley train wreck – what is that? Couldn't tell you. I also don't have any idea where The Ogden Intermodal Transit Center is.

I'm completely ignorant of Airports in Utah. I also don't know how to get to Tooele Valley Airport, St. George Municipal Airport, Kanab Municipal Airport, Fillmore Municipal Airport or Green River Municipal Airport.

And don't ask me about Transportation in Washington County, Utah. Where in the world was The Zion – Mount Carmel Highway? Where the fuck is The Floor of the Valley Road? I have no idea.

I also don't know any Roads on the National Register of Historic Places in Utah. Where the hell is The Hole in the Rock Trail? Transportation in Kane County, Utah is a mystery to me. I have never been to U.S. Route 89A. I'm sorry, did you say 'Cottonwood Canyon Road'? Ask someone who knows something.

I'm not hip to Bannered and suffixed U.S. Highways. What's the deal with Bannered routes of U.S. Route 3, and what's Bannered routes of U.S. Route 16 got to do with it? Where is Bannered routes of U.S. Route 49, Bannered routes of U.S. Route 30 or U.S. Route 395 Alternate located? I frankly just don't know.

Concerning U.S. Route 30, I am fully ignorant. What the fuck is Tomasello Winery? Where is U.S. Route 130? Come on. Can you tell me how to get to Pennsylvania Route 462? I just don't know about that. I also have no clue where The St. Johns Bridge or Burnside Bridge is.

I haven't the foggiest notion what Buildings and structures in St. Johns, Portland, Oregon are about. Am I supposed to be familiar with James John High School? I have no idea where The Burlington Northern Railroad Bridge 5.1 or St. Johns Library is. I haven't the faintest idea.

I'm not conversant with Defunct schools in Oregon. What is The Springdale School, and what was the deal with Bishop Scott Academy? Azbuka Academy? Doesn't ring a bell. Couldn't say.

I also couldn't tell you what High schools in Portland, Oregon are about. Columbia Christian Schools – not my area of expertise. How am I supposed to make sense of Portland Adventist Academy, and what is the mystery about Metropolitan Learning Center Portland, Oregon? I haven't the foggiest idea.

I don't know anything about Schools accredited by the Northwest Accreditation Commission. Chemawa Indian School – I don't understand this. Castle Rock High School – I don't know what that is. I have absolutely no idea.

And I don't know what people mean by 'High schools in Cowlitz County, Washington'. Please don't talk to me about Mark Morris High School. What's up with Kalama Middle/High School, and what the hell is Kelso High School? I don't have any idea.

Longview, Washington is unfamiliar to me. Lower Columbia College – not my field. Oregon Primate Rescue – I don't know how to begin. Search me. Do people even go to Southwest Washington Regional

Airport?

I'm not well-versed in Universities and colleges accredited by the Northwest Commission on Colleges and Universities. And I'm certain that I've never heard of Peninsula College or what the hell Olympic College is or how to make sense of it. What is 'Salish Kootenai College' supposed to mean again, and what in tarnation is Corban University? Not a clue.

And I know nothing about The Ktunaxa. Don't ask me where The Flathead Indian Reservation is! What the hell is The Kutenai language? Damned if I know. I certainly don't know where St. Eugene Golf Resort and Casino is. I haven't the slightest idea. The Sturgeon-nosed canoe, is that even a thing?

I frankly don't know about Residential schools in Canada. Sleeping Children Awake – I don't even know where to start. What about Lejac Residential School? I haven't the remotest idea.

I haven't kept up on Documentary films about education. I don't know what Our School is.

I'm not familiar with Documentary films about Japan. Know Your Enemy: Japan – what does that mean? And I have no idea what Kokoyakyu: High School Baseball is or what the deal with Design for Death is. No idea. What, in the name of all that is holy, is Surviving Japan?

I don't know the first thing about Occupied Japan. The Cave of the Negroes incident? How should I know? I don't have any idea what The British Commonwealth Occupation Force is. I just don't know. And I'm completely ignorant of British Commonwealth units and formations. The Commonwealth Corps – don't know. What in the world is KATCOM? Don't ask me.

Don't ask me about British field corps. The Headquarters Allied Rapid Reaction Corps – doesn't ring a bell.

I'm not hip to Military units and formations of NATO. And what is 'The Supreme Allied Commander Atlantic' supposed to mean, and what is The Khyber Border Coordination Center? What in God's name was The SACLANT ASW Research Centre, and what is The NATO Training Mission-Afghanistan supposed to be? I can't tell you that. And I don't know any Military installations of Afghanistan. I have no clue what Gardez Air Base is or what The National Military Academy of Afghanistan is. I obviously don't have any idea where Bagram Airfield, Camp Marmal or Forward Operating Base Delaram is. How should I know?

I also haven't the foggiest notion what Military bases of the United States in Afghanistan are about. What the shit is Camp Eggers? Camp Dwyer, is that even a real place? I'm clueless about that.

I've never heard of United States Marine Corps bases. Marine Corps Brig, Quantico – what is that? I don't know how to get to Marine Corps Base Quantico, Courthouse Bay or Marine Corps Base Camp Lejeune. Doesn't sound remotely familiar.

I also couldn't tell you what Military facilities in North Carolina are about. Where the fuck is Pope Field, Seymour Johnson Air Force Base or Camp Mackall?

Concerning Airfields of the United States Army Air Forces in North Carolina, I am fully ignorant. Where in the world is Currituck County Regional Airport, Laurinburg-Maxton Army Air Base or Smith Reynolds Airport?

I don't know what people mean by 'Buildings and structures in Winston-Salem, North Carolina'. The James R Scales Fine Arts Center – what's that supposed to mean?

I don't know anything about Art schools in North Carolina. The Art Institute of Raleigh–Durham – how should I know what that is? What the fuck is The Penland School of Crafts? Couldn't tell you.

I'm not well-versed in Buildings and structures in Mitchell County, North Carolina. Where the hell is Pinebridge Coliseum?

Sports venues in North Carolina are unfamiliar to me. Where is Paul Porter Arena?

I also know nothing about College basketball venues in the United States. Where is Christenberry Fieldhouse, Reed Green Coliseum, McKenzie Arena, McAlister Field House or Mizzou Arena located?

Indoor arenas in the United States are a mystery to me. Can you tell me how to get to Hardee's Iceplex? And I have no idea where The Miami Arena was. Wouldn't know.

I'm not familiar with Miami Heat venues. I also have no clue where The American Airlines Arena is.

And I'm not conversant with Visitor attractions in Miami, Florida. Miami City Ballet – dunno.

I haven't kept up on Ballet companies in the United States. What's the deal with The James Sewell Ballet, and what was The American Chamber Ballet again? The Oakland Ballet – never heard of it. I have no idea.

I'm completely ignorant of Arts organizations in Minneapolis, Minnesota. And don't ask me what Minnesota Center for Book Arts is. Theatre Pro Rata – I don't understand this. I just don't know.

I'm not hip to Bookbinding. I also couldn't tell you about Stiffening or what is supposed to be special about A Miniature book. I'm sorry, did you say 'Bindery', and what the heck is Biernagel? Ask someone who knows something.

I don't know the first thing about Academic meals. The Boar's Head Feast – I don't know what that is. What is The Freshman 15, and what on earth is a Local School Food Authority? I just don't know that. Don't ask me about Nutrition. Please don't talk to me about Peptide YY. 5 A Day? Doesn't ring a bell. I have no clue.

I've never heard of Nutritional advice pyramids. The twelve pyramids – not my field.

I also don't know about Illinois railroads. Am I supposed to be familiar with The Toledo, Peoria and Western Railway? The Bloomer Shippers Connecting Railroad – not my area of expertise. I haven't got a clue. I'm certain that I've never heard of The Keokuk Junction Railway or how I'm supposed to know something about The Indiana Rail Road or what to make of it.

And I couldn't tell you what Companies operating former Pennsylvania Railroad lines are about. I also have no idea what Conrail Shared Assets Operations is.

I haven't the foggiest notion what New Jersey railroads are about. What's up with The Southern Railroad of New Jersey, and what is The Norfolk Southern Railway about? CSX Transportation? Come again? Never heard of it. I haven't the faintest idea.

I certainly don't know any Companies operating former Erie Railroad lines. The Indiana and Ohio Railway – I don't know how to begin. The Warren and Trumbull Railroad – I don't understand that. I just don't know about that.

And I don't know anything about Genesee & Wyoming Inc.. Louisiana and Delta Railroad, is that even a thing?

I'm not well-versed in Spin-offs of the Southern Pacific Transportation Company. The Alamo Gulf Coast Railroad – don't know. The Willamette Valley Railway – doesn't ring a bell. I don't have any idea. I don't know what The Austin and Northwestern Railroad is.

I know nothing about 3 ft gauge railways in the United States. And what the hell is The Huckleberry Railroad, and what was the idea with The Little Saw Mill Run Railroad? The Americus, Preston and Lumpkin Railroad – what's that supposed to mean? I haven't the foggiest idea. How am I supposed to make sense of The Path Valley Railroad? I have absolutely no idea. And what is The Cherokee Railroad?

Concerning Narrow gauge railroads in Pennsylvania, I am fully ignorant. The Altoona and Beech Creek Railroad – what does that mean? And I don't have any idea what The Susquehanna and Eagles Mere Railroad was or what the current state of research is on The Coudersport and Port Allegany Railroad. Damned if I know. Don't ask me what The Baltimore and Lehigh Railroad is. Search me. The Lancaster, Oxford and Southern Railway – never heard of it.

Transportation in Blair County, Pennsylvania are unfamiliar to me. What, in the name of all that is holy, is The Nittany and Bald Eagle Railroad, and what's The Bald Eagle Creek Path got to do with it? Don't ask me where Pennsylvania Route 36, Pennsylvania Route 866 or Pennsylvania Route 764 is! I haven't the slightest idea.

I don't know what people mean by 'Native American trails in the United States'. And do people even go to White Pass? I couldn't tell you about The Coushatta-Nacogdoches Trace or what on earth The Cherokee Trail is. Not a clue.

Historic trails and roads in Texas are a mystery to me. The Goodnight–Loving Trail – I don't even know where to start. The Great Western Cattle Trail – I don't understand this. Come on. I surely don't have any idea where The El Camino Real de los Tejas National Historic Trail is. I haven't the remotest idea. What is 'The San Antonio-El Paso Road' supposed to mean again?

I'm also not conversant with Historic trails and roads in Colorado.

The Trapper's Trail? How should I know? And what about The Great Osage Trail? What the hell? The Santa Fe Trail, was that even a real place?
I haven't kept up on New Mexico Territory. What in God's name is The Kearny Code, and what was the mystery about The New Mexico Campaign? The Apache Wars – what is that? How should I know? I'm not hip to Pre-statehood history of Arizona. Salado culture – how should I know what that is? Please don't talk to me about The Gila Expedition. Couldn't say. The Peralta Stones – dunno. I'm clueless about that. I don't know how to get to New Spain.
And I'm not familiar with Spanish colonial period in the Philippines. What the fuck is The Colegio de San Ildefonso, and what the hell was The Igorot Revolt? I've never heard of The Thirteen Martyrs of Cavite. I can't tell you that. I have never been to The Captaincy General of the Philippines.
Don't ask me about Defunct educational institutions. And I have no clue what The Universidad de San Felipe de Austria was or what the heck The Hyderabad Sind National Collegiate Board is or what it is all about. What in the world is The Higher Scientific Institute for Diocesan Priests at St. Augustine's? Doesn't sound remotely familiar. I couldn't tell you what Defunct organizations of the Philippines are about. The Makapili? Doesn't ring a bell. The Katipunan – not my field. I have no idea.
I don't know the first thing about Military history of the Philippines during World War II. And what the shit is The Battle of Maguindanao, and what was The Battle of Ormoc Bay anyway? The Japanese occupation of the Philippines – I don't know what that is. I frankly just don't know.
I don't know any South West Pacific theatre of World War II. And what is The Fuerza Aérea Expedicionaria Mexicana, and what in tarnation was The Battle of Mindanao? I'm sorry, did you say 'Operation Transom'? Ask someone who knows something.
I definitely haven't the foggiest notion what The Mexican Air Force is about. And I have no clue who Emilio Carranza is.
And I'm not well-versed in Mexican aviators. I don't have any idea who Miguel Moreno Arreola was. Who the fuck is Roberto Salido

Beltrán or Alberto Braniff? Couldn't tell you.
I don't know anything about Mexican military personnel. And who the shit is Charles Edward Hawkins? I've never heard of a person called Ramón Corona, Diódoro Corella or Jesús Carranza. Don't ask me.
Concerning People from Sonora, I am fully ignorant. And who is this Alfonso Elías Serrano, Fernando Salas or Alfredo Codona guy?
I know nothing about Institutional Revolutionary Party politicians.
Do I need to know who Raúl José Mejía González, María Esther Garza Moreno, Pedro Joaquín Coldwell or Eduardo Ovando Martínez is?
I'm completely ignorant of People from Guanajuato. Feliciano Peña – who was that? Who on earth is María Concepción Navarrete, Miguel Alonso Raya or Flor Silvestre? I frankly just don't know that.
I also don't know about Mexican engravers. Who is Amador Lugo Guadarrama? I'm certain that I've never heard of Abelardo Ávila.
I haven't got a clue. I have no idea who Luis Arenal Bastar, Carlos Alvarado Lang or Julio Castellanos was.
Mexican muralists are unfamiliar to me. And I don't know who Rafael Coronel is. Who the hell is Olga Costa? I just don't know. What's up with Roberto Cueva del Río, Fanny Rabel or Gabriel Fernández Ledesma?
I don't know what people mean by 'Mexican women painters'. I also have no clue who Bridget Bate Tichenor was.
And I'm not conversant with 20th-century Mexican painters. Leonel Maciel? Come again? Never heard of it. Enrique Echeverría – doesn't ring a bell. I haven't the faintest idea.
I'm also not familiar with Mexican illustrators. What is 'Rodolfo Hurtado' supposed to mean? I don't have any idea who José Guadalupe Posada is. I haven't the foggiest idea.
I've never heard of Mexican caricaturists. Who the fuck is Emilia Ortiz or Miguel Covarrubias?
And don't ask me about Olmec scholars. I don't know anything about Christine Niederberger Betton, Elizabeth P. Benson, Alfonso Caso, Michael D. Coe or Caterina Magni.
I haven't kept up on 20th-century Mesoamericanists. Who the shit is Aleš Hrdlička? Robert M. Carmack or Teoberto Maler – who are they?

No idea.

I also couldn't tell you what Austro-Hungarian emigrants to the United States are about. I've never heard of a person called Julia Warhola.

I'm not hip to Warhola family. Who is this Andy Warhol guy? Am I supposed to know John Warhola or James Warhola? I have no clue.

I also haven't the foggiest notion what American film directors of Hungarian descent are about. Who on earth was Jules White?

I'm not well-versed in 20th-century American male actors. Do I need to know who Carter DeHaven was?

Concerning American male film actors, I am fully ignorant. Ernest Cline – who is that? Are Richard Carle, Julius Tannen or Gayne Whitman famous or something? Wouldn't know.

I don't know the first thing about American Jews. I also don't know who Abraham Osheroff or Robert Soblen is.

I'm completely ignorant of American Marxists. Is Louise Bryant famous or something? Who is Alfred Wagenknecht, Grace Lee Boggs, Will Herberg or Oakley C. Johnson? Damned if I know.

I surely know nothing about German emigrants to the United States. I have no clue who Frederick Ludwig Hoffman is.

Presidents of the American Statistical Association are a mystery to me. What's up with Leslie Kish? I don't have any idea who Isador Lubin, Louis Israel Dublin or Raymond Pearl was. Search me.

I don't know about Abraham Lincoln Brigade members. The Abraham Lincoln Brigade – I don't know how to begin. And who the hell is Robert Hale Merriman? Come on.

I don't know what people mean by 'Military personnel killed in the Spanish Civil War'. Oliver Law – doesn't ring a bell.

American communists are unfamiliar to me. Who the fuck is Wyndham Mortimer or Melech Epstein?

And I don't know any American anti-communists. I've never heard of a person called Ingrid Rimland. Who the shit is Martin Dies, Jr., Walter Brennan, Walt Whitman Rostow or Ray Bridwell White? I have absolutely no idea.

I've never heard of Texas Democrats. I certainly don't know anything about Clinton McKamy Winkler. Edgar E. Witt or John Wiley Bryant

– who are they? I haven't the slightest idea.
Don't ask me about American soldiers. And I have no idea who Lawrence Rockwood is.
I'm not conversant with American Buddhists. And do I need to know who Mark Nakashima is? Lewis Lancaster – not my area of expertise. I don't have any idea. Who on earth is Michelle Gordon?
I couldn't tell you what Hawaii Democrats are about. I also don't know who Dennis Arakaki is.
I haven't kept up on University of Hawaii at Manoa alumni. Am I supposed to know Beth Fukumoto or Della Au Belatti?
I haven't the foggiest notion what Hawaii lawyers are about. William Owen Smith – who was that? I have no clue who Eric Yamamoto, David F. Simons, Mark S. Davis or Richard W. Pollack is. I just don't know about that.
And concerning Members of the Hawaiian Kingdom House of Representatives, I am fully ignorant. Who is John Edward Bush? I don't have any idea who William Ansel Kinney or William Hyde Rice was. What the hell?
And I don't know the first thing about Hawaiian Kingdom Interior Ministers. What's up with William Lowthian Green, Keoni Ana, Kamehameha V or Samuel Gardner Wilder?
I'm not familiar with Hawaiian Kingdom politicians. Who the hell is Kamanawa?
I'm also not well-versed in Royalty of the Kingdom of Hawaii. And who the fuck is Kinoiki Kekaulike? Are Leleiohoku II or Pākī famous or something? Couldn't say.
I'm not hip to Princes of Hawaii. Is Kalaninuiamamao famous or something? I've never heard of a person called John Owen Dominis, Albert Kamehameha or Jonah Kūhiō Kalanianaʻole. I haven't the remotest idea.
I frankly know nothing about Hawaii Republicans. Sam Slom, Linda Lingle or Barbara Marumoto – doesn't ring a bell.
I'm completely ignorant of Jewish American state governors of the United States. I don't know anything about Bruce Sundlun.
I don't know what people mean by 'Chevaliers of the Légion d'honneur'. I have no idea who Heiko Engelkes is. Do I need to know

who Jenny Alpha or Joseph-Émery Robidoux was? Not a clue.
I don't know any Quebec Liberal Party MNAs. Who the shit is André Raynauld? Who on earth is Marguerite Blais or Yvon Charbonneau? I'm clueless about that.
I don't know about Quebec trade unionists. And who is this François Pilon guy?
I've never heard of People from Laval, Quebec. And I have no clue who Lucien Rivard, Martin St. Louis, Mariève Provost, Alexandre Despatie or Rosane Doré Lefebvre is.
I'm not conversant with Sportspeople from Montreal. Am I supposed to know Miguel Duhamel, Eric Lamaze or Claude Legris?
Canadian ice hockey goaltenders are a mystery to me. I really don't have any idea who Malcolm Subban, Matt Keetley, Glenn Ramsay, Paxton Schafer or Maxime Daigneault is.
I couldn't tell you what South Carolina Stingrays players are about. What's up with Matt Stefanishion, Ryan Hayes, Tyler McNeely or Jamie Fraser?
Don't ask me about Plymouth Whalers players. Karl Stewart, Brett Bellemore, Andrew Fournier, Nate Kiser or Tomáš Kůrka – who are they?
Concerning Carolina Hurricanes draft picks, I am fully ignorant. Who is Kyle Lawson or Zac Dalpe?
I also don't know the first thing about Ice hockey people from Ontario. Ric Jordan – who is that?
New England Whalers players are unfamiliar to me. Are Don Borgeson or Danny Arndt famous or something?
I surely haven't the foggiest notion what New England Whalers draft picks are about. Who the hell is Tom Colley, Michel Deziel or Peter Sturgeon?
And I haven't kept up on Canadian ice hockcy players. I've never heard of a person called Corban Knight.
I'm also not well-versed in Calgary Flames players. Blair Jones or Reto Berra – doesn't ring a bell.
I'm not hip to St. Louis Blues draft picks. Who the fuck is Ryan Reaves?
I'm not familiar with St. Louis Blues players. I also don't know

anything about Brian Elliott, Seth Martin or Maxim Lapierre.
I'm also completely ignorant of P.E.I. Rocket players. I have no idea who Marco Cousineau, Jimmy Bonneau or Michaël Dubuc is.
I know nothing about French Quebecers. I also don't know who Pierre Perrault was. Who is this Pierre-Luc Gagnon or Mario Jean guy? Doesn't sound remotely familiar.
I don't know any Canadian skateboarders. Who on earth is Kevin Harris?
I don't know what people mean by 'Sportspeople from British Columbia'. Do I need to know who Christopher Bowie, James Lepp, Darren Reisig, Darcy Marquardt or Carol Huynh is?
I also don't know about Commonwealth Games gold medallists for Canada. I have no clue who Patricia Noall is. And I don't have any idea who Percy Williams was. How should I know?
And I couldn't tell you what Canadian Olympic Hall of Fame inductees are about. Who the shit is Betsy Clifford?
Don't ask me about Sportspeople from Ottawa. Jeff Bean or Jamie Lee Rattray – who are they?
I've never heard of Olympic freestyle skiers of Canada. What's up with Alex Beaulieu-Marchand, Rosalind Groenewoud or Vincent Marquis?
Concerning Sportspeople from Calgary, I am fully ignorant. Is Lynn Bottoms famous or something? And who the hell is Ben Hindle, Brent Franklin or Samuel Edney? I just don't know.
Olympic lugers of Canada are unfamiliar to me. Am I supposed to know Regan Lauscher, Arianne Jones, Grant Albrecht or Ian Cockerline?
Mount Royal University alumni are a mystery to me. Are Denise Wong, Stewart Cameron or Doug Vogt famous or something?
I obviously don't know the first thing about Canadian military personnel of World War II. Who was Barney Danson? Lobo Nocho, is that even a thing? I can't tell you that. I don't know anything about Sydney Valpy Radley-Walters or Edmund H. Marriott.
I haven't kept up on 20th-century French painters. I've also never heard of a person called Jean-François Raffaëlli.
And I haven't the foggiest notion what Burials at Père Lachaise

Cemetery are about. Yves Montand – who was that?
I'm not conversant with People from the Province of Pistoia. And I have no idea who Vittorio Chierroni was. Who is this Allucio of Campigliano, Riccardo Magrini, Zeno Colò or Giuseppe Giusti guy? Ask someone who knows something.
I'm also completely ignorant of Italian saints. Who on earth was Peter Igneus? Do I need to know who Anathalon or Gerontius of Cervia is? I haven't got a clue.
I'm also not familiar with 11th-century Roman Catholic bishops. Robert the Lotharingian – doesn't ring a bell. I don't know who Geoffrey de Montbray is. I have no idea.
I'm not hip to Bishops of Coutances. I have no clue who Gilles Deschamps is. Who the fuck is Pope Julius II? I haven't the foggiest idea.
And I don't know about Ecumenical councils. Am I supposed to be familiar with The Council of Trent? What's the deal with The Council of Vienne, and what is The Third Council of Constantinople? I haven't the faintest idea. The Long Island Council of Churches – what's that supposed to mean?
I know nothing about Long Island. And what the hell is The Hauppauge Industrial Association?
Don't ask me about Business and industry organizations based in the United States. I also have no idea what Alpha Beta Gamma is or what the hell it has to do with The National Automotive Parts Association. What is 'AllBusiness.com' supposed to mean again, and what is the deal with The Louisiana Association of Business and Industry? I have no clue. How am I supposed to make sense of The National Negro Business League?
I'm not well-versed in Internet companies of the United States. Become.com – I don't understand that. Jog.fm – what docs that mean? I just don't know that. And don't ask me what Sumazi is.
I also don't know what people mean by 'Domain hacks'. I don't have any idea what Blo.gs is or what in tarnation A Domain hack is. Goatse.cx? How should I know? Damned if I know. Gnolia – I don't understand this.
I've also never heard of A Social bookmarking. And please don't talk

to me about Regator. Menéame – what is that? Don't ask me.
I also couldn't tell you what The Semantic Web is about. What, in the name of all that is holy, is The Agricultural Ontology Service, and what the heck is A Microformat?
Knowledge representation is a mystery to me. What about the Open world assumption, and what on earth is The PROTON?
I don't know anything about Logic programming. What the fuck is Narrowing of algebraic value sets, and what is the Occurs check about? What in the world is The Situation calculus? Search me.
I haven't kept up on Logical calculi. What in God's name is the Monadic predicate calculus, and what is The Region connection calculus supposed to be? The Oriented Point Relation Algebra – how should I know what that is? No idea. What the shit is Spatial–temporal reasoning?
I certainly don't know the first thing about Algebra. An Identity element? Come again? Never heard of it. What's up with a Topological module, and what is the idea with an Invertible module? I have absolutely no idea. A Bose–Mesner algebra – dunno. I haven't the slightest idea. Graph dynamical system, is that even a thing?
Analysis of variance are unfamiliar to me. The False positive rate – never heard of it. The F-distribution? Doesn't ring a bell. Couldn't tell you. Completely randomized design – I don't even know where to start.
I'm completely ignorant of Probability distributions. I have no clue what the Gumbel distribution is or why people are so interested in the Arcsine distribution or if it's worth knowing. The Marchenko–Pastur distribution – not my field. I don't have any idea. I'm sorry, did you say 'the Beta-binomial distribution'?
I haven't the foggiest notion what Continuous distributions are about. What is 'the ARGUS distribution' supposed to mean?
Concerning Particle physics, I am fully ignorant. And what the hell is Mirror matter? And what is Warm inflation? Come on. What's the deal with The Chromo–Weibel instability, and what is the mystery about Quantum chromodynamics?
And I don't know any Hypothetical particles. What is 'Unparticle physics' supposed to mean again?

I also don't know about Theoretical physics. Bi-scalar tensor vector gravity – I don't know how to begin.
I'm not familiar with Astrophysics. A Spectral atlas – what does that mean? Luminosity – not my area of expertise. I haven't the remotest idea.
I definitely know nothing about Astronomical objects. A Hypothetical astronomical object? How should I know?
I'm not conversant with Astronomy. Am I supposed to be familiar with The First Point of Aries?
I'm not hip to Constellations. Corona Borealis – doesn't ring a bell. How am I supposed to make sense of Musca, and what's Capricornus got to do with it? I just don't know about that. And I couldn't tell you about Pictor.
Don't ask me about Northern constellations. I also don't know what Sagitta is or what Camelopardalis is about or whether I should care. Canes Venatici – what's that supposed to mean? Not a clue. And what about Triangulum?
And I'm not well-versed in Constellations listed by Ptolemy. What the fuck is Cetus, and what is Canis Major again? What is Boötes? Couldn't say.
Equatorial constellations are a mystery to me. Sextans – don't know. I couldn't tell you what History of the Commonwealth of Nations are about. I'm certain that I've never heard of The Secretary of State for Commonwealth Relations. Where the fuck is The British Empire and Commonwealth Museum? How should I know?
I don't know what people mean by 'Grade I listed museum buildings'. I also don't have any idea what Sandham Memorial Chapel is. I don't know where Sir John Soane's Museum was. Doesn't sound remotely familiar. Where in the world is Brighton Museum & Art Gallery?
I've also never heard of Amusement museums in the United Kingdom. Where the hell is Watermouth Castle? Puppet Animation Scotland – I don't know what that is. What the hell? Folly Farm Adventure Park and Zoo – what is that? I'm clueless about that. What in the world is The Hollycombe Steam Collection? Can you tell me how to get to The Scarborough Fair Collection?
Steam museums in England are unfamiliar to me. Please don't talk

to me about Papplewick Pumping Station. Is Tom Varley famous or something? Wouldn't know. And I have no idea what Wortley Top Forge is. I can't tell you that. Where is The Weavers' Triangle or Westonzoyland Pumping Station Museum?

I haven't kept up on Buildings and structures in Barnsley. The Open College of the Arts – how should I know what that is?

I haven't the foggiest notion what Distance education in the United Kingdom is about. Am I supposed to know Raia Prokhovnik? And what the shit is BBC School Radio, and what is The Open University anyway? I have no idea. What's up with The Millennium Mathematics Project, and what in tarnation is BPP Law School?

And concerning Charities based in Scotland, I am fully ignorant. The John Muir Trust? Come again? Never heard of it. I don't know the first thing about PACE Theatre Company. I haven't got a clue.

I certainly don't know anything about Theatre companies in Scotland. Borderline Theatre Company – dunno. 7:84 – I don't understand this. I just don't know.

I'm completely ignorant of Political theatre. Los Vendidos – I don't even know where to start.

I don't know any Plays about race and ethnicity. Don't ask me what A Taste of Honey is. I'm sorry, did you say 'The Nigger', and what is the deal with Superior Donuts? I obviously don't know.

I know nothing about Chicago, Illinois in fiction. I also have no clue what Godshow is or what the hell The Nuala Anne McGrail series is or what to think about it. The Great White Hope – I don't understand that. I haven't the faintest idea.

I also don't know about Mystery novels by series. Something Queer Is Going On – not my area of expertise.

I'm not familiar with Fictional amateur detectives. Trixie Belden – never heard of it.

I'm not well-versed in Juvenile series. Grace Harlowe – not my field.

I'm not conversant with Characters in children's literature. And who is Marcia Overstrand? What is 'Anne Shirley' supposed to mean? I obviously don't know that.

Don't ask me about Anne of Green Gables characters. Gilbert Blythe, is that even a thing?

I couldn't tell you what Fictional Canadian people are about. Who the hell is Benton Fraser, Rodney McKay or Frank Zhang?
I certainly don't know what people mean by 'Fictional shapeshifters'. Who the shit is Veranke, Clayface or Jaime Reyes?
I've never heard of Golden Age supervillains. I also don't have any idea who Agent Axis, Per Degaton or Killer Moth is.
Nazis in comic book fiction are a mystery to me. The Hate-Monger – who is that? Who on earth is The Red Skull? Don't ask me. I've never heard of a person called Werner von Strucker, Karl Ruprecht Kroenen or Baron Zemo.
Fictional business executives are unfamiliar to me. Are Adam Chandler, Lew Moxon, Tanja von Lahnstein or Edwin Cord famous or something?
I'm not hip to DC Comics supervillains. And do I need to know who Lucy Lane or Bizarra is?
Concerning Fictional majors, I am fully ignorant. What's the deal with Revolver Ocelot? Misa Hayase or Suzaku Kururugi – who are they? No idea.
And I don't know anything about Fictional characters with multiple personalities. Who is this Francis Dolarhyde guy?
I'm completely ignorant of Fictional United States Army personnel. I have no clue who Jack Bauer, Owen Hunt, Diana Prince, Curtis Manning or Benjamin L. Willard is.
I haven't the foggiest notion what Fictional African-American people are about. I have no idea who Mammy Two Shoes, Namond Brice or Hazel Levesque is.
I also don't know the first thing about Fictional undead. What in God's name is Kharis? Is The Un-Men famous or something? I have absolutely no idea. I don't know who Spidercide or The Crow is.
I also don't know any Marvel Comics supervillains. Who the fuck is The Lobo Brothers? David Moreau, Kaluu, Peace Monger or Maha Yogi – doesn't ring a bell. Damned if I know.
I don't know about Marvel Comics characters who use magic. Salem's Seven – what's that supposed to mean? What's up with Baron Mordo or Devil-Slayer? I haven't the slightest idea.
I'm also not familiar with Characters created by Stan Lee. And who

the shit is Mangog?

I'm also not well-versed in Characters created by Jack Kirby. The Newsboy Legion – I don't know how to begin. Who the hell is Ego the Living Planet, Mister Miracle or Agatha Harkness? Couldn't tell you. Don't ask me about Marvel Comics witches. The Scarlet Witch – who is that?

I'm also not conversant with Marvel Comics superheroes. Am I supposed to know Felicity Hardy or Spider-Woman Mattie Franklin? I also don't know what people mean by 'Characters created by Tom DeFalco'. I've never heard of a person called Sunset Bain. The New Warriors – what does that mean? I have no clue.

And I know nothing about Female supervillains. Are Sat-Yr-9, Doctor Cyber, Andrea Beaumont or Lady Mastermind famous or something? Wonder Woman characters are a mystery to me. I also don't have any idea who The Duke of Deception is. Who on earth is Giganta, Steve Trevor or Queen Desira? I haven't the remotest idea.

DC Comics aliens are unfamiliar to me. Ganthet or Tomar-Tu – who are they?

I also haven't kept up on Characters created by John Byrne. I don't know anything about Trevor Bruttenholm. What the hell is Alpha Flight? Search me.

Concerning Fictional World War II veterans, I am fully ignorant. And do I need to know who Ultimate Wolverine is?

And I couldn't tell you what Marvel Comics characters with superhuman strength are about. Who is Genis-Vell or Norman Osborn?

I'm completely ignorant of Spider-Man characters. And I have no idea who Normie Osborn, Uncle Ben, Janice Lincoln or Hydro-Man is.

I'm not hip to Fictional inventors. And who is this Doctor Doom guy? I don't know the first thing about Marvel Comics characters who have mental powers. And I don't know who The Living Monolith is. What's up with Moondragon or Jean Grey? Not a clue.

I've never heard of Fictional schoolteachers. Lucas Tanner? How should I know? I have no clue who Northstar is. I don't have any idea. I don't know about Fictional adoptees. Who the hell is Teela, Heffer Wolfe or Jade Taylor?

I'm not well-versed in Masters of the Universe Heroic Warriors. The Sorceress of Castle Grayskull – doesn't ring a bell. Who the shit is Queen Marlena or He-Man? Ask someone who knows something.
I also haven't the foggiest notion what Fictional royalty is about. Am I supposed to be familiar with Firebird Angelo? And what about Finrod Felagund, and what the hell is Idril? Doesn't sound remotely familiar. What is 'Seoman Snowlock' supposed to mean again? What the hell? Am I supposed to know Guran?
And I'm not conversant with Characters in fantasy literature. Who the fuck is Tem Barkwater? What the fuck is Bunduki? I just don't know about that.
I'm also not familiar with The Edge Chronicles. Sky Ship – don't know.
And I don't know any Fictional ships. The Love Boat? Doesn't ring a bell.
And I know nothing about American television sitcoms. What, in the name of all that is holy, is Raising Dad?
English-language television programming is unfamiliar to me. What in the world is Eternal Law?
I haven't kept up on British drama television series. And I don't know what Top Boy is or what is supposed to be special about Footballers' Wives.
I really don't know anything about Television shows set in London. How am I supposed to make sense of Citizen Smith, and what is Sykes and a...? Spatz – what is that? I haven't the foggiest idea. The Beat of London – how should I know what that is? Wouldn't know. And I'm sorry, did you say 'Dear Mother...Love Albert'?
I don't know what people mean by 'ITV sitcoms'. What the shit is Take My Wife?
I've never heard of 20th-century German people. And who is Walter Wreszinski or Heinrich Rubens?
Concerning Humboldt University of Berlin alumni, I am fully ignorant. I don't know who Margarete Bieber or Fritz Fischer was.
I don't know the first thing about German Jews. Emanuel Lasker – who was that? I don't have any idea who Aryeh Leo Olitzki was. Couldn't say. I have no clue who Pedro Friedeberg or Ignaz Maybaum

is.

I'm not well-versed in University of Wrocław faculty. Who is this Edward Marczewski guy?

I'm not conversant with Polish mathematicians. Karol Życzkowski – doesn't ring a bell.

I also haven't the foggiest notion what Polish physicists are about. Who the shit is Witold Nazarewicz?

I don't know about People from Warsaw. What's up with Agnieszka Holland, Kate Simon, Henryk Hilarowicz or Wiktor Grodecki?

I definitely don't know any Recipients of the Gold Medal for Merit to Culture – Gloria Artis. Who the fuck is Ryszard Kapuściński? Am I supposed to know Jerzy Janicki, Tomasz Merta, Rudolf Buchbinder or Adam Hanuszkiewicz? I'm clueless about that.

I know nothing about Austrian people of German Bohemian descent. And who the hell is Joseph von Führich? Who on earth was Maria Eis or Theodor Innitzer? I have no idea.

I obviously haven't kept up on 20th-century Austrian actresses. I've never heard of a person called Olga Engl.

I'm not familiar with Austrian film actresses. Maria Perschy, Hilde Krahl, Mia May, Dagny Servaes or Vivian Gibson – who are they?

I also don't know what people mean by 'Austrian people of Czech descent'. I don't know anything about Rudolf Vytlačil.

Don't ask me about People from Arad, Romania. Stela Perin – who is that?

I'm not hip to Olympic gymnasts of Romania. And who is Celestina Popa, Irina Deleanu, Anamaria Tămârjan or Răzvan Dorin Șelariu?

Olympic medalists in gymnastics are a mystery to me. Are Luigi Contessi or Gunnar Höjer famous or something?

I've never heard of Olympic gold medalists for Sweden. And I have no clue who Egon Jönsson was. Who is this Janne Lundblad, Josef Ternström or Gehnäll Persson guy? I just don't know.

And I don't know the first thing about Olympic silver medalists for Sweden. Do I need to know who Christina Bertrup is?

I'm not well-versed in Swedish curlers. Who the shit is Carl Axel Pettersson?

I haven't the foggiest notion what Olympic curlers of Sweden are

about. Johan Petter Åhlén – doesn't ring a bell.
I'm not conversant with Imperial Austrian emigrants to Mexico.
What's up with Juan de Esteyneffer?
And concerning 17th-century Czech people, I am fully ignorant.
I really don't know who Václav Karel Holan Rovenský is. Am I supposed to know John Amos Comenius or Jakub Kresa? Come on.
I don't know any Czech expatriates in the Netherlands. And who on earth is Michal Švec?
I'm also completely ignorant of Swedish expatriate sportspeople in Denmark. And I have no clue who Mikael Antonsson, Lukas Karlsson or Teresa Utković is.
I frankly haven't kept up on People from Castro Urdiales. Who the fuck is Ignacio Diego? I don't have any idea who Antonio Hurtado de Mendoza or Melitón Pérez del Camino is. I have absolutely no idea.
I haven't the foggiest notion what Cantabrian military personnel is about. And who on earth was Rafael de Izquierdo y Gutiérrez? I don't know anything about Antonio Valverde y Cosío. Couldn't tell you. I have no clue who José de Bustamante y Guerra or Felipe González de Ahedo is.
I'm also not conversant with History of Easter Island. Jean-Baptiste Dutrou-Bornier – who is that? The Williamson-Balfour Company, is that even a thing? I haven't got a clue.
I know nothing about Easter Island people. Is Hotu Matu'a famous or something? I've never heard of a person called Carmen Cardinali Paoa. Damned if I know.
I also couldn't tell you what Mythological kings are about. Gard Agdi – I don't know what that is. I'm certain that I've never heard of Þrymr or how I'm supposed to know something about Polynices or if it's good to know. I haven't the remotest idea. And who the hell is Pryderi or Arcesius?
I'm not familiar with The Seven Against Thebes. What's the deal with Parthenopeus?
And concerning Characters in Book VI of the Aeneid, I am fully ignorant. What is Musaeus of Athens, and what is Caeneus about?
I'm completely ignorant of Metamorphoses in Greek mythology.
Please don't talk to me about Ocyrhoe. What is 'Nereus' supposed to

mean, and what is Actaeon supposed to be? Not a clue.
I've never heard of Greek deities. Ariadne? Come again? Never heard of it. The Odyssean gods? How should I know? I definitely don't have any idea.
I don't know about Characters in the Odyssey. Am I supposed to be familiar with Mentor? Who is Agelaus or Amphimedon? Ask someone who knows something.
I also don't know what people mean by 'Jungian archetypes'. The Cosmic Man – dunno. Sky father – what does that mean? Search me. I have no idea what The Pearson-Marr Archetype Indicator PMAI is or what the deal with The Apollo archetype is or what people say about it.
Analytical psychology is unfamiliar to me. Don't ask me what Synchronicity is.
Philosophy of mind is a mystery to me. What is 'The Specious present' supposed to mean again, and what is the idea with The Binding problem?
I'm not hip to Memory. And what in God's name is Spreading activation? And what is Visual memory? I can't tell you that. I frankly don't have any idea what Long-term memory is.
And I don't know any Semantics. A Referring expression – I don't even know where to start. I also have no clue what Seven Types of Ambiguity was or what the current state of research is on Context change potential or if the whole concept makes sense to me. I just don't know about that. What the fuck is A Representation term, and what on earth is A Sobriquet?
I also don't know the first thing about A Metadata registry. Schema.org – I don't understand that. What, in the name of all that is holy, is The National Environmental Information Exchange Network, and what is the mystery about A Data element name? I haven't the slightest idea.
I'm also not well-versed in HTML5. What the hell is Maqetta, and what the heck is Adobe Wallaby?
I don't know anything about Cross-platform free software. How am I supposed to make sense of Mathomatic?
I haven't kept up on Free computer algebra systems. CoCoA – never

heard of it.

I also haven't the foggiest notion what Science software that uses Qt are about. Voreen – not my field. BALL – I don't know how to begin. I just don't know. I couldn't tell you about FreeMat.

I couldn't tell you what Free software programmed in C++ is about. LinBox – not my area of expertise. I don't know what MPQC is or what Qt Creator is or how to make sense of it. What the hell?

And I'm not conversant with Integrated development environments. Metismo – what is that? Visual Prolog – what's that supposed to mean? I really haven't the foggiest idea. I'm sorry, did you say 'EiffelStudio', and what is Python Tools for Visual Studio again? Couldn't say. What the shit is TommyGun?

Concerning Free compilers and interpreters, I am fully ignorant. MTASC – doesn't ring a bell. SmallBASIC – I don't understand this. Doesn't sound remotely familiar. Algebraic Logic Functional programming language – I don't know what that is.

I know nothing about Adobe Flash. SWFObject? Doesn't ring a bell. What's up with Auroraflash? Wouldn't know.

I'm completely ignorant of Software using the MIT license. Blackbox – how should I know what that is?

I've never heard of Free X window managers. What in the world is Dwm?

And I'm not familiar with Application launchers. I have no idea what Avant Window Navigator is or what the mystery about RK Launcher is or what it actually means.

I also don't know what people mean by 'Applications using D-Bus'. Apper, is that even a thing?

Free package management systems are unfamiliar to me. What's the deal with The Advanced Packaging Tool?

I also don't know about Linux package management-related software. Don't ask me what Drakconf is. Please don't talk to me about Ubuntu-restricted-extras. I have no clue. Software Updater – I don't even know where to start. I have no idea. What is 'Ipkg' supposed to mean?

Don't ask me about Free software programmed in Perl. And I don't have any idea what Automake is or what the hell it has to do with BackupPC. GNU parallel? Come again? Never heard of it. I just don't

know.
I'm not well-versed in Build automation. NAnt? How should I know? Compiling tools are a mystery to me. SCons – don't know. What is Distcc, and what is TeamCity anyway? Come on.
And I don't know the first thing about Cross-platform software. Apache Ant – what does that mean? I have no clue what SableVM was or what in tarnation TextCrypt is or what to make of it. No idea. What is 'InfinityDB' supposed to mean again, and what in tarnation is Metafont?
I'm not hip to Font formats. What in God's name is The Glyph Bitmap Distribution Format, and what is the deal with TrueDoc? What the fuck is TeX font metric, and what the hell is TrueType? I have absolutely no idea.
And I don't know anything about Digital typography. Intellifont – never heard of it.
I also don't know any Wilmington, Massachusetts. What, in the name of all that is holy, is The Wildcat Branch? I have no idea where The Wilmington Centre Village Historic District is. How should I know? Don't ask me where The Middlesex Canal was! I haven't the faintest idea. The Baldwin apple – not my field.
I'm not conversant with Geography of Middlesex County, Massachusetts. What about Ball Square? Do people even go to The Haverhill Street Milestone? I just don't know that.
I haven't kept up on Somerville, Massachusetts. Am I supposed to be familiar with The Somerville Assembly? What the hell is Davis Square, and what was The Charlestown Neck about? Don't ask me.
Concerning Buildings and structures in Middlesex County, Massachusetts, I am fully ignorant. Where is The Natick Mall located? I also don't have any idea where Jones Tavern or Casey's Diner is. I haven't the remotest idea.
I also haven't the foggiest notion what Drinking establishments on the National Register of Historic Places in Massachusetts are about. I don't know how to get to Brow's Tavern.
I know nothing about Buildings and structures in Taunton, Massachusetts. I also have no clue where The Taunton State Hospital is. Whittenton Fire and Police Station or Leonard School, is that even a

real place? I don't have any idea.
I couldn't tell you what Defunct hospitals in Massachusetts are about. I'm certain that I've never heard of The Boston City Hospital. I have never been to North Adams Regional Hospital, Gaebler Children's Center or Worcester State Hospital. Ask someone who knows something.
I'm completely ignorant of Kirkbride Plan hospitals. What the shit is The Trenton Psychiatric Hospital? And I don't know where Oregon State Hospital is. I'm clueless about that. I couldn't tell you about Spring Grove Hospital Center or what the heck The Danvers State Hospital is or if it's worth knowing. Not a clue. Where the fuck is The Clinton Valley Center?
I've never heard of Oakland County, Michigan. I also don't know what Child Bite is. And where the hell is The Hilzinger Block? I can't tell you that.
I'm not familiar with Musical groups from Michigan. Love Arcade – what's that supposed to mean?
I surely don't know about Atlantic Records artists. Dream Theater – I don't understand that.
Don't ask me about Rock music groups from New York. Darediablo – I don't understand this.
Musical trios are a mystery to me. Cici Kızlar – dunno. What's up with The Ceasars, and what is Ling Tosite Sigure? Search me.
Turkish rock music groups are unfamiliar to me. Yüksek Sadakat – I don't know how to begin. Gripin – how should I know what that is? Couldn't tell you. I have no idea what Nükleer Başlıklı Kız is.
I'm not well-versed in Musical groups from Istanbul. How am I supposed to make sense of Nekropsi, and what is Baba Zula supposed to be? Mor ve Ötesi – doesn't ring a bell. Damned if I know. Islak Köpek? Doesn't ring a bell.
I frankly don't know the first thing about Progressive rock groups. Labirent – not my area of expertise.
I don't know anything about Musical groups from Ankara. Çilekeş – I don't know what that is. Don't ask me what Gece is. I haven't got a clue.
And I don't know what people mean by 'Turkish alternative rock

groups'. I also don't have any idea what Hayko Cepkin is or why people are so interested in Ezginin Günlüğü or whether I should care. I haven't kept up on Folk rock groups. I'm sorry, did you say 'Hoven Droven', and what's Of Monsters and Men got to do with it? Schandmaul, is that even a thing? I haven't the foggiest idea.
I don't know any German musical groups. In My Rosary – never heard of it. Virtual Embrace – don't know. I haven't the slightest idea. Concerning German dark wave musical groups, I am fully ignorant. What in the world is Girls Under Glass, and what is the idea with Project Pitchfork?
And I haven't the foggiest notion what Musical groups from Hamburg are about. Dynamite Deluxe? Come again? Never heard of it. Gleis 8? How should I know? I just don't know about that. Fünf Sterne deluxe – not my field. Doesn't sound remotely familiar. Texas Lightning – I don't even know where to start.
I'm not hip to Culture in Hamburg. Am I supposed to know Lilo Wanders?
I'm completely ignorant of German theatre managers and producers. I have no idea who Ilia Trilling is.
I've never heard of People from Wuppertal. Alexandra Buch, Michael Holthaus, Rudolf Carnap or Hans Grüneberg – who are they?
I couldn't tell you what Royal Army Medical Corps officers are about. I couldn't tell you about Cameron Moffat. Who is this Jack Matthews guy? I have no clue. Do I need to know who Robert Aim Lennie or Howard Somervell is?
I also know nothing about People from Kincardine. What was 'Laird of Burnbrae' supposed to mean? Are Shirley Henderson or Sir Robert Graham famous or something? I just don't know.
And I'm not conversant with Shakespearean actresses. I don't have any idea who Emma Thompson, Sinead Keenan, Hayley Carmichael or Zoe Tapper is.
I'm not familiar with People educated at Camden School for Girls. Who the shit is Tilly Vosburgh?
English film actresses are a mystery to me. Who the fuck is Chloe Howman, Sarita Khajuria, Patricia Routledge or Cara Horgan?
I certainly don't know about English people of Indian descent. I've

never heard of a person called Jimi Mistry, Upen Patel, Waqar Azmi, Priya Kaur-Jones or Harpal Singh.
I'm not well-versed in Civil servants in the Cabinet Office. And who the hell is Moira Wallace, Quentin Thomas or Philip Allen, Baron Allen of Abbeydale?
Don't ask me about Crossbench life peers. Who is Ronald Oxburgh, Baron Oxburgh, Betty Boothroyd or Frank Chapple?
I don't know the first thing about Fellows of the Australian Academy of Science. And I don't know who Joseph Lade Pawsey was. Who on earth was Douglas Mawson? Couldn't say. What's up with Frank Leslie Stillwell, William Compston or Ian Clunies Ross?
I also don't know anything about Australian scientists. Andrew G. White – doesn't ring a bell.
I haven't kept up on Australian physicists. Am I supposed to know Edward Roy Pike, Debra Searles, Michael A. O'Keefe, Stuart Thomas Butler or Robert Delbourgo?
Concerning Australian nuclear physicists, I am fully ignorant. Oleg Sushkov – who is that? I have no idea who John Clive Ward was. No idea.
Russian physicists are unfamiliar to me. I have no clue who George M. Zaslavsky, Alex Kamenev, Vladimir Korepin or Alexei Yuryevich Smirnov is.
I don't know what people mean by 'Moscow State University faculty'. And I don't have any idea who Valerian Borisovich Aptekar was. Johann Georg Schwarz, Revaz Dogonadze or Yuri Rozhdestvensky – who are they? Wouldn't know.
I'm completely ignorant of Rosicrucians. And do I need to know who Israel Regardie was? Is Paschal Beverly Randolph famous or something? Come on. Who is this Constant Chevillon, Max Heindel or Harvey Spencer Lewis guy?
I've never heard of African-American physicians. Helen Elizabeth Nash – what is that?
I don't know any Washington University in St. Louis faculty. Who the shit is George Pake? Who the hell is Philippe Bourgois? I have absolutely no idea.
I'm also not hip to National Medal of Science laureates. I've never

heard of a person called Phillip Allen Sharp. Are Katherine Esau or Bernard M. Oliver famous or something? I just don't know that.
I couldn't tell you what American Nobel laureates are about. I don't know who Sinclair Lewis was. What's up with Philip Warren Anderson or Riccardo Giacconi? I haven't the faintest idea.
And I haven't the foggiest notion what Recipients of the Gold Medal of the Royal Astronomical Society are about. Who the fuck is James South? Who was Bertil Lindblad, Heinrich Louis d'Arrest or Walter Baade? I haven't the remotest idea.
I'm also not familiar with British astronomers. Am I supposed to know Isis Pogson? I don't know anything about Steve Fossey, Francis Graham-Smith or Manuel John Johnson. What the hell?
Royal Medal winners are a mystery to me. Joseph Dalton Hooker – doesn't ring a bell. Who on earth was David Edward Hughes? Ask someone who knows something. I have no idea who Donald Charlton Bradley, Thomas Galloway or Albert Charles Seward is.
I know nothing about Paleobotanists. I also have no clue who Constantin von Ettingshausen is. Is Charles Eugène Bertrand famous or something? I don't have any idea. Do I need to know who John Lindley, Adolf Carl Noé or John Ray was?
I don't know about Botanists active in New Zealand. And who is this Joseph Banks guy? Who the shit is John Carne Bidwill? I'm clueless about that. I also don't have any idea who William Colenso or Sven Berggren is.
Don't ask me about Members of the New Zealand House of Representatives. William Rolleston – who was that? I've never heard of a person called Bob Clarkson, Rob Munro or Lancelot Walker. I have no idea.
I'm not conversant with People educated at Rossall School. What's up with Thomas Jacomb Hutton?
I'm not well-versed in British Army personnel of World War I. Who the hell is Hubert James Willey, Thomas James Harris or Edmund Ironside, 1st Baron Ironside?
British Army personnel of the Russian Civil War is unfamiliar to me. Who is Charles Ogston? And I don't know who Montague Shadworth Seymour Moore or Henry Edward Manning Douglas was. I can't tell

you that.

I don't know what people mean by 'Companions of the Distinguished Service Order'. Who the fuck is Paramasiva Prabhakar Kumaramangalam? Am I supposed to know John Oliver Andrews? I certainly don't know. Are Rudolf Medek, Morris Gelsthorpe or George Kitching famous or something?

I'm completely ignorant of Recipients of the Canadian Forces Decoration. I don't know anything about Vincent Massey. John Carl Murchie – doesn't ring a bell. Damned if I know. And who on earth is Guy Tousignant or Princess Alexandra, The Honourable Lady Ogilvy?

I've never heard of Fellows of the Royal Society of Canada. Is Larkin Kerwin famous or something? I have no clue who David McCurdy Baird, Ford Doolittle, Rita R. Colwell or Suresh P. Sethi is. Not a clue.

I don't know the first thing about Dalhousie University faculty. I also have no idea who Michael Ungar is. Who is this John Erskine Read, Peter G. Fletcher or Abraham Pineo Gesner guy? Couldn't tell you.

I haven't kept up on Canadian geologists. And do I need to know who Muayyed Nureddin is? I've never heard of a person called George Frederick Matthew or Duncan R. Derry. I haven't the slightest idea.

I'm not hip to Alumni of the University of Cambridge. What's up with Ganesar Chanmugam? I don't have any idea who Ghulam Mustafa Jatoi was. I just don't know about that. Who the shit is Charles Thomas Oldham or Shinji Inoue?

Concerning Pakistan Peoples Party politicians, I am fully ignorant. And who was Murtaza Bhutto? Who the hell is Khalid Shahanshah? Search me.

I don't know any Pakistani exiles. Malik Siraj Akbar – what's that supposed to mean? And I don't know who Asif Ali Zardari, Tahir Aslam Gora or Nawaz Sharif is. Don't ask me.

Members of the National Assembly of Pakistan are a mystery to me. I don't know anything about M Hayat Khan. Are Begum Ishrat Ashraf, Mehdi Hassan Bhatti or Hamza Shahbaz Sharif famous or something? I haven't got a clue.

I'm not familiar with Pakistani people. Am I supposed to know Bilquis Sheikh, Hussain Shah, Muhammad Arif Balgamwala, Hasan Raza Pasha or Sadia Qureshi?

I couldn't tell you what Women short story writers are about.
Katherine Anne Porter – who was that? Lolita Files, Karen Bender, Anne Laughlin or Eva Anstruther – who are they? I just don't know.
I know nothing about People from Fort Worth, Texas. Is Dallas Wiens famous or something?
I frankly haven't the foggiest notion what Organ transplant recipients are about. Charlie Spoonhour – doesn't ring a bell. I have no clue who Freddy Fender or Peter Houghton was. Doesn't sound remotely familiar.
I also don't know about Deaths from multiple organ failure. And I have no idea who Chao Yao-dong is.
Taiwanese economists are unfamiliar to me. Who is this Mao Chi-kuo, Larry Hsien Ping Lang or Quan Hansheng guy?
I also don't know what people mean by 'Wharton School of the University of Pennsylvania alumni'. Who the fuck is Vincent S. Perez, Ajay Waghray, Nikhil Nanda or Irma Arguello?
And I'm not well-versed in University of the Philippines alumni. I've never heard of a person called Florencio Campomanes, Virgilio S. Almario or Sonny Angara.
Don't ask me about Chess arbiters. What's up with Elisabeta Polihroniade? Who on earth was George Koltanowski? No idea.
I'm also completely ignorant of Chess writers. I don't have any idea who José Raúl Capablanca or Richard Réti was.
I also haven't kept up on Columbia University alumni. What is Susan Brind Morrow? Who was William Pollin? How should I know? Do I need to know who Sidney Altman, Jay Furman or Markos Kounalakis is?
I don't know the first thing about Molecular biologists. I don't know anything about Ehud Gazit or Peter K. Vogt.
Concerning University of Southern California faculty, I am fully ignorant. Are Steven Lamy, Robert McKee or Thomas D. Griffith famous or something?
I'm not hip to American legal scholars. Who the shit is Telford Taylor? Am I supposed to know Walton Hale Hamilton, Abram Chayes, Theodore J. St. Antoine or Evan Wolfson? Couldn't say.
I'm not familiar with University of Michigan alumni. Who the hell is

Natalie Zemon Davis or Joseph Gramley?
I couldn't tell you what Smith College alumni are about. I also don't know who Constance Carrier is. Is Anna Chapin Ray famous or something? Wouldn't know.
I'm not conversant with Latin–English translators. And I have no idea who Aubrey de Sélincourt is.
I know nothing about Royal Air Force officers. Felicity Peake – doesn't ring a bell.
I've never heard of Converts to Anglicanism. Who the fuck is Emmanuel Amand de Mendieta? I have no clue who Bess Truman or Kamehameha IV was. I just don't know that.
And I don't know any Christians of the Kingdom of Hawaii. Who is this Hoapili, Keōpūolani or Joel Hulu Mahoe guy?
Converts to Christianity are a mystery to me. I've never heard of a person called Kaukuna Kahekili.
And I don't know what people mean by 'Members of the Hawaiian Kingdom House of Nobles'. What's up with Peter Cushman Jones, Kalākua Kaheiheimālie or Charles Reed Bishop?
Hawaiian royal consorts are unfamiliar to me. Wahinepio, Kānekapōlei or Kaʻahumanu – who are they?
I'm also not well-versed in Hawaiian women in politics. And who on earth was Kekāuluohi, Likelike or Kuini Liliha?
I frankly don't know about Women of the Victorian era. Violet Melnotte – who is that? I don't have any idea who Norah Elam is. I haven't the faintest idea. Who was Charlotte Despard, Rebecca West or Emily Chubbuck?
I'm completely ignorant of Baptist missionaries. And I don't know anything about George Grenfell.
I haven't kept up on Cornish Christian missionaries. Do I need to know who Charles Oswald Lelean is?
And I don't know the first thing about Christian missionaries in Fiji. Aminio Baledrokadroka – what does that mean? I don't know who Hannah Dudley is. Come on. Are Sioeli Nau, Ilaijia Varani or Josua Mateinaniu famous or something?
Concerning Methodist missionaries, I am fully ignorant. And who the hell is John McKendree Springer or William Edward Soothill?

I haven't the foggiest notion what American expatriates in Zimbabwe are about. Am I supposed to know Michael Swango or Diane Birch? And don't ask me about American singer-songwriters. Devon Sproule, Andy Offutt Irwin, Jimbo Mathus or Laura Shay – doesn't ring a bell. I'm not familiar with American humorists. And who the fuck is Cornelia Otis Skinner?

And I couldn't tell you what American stage actresses are about. Is Mews Small famous or something? Who is this Jean Bartel or Susie Garrett guy? I have absolutely no idea.

And I'm not conversant with American television actresses. Who the shit is Debrah Farentino or Demi Moore?

I know nothing about American women film directors. What's up with Nanette Burstein?

I also don't know any People from Buffalo, New York. I have no idea who Diane Beall Templin is.

And I don't know what people mean by 'Female United States presidential candidates'. I've never heard of a person called Victoria Woodhull. I have no clue who Maureen Smith was. I have no clue. Cathy Gordon Brown, Evelyn Reed or Laurie Roth – who are they?

American female singers are unfamiliar to me. Who is Mimi Page or Katrina Leskanich?

I'm not hip to British women writers. I don't have any idea who Eileen Ascroft was. Do I need to know who Farah Mendlesohn, Helen Maria Williams or Kay Parker is? What the hell?

I've never heard of Religion academics. And I don't know who Max Müller was. Are Paul Nathanson or John D. Turner famous or something? I'm clueless about that.

Members of the Privy Council of the United Kingdom are a mystery to me. Who the hell is Harold Wilson? And I don't know anything about Reginald Bevins, Lancelot Sanderson or John Taylor Coleridge. I haven't the foggiest idea.

I don't know about Councillors in Liverpool. Bessie Braddock – doesn't ring a bell. Am I supposed to know Mike Storey or Alex Hargreaves? I just don't know.

I don't know the first thing about Commanders of the Order of the British Empire. I don't know what Thomas Crick is.

I haven't kept up on Companions of the Order of the Bath. And who the fuck is John Northcott? Is George Grove famous or something? Damned if I know.
And I'm completely ignorant of Governors of New South Wales. Who the shit is Richard Bourke? What's the deal with The Governor of New South Wales? I haven't the remotest idea.
And I'm not well-versed in The Parliament of New South Wales. What the fuck is The New South Wales Legislative Council, and what on earth is The Lieutenant-Governor of New South Wales?
Concerning Lists of viceroys in Australia, I am fully ignorant. The Governor of Tasmania – I don't understand that. The Governor of South Australia – I don't understand this. I definitely don't have any idea. I have no clue what The Governor of Victoria is or what on earth The Governor of Western Australia is.
I haven't the foggiest notion what The Parliament of Tasmania is about. Where in the world is Parliament House, Hobart?
And I couldn't tell you what Buildings and structures in Hobart are about. Hobart Bus Station – dunno. Please don't talk to me about Cascade Brewery. Couldn't tell you. Can you tell me how to get to The Denison Canal or Cascades Female Factory?
I'm also not familiar with Defunct prisons in Hobart. Don't ask me where Campbell Street Gaol is!
I obviously know nothing about Prison museums in Australia. I have no idea where Fremantle Prison is.
And don't ask me about Heritage places of Western Australia. I have no idea what Stone Wall is. Where is The Perth Mint? I have no idea. Who is this The Perth Observatory guy? I definitely don't know about that. What, in the name of all that is holy, is Astor Cinema?
I'm not conversant with West Perth, Western Australia. And where is Parliament House, Perth located? What about Solidarity Park? Search me. And what is Dumas House? Not a clue. Am I supposed to be familiar with The Edith Dircksey Cowan Memorial?
And I don't know any Landmarks in Perth, Western Australia. What in God's name is Old Perth Fire Station? I also don't have any idea where The Spare Parts Puppet Theatre is. I just don't know.
I've never heard of Buildings in Fremantle. The Fremantle Markets

– not my area of expertise. The Fremantle Post Office – how should I know what that is? I can't tell you that. I have no clue where The Strelitz Buildings is.

Retail markets in Australia are unfamiliar to me. And what the hell is Salamanca Market, and what is the mystery about The Adelaide Central Market?

I also don't know what people mean by 'Visitor attractions in Hobart'. I'm certain that I've never heard of Constitution Dock or what the hell The Royal Tasmanian Botanical Gardens is. The Hobart Synagogue? Doesn't ring a bell. No idea. How am I supposed to make sense of Hobart Cenotaph? Doesn't sound remotely familiar. Salamanca Place, is that even a real place?

I'm also not hip to Australian military memorials. Avenue of honour – never heard of it. The Kokoda Track Memorial Walkway, is that even a thing? Couldn't say. I'm sorry, did you say 'The Sydney Cenotaph'?

I also don't know the first thing about Monuments and memorials in Sydney. The Sydney Gay and Lesbian Holocaust Memorial? Come again? Never heard of it.

I surely don't know anything about LGBT culture in Sydney. I don't have any idea what SX News is or what The Star Observer is about or what it is all about.

I'm completely ignorant of Newspapers published in Sydney. Bell's Life in Sydney and Sporting Reviewer – don't know. What the shit was The Labor News, and what is The Sydney Morning Herald again? Wouldn't know.

I also don't know about Newspaper companies of Australia. What in the world is Australian Chinese Daily, and what is Provincial Newspapers QLD Ltd anyway?

Chinese-Australian culture in Sydney is a mystery to me. 2CR China Radio Network – I don't know how to begin. And what is 'The Chinese Garden of Friendship' supposed to mean, and what in tarnation is New Land magazine? I haven't got a clue.

I'm not well-versed in Asian-Australian culture in Melbourne. What is The Chinese Methodist Church in Australia, and what is the deal with The Japanese School of Melbourne?

I haven't the foggiest notion what Chinese-Australian culture is about.

Don't ask me what The History of Chinese Australians is. Chinese New Year – what's that supposed to mean? I frankly just don't know that. The Hou Wang Temple – what is that? I haven't the faintest idea. Chinatowns in Australia? How should I know?
And I haven't kept up on Chinese Australian. I couldn't tell you about Chinese immigration to Sydney or what is supposed to be special about Lost Years: A People's Struggle for Justice or what to think about it.
Concerning Chinese culture, I am fully ignorant. Baiheliang – I don't know what that is. And I don't know what The Little Emperor Syndrome is or how I'm supposed to know something about A Sky lantern. I frankly haven't the slightest idea.
Don't ask me about Japanese culture. The Tonbogiri – I don't even know where to start. The Taikomochi – not my field. How should I know? What's the deal with Hatsuyume, and what is Important Cultural Properties of Japan about?
I definitely couldn't tell you what Spears of Japan are about. Yari – I don't understand that.
I know nothing about Blade weapons. The Sica – what does that mean?
Illyrian warfare is unfamiliar to me. What is 'The Shmarjet' supposed to mean again, and what is Illyrian weaponry? Liburna – I don't understand this. Come on. A Sibyna – doesn't ring a bell.
And I'm not familiar with Ancient ships. What about A Navis lusoria? I've never heard of Navy of ancient Rome. Portus Julius – dunno.
I'm not conversant with Military of ancient Rome. Am I supposed to be familiar with Laeti? I have no clue what The Alpine regiments of the Roman army were. I have absolutely no idea.
I'm not hip to Military units and formations of the Roman Empire. What the fuck were Frumentarii, and what is The Praetorian Guard supposed to be? A Roman legion? Doesn't ring a bell. What the hell? And I don't know anything about Military units and formations established in the 1st century BC. Please don't talk to me about The Classis Ravennas. What, in the name of all that is holy, is The Classis Flavia Moesica, and what the hell is Legio X Equestris? I'm clueless about that.

I don't know what people mean by 'Naval units and formations of ancient Rome'. I don't know the first thing about The Classis Britannica.
I'm completely ignorant of Military history of Roman Britain. What's up with Dux Britanniarum, and what's Comes Britanniarum got to do with it? I'm certain that I've never heard of The Ala Gallorum Indiana. I have no clue.
I haven't the foggiest notion what Roman Gaul is about. Who on earth is Mallobaudes? I have no idea what Coligny calendar was. Damned if I know. Orientius – who was that?
I'm not well-versed in Obsolete calendars. I don't have any idea what The Bulgar calendar was.
I haven't kept up on Bulgar language. What in God's name is Kanasubigi, and what the heck is The Nominalia of the Bulgarian khans? Boila – don't know. I haven't the remotest idea.
And I don't know about Bulgarian noble titles. Tsar – what's that supposed to mean? Don't ask me what The Kavhan is. Don't ask me. I have no clue who Knyaz is. I just don't know. What the hell is A Boyar?
Concerning Rus, I am fully ignorant. I've never heard of a person called Rurik. Polish–Lithuanian–Ruthenian Commonwealth – I don't know how to begin. Couldn't tell you. The Caspian expeditions of the Rus' – I don't know what that is. Ask someone who knows something. And do people even go to The Principality of Trubetsk?
I don't know any Former Slavic countries. And I don't know how to get to The Grand Duchy of Lithuania. Where the fuck is Congress Poland? I have no idea. I have never been to The Republic of Ragusa or Polish People's Republic.
Communist states are a mystery to me. Soviet Central Asia, is that even a thing? Marxism–Leninism – not my area of expertise. I just don't know. Where the hell is The Socialist Federal Republic of Yugoslavia or People's Republic of Benin?
I know nothing about Former countries in the Balkans. Where in the world is Yugoslavia? I don't know where the Bulgarian Empire is. I haven't the foggiest idea. I have no idea where The Kingdom of Syrmia or Principality of Achaea is.

I couldn't tell you what Lists of princes are about. Prince of Polotsk – never heard of it. Prince of Orange – how should I know what that is? I just don't know about that. Prince Murat? Come again? Never heard of it. Not a clue. Where was The Principality of Anhalt-Aschersleben? And don't ask me about Belarusian rulers. Who was Rogvolod? I have no idea who Mindaugas was. Search me. How am I supposed to make sense of The Prince of Turov? I definitely don't have any idea. I don't have any idea who Butvydas or Narimantas is.

Belarusian nobility is unfamiliar to me. I surely couldn't tell you about The Szlachta. Do I need to know who Aleksander Słuszka is? Wouldn't know. Who the fuck is Stanisław Bułak-Bałachowicz?

I'm also not hip to Noble titles. What in the world is Madame Royale? And I don't know who Khagan is. I haven't got a clue. What is 'Elteber' supposed to mean, and what is the idea with Uparaja? I haven't the faintest idea. What is A Duke?

And I'm not familiar with Volga Bulgaria. Esegel – I don't understand that. I don't know what Aşlı is or what the deal with Qol Ghali is or if it's good to know. I haven't the slightest idea. The Battle of Samara Bend – doesn't ring a bell.

I'm also not conversant with Nomadic groups in Eurasia. Can you tell me how to get to Tongwancheng? Yugh people – I don't even know where to start. No idea. The Roxolani – what is that? Come on. I'm sorry, did you say 'The Turkic peoples', and what is the mystery about The Yuezhi?

I don't know anything about The History of India. And I have no clue what Wadbudhe is or what the current state of research is on A Coolie or what people say about it. I've never heard of Bara culture. I have absolutely no idea.

I don't know what people mean by 'Racism'. What the shit is The Expert Committee on Questions of Population and Racial Policy, and what on earth were Slave ship?

I also haven't the foggiest notion what Ship types are about. What was 'Destroyer minesweeper' supposed to mean again, and what was Blackwall frigate again?

And I'm completely ignorant of Merchant ships of India. Please don't talk to me about Essar Shipping. The Ganj-i-Sawai – dunno. Doesn't sound remotely familiar. The Patamar? How should I know? I also haven't kept up on Companies based in Mumbai. Accommodation Times? Doesn't ring a bell. What about Web18, and what in tarnation is Shree Ashtavinayak Cine Vision Ltd? I can't tell you that.

I also don't know about Real estate in India. What the fuck is MagicBricks, and what is the deal with Real Estate Bank India? Am I supposed to be familiar with Indiaproperty? How should I know? The Indian property bubble – what does that mean?

I really don't know any Real estate companies of India. What, in the name of all that is holy, is Prestige Group, and what is Equinox Realty anyway? What's up with ABW Group? I'm clueless about that. And what is Tata Housing Development Company?

I don't know the first thing about Real estate and property developers. What the hell is Sheltech? Robin Loh or Morris Cafritz – who are they? I haven't the remotest idea.

And I'm not well-versed in Lithuanian expatriates in the United States. Are Deividas Taurosevičius, Aaron Harry Gorson or Aidas Bareikis famous or something?

Concerning People from Vilnius, I am fully ignorant. Who the shit is Dalius Čekuolis, Mark Kisin, Algirdas Kaušpėdas, Jūratė Kiaupienė or Vytautas Miškinis?

I couldn't tell you what Classical composers of church music are about. Who the hell is Cristoforo Caresana?

I know nothing about Baroque composers. Who is this Mikołaj Zieleński, François Dufault or Johann Christoph Pezel guy?

French composers are unfamiliar to me. And I have no clue who Dumè, Antoine Mahaut, Jaufre Rudel, Maxence Cyrin or Joseph-François Garnier is.

Don't ask me about People from Vaucluse. Is Jean Besson famous or something? I also have no idea what Delphine of Glandèves is. Couldn't say. Am I supposed to know Frédéric Benoît Victoire Jullien or Jean-Esprit Isnard?

I'm also not hip to Chevaliers of the Ordre national du Mérite. And who is Anne-Caroline Graffe, Georges Morel, Françoise Fabian, Janusz Bojarski or Jean-Paul Gauzès?

I'm not familiar with Polish generals. Who on earth was Władysław Filipkowski? Do I need to know who Dezydery Chłapowski or Kazimierz Rumsza is? Damned if I know.
And I'm not conversant with Polish military personnel of World War II. I've never heard of a person called Ksawery Pruszyński. I also don't know who Konstanty Ildefons Gałczyński, Mamert Stankiewicz, Władysław Grydziuszko or Marian Suski was. I just don't know.
I've never heard of People from Courland Governorate. Armin von Gerkan or Eduard Schmidt von der Launitz – doesn't ring a bell.
I also haven't the foggiest notion what German archaeologists are about. Paul Borchardt – who is that?
I also don't know what people mean by 'Members of the United Kingdom Parliament for English constituencies'. I don't know anything about Martin Linton, Edmund Broughton Barnard or William Noel-Hill, 3rd Baron Berwick.
I haven't kept up on Alumni of Downing College, Cambridge. Who the fuck is Richard Gregory? I also have no idea who Antony Roy Clark, Richard Addis or Steven Abbott is. Couldn't tell you.
Fellows of the Royal Society of Edinburgh are a mystery to me. Who the shit is Cyril Offord? And I don't have any idea who Matthew Boulton was. I have no idea.
I'm completely ignorant of English engineers. I have no clue who Rowland Mason Ordish is. What in God's name is John Joseph Bramah? I just don't know.
And I don't know the first thing about Bridge engineers. Who the hell is Sir Francis Fox?
Concerning The Mughal Empire, I am fully ignorant. Talkatora Gardens, is that even a thing? I don't have any idea where The Principality of Bengal was. I have no clue. Is Daud Khan Panni famous or something?
I'm also not well-versed in Former countries in South Asia. Don't ask me where Kantipur is! The Maya Rata – how should I know what that is? What the hell? And I have no clue where The Jaffna kingdom or Democratic Republic of Afghanistan is.
I really couldn't tell you what Soviet satellite states are about. East Germany, is that even a real place? Where is The Mongolian People's

Republic, Finnish Democratic Republic or Socialist Republic of Romania located? I just don't know about that.

Communism in Germany is unfamiliar to me. And I don't have any idea what Die Rote Fahne is or what the mystery about The Hamburg Uprising is. How am I supposed to make sense of The Cuno strikes? Ask someone who knows something. Where the fuck is The Bavarian Soviet Republic?

I'm also not hip to Socialism. Dual power – not my field. The International Socialist Commission – I don't understand this. I just don't know that. And I'm certain that I've never heard of The Proletariat.

I don't know about Poverty. What in the world is A Soup kitchen, and what is The Social determinants of health in poverty about? What is Fish fur? Don't ask me.

And don't ask me about Textiles. Kiswah – what's that supposed to mean?

I'm not familiar with The Kaaba. The Year of the Elephant – don't know.

And I'm not conversant with History of Mecca. The Battle of Fakhkh – I don't know how to begin. The Grand Mosque Seizure – what is that? Not a clue.

I've never heard of Massacres in places of worship. I have never been to Neve Shalom Synagogue. I'm sorry, did you say 'The Mecca Masjid bombing', and what is Madhu church shelling supposed to be? Wouldn't know. Don't ask me what Ave Maria church is.

And I know nothing about Beyoğlu. İstiklal Avenue – I don't understand that. Do people even go to The Crimea Memorial Church? I haven't the slightest idea. I certainly don't know how to get to İstanbul Modern or Istanbul UFO Museum.

I don't know any Churches in Istanbul. Toklu Dede Mosque – I don't know what that is. What the shit is The Cathedral of the Holy Spirit? I haven't the faintest idea. I also don't know where Hagia Irene is. I don't have any idea. I couldn't tell you about The Church of the Virgin of the Pharos.

I really don't know what people mean by 'Byzantine sacred architecture'. Where the hell is Koca Mustafa Pasha Mosque? Panagia

Apsinthiotissa – I don't even know where to start. No idea. Please don't talk to me about The Monastery of Komnenion. Search me. What's the deal with Ese Kapi Mosque?
I also haven't kept up on Byzantine art. What is 'The Byzantine Museum of Kastoria' supposed to mean again, and what the hell is The Art of Eternity?
I definitely haven't the foggiest notion what Museums in Kastoria are about. The Delinanios Folklore Museum – not my area of expertise. I have no clue what The Folklore Museum of Kastoria is. I haven't the foggiest idea.
I surely don't know anything about Historic house museums in Greece. The Vourkas Mansion – dunno. The Kapodistrias Museum? How should I know? Come on.
I'm completely ignorant of Greek culture. Greek musical instruments – never heard of it. I don't know the first thing about The Greek War of Independence. I can't tell you that.
Wars involving Greece are a mystery to me. I don't have any idea what World War II is or what in tarnation The Incident at Petrich is. What is 'The Greek Civil War' supposed to mean, and what is The Gulf War? I'm clueless about that.
Wars involving Iraq are unfamiliar to me. The Iraqi Kurdish Civil War? Doesn't ring a bell. Mahmud Barzanji revolts – doesn't ring a bell. Doesn't sound remotely familiar.
I'm also not well-versed in Kurdish protests and rebellions in Iraq. I don't know what Ahmed Barzani revolt is or what The Halabja chemical attack is.
And I don't know about Kurdish–Iraqi conflict. The PUK insurgency – not my field. The Iraqi–Kurdish conflict – what's that supposed to mean? How should I know?
Concerning Kurdistan independence movement, I am fully ignorant. And I'm certain that I've never heard of The Patriotic Union of Kurdistan.
I'm not hip to Political parties in Iraqi Kurdistan. I've also never heard of The Yazidi Movement for Reform and Progress.
And I'm not familiar with Political parties in Iraq. I have no idea what The Islamic Supreme Council of Iraq IS or what the heck The State of

Law Coalition is. Baghdad of Peace – I don't understand that. I haven't got a clue. The Kurdistan Conservative Party – don't know. Couldn't tell you. Am I supposed to be familiar with The Democratic Centrist Tendency?
I couldn't tell you what Coalitions of parties in Iraq are about. I also couldn't tell you about The Democratic Patriotic Alliance of Kurdistan or why people are so interested in The Iraqi National Movement. The Iraqi Accord Front – I don't know how to begin. I have no idea.
Don't ask me about Sunni Islamic political parties. The Muslim Brotherhood – what does that mean?
I also know nothing about Sunni Islam in Egypt. And don't ask me what Brotherhood Without Violence is.
I don't know what people mean by 'Islamic organizations'. What the fuck is AMUPI, and what is the idea with The Islamic Society in Denmark? The Chinese Islamic Cultural and Educational Foundation? Come again? Never heard of it. I just don't know.
I haven't the foggiest notion what Advocacy groups are about. The National Association for Biomedical Research – I don't know what that is. What's up with The London Municipal Reform League, and what is the mystery about The Friends Committee on National Legislation? I have absolutely no idea. NGO Monitor – I don't even know where to start.
I don't know any Environmental organizations based in the United States. Earth First! – not my area of expertise. And what about Native Seeds/SEARCH, and what the heck is LinkCycle? I have no clue.
I'm not conversant with Anti-road protest. What, in the name of all that is holy, is The Newbury bypass, and what on earth was The M11 link road protest? Where is A30 road? I frankly just don't know.
I don't know anything about DIY culture. Please don't talk to me about The London Action Resource Centre. And what the hell is Hausmania? Ask someone who knows something.
Infoshops are a mystery to me. The Brian MacKenzie Infoshop, is that even a thing? A Centre International de Recherches sur l'Anarchisme – dunno. Couldn't say. Where in the world is Kafé 44? I just don't know about that. Spartacus Books – never heard of it.
Music organizations are unfamiliar to me. I also don't know the

first thing about TONO or what the hell it has to do with The Swiss Ecclesiastical Chant Federation or if the whole concept makes sense to me.
And I'm not well-versed in Organisations based in Switzerland. COSC? Doesn't ring a bell. I don't know what The New European Order is or what on earth The Gruppe Olten is. What the hell? Permindex – doesn't ring a bell. I definitely haven't the remotest idea. I have no clue what The Geneva Institute for Democracy and Development is.
I'm completely ignorant of Swiss literature. And what in the world is Summa Iniuria: Ein Pitaval der Justizirrtümer?
And I don't know about Libertarian books. I'm also certain that I've never heard of The Road to Serfdom or what is supposed to be special about No, They Can't or what it actually means. The Revolution: A Manifesto – how should I know what that is? I just don't know that. I've never heard of Freedomnomics. Don't ask me. What is The Myth of National Defense?
I'm not familiar with Books by Friedrich Hayek. And I'm sorry, did you say 'The Fatal Conceit', and what is The Use of Knowledge in Society again? I have no idea what Individualism and Economic Order is. I haven't the slightest idea.
Concerning Capitalism, I am fully ignorant. How am I supposed to make sense of State monopoly capitalism, and what in tarnation is The Culture of capitalism?
I obviously haven't kept up on Economic anthropology. A Gift economy – what is that? What is 'Axe-monies' supposed to mean again, and what is Inalienable possessions anyway? Damned if I know. The Vertical archipelago – I don't understand this. Search me. The Original affluent society – not my field.
I surely know nothing about Property. The Lockean proviso – what's that supposed to mean? And what the shit is The Right to property, and what is the deal with The Gross annual value? No idea. What is 'A Non-property system' supposed to mean, and what is Ownership society about?
I also couldn't tell you what John Locke is about. The John Locke Lectures – I don't understand that. What in God's name is Limited

government, and what's The Fundamental Constitutions of Carolina got to do with it? I haven't the foggiest idea. Am I supposed to know Damaris Cudworth Masham? Not a clue. Don't ask me what The Labor theory of property is.
I also don't know what people mean by 'English women philosophers'. And who is Jill Marsden?
I haven't the foggiest notion what Nietzsche scholars are about. Are Peter Poellner or Rüdiger Schmidt-Grépály famous or something?
I'm not hip to 21st-century philosophers. Who is this Judith Jarvis Thomson, Steven P. Scalet, Dalmacio Negro Pavón or Robert Frodeman guy?
And I don't know anything about Historians of philosophy. Do I need to know who Ricardo Forster or Don Collins Reed is?
I also don't know any Argentine television personalities. I've never heard of a person called Juan Carlos Mesa, Ambar La Fox, Reina Reech, Maria Concepcion Cesar or Jaime Yankelevich.
Argentine musical theatre creative directors are unfamiliar to me. Valeria Archimó – who is that?
Don't ask me about Argentine musical theatre female dancers. Who the fuck is Norma Pons? Who on earth is Jésica Cirio, Adabel Guerrero or Moria Casán? I haven't the faintest idea.
I don't know the first thing about Argentine female dancers. I surely don't know who Romina Yan was. I don't have any idea who Julieta Sciancalepore or Teddie Gerard is. Come on.
I'm not well-versed in Argentine film actresses. I have no idea who Martina Stoessel, Tulia Ciámpoli, Inda Ledesma, Nancy Dupláa or Julieta Díaz is.
I'm also not conversant with Deaths from heart failure. I have no clue who Chong Chee Kin is. Who the hell is Lina Ron or Ettore Mattia? How should I know?
I'm completely ignorant of People from Anzoátegui. What's up with Alfredo Armas Alfonzo? Am I supposed to know Giovanni Carrara, Ruddy Rodríguez or Octavio Lepage? I'm clueless about that.
I've also never heard of Venezuelan lawyers. Is Robert Carmona-Borjas famous or something?
I definitely don't know about Venezuelan journalists. Who is Miguel

Ángel Capriles Ayala?
I'm not familiar with Venezuelan businesspeople. Pedro Tinoco – doesn't ring a bell. Are Ricardo Fernández Barrueco, Ricardo Domínguez Urbano-Taylor, Ali Lenin Aguilera or Nazri David Dao famous or something? Doesn't sound remotely familiar.
And concerning Members of the Venezuelan Chamber of Deputies, I am fully ignorant. I don't know anything about Germán Suárez Flamerich. José Gregorio Briceño, Jorge Olavarría or Nicolás Maduro – who are they? I certainly haven't got a clue.
Governors of Monagas are a mystery to me. Who the shit is Alirio Ugarte Pelayo?
I don't know what people mean by 'Presidents of the Venezuelan Chamber of Deputies'. I've never heard of a person called Ramón Guillermo Aveledo. Who is this Ignacio Luis Arcaya, Andrés Eloy Blanco or Guillermo Tell Villegas Pulido guy? Wouldn't know.
I also know nothing about Venezuelan poets. Pedro Sotillo – who was that? Who on earth was José Antonio de Armas Chitty? I can't tell you that. Who the fuck is Eugenio Montejo or Yucef Merhi?
I definitely haven't the foggiest notion what New media artists are about. And I don't know who Zhang Deli or Ursula Endlicher is.
I certainly haven't kept up on Digital artists. Paper Rad – don't know. I don't have any idea who Phil Morton, Wolfgang Staehle or Olly Moss is. I just don't know.
I'm not hip to American artist groups and collectives. California Society of Printmakers? How should I know? I also couldn't tell you about The American Society of Miniature Painters or how I'm supposed to know something about Bureau for Open Culture. I don't have any idea.
I couldn't tell you what Printmaking is about. Keyline – not my area of expertise. What's the deal with Popular print, and what is Nature printing supposed to be? I have no clue.
Art genres are unfamiliar to me. Animal style? Come again? Never heard of it.
And don't ask me about Animals in art. I and the Village – I don't know how to begin. Am I supposed to be familiar with Metamorphosis III? Ask someone who knows something.

I'm not well-versed in Paintings by Marc Chagall. Bouquet with Flying Lovers – I don't even know where to start.

I'm not conversant with Actresses from Buenos Aires. I have no idea who Olivia Hussey is.

I've never heard of British film actresses. Who the hell is Pamela Salem? And do I need to know who Vi Kaley, Elliott Mason or Joan Lockton was? I certainly don't know.

And I don't know the first thing about British soap opera actresses. Who is Rachel Leskovac, Amy Yamazaki, Janet Lees Price or Kerry Peers?

And I don't know about British television actresses. Melanie Gutteridge or Shakira Caine – doesn't ring a bell.

I'm completely ignorant of Guyanese beauty pageant winners. I have no clue who Ruqayyah Boyer, Katherina Roshana, Christa Simmons, Arti Cameron or Kara Lord is.

And concerning Guyanese female models, I am fully ignorant. I don't know anything about Shari McEwan.

Antigua and Barbuda beauty pageant winners are a mystery to me. Am I supposed to know Athina James?

I also don't know what people mean by 'Burmese culture'. I don't have any idea what Myazedi inscription is or what the deal with Tagu is or what to make of it.

And I haven't the foggiest notion what Months of the Burmese calendar are about. Pyatho? Doesn't ring a bell. Tabaung – what does that mean? I have no idea. Tazaungmon – never heard of it. Couldn't tell you. What the hell is Nayon, and what the hell is Thadingyut?

I'm not familiar with Burmese words and phrases. Karaweik – dunno. What, in the name of all that is holy, is Salwe? I haven't the remotest idea.

I'm also not hip to Yangon. Please don't talk to me about The Supreme Court of Burma. Myanmar Christian Fellowship of the Blind, is that even a thing? What the hell? Can you tell me how to get to Kaba Aye Pagoda?

I don't know any 20th-century Buddhist temples. And I'm certain that I've never heard of The Datsan Gunzechoinei or what the current state of research is on Das Buddhistische Haus or how to make sense of it.

The Na Tcha Temple – I don't know what that is. Couldn't say. Chung Tian Temple – I don't understand this.
I couldn't tell you what Buildings and structures in Macau are about. I have no clue what World Trade Center Macau is or what the mystery about Macao Studio City is. I definitely don't know what A-Ma Temple is or what the hell Sun Yat Sen Memorial House is. Damned if I know. Kuan Tai Temple – I don't understand that.
Don't ask me about Sun Yat-sen. And what in the world is Zhongshan Park, and what is the idea with Hung Lau?
I haven't kept up on Tuen Mun. Tai Hing Estate – what's that supposed to mean? Don't ask me what Tuen Mun Government Secondary School is. I have absolutely no idea. I have no idea where Castle Peak Hospital is. I just don't know that. I have no idea what The Tuen Mun Town Hall is.
And I'm not conversant with Hospitals in Hong Kong. What is Hong Kong Central Hospital? And what is Tuen Mun Hospital? Don't ask me. Don't ask me where Prince of Wales Hospital is!
I'm also not well-versed in Teaching hospitals in Hong Kong. I don't have any idea where Hong Kong Sanatorium and Hospital is.
Nursing schools in Hong Kong are unfamiliar to me. What the fuck is The Open University of Hong Kong, and what is The Chinese University of Hong Kong? Hong Kong Baptist Hospital, is that even a real place? I just don't know about that.
I don't know about Ma Liu Shui. What about Yucca de Lac, and what is the mystery about Sha Tin Sewage Treatment Works?
I've never heard of Defunct restaurants. And where the fuck was Pizza Showtime, The Loose Box or Bacchi Wapen?
I'm also completely ignorant of Restaurants in Western Australia. Miss Maud – I don't know how to begin.
I don't know anything about Restaurant franchises. How am I supposed to make sense of J. Alexander's, and what is Paradise Bakery & Café again?
And I know nothing about Companies formerly listed on NASDAQ. Hot Topic – how should I know what that is? Asset Acceptance – I don't even know where to start. I certainly haven't the foggiest idea. I really don't know the first thing about Companies based in Macomb

County, Michigan. The Kuhnhenn Brewing Company – don't know. And what is 'Tubby's' supposed to mean again, and what in tarnation is Jet's Pizza? I haven't the slightest idea. I'm sorry, did you say 'Chevrolet Performance', and what on earth is Spirit Airlines? And I haven't the foggiest notion what Companies based in Broward County, Florida are about. What is 'Stratogon Entertainment' supposed to mean, and what is Locair anyway? Ultimate Software – not my area of expertise. Search me. Tropical Financial Credit Union? Doesn't ring a bell.
And I'm not familiar with Plantation, Florida. I have no clue where Westfield Broward is. What in God's name were The Miami Kickers? I'm clueless about that.
Concerning Women's soccer clubs in the United States, I am fully ignorant. The Miami Surf – doesn't ring a bell.
I'm also not hip to Soccer clubs in Miami, Florida. I couldn't tell you about Fort Lauderdale Schulz Academy.
I couldn't tell you what Florida soccer clubs are about. What the shit was Tampa Bay Hawks, and what is the deal with Ocala Stampede? And I don't have any idea what The Florida Gators women's soccer is or what Storm FC is. I haven't the faintest idea.
Southeastern Conference soccer is a mystery to me. What's the deal with The Tennessee Lady Volunteers soccer, and what is The South Carolina Gamecocks women's soccer about?
I don't know what people mean by 'South Carolina soccer clubs'. The Myrtle Beach Boyz – what is that? Am I supposed to be familiar with The South Carolina Shamrocks? I definitely haven't got a clue. The South Carolina Gamecocks men's soccer – not my field.
I haven't kept up on Defunct soccer clubs in the United States. The Newark Falcons – what does that mean? Hellrung & Grimm – never heard of it. No idea. The Reno Rattlers? How should I know?
I'm not conversant with Missouri soccer clubs. I'm also certain that I've never heard of St. Louis Shamrocks or what the heck St. Louis USL Pro team is or whether I should care. And I have no clue what Springfield Storm were. Come on. Who the shit is The Kansas City Comets?
Don't ask me about Soccer clubs in the United States. What's up with

Indiana Invaders?

I also don't know about Teams in the Premier Development League. Lane United FC – I don't know what that is. Hollywood United Hitmen – I don't understand that. Not a clue. Fresno Fuego, is that even a thing? I just don't know. What the hell are Oklahoma City FC, and what's K-W United FC got to do with it?

I've also never heard of Oregon soccer clubs. What, in the name of all that is holy, is Spartans Futbol Club, and what are The Portland Timbers supposed to be? Southern Oregon Fuego – what's that supposed to mean? I can't tell you that. And what is The Portland Thorns FC, and what is the idea with Gorge FC?

I don't know any National Premier Soccer League teams. I don't know what Knoxville Force is or what The Cape Coral Hurricanes are about. AFC Cleveland? Come again? Never heard of it. I have no clue.

I'm also completely ignorant of Tennessee soccer clubs. The Memphis Storm – I don't understand this. Memphis Mercury – dunno. Wouldn't know. Don't ask me what Memphis Express were. I don't have any idea. How am I supposed to make sense of The Memphis Rogues?

I know nothing about Sports in Memphis, Tennessee. The Memphis Mad Dogs – how should I know what that is?

I don't know the first thing about Sports teams in Tennessee. The Carolina Diamonds – don't know. What about The Knoxville Rugby Club? Doesn't sound remotely familiar.

Sports in Knoxville, Tennessee are unfamiliar to me. Please don't talk to me about Hard Knox Roller Girls.

I'm not well-versed in Roller derby leagues in Tennessee. What is 'The Little City Roller Girls' supposed to mean again?

And I haven't the foggiest notion what The Women's Flat Track Derby Association Division 3 is about. Pacific Roller Derby? Doesn't ring a bell. The Crime City Rollers – doesn't ring a bell. How should I know?

I'm not familiar with Sports in Honolulu, Hawaii. The Waikiki BeachBoys – I don't even know where to start. I couldn't tell you about The Sony Open in Hawaii or why people are so interested in EliteXC: Return of the King or what it is all about. Couldn't tell you. And I'm sorry, did you say 'The Fields Open in Hawaii'? I have no idea. And what were The Long Beach Chiefs?

And concerning PGA Tour events, I am fully ignorant. What is 'The RBC Heritage' supposed to mean?

I'm not hip to Golf in South Carolina. I don't have any idea what The BMW Charity Pro-Am is.

I also don't know what people mean by 'Golf in North Carolina'. What the fuck was The Greensboro Open, and what the heck is The North and South Men's Amateur Golf Championship?

I also don't know anything about Former Web.com Tour events. The New Mexico Charity Classic – never heard of it. The Peek'n Peak Classic – I don't know how to begin. I just don't know. I'm certain that I've never heard of The Miami Valley Open.

I'm not conversant with Golf in New York. What the shit is The Pepsi Championship, and what was The Empire State Open?

Don't ask me about Sports in Albany, New York. Albany All Stars Roller Derby – I don't know what that is. What in God's name is Freihofer's Run for Women, and what is the mystery about ECAC Hockey? What the hell? Am I supposed to be familiar with The Albany Choppers? I have absolutely no idea. I have no clue what The Albany Metro Mallers are.

And I don't know about Road running competitions in the United States. The Empire State Marathon – what does that mean? The Monument Avenue 10K – I don't understand that. I haven't the remotest idea.

I also haven't kept up on Marathons in the United States. The Oklahoma City Memorial Marathon – what is that? The Dallas Marathon – not my area of expertise. Ask someone who knows something.

I've also never heard of Sports in Dallas, Texas. What's the deal with The Dallas Grand Prix, and what was The Dallas Generals again? The Dallas Rage? How should I know? Don't ask me. I don't know what The Bank One Senior Championship was or what the hell it has to do with Global Wrestling Federation.

I'm also completely ignorant of Basketball teams in Texas. What the hell is The Dallas Impact, and what in tarnation are The Houston Red Storm? What's up with The West Texas Whirlwinds? I haven't the foggiest idea.

Sports in Houston, Texas are a mystery to me. And where is NRG Park located? The Houston Takers, is that even a thing? I frankly just don't know that.

I don't know any Sports venues in Harris County, Texas. I also have no idea what Lakewood Yacht Club is or what in tarnation Stallworth Stadium is. And I have never been to Sam Houston Race Park or Galena Park ISD Stadium. Damned if I know.

I also don't know the first thing about Greater Houston. Don't ask me what College of the Mainland is. What is Baytown Christian Academy? Couldn't say. I don't know where Dickinson Bayou is. Texas City, Texas is unfamiliar to me. Do people even go to The Texas City Prairie Preserve?

I surely know nothing about Protected areas of Galveston County, Texas. And I don't know how to get to Galveston Island State Park. I'm not familiar with Visitor attractions in Galveston, Texas. And where is Scholes International Airport at Galveston? Can you tell me how to get to The Strand Historic District? I haven't the slightest idea. Schlitterbahn – I don't understand this. I haven't got a clue. Oni-Con – what's that supposed to mean? The Galveston Seawall? Come again? Never heard of it.

I couldn't tell you what Culture of Galveston, Texas is about. The International Pageant of Pulchritude? Doesn't ring a bell. Where the hell is Rosenberg Library? No idea. And please don't talk to me about Seawolf Park.

I'm not well-versed in Naval museums in the United States. What in the world is The USS Midway Museum? And where in the world is The USS Hornet Museum? I'm clueless about that.

And concerning Aerospace museums in California, I am fully ignorant. The Museum of Flying – how should I know what that is? Don't ask me where The California Science Center, Pacific Coast Air Museum or Naval Museum of Armament & Technology is! I just don't know about that.

I also don't know what people mean by 'Space Shuttle tourist attractions'. How am I supposed to make sense of The Space Shuttle Enterprise? I don't have any idea where The US Space Walk of Fame is. Search me.

And I'm not conversant with Buildings and structures in Titusville, Florida. What about Titusville High School, and what is The United States Astronaut Hall of Fame anyway? I have no idea where The Judge George Robbins House, Wager House or Pritchard House is. Not a clue.

Don't ask me about Houses in Brevard County, Florida. Where the fuck is Winchester Symphony House? The Porcher House, Rockledge Drive Residential District, Nannie Lee House or Taylor-Dunn House, is that even a real place? I have no clue.

And I don't know about Florida cracker culture. I've also never heard of a person called Florida cracker.

I'm not hip to American cattlemen. Archie Parr – who was that? Are Frank M. Canton, Claude Benton Hudspeth, Carol Hudkins or George McJunkin famous or something? I can't tell you that.

I've never heard of University of Nebraska–Lincoln alumni. Is Michael D. Navrkal famous or something?

I haven't kept up on Bellevue University alumni. And who the fuck is Graeme Eaglesham, Abbie Cornett, Eric Madsen or Beau McCoy?

Hakka people are unfamiliar to me. Liow Tiong Lai, Panthongtae Shinawatra, Lee Khoon Choy or Penny Tai – who are they?

Don't ask me about Thai Hakka people. And I have no idea who Choti Lamsam was. I also have no clue who Sudarat Keyuraphan or Yingluck Shinawatra is. Doesn't sound remotely familiar.

And I couldn't tell you what Yingluck cabinet is about. What's up with Wannarat Channukul, Nattawut Saikua or Surawit Khonsomboon?

I'm not familiar with Government ministers of Thailand. Krasae Chanawongse or Lek Nana – doesn't ring a bell.

And I don't know about Thai physicians. Who the fuck is Mongkol Na Songkhla? Who is Therdchai Jivacate, Thian Hee or Boonsong Lekagul? How should I know?

I'm not conversant with Knights Commander of the Order of the Crown of Thailand. Am I supposed to know Eiji Toyoda? Who on earth is Rolf Stranger or Herman B Wells? I don't have any idea.

I'm completely ignorant of Commanders of the Order of Vasa. I don't have any idea who Jonas Aspelin, Leopold Freiherr von Hauer, Halfdan Christensen, Ludvig Stoud Platou or Thomas Johannessen

Heftye is.

I don't know what people mean by 'Knights of the Order of the Polar Star'. Who the hell is Carl Linnaeus? Are Stub Wiberg or Jonas Alströmer famous or something? I obviously haven't the remotest idea.

Concerning Members of the Royal Swedish Academy of Sciences, I am fully ignorant. I've never heard of a person called Matthew Black. And who the shit is Alexandre Brongniart or Jean Albert Gaudry? Ask someone who knows something.

I'm also not well-versed in People from Kilmarnock. I don't know anything about Eleanor Kasrils, Steve McAnespie, Darren Henderson or Iain McDowall.

And I don't know anything about People from Kobe. I have no idea who Charles Calveley Foss was. Do I need to know who Chin Shunshin or Miwa Yanagi is? I just don't know.

Concerning Japanese fantasy writers, I am fully ignorant. Who the hell is Bochō Yamamura, Hajime Kanzaka, Hiroko Minagawa or Soichiro Watase?

And I haven't kept up on Japanese crime fiction writers. I also don't know who Kanae Minato, Natsuo Kirino, Joh Sasaki, Hisashi Nozawa or Yoshinaga Fujita is.

And I haven't the foggiest notion what Japanese women writers are about. Who was Kanoko Okamoto, Sei Shōnagon, Tatsuko Hoshino or Tama Morita?

I'm not hip to Women of medieval Japan. Izumi Shikibu – I don't even know where to start. What's up with Nakatsukasa, Tachibana Ginchiyo, Empress Jitō or Lady Sanjō? I haven't the foggiest idea.

I know nothing about Japanese monarchs. What is 'Suishō' supposed to mean? Empress Kōken, Empress Go-Sakuramachi, Empress Genmei or Empress Genshō – who are they? I just don't know.

I'm completely ignorant of 8th-century monarchs in Asia. Saman Khuda – doesn't ring a bell. Who on earth was Emperor Shōmu or Gyeongdeok of Silla? Couldn't say.

756 deaths are a mystery to me. Who the fuck is Forggus mac Cellaig, An Sishun or Aistulf?

And I don't know the first thing about Executed Tang dynasty people.

Is Jing Hui famous or something?
And don't ask me about 706 deaths. Am I supposed to know Cui Xuanwei or Wei Chengqing?
I also don't know any Chancellors under Wu Zetian. I have no clue who Xing Wenwei, Doulu Qinwang, Zong Chuke or Ji Xu is.
I'm not conversant with 690 deaths. I've never heard of a person called Landrada.
I've never heard of Year of birth missing. I'm sorry, did you say 'Febo di Poggio'? Who the shit is Mario Sosa? I surely haven't the slightest idea.
And I don't know about LGBT models. Who is this Bree Olson guy? American female pornographic film actors are unfamiliar to me. I have no idea who Bridget Powers is. I don't know anything about Bonnie Holiday. Don't ask me.
I couldn't tell you what The Surreal Life participants are about. Chyna – who is that?
I don't know what people mean by 'The Corporate Ministry members'. Who the hell is Pete Gas or Triple H?
I'm not familiar with The Kliq. And do I need to know who Shawn Michaels is?
Concerning Professional wrestlers from Texas, I am fully ignorant. Who is Barry Orton or Kevin Von Erich?
I'm not well-versed in American male television actors. I don't know who Jack Palance was. Seth Morris, Michael Carbonaro, Jon Reep or French Stewart – who are they? I have absolutely no idea.
I obviously haven't the foggiest notion what North Carolina State University alumni are about. What the fuck is Julie Shea? Steve Troxler – doesn't ring a bell. I haven't got a clue.
I'm not hip to ACC Athlete of the Year. Are Barry Parkhill, Jen Adams, Bobby Bryant or Joel Shankle famous or something?
I'm completely ignorant of Australian lacrosse players. And who the fuck is John Tokarua or Hannah Nielsen?
I obviously haven't kept up on Northwestern Wildcats athletes. And who on earth is Kristen Kjellman?
I also don't know the first thing about People from Westwood, Massachusetts. Am I supposed to know Peter Vaas, Joe Santilli, Brian

Mann or Aleca Hughes?
Yale University alumni are a mystery to me. Is Frederic Lansing Day famous or something? I also don't have any idea who Cathy Schulman is. I just don't know about that.
I know nothing about American film producers. Who the shit is Steve Schwartz and Paula Mae Schwartz? What's up with Jules Buck, Mary Jane Skalski or Richard Arlook? No idea.
I've never heard of American talent agents. I also have no idea who Alan Walden was. And I have no clue who Steve Rennie, Mark Spiegler, Wendy Day or Christian Picciolini is. Damned if I know.
I definitely don't know about American music industry executives. Who is this Gonzalo de la Torre, Marcus T Grant, Styles P, Aton Ben-Horin or Immortal Technique guy?
I don't know any African-American non-fiction writers. I also don't know anything about James Weldon Johnson. I've never heard of a person called Clyde Taylor, Tina Turner or Clayborne Carson. I just don't know that.
And I couldn't tell you what African-Americans' civil rights activists are about. Who the hell is T. J. Jemison or Johnnie Ruth Clarke?
I'm not conversant with African-American religious leaders. And I don't know who John Melville Burgess was.
Don't ask me about African-American Episcopalians. Who was Andree Layton Roaf? Alexander Crummell or Lisette Denison Forth – who are they? Not a clue.
Concerning People from Muskegon, Michigan, I am fully ignorant. Who the fuck is Harry Morgan?
And I'm not familiar with The Hollywood blacklist. Do I need to know who Karen Morley, Robert Rossen or Phoebe Brand was?
Metro-Goldwyn-Mayer contract players are unfamiliar to me. Howard Keel, Ned Glass, Ruth Gordon or Keye Luke – doesn't ring a bell.
And I'm not hip to Musicians from Illinois. Who on earth is Corey Stevens?
I'm also not well-versed in American blues guitarists. Cootie Stark – who was that? Who the shit is Lead Belly? I have no clue. I don't have any idea who Arlo West, Johnny Rawls or Jerry Ricks is.
And I haven't the foggiest notion what Soul-blues musicians are

about. Am I supposed to know Darrell Nulisch? Is Junior Parker famous or something? I can't tell you that.
I also don't know the first thing about Musicians from Dallas, Texas. And who is this Sam the Sham guy?
Grammy Award-winning artists are a mystery to me. I don't know anything about Dottie Rambo. I have no clue who Sade Adu, Al Green or Hilary Hahn is. Search me.
I'm completely ignorant of Smooth jazz singers. Jackie and Roy – not my field. I've never heard of a person called Curtis Stigers or Halie Loren. I have no idea.
I haven't kept up on Post-bop singers. What's up with Tania Maria, Susanne Abbuehl or Patricia Barber?
I don't know about Lesbian musicians. I also don't know who Emmy Krüger, Jennifer Corday or Wynne Greenwood is.
I've also never heard of People from Frankfurt. Who the hell is Baermann of Limburg? Are William I, Duke of Bavaria, Bernhard Sinkel or Jochem Hendricks famous or something? Couldn't tell you.
I don't know what people mean by 'The History of the Netherlands'. And what is 'The Second Stadtholderless Period' supposed to mean again? Where is the Burgundian Netherlands located? Doesn't sound remotely familiar. I have never been to The Sovereign Principality of the United Netherlands. What the hell? I also have no idea who Willem Usselincx or Court Lambertus van Beyma is.
I obviously know nothing about Dutch people of Flemish descent. And who the fuck is Daniel Heinsius? Robert van Genechten – doesn't ring a bell. Wouldn't know.
I'm also not conversant with Participants in the Synod of Dort. Do I need to know who Johannes Polyander or Georg Cruciger is?
Don't ask me about University of Heidelberg alumni. Who on earth was Friedrich Arnold? Who the shit is Charles Waldstein? I haven't the faintest idea. John Fletcher Hurst, Karl-Henning Rehren or Justus Baronius Calvinus – who are they?
I don't know any American theologians. Who is Samuel Gilman, Gary M. Burge, Irving Francis Wood or Emanuel Vogel Gerhart?
Concerning Christian writers, I am fully ignorant. Am I supposed to know Os Guinness, Els Coppens-van de Rijt, Nasrallah Boutros Sfeir,

William Hugh Clifford Frend or Mikhail Morgulis?
Academics of the University of Glasgow are unfamiliar to me. I don't have any idea who Gilbert Burnet was. I have no clue who Anne Buttimer, David Maxwell Walker or William Tennant Gairdner is. I haven't the remotest idea.
I'm not well-versed in British Army personnel of World War II. I've never heard of a person called Patrick Shovelton, John Le Mesurier or Douglas Clague.
I also couldn't tell you what Manx people are about. Robert Benjamin Young – who was that?
I haven't the foggiest notion what People from Douglas, Isle of Man are about. I also don't know anything about John Allen Mylrea.
Manx politicians are a mystery to me. I don't know who Dudley Butt or Richard Kissack is.
I'm also not familiar with British accountants. Who the hell is Zarin Patel or William Hopkins Holyland?
I'm also not hip to Year of death missing. Is Joshua Boyle famous or something? And who the fuck is Walter Spratt? I just don't know.
I don't know about People educated at Boston Grammar School. What's up with George Bass? Do I need to know who Barry Spikings, Joseph Langley Burchnall, Simon Patrick or Arthur James Grant is? Ask someone who knows something.
I also know nothing about 17th-century Anglican bishops. I don't have any idea who William Lucy is.
I'm also not conversant with English Anglican priests. Are William Berriman or Robert Bolton famous or something?
Don't ask me about English conforming Puritans. And who is Robert Crosse, John Sprint or Jeremiah Dyke?
I don't know any Fellows of Sidney Sussex College, Cambridge. Henry George Keene – dunno. I also have no clue who Asa Briggs, Baron Briggs, George Cecil Renouard, Thomas Woolston or Keith Glover is. I'm clueless about that.
I've never heard of East India Company civil servants. What in God's name is John Carnac Morris? George Foxcraft – who was that? Couldn't say. James Thomason – never heard of it.
And I'm completely ignorant of English Indologists. I've never heard

of a person called Arthur Llewellyn Basham. I surely don't know anything about Isaline Blew Horner or Thomas Burrow. I just don't know.

I'm not well-versed in English historians. I also don't know who William Henry Page was. Am I supposed to know Richard of Hexham, Stuart Peachey, Arthur Francis Leach or Ralph Thoresby? I haven't the slightest idea.

I couldn't tell you what English antiquarians are about. Who the shit is Charles Hamilton Smith?

I don't know what people mean by 'English illustrators'. Is Clive Barker famous or something?

Gay writers are a mystery to me. Who the fuck is Mario Mieli, Edwin Cameron or Ronald Eyre?

I also haven't the foggiest notion what Alumni of Pretoria Boys High School are about. Damon Galgut or Richard Kunzmann – who are they?

I'm not familiar with South African male novelists. Who on earth is Christopher Hope, Leon Louw, Clive Algar, Alex La Guma or Karel Schoeman?

Concerning Translators to Afrikaans, I am fully ignorant. Uys Krige or Jaap Marais – doesn't ring a bell.

I also don't know the first thing about Herstigte Nasionale Party politicians. I have no idea who Willie Marais is.

And I don't know about Apartheid in South Africa. Afrikaner nationalism – what does that mean?

I definitely haven't kept up on Political movements in South Africa. What the shit is The Environmental movement in South Africa, and what the hell is Libertarianism in South Africa? Am I supposed to be familiar with South African resistance to war? Come on. What's the deal with Anarchism in South Africa?

I know nothing about Anarchism by country. Anarchism in the United States – I don't know how to begin.

Don't ask me about Anarchism in the United States. The Free Voice of Labor – what is that? I also couldn't tell you about The First Red Scare or what on earth Bash Back! is. Don't ask me.

And I'm not hip to Documentary films about United States history.

What the hell is The Search for Kennedy's PT 109?
I certainly don't know any Documentary films about World War II.
What is Plan for Destruction?
I've never heard of American films. I'm certain that I've never heard of For the Love of Movies: The Story of American Film Criticism or what the deal with The Hot Chick is or what to think about it.
I'm completely ignorant of American sex comedy films. Good Luck Chuck – I don't know what that is. I don't have any idea what Couples Retreat is or what the current state of research is on You're a Big Boy Now. How should I know? I frankly don't know what Porky's is.
And I'm not well-versed in Films directed by Bob Clark. I have no clue what Superbabies: Baby Geniuses 2 is.
Children's fantasy films are unfamiliar to me. The Care Bears Adventure in Wonderland? Come again? Never heard of it.
I'm not conversant with Films featuring anthropomorphic characters. Don't ask me what The Pebble and the Penguin is. Mickey's House of Villains, is that even a thing? No idea.
I also don't know what people mean by 'Donald Duck films'. The Three Caballeros? How should I know?
And I couldn't tell you what Walt Disney Pictures films are about.
I have no idea what The Computer Wore Tennis Shoes is or what is supposed to be special about Condorman. What, in the name of all that is holy, is The Lizzie McGuire Movie, and what on earth is The Muppet Christmas Carol? I just don't know about that.
I haven't the foggiest notion what Films directed by Robert Butler are about. White Mile – how should I know what that is? What in the world is Guns in the Heather, and what is Scandalous John about? I have no clue. Night of the Juggler – what's that supposed to mean? I have absolutely no idea. Underground Aces – not my area of expertise.
English-language films are a mystery to me. The Abyss – I don't understand this. I'm sorry, did you say 'Darkest Africa', and what's The Tracker got to do with it? I just don't know that. What is 'Spookies' supposed to mean, and what is the deal with The Choppers?
I'm also not familiar with Monster movies. The Undying Monster – I

don't understand that. Please don't talk to me about Alvin and the Chipmunks Meet Frankenstein. I haven't got a clue. What is 'Mega Shark Versus Mecha Shark' supposed to mean again? Damned if I know. And what is An American Werewolf in Paris?

And I don't know anything about Films based on horror novels. Nosferatu – I don't even know where to start. Howling III – not my field. I have no idea. What the fuck is Seven Footprints to Satan? And I don't know the first thing about American mystery films. In the Next Room – don't know. The Woman Hunter – I don't know how to begin. Doesn't sound remotely familiar. How am I supposed to make sense of Murder on the Campus, and what the heck is The Maddening?

Concerning Psychological thriller films, I am fully ignorant. And what about The Quiet, and what is the idea with Lady Beware? Pandorum – dunno. What the hell?

And don't ask me about Films set in the 31st century. What's up with Oblivion 2: Backlash, and what is Futurama: Bender's Game supposed to be? I couldn't tell you about Deathsport or how I'm supposed to know something about Captive Women or if it's worth knowing. Search me.

I also know nothing about American comedy science fiction films. Airplane II: The Sequel? Doesn't ring a bell. What the shit is The Adventures of Pluto Nash, and what is Aliens in the Attic again? I haven't the remotest idea.

I don't know about Castle Rock Entertainment films. What in God's name is The Last Days of Disco, and what is Mr. Saturday Night? I'm not hip to Saturday Night Live films. Am I supposed to be familiar with Bob Roberts? A Mighty Wind – I don't know what that is. Couldn't tell you. I'm certain that I've never heard of Mr. Mike's Mondo Video.

I've never heard of Paramount Pictures films. The Perfect Score – never heard of it. Star Trek: First Contact – what is that? I certainly haven't the faintest idea. Don't ask me what Fire in the Sky is. I can't tell you that. I have no clue what The Cocoanuts is or what the hell The Air Mail is or if it's good to know.

I'm not well-versed in Films about revenge. Yuga Purusha – what's that supposed to mean?

I haven't kept up on Films about reincarnation. I have no idea what Dead Again is or what the heck Karzzzz is or if the whole concept makes sense to me. What is Prem Shakti? Ask someone who knows something.

And I don't know any Films directed by Kenneth Branagh. What's the deal with Jack Ryan: Shadow Recruit?

And I'm completely ignorant of Films shot in England. Withnail and I – doesn't ring a bell. Eyes Wide Shut? Come again? Never heard of it. I haven't the foggiest idea.

I also don't know what people mean by 'Films based on works by Arthur Schnitzler'. And what the hell is Young Medardus, and what in tarnation is The Distant Land? Fräulein Else – I don't understand this. I don't have any idea. The Affairs of Anatol, is that even a thing? I'm clueless about that. I don't know what The Return of Casanova is.

I'm not conversant with Austrian films. Beresina, or the Last Days of Switzerland – I don't even know where to start. Please don't talk to me about Am Sklavenmarkt. I haven't the slightest idea. Chalet Girl – how should I know what that is?

German films are unfamiliar to me. Chance the Idol – not my field. What, in the name of all that is holy, is No Money Needed, and what is Thieves by Law anyway? I just don't know.

German drama films are a mystery to me. Where Others Keep Silent? How should I know? The Girl Irene – don't know. Couldn't say.

And I'm not familiar with Films directed by Reinhold Schünzel. I'm sorry, did you say 'Column X', and what on earth is The Count of Cagliostro? Peter the Mariner – not my area of expertise. Not a clue. What in the world is Season in Cairo?

I surely don't know the first thing about German-language films. Eisetüde – what does that mean? What the fuck is The Inn on the River, and what is the mystery about The Tango Player? Don't ask me.

I surely haven't the foggiest notion what German crime films are about. And what about Dr. Mabuse the Gambler?

Concerning German silent films, I am fully ignorant. The Red Mouse – dunno. The Three Dances of Mary Wilford? Doesn't ring a bell. How should I know? What is 'Her Dark Secret' supposed to mean?

I don't know anything about Films directed by Johannes Guter. What is 'The Adventure of Mr. Philip Collins' supposed to mean again, and what the hell is Rhenish Girls and Rhenish Wine? Express Train of Love – I don't know how to begin. I have no clue.
I also couldn't tell you what German comedy films are about. What's up with Otto – Der Film, and what's Alive and Ticking got to do with it? Am I supposed to be familiar with Wenn Ludwig ins Manöver zieht? No idea.
I don't know about Films set in Germany. And what the shit is Gasbags, and what is the deal with The Mortal Storm?
I'm not hip to World War II films made in wartime. I couldn't tell you about Cottage to Let.
And I know nothing about British films. Hellraiser – what is that?
I've also never heard of Films set in London. Don't Open till Christmas – I don't know what that is. And what is Mod Fuck Explosion? I just don't know about that. And what is Get Him to the Greek?
I haven't kept up on Universal Pictures films. Jaws 3-D – I don't understand that. Don't ask me what Ride Clear of Diablo is. Come on. This Woman is Mine – what's that supposed to mean?
I also don't know what people mean by 'SeaWorld Orlando'. And do people even go to Turtle Trek, Journey to Atlantis, Antarctica: Empire of the Penguin or Wild Arctic?
I don't know any Water rides by name. Stormforce 10? Come again? Never heard of it. I have no clue where Daredevil Falls, Roaring Rapids or Living with the Land is. I have absolutely no idea.
And I'm completely ignorant of Six Flags Over Texas. I don't know where The Glow in the Park Parade is. Can you tell me how to get to Runaway Mountain, El Aserradero, Superman: Tower of Power or Judge Roy Scream? I haven't got a clue.
And don't ask me about Six Flags New England. I also don't know how to get to The Dark Knight Coaster.
I'm not well-versed in Wild Mouse roller coasters. Where is Coast Rider? How am I supposed to make sense of A Wild Mouse roller coaster? Wouldn't know.
Types of roller coasters are a mystery to me. What's the deal with An Inverted roller coaster, and what is the idea with A Powered roller

coaster? I have no idea what A Spinning roller coaster is or what A Dive Coaster is. Damned if I know.

I'm not familiar with Inverted roller coasters. Where the hell is The Mind Eraser? And where in the world is Nemesis Inferno or Ednör – L'Attaque? I just don't know that.

And I haven't the foggiest notion what Roller coasters operated by Herschend Family Entertainment are about. Don't ask me where Outlaw Run or Thunderation is!

Concerning Roller coasters in Missouri, I am fully ignorant. And I have no idea where The Screamin' Eagle is.

And I don't know the first thing about Six Flags St. Louis. I also don't have any idea where Batman: The Ride or SkyScreamer is.

I couldn't tell you what Six Flags Fiesta Texas is about. Kiddee Koaster, Bugs' White Water Rapids, The Gully Washer, Boomerang: Coast to Coaster or Superman: Krypton Coaster, is that even a real place?

Six Flags attractions are unfamiliar to me. And where was Sky Whirl located? Where the fuck is Shipwreck Falls or Monster Mansion? Doesn't sound remotely familiar.

And I don't know about Animatronic attractions. What in God's name was Trauma Towers, and what the heck is The Fairfield Industrial Dog Object? I have no clue what Rainforest Cafe is. I have no idea.

I'm not hip to Haunted attractions. What the hell is The Chimera House, and what is Ghost Blasters about? I'm certain that I've never heard of The National Railroad Museum. I just don't know. And I have never been to The Twilight Zone Tower of Terror or Halloween Horror Nights.

I don't know anything about Dark rides. Do people even go to Monsters, Inc. Mike & Sulley to the Rescue!?

I know nothing about Disney California Adventure. Buena Vista Street, is that even a thing? I've never heard of The Little Mermaid: Ariel's Undersea Adventure, Toy Story Midway Mania!, Ariel's Grotto or King Triton's Carousel of the Sea. I frankly haven't the remotest idea.

I haven't kept up on Fantasyland. I also have no clue where The Mickey Mouse Revue was. Can you tell me how to get to Haunted Mansion Holiday or It's a Small World? Ask someone who knows something.

And I'm completely ignorant of Walt Disney Parks and Resorts gentle boat rides. I don't know how to get to The Admiral Joe Fowler Riverboat. I also don't know where Storybook Land Canal Boats, El Rio del Tiempo or Mark Twain Riverboat is. Search me.

I'm not conversant with Magic Kingdom. Push the Talking Trash Can – I don't understand this. Where is HalloWishes? I don't have any idea. And where in the world is The Astro Orbiter?

I also don't know what people mean by 'Hong Kong Disneyland'. Don't ask me where Disney on Parade was! And I have no idea where Sleeping Beauty Castle or Prince Charming Regal Carrousel is. Couldn't tell you.

And I'm not familiar with Disneyland. Mickey's House and Meet Mickey or The Disney Gallery, is that even a real place?

Mickey's Toontown is a mystery to me. Where the hell is Pixie Hollow? I'm sorry, did you say 'The Walt Disney World Railroad'? I haven't the slightest idea.

I definitely don't know any Walt Disney Parks and Resorts attractions. And where the fuck is Golden Zephyr, The Enchanted Tiki Room: Stitch Presents Aloha e Komo Mai! or Star Tours—The Adventures Continue?

I haven't the foggiest notion what Tomorrowland is about. I frankly don't have any idea where Finding Nemo Submarine Voyage is.

I definitely don't know the first thing about Pixar in amusement parks. And where is The Seas with Nemo & Friends, Turtle Talk with Crush, Toy Soldiers Parachute Drop or Woody's Roundup Village located?

Concerning Toy Story, I am fully ignorant. Toy Story Playland – how should I know what that is? You've Got a Friend in Me – I don't even know where to start. I haven't the faintest idea. I don't know what Buzz Lightyear of Star Command: The Adventure Begins is or what the mystery about Toy Story Toons is or what people say about it. I really haven't the foggiest idea. What, in the name of all that is holy, is Toy Story: The Musical?

Don't ask me about Disney Cruise Line. Who the hell is Matt Ouimet? What in the world is Disney's Fairy Tale Weddings & Honeymoons, and what is The Disney Cruise Line Terminal again? I just don't know.

And do people even go to Castaway Cay or The Golden Mickeys? And I don't know about The Disneyland Resort. Disney Jazz Celebration? How should I know?

I'm also not hip to Jazz festivals in the United States. Please don't talk to me about The Miami Nice Jazz Festival. The Tanglewood Jazz Festival – what does that mean? I can't tell you that. What is 'The Chicago Jazz Festival' supposed to mean, and what in tarnation is The Omaha Blues, Jazz, & Gospel Festival?

And I couldn't tell you what Visitor attractions in Berkshire County, Massachusetts are about. The Tanglewood Music Festival – not my field. I've also never heard of Catamount Ski Area. Couldn't say. Can you tell me how to get to The Stafford Hill Memorial or Berkshire Theatre Festival?

Music of Massachusetts are unfamiliar to me. What the fuck is The Road to Boston?

And I don't know anything about Military marches. What's up with The Old Brigade, and what is On the Mall? What is 'The Thunderer' supposed to mean again, and what is Soldiers of the King supposed to be? How should I know?

And I haven't kept up on Compositions by John Philip Sousa. The Gallant Seventh – doesn't ring a bell. The Kansas Wildcats – not my area of expertise. Don't ask me. High School Cadets – dunno. I just don't know about that. The Fairest of the Fair? Doesn't ring a bell.

I'm not conversant with American marches. Hands Across the Sea – what is that? What the shit is American march music, and what is the mystery about The Stars and Stripes Forever? Come on.

I don't know what people mean by 'American styles of music'. Am I supposed to be familiar with The Tulsa Sound? I also don't have any idea what Hip hop soul is. Not a clue.

I'm not well-versed in American hip hop genres. I couldn't tell you about Twin Cities hip hop or what the hell it has to do with Hyphy. Southern hip hop? Come again? Never heard of it. What the hell? What is West Coast hip hop, and what the hell is Bounce music?

I'm also not familiar with Culture of Minneapolis, Minnesota. The Minnesota Opera – don't know. The Minnesota International Center – I don't understand that. I'm clueless about that. Mayday Books –

what's that supposed to mean? I have absolutely no idea. I have no clue where The Minnesota Orchestra or Traffic Zone Center for Visual Art is.
Independent bookstores of the United States are a mystery to me. What's the deal with Open Books & Records, and what is John Cole's Book Shop anyway? And what the hell is Harvard Book Store, and what on earth is Tia Chucha's Centro Cultural? Wouldn't know.
I also haven't the foggiest notion what Bookstores in California are about. Vroman's Bookstore – I don't know what that is.
I also don't know the first thing about Companies based in Pasadena, California. How am I supposed to make sense of Avery Dennison, and what's Red Hen Press got to do with it?
I definitely know nothing about Radio-frequency identification companies. I'm sorry, did you say 'Guard RFID Solutions Inc.'? And what is RCD Technology? I have no clue. What about Psion, and what the heck is Impinj? Doesn't sound remotely familiar. Rasilant Technologies, is that even a thing?
Don't ask me about Software companies of Canada. SmartUse – how should I know what that is? What, in the name of all that is holy, is 01 Communique, and what is the idea with Geac Computer Corporation? I have no idea. ObjecTime? How should I know?
Concerning Companies listed on the Toronto Stock Exchange, I am fully ignorant. What is 'Electrovaya' supposed to mean, and what is Manulife Financial about? Talisman Energy – what does that mean? I really just don't know. What in the world is The Canadian Western Bank, and what is the deal with Buhler Industries?
I'm not hip to The S&P/TSX Composite Index. What in God's name is Just Energy, and what is Canfor again? I have no clue what The Royal Bank of Canada is or why people are so interested in The Canadian Imperial Bank of Commerce or what to make of it. I haven't the remotest idea. And what the fuck is Detour Gold?
I don't know about Banks of the Caribbean. Don't ask me what CIBC FirstCaribbean International Bank is. The Central Bank of Barbados – I don't know how to begin. No idea. What's up with The Caribbean Development Bank?
I also couldn't tell you what Saint Michael, Barbados is about. I don't

know how to get to Bridgetown Heliport. Combermere School – what is that? I just don't know that. I have no idea what The Lloyd Erskine Sandiford Centre is.

I've never heard of Visitor attractions in Barbados. What is 'Harrison's Cave' supposed to mean again, and what in tarnation is The Barbados Wildlife Reserve?

I obviously don't know any Caves of Barbados. The Animal Flower Cave – I don't even know where to start.

I'm also completely ignorant of Sea caves. And I don't know where Smoo Cave is. I have never been to Sea Lion Caves. Damned if I know. The Great Blue Hole – I don't understand this. I haven't got a clue. What the shit is Portbraddon Cave?

I don't know anything about Parish of Durness. And where in the world is Sangobeg or Leirinmore?

I'm not conversant with Populated places in Sutherland. I also have no idea where Strathy, Altnaharra or Swordly is.

Parish of Farr is unfamiliar to me. Where is Strathnaver?

I'm not familiar with Sutherland. I'm certain that I've never heard of Eas a' Chual Aluinn or what on earth The Old Man of Stoer is or what it actually means. Dornoch Cathedral – doesn't ring a bell. Couldn't tell you.

I don't know what people mean by 'Climbing areas of Scotland'. Coire an t-Sneachda, Ben Nevis or Beinn Odhar, is that even a real place?

I'm also not well-versed in Mountains and hills of the Central Highlands. And don't ask me where Beinn a' Bheithir is!

I haven't kept up on Marilyns of Scotland. I also don't have any idea where Mòruisg is.

And I don't know the first thing about Mountains and hills of the Northwest Highlands. Where the hell is Fionn Bheinn, Meall na h-Eilde or Sgùrr nan Eugallt?

I know nothing about Corbetts. Where are Sgùrr an Utha and Fraoch-bheinn located?

Lochaber is a mystery to me. What is Kinlochaline Castle?

I also haven't the foggiest notion what Listed castles in Scotland are about. I don't know what Inverquharity Castle is.

I definitely don't know about Castles in Angus. Can you tell me how to get to Glamis Castle? Farnell Castle – dunno. I haven't the faintest idea.

Don't ask me about Reportedly haunted locations in Scotland. Castle Levan – never heard of it. Where the fuck is Kilmory Castle, Culcreuch Castle or Loch Leven Castle? I definitely haven't the foggiest idea.

I've also never heard of Historic house museums in Perth and Kinross. Am I supposed to be familiar with Elcho Castle? And I don't have any idea what Castle Menzies is. I haven't the slightest idea. I don't know how to get to Blair Castle or Huntingtower Castle.

I'm not hip to Castles in Perth and Kinross. What the hell is Balhousie Castle?

I'm completely ignorant of Regimental museums in Scotland. I also don't know where Edinburgh Castle is. The Argyll and Sutherland Highlanders Regimental Museum? Come again? Never heard of it. Ask someone who knows something.

I don't know anything about Listed prison buildings in Scotland. Do people even go to HM Prison Perth or Inveraray Jail?

I'm also not conversant with James Gillespie Graham buildings. I couldn't tell you about Armadale Castle.

I don't know any Ethnic museums in Scotland. Where in the world is Achnacarry Castle?

And I'm not familiar with Inventory of Gardens and Designed Landscapes. I have no clue where Balnagown Castle, Cally Palace, Culzean Castle, Callendar House or Drum Castle is.

Hotels in Scotland are unfamiliar to me. And please don't talk to me about The Kings House Hotel.

I also couldn't tell you what Junior roller coasters are about. And where is Hoot N Holler or Wilderness Run?

And I haven't kept up on Darien Lake. What about Splashtown at Darien Lake?

I also don't know the first thing about Buildings and structures in Genesee County, New York. How am I supposed to make sense of Genesee Community College? I have never been to Alexander Classical School. Search me. And don't ask me where The Batavia Club, Genesee County Courthouse or Richmond Memorial Library is!

I know nothing about Onondaga limestone. And I have no idea where The Gridley Building is. I'm sorry, did you say 'The Onondaga Formation'? How should I know?
I also don't know what people mean by 'Escarpments of the United States'. The Helderberg Escarpment – not my area of expertise. What's the deal with The Balcones Fault? Couldn't say.
I haven't the foggiest notion what Geology of Texas is about. The Woodbine Formation? Doesn't ring a bell. Where the hell is The Solitario? I just don't know about that. The Antlers Formation, is that even a thing? Come on. Where is Duffy's Peak or Enchanted Rock located?
Concerning Protected areas of Llano County, Texas, I am fully ignorant. The Texas Highland Lakes? How should I know? Can you tell me how to get to Inks Lake or Lake Lyndon B. Johnson? What the hell?
Lyndon B. Johnson is a mystery to me. I also don't have any idea who William Conrad Gibbons was. The Lyndon Baines Johnson Library and Museum – how should I know what that is? Don't ask me.
I don't know about History museums in Texas. Stephen F. Austin State Park – I don't know what that is. The OS Museum – what's that supposed to mean? I have absolutely no idea.
I've never heard of Art museums in Texas. Where the fuck is The Museum of Fine Arts, Houston, Tyler Museum of Art, Elisabet Ney Museum or Kimbell Art Museum?
I'm not well-versed in National Register of Historic Places in Austin, Texas. I don't know how to get to Battle Hall. I don't know where The Levi Rock Shelter, Dewitt C. Greer State Highway Building or Andrew M. Cox Ranch Site is. I obviously don't have any idea.
I'm also not hip to University of Texas at Austin campus. I don't have any idea where Flawn Academic Center or Benedict Hall is.
I surely don't know anything about National Trust of Australia. Dalwood House – I don't understand that.
I'm completely ignorant of The Hunter Region. What is 'The Hunter Valley Coal Chain' supposed to mean, and what is the mystery about Burraga Swamp? Don't ask me what The Hunter Valley cannabis infestation was. I'm clueless about that. Where in the world is Lostock

Dam?
I don't know any Hydroelectric power stations in New South Wales. I have no clue where Glenbawn Dam is.
The Upper Hunter Shire is unfamiliar to me. And do people even go to Krui River or Pages Creek?
And I'm not conversant with Rivers of New South Wales. Where is Iron Cove Creek?
I'm not familiar with Creeks and canals of Sydney. I have never been to Tank Stream, Wolli Creek, Darling Mills Creek, Salt Pan Creek or Terrys Creek.
I also couldn't tell you what Subterranean rivers are about. I have no idea where The Zenne is. What in God's name is The Hobart Rivulet? I can't tell you that.
I know nothing about Rivers of Tasmania. The Pieman River – not my field. I have no idea what Gordon Splits is. I frankly just don't know. And where the hell is The Gordon River or Weld Valley?
I also don't know what people mean by 'Franklin Dam'. And what in the world is The Franklin River?
I don't know the first thing about Lists of coordinates. What, in the name of all that is holy, is Ko Phaluai, and what is the Extreme points of Moldova?
And I haven't the foggiest notion what the Extreme points of Moldova are about. Where is Naslavcea located?
Concerning People from Puerto Cabello, I am fully ignorant. Do I need to know who Carlos Capriles Ayala or José Lebrún Moratinos is?
I don't know about Cardinals created by Pope John Paul II. And who is Angelo Felici?
Italian Roman Catholics are a mystery to me. And I have no clue who Rinaldo Brancaccio or Agostino Ciasca is.
And I haven't kept up on Italian orientalists. Are Giuseppe Tucci, Franciscus Quaresmius or Thomas Obicini famous or something?
I've never heard of Visva-Bharati University alumni. Who is this Birendra Nath Datta guy? Nilima Sen – who is that? I have no idea. Am I supposed to know Chittaranjan Deb, Satyajit Ray or Sudhi Ranjan Das?
Don't ask me about Assamese writers. I don't know who Jaideep

Saikia is. Who the fuck is Saurabh Kumar Chaliha? I have no clue.
I don't know anything about Writers from Northeast India. Who the shit is Lakshminath Bezbaroa? I've never heard of a person called Anuradha Sharma Pujari. I haven't the remotest idea.
I'm completely ignorant of Asom Sahitya Sabha Presidents. I have no idea who Chandradhar Barua, Bhupen Hazarika, Rajanikanta Bordoloi or Amrit Bhushan Dev Adhikari was.
Indian cinematographers are unfamiliar to me. Who on earth is R. D. Rajasekhar or Prasad Murella?
I'm not well-versed in Tamil cinematographers. Ilavarasu – doesn't ring a bell.
I also don't know any People from Tamil Nadu. And I don't have any idea who Chezhiyan, Perumal Rasu or P. S. Vinod is.
I'm not familiar with Indian painters. Who the hell is Jayanth Manda? Do I need to know who Dalchand or Farrukh Beg was? Not a clue.
I'm not hip to Indian artists. Who was Jagdeep Smart? I also have no clue who Chittrovanu Mazumdar or Ajit Ninan is. Doesn't sound remotely familiar.
I couldn't tell you what University of Calcutta alumni are about.
Is Shamsunnahar Mahmud famous or something? What's up with Shaktipada Rajguru? I just don't know.
I definitely don't know what people mean by 'People from Bankura district'. I don't know who Jamini Roy was.
I know nothing about Government College of Art & Craft alumni. Nikhil Baran Sengupta – who was that? I also don't know anything about Somnath Hore. No idea. Am I supposed to know Jogen Chowdhury or Hiran Mitra?
Concerning Visva-Bharati University faculty, I am fully ignorant. Guru Chandrasekharan or Ramchandra Gandhi – who are they?
I don't know about Indian dancers. Are Gulabo Sapera, Nakuul Mehta, Shovana Narayan or Salman Yusuff Khan famous or something?
I'm not conversant with Recipients of the Padma Shri. Who is this Ritwik Ghatak, Juthika Roy or Habib Tanvir guy?
I haven't the foggiest notion what Bengali film directors are about. And who the shit is Premankur Atorthy? Who on earth is Agradoot, Buddhadeb Dasgupta, Ashoke Viswanathan or Amit Bose? I really

haven't got a clue.

People of British India are a mystery to me. Gilbert Slater – doesn't ring a bell. And I have no idea who Budhal Faqir was. Couldn't tell you.

I've never heard of People from Shikarpur District. I certainly don't have any idea who Imran Channa is.

I also haven't kept up on People from Lahore. And I have no clue what Mian Ijaz ul Hassan is. Who the fuck is Masud Ahmad, Sana Nawaz or Asif Raza Mir? I haven't the faintest idea.

I'm completely ignorant of 21st-century Pakistani actresses. Who was Sadia Imam? I've never heard of a person called Neelo, Sanam Jung or Vaneeza Ahmad. I frankly haven't the foggiest idea.

Don't ask me about Pakistani Muslims. Is Abdul Sattar Edhi famous or something?

People from Karachi are unfamiliar to me. Do I need to know who Kainat Imtiaz, Danish Taimoor, Abida Sultan, Ibad Rehman or Saeeduzzaman Siddiqui is?

I obviously don't know any Politics of Karachi. Khidmat-e-Khalq Foundation – I don't understand this. Operation Clean-up – I don't know how to begin. I just don't know that. I have no clue who Shahi Sayed or Syed Mustafa Kamal is.

And I'm not familiar with Operations involving Pakistani special forces. I'm certain that I've never heard of Operation Black Thunderstorm or what the deal with Operation Janbaz is. The Siachen conflict – never heard of it. Damned if I know.

I also couldn't tell you what Hostage taking is about. The Norrmalmstorg robbery – what does that mean? And what the shit is The Beslan school hostage crisis? Search me.

I'm not well-versed in Massacres in Russia. The Komsomolskoye massacre – what is that? The Alkhan-Yurt massacre – I don't even know where to start. Couldn't say.

I definitely don't know what people mean by 'Police brutality'. I couldn't tell you about A Police riot or what Excited delirium is about. I also don't know the first thing about Medical emergencies. And I don't know what Mollaret's meningitis is or what the current state of research is on Paralytic shellfish poisoning. Hyperthermia – dunno. I

haven't the slightest idea. Cardiac tamponade – don't know.
And I'm not hip to Heat waves. What is 'A Heat wave' supposed to mean again, and what is A Cooling center anyway?
And I don't know anything about Heating, ventilating, and air conditioning. I don't have any idea what Thermal mass is.
Concerning Heat transfer, I am fully ignorant. What the hell is Natural convection, and what the hell is A Mesocosm? And what is A Heat kernel signature? I just don't know about that.
I haven't the foggiest notion what Fluid dynamics is about. Am I supposed to be familiar with Wave drag? How am I supposed to make sense of the Bulk temperature, and what's A Flow limiter got to do with it? Wouldn't know. I'm sorry, did you say 'Pulsatile flow', and what is The Sandia method supposed to be?
And I'm not conversant with Pneumatics. What about The Pneumatic refuse conveying system? Can you tell me how to get to The Beach Pneumatic Transit? What the hell? Compressed air gramophone – what's that supposed to mean?
Mechanical amplifiers are a mystery to me. A Servomechanism? Come again? Never heard of it.
And I don't know about Control devices. A Restrictive flow orifice? Doesn't ring a bell.
I've never heard of Gas technologies. The Boudouard reaction – I don't understand that. What's the deal with Gasification? How should I know? And what is a Cryogenic nitrogen plant?
I'm completely ignorant of Industrial processes. Please don't talk to me about Copper slag. Pasteurization – how should I know what that is? I'm clueless about that.
I also know nothing about Unit operations. Acid-base extraction? How should I know? What the fuck is Freeze-drying, and what on earth is A Belt dryer? I have absolutely no idea. The Sedimentation coefficient – not my field.
Food preservation is unfamiliar to me. An Olla – not my area of expertise. I have no clue what Tyndallization is or what in tarnation A Cooler is. Don't ask me. Don't ask me what A Reefer ship is. I have no idea. What in the world is The Radura?
And I'm not familiar with Cookware and bakeware. What is 'A Cezve'

supposed to mean, and what the heck is Wonder Pot?
I also don't know any Israeli inventions. I have no idea what Video Synopsis is or what the hell ReWalk is or whether I should care. Sabich – doesn't ring a bell. Ask someone who knows something. Ptitim – I don't understand this.
Don't ask me about Assistive technology. What, in the name of all that is holy, is Live conferencing?
I don't know what people mean by 'Teleconferencing'. What in God's name is Teletraining, and what is the idea with Web conferencing? AIM Phoneline – I don't know what that is. I can't tell you that. And what the shit is VenueGen?
I haven't kept up on Web conferencing. VSee – what is that? What's up with PGi? Come on.
I surely couldn't tell you what Freeware is about. What the hell is RetroShare, and what is the deal with RJ TextEd? What is XWindows Dock? I don't have any idea.
I don't know the first thing about Instant messaging clients for Linux. I'm also certain that I've never heard of Linphone.
Concerning IOS software, I am fully ignorant. Loopt – never heard of it. AOL Instant Messenger – what does that mean? Doesn't sound remotely familiar. StudioMini, is that even a thing? I haven't the remotest idea. Am I supposed to be familiar with NewsBlur?
I'm not hip to Free software. I also don't know what KDE Software Compilation 4 is or what is supposed to be special about SiSU. A Free standard – dunno. I just don't know. What about DESMO-J?
And I'm not well-versed in Software. How am I supposed to make sense of Greenzones, and what in tarnation is WinAPIOverride? Dream report? Come again? Never heard of it. Not a clue.
I don't know anything about Business software. SHAPE Services – how should I know what that is? What is 'Xcon' supposed to mean again, and what is Telecommunications billing about? No idea. The USAS application – I don't know how to begin.
I also haven't the foggiest notion what Fortran software is about. Monte Carlo N-Particle Transport Code? How should I know? Scientific simulation software is a mystery to me. What the fuck is BLOPEX, and what is SLEPc again?

I'm not conversant with Numerical libraries. What's the deal with MPFR, and what is the mystery about FFTW? And I'm sorry, did you say 'Hypre', and what is The GNU Multiple Precision Arithmetic Library? I haven't got a clue.

I don't know about Free software programmed in C. What, in the name of all that is holy, is Mdadm, and what is Komodo Edit anyway? And I don't have any idea what Gretl is. I just don't know that.

I've never heard of Statistical software. OxMetrics – I don't even know where to start. StatCVS – I don't understand that. I really haven't the faintest idea. What the shit is TinkerPlots, and what is BMDP supposed to be? I have no clue. RExcel – what is that?

I know nothing about Data analysis software. What's up with JHepWork? And what is SekChek Local? Couldn't tell you. What in the world is Teradata Warehouse Miner?

And I'm not familiar with Computer security software. WS-Security – what's that supposed to mean?

I don't know any Web service specifications. What the hell is WS-Policy, and what the hell is Apache Axis2? The Web Services Invocation Framework – don't know. Couldn't say. Flow Description Markup Language – what does that mean?

Don't ask me about XML-based standards. What in God's name is The Pronunciation Lexicon Specification, and what the heck is OPML? Am I supposed to be familiar with RDF/XML? I obviously haven't the slightest idea.

World Wide Web Consortium standards are unfamiliar to me. The Web Services Description Language – not my field. What is XSLT, and what is the idea with The Open Web Platform? I just don't know about that.

And I don't know what people mean by 'Web services'. How am I supposed to make sense of OWL-S, and what's Event-driven SOA got to do with it? What is 'XML Interface for Network Services' supposed to mean? I just don't know.

And I couldn't tell you what Markup languages are about. Please don't talk to me about XLink. OGDL, is that even a thing? How should I know? XGMML – not my area of expertise.

I haven't kept up on Data serialization formats. And what are

'Protocol Buffers' supposed to mean again, and what is the deal with a Comparison of data serialization formats? The Open Data Description Language? Doesn't ring a bell. Wouldn't know. SDXF? How should I know?

I'm completely ignorant of Persistence. Core Data – doesn't ring a bell. I have no clue what The Java Persistence API is. Damned if I know.

And I'm not well-versed in NeXT. What the fuck is The NeXT Computer, and what is Objective-C about? Interface Builder – how should I know what that is? I have absolutely no idea.

I also don't know the first thing about User interface builders. WaveMaker – I don't know what that is. And I'm certain that I've never heard of The Resource construction set or how I'm supposed to know something about Open Cobalt or how to make sense of it. Search me. I couldn't tell you about Microsoft Blend or what the mystery about AppFlower is.

I haven't the foggiest notion what JavaScript libraries are about. What's the deal with Bindows, and what in tarnation is Appcelerator? I don't know what The Prototype JavaScript Framework is or what JQuery UI is. What the hell?

I'm not hip to Year of introduction missing. I also have no idea what Tapatalk is or why people are so interested in BackTrack or what it is all about. The Olympus E-20 – I don't understand this. Ask someone who knows something. The EMD G12 – dunno.

Concerning Bridge digital cameras, I am fully ignorant. I'm sorry, did you say 'Panasonic Lumix DMC-FZ100'?

Panasonic Lumix cameras are a mystery to me. I've never heard of Panasonic Lumix DMC-GX1. I really don't have any idea what The Panasonic Lumix DMC-TZ3 was or what the hell it has to do with Panasonic Lumix DMC-FZ50. I haven't the foggiest idea. What about The Panasonic Lumix DMC-GH2?

I don't know about Superzoom. And don't ask me what The Nikon Coolpix P90 was.

I don't know anything about Nikon Coolpix cameras. The Nikon Coolpix S800c – I don't understand that.

I'm not conversant with American coming-of-age films. October Sky?

Come again? Never heard of it. The Breakfast Club – never heard of it. I certainly don't have any idea. The Genesis Children – I don't know how to begin. Come on. The Last Starfighter – what's that supposed to mean?

Don't ask me about Flying cars in fiction. What's up with Blade Runner, and what on earth is Harry Potter and the Chamber of Secrets?

I obviously know nothing about Android films. What in the world is Not Quite Human II?

I'm not familiar with Teen comedy films. The Inbetweeners Movie – not my field. What, in the name of all that is holy, is The Hollywood Knights? I surely haven't the remotest idea.

And I don't know what people mean by 'Films about virginity'. Please don't talk to me about Stealing Beauty. Losin' It – I don't even know where to start. I'm clueless about that. The Ballad of Jack and Rose – don't know.

I'm completely ignorant of Incest in film. Stay As You Are? Doesn't ring a bell. What the shit is August Underground's Mordum, and what is Andy Warhol's Frankenstein? I can't tell you that. And I Spit on Your Grave 2 – doesn't ring a bell. Doesn't sound remotely familiar. What the hell is Twin Peaks: Fire Walk with Me?

I couldn't tell you what Film scores by Ennio Morricone are about. Cinema Paradiso – I don't know what that is. I don't know the first thing about Allonsanfàn or what on earth Todo modo is or if it's worth knowing. Not a clue. And what in God's name is Especially on Sunday?

I don't know any Best Foreign Language Film BAFTA Award winners. And I don't know what the BAFTA Award for Best Film is or what Amores perros is about.

Mexican thriller films are unfamiliar to me. Satánico pandemonium – what does that mean? How am I supposed to make sense of Santa Sangre, and what is The Brainiac again? I frankly just don't know. I have no clue what El vampiro is or what the deal with Daniel & Ana is or if it's good to know.

I haven't kept up on Films about psychopaths. I have no idea what The American Friend is or what the heck Fatal Attraction is or if the whole

concept makes sense to me. The Young Poisoner's Handbook – not my area of expertise. I have no idea.
And I'm not well-versed in Neo-noir. The Sugarland Express – what is that? I certainly couldn't tell you about Who Framed Roger Rabbit or what the hell Long Hello and Short Goodbye is or what to think about it. No idea. What is Sam Noir?
And I'm not hip to Comedy mystery films. Radioland Murders – I don't understand this. Am I supposed to be familiar with Get a Clue? Couldn't tell you.
I've never heard of Lucasfilm films. The Star Wars sequel trilogy, is that even a thing?
Bad Robot Productions films are a mystery to me. Mission: Impossible – Ghost Protocol – dunno.
I also don't know about Dolby Surround 7.1 films. I'm certain that I've never heard of Gnomeo & Juliet.
I'm not conversant with Films based on Romeo and Juliet. What is 'Shakespeare in Love' supposed to mean, and what is the mystery about The Sea Prince and the Fire Child? Beneath the 12-Mile Reef – I don't know how to begin. I just don't know that. Amar te duele – what's that supposed to mean? I have no clue. Rome & Jewel – how should I know what that is?
And concerning Best Picture Academy Award winners, I am fully ignorant. I frankly don't have any idea what The Apartment is.
I definitely know nothing about Films whose writer won the Best Original Screenplay Academy Award. The King's Speech – never heard of it. Interrupted Melody? How should I know? Don't ask me. Don't ask me about George VI. And please don't talk to me about The Royal Family Order of King George VI. I'm sorry, did you say 'The King George VI Coronation Medal'? I just don't know about that.
I don't know what people mean by 'British royalty'. What about Succession to the British throne, and what is The Line of succession to the British throne anyway?
I surely haven't the foggiest notion what Succession to the British crown is about. Duke of Rothesay? Come again? Never heard of it. Don't ask me what The First Succession Act is. I haven't the faintest idea. What is 'The Exclusion Crisis' supposed to mean again?

I don't know anything about James II of England. The Declaration of Indulgence – I don't even know where to start. The Patriot Parliament – not my field. How should I know? Anne Hyde – who was that? I just don't know. And what in the world was The Loyal Parliament, and what is The Glorious Revolution supposed to be?
I'm not familiar with 17th century in Scotland. What's up with Jarlshof, and what the hell was A Commission of Justiciary? And what the shit is The Edinburgh Gazette, and what the heck is The Jacobean era? Wouldn't know.
I also don't know any Former populated places in Scotland. Dùn an Achaidh – don't know. Dùn Tealtaig – I don't understand that. I have absolutely no idea. Dun Ringill? Doesn't ring a bell. What the hell? Traprain Law or Isle Martin, is that even a real place?
Archaeological sites in East Lothian are unfamiliar to me. What's the deal with Nunraw, and what is the idea with Chesters Hill Fort? What in God's name is Black Castle, East Lothian? Search me.
And I'm completely ignorant of Scheduled Ancient Monuments in Scotland. Where the fuck was Pittarthie Castle? Don't ask me where The Ring of Brodgar is! I haven't the foggiest idea. What the fuck is Sunhoney?
I also haven't kept up on Visitor attractions in Orkney. I have no clue what The Old Man of Hoy is.
I couldn't tell you what Geography of Orkney is about. I have no idea what Veantro Bay is or what in tarnation Lairo Water is or what to make of it.
I'm not hip to Shapinsay. Quholm – not my area of expertise. I couldn't tell you about Balfour Castle or what is supposed to be special about Burroughston Broch or what it actually means. Couldn't say. What the hell is Mor Stein, and what's Castle Bloody got to do with it?
And I'm not well-versed in Buildings and structures in Orkney. I don't know where RAF Skaebrae is.
I really don't know the first thing about Royal Air Force stations in Scotland. RAF West Freugh – what is that? I don't have any idea where RAF Kilchiaran was. I haven't got a clue. And I have no clue where RAF Dallachy or RAF Grangemouth is.

And I'm not conversant with Buildings and structures in Dumfries and Galloway. I don't know how to get to Southerness lighthouse. The Scots' Dike – I don't know what that is. I don't have any idea. Kirkcudbright Castle – dunno.

Former castles in Scotland are a mystery to me. What, in the name of all that is holy, was Jedburgh Castle, and what was Pollock Castle about? How am I supposed to make sense of Montrose Castle? I'm clueless about that. And what is Kirkwall Castle? I haven't the remotest idea. Do people even go to Ayr Castle?

And I don't know about Castles in the Scottish Borders. Where is Cranshaws Castle? Nisbet House – what does that mean? Doesn't sound remotely familiar. I'm certain that I've never heard of Oliver Castle.

Concerning Houses completed in the 14th century, I am fully ignorant. And what is Levens Hall, and what is the deal with Palazzo dei Consoli? Dalton Castle – doesn't ring a bell. Ask someone who knows something. I also have no idea where Dacre Castle is. Come on. Am I supposed to be familiar with Palazzo Panciatichi?

Don't ask me about Castles in Cumbria. Liddel Strength – I don't understand this. I've never heard of Corby Castle. I haven't the slightest idea. Where in the world is Naworth Castle, Carlisle Castle or Sizergh Castle and Garden?

I don't know what people mean by 'Historic house museums in Cumbria'. Dove Cottage – never heard of it. Dalemain? How should I know? Damned if I know. And I have never been to Muncaster Castle or Brantwood.

I'm not familiar with Grade I listed houses. Old Soar Manor – I don't know how to begin. What is 'Vanbrugh Castle' supposed to mean, and what is Netherwitton Hall? I have no idea. Where the hell is Highfields, Buerton or Cambridge House?

I certainly don't know anything about National Trust properties in Kent. Can you tell me how to get to Ightham Mote? Scotney Castle, is that even a thing? I can't tell you that.

I haven't the foggiest notion what Gardens in Kent are about. Leeds Castle, is that even a real place?

I know nothing about Former zoos. What about SeaWorld Ohio?

I don't know any Amusement parks in Ohio. Where the fuck is Olentangy Park?

I'm also completely ignorant of Buildings and structures in Columbus, Ohio. Don't ask me where The Newport Music Hall is!

Visitor attractions in Columbus, Ohio are unfamiliar to me. I don't know what The Greater Columbus Convention Center is or how I'm supposed to know something about Scioto Greenway Trail or what people say about it. I don't have any idea where Lifestyle Communities Pavilion is. I have no clue.

I'm also not hip to Economy of Columbus, Ohio. I'm sorry, did you say 'The Game Manufacturers Association'? I don't know where The Short North is. Couldn't tell you. What in the world is Staber Industries, and what in tarnation is Zoombezi Bay? Don't ask me. Please don't talk to me about The North Market.

I haven't kept up on Game manufacturers. Rackham – what's that supposed to mean?

I'm not conversant with Role-playing game publishing companies. Nightfall Games – don't know. Games Workshop – how should I know what that is? I just don't know that. And what is 'Fantasy Flight Games' supposed to mean again, and what is Issaries, Inc. again? I just don't know. What the shit was Guardians of Order?

I couldn't tell you what Board game publishing companies are about. Game Designers' Workshop – I don't even know where to start. Lookout Games? Doesn't ring a bell. I just don't know about that.

I'm also not well-versed in Companies based in Lower Saxony. I have no clue what Volkswagen is.

And I don't know the first thing about Volkswagen vehicles. Am I supposed to know Herbie? I also don't have any idea what Busfest is. I haven't the faintest idea.

Concerning Herbie films, I am fully ignorant. What's the deal with Herbie: Fully Loaded, and what is Herbie, the Love Bug anyway? What the fuck is The Love Bug, and what is the mystery about Herbie Rides Again? Not a clue.

Films based on novels are a mystery to me. What's up with Tow Truck Pluck, and what on earth is Black Narcissus?

I also don't know about Dutch-language films. Tropic of Emerald –

not my area of expertise. And don't ask me what To Play or to Die is. Wouldn't know. Mijn nachten met Susan, Olga, Julie, Piet en Sandra – I don't know what that is. What the hell? Allemaal naar Bed? Come again? Never heard of it. De Pijnbank – not my field.

I've never heard of Dutch films. The Hypocrites – what is that? And I couldn't tell you about The Human Centipede First Sequence. I haven't the foggiest idea.

I don't know what people mean by 'Splatter films'. Zombie Women of Satan – doesn't ring a bell.

I'm also not familiar with Zombie comedy films. I'm certain that I've never heard of Die You Zombie Bastards! or what the mystery about SARS Wars is.

And I know nothing about Cannibalism in fiction. A Boy and His Dog – I don't understand that. The Texas Chainsaw Massacre 2 – never heard of it. Couldn't say.

I also don't know anything about Sequel films. How am I supposed to make sense of Saw 3D?

And I don't know any Films directed by Kevin Greutert. I have no idea what Jessabelle is or why people are so interested in Saw VI or how to make sense of it.

I'm completely ignorant of Films shot in Toronto. The 6th Day – what does that mean? What, in the name of all that is holy, is Seventeen Again, and what the hell is Hidden in America? How should I know? What the hell is Gone Dark, and what the heck is A Cool, Dry Place? Don't ask me about Columbia Pictures films. Please don't talk to me about The Animal. Goin' Coconuts? How should I know? Search me. Wild Things: Foursome – I don't know how to begin.

I'm also not hip to Revolution Studios films. Tears of the Sun – what's that supposed to mean? Am I supposed to be familiar with The New Guy? I haven't got a clue.

I really haven't kept up on United States Navy in films. Someone Special – dunno. The Secret Land? Doesn't ring a bell. No idea. Cinderella Liberty – I don't even know where to start. I just don't know. What is 'The Hunt for Red October' supposed to mean, and what's Executive Decision got to do with it?

Films about prostitution are unfamiliar to me. I also have no clue what

Amar Prem is or what Hotel Angel is.
I'm not conversant with Films shot in Mumbai. And what about Thalaivaa, and what is the idea with Lage Raho Munna Bhai?
I certainly couldn't tell you what Dolby Atmos films are about. What in God's name is Race 2?
I'm not well-versed in Detective films. What in the world is Lady in Cement?
I don't know the first thing about Comedy thriller films. I don't have any idea what Strange Boarders is or what the current state of research is on Karmic Mahjong. I surely don't know what Adieu poulet is or what the hell it has to do with La Torre de los Siete Jorobados. I haven't the remotest idea. And what is Boys of the City?
I obviously don't know about Compositions by Charles Williams. Majestic Fanfare – not my area of expertise. Don't ask me what Devil's Galop is. I'm clueless about that. The Young Mr Pitt, is that even a thing?
Concerning Films about Prime Ministers of the United Kingdom, I am fully ignorant. The Tony Blair Witch Project – I don't know what that is. What is 'Tracking Down Maggie' supposed to mean again? I haven't the slightest idea.
I also don't know what people mean by 'Cultural depictions of Tony Blair'. I've never heard of Jeffrey Archer: The Truth.
I haven't the foggiest notion what BBC Television programmes are about. Picture Page – doesn't ring a bell. Bang Goes the Theory – don't know. Ask someone who knows something. And I couldn't tell you about Glendogie Bogey or what Tomorrow's World was about.
BBC Scotland television programmes are a mystery to me. The Mad Death – I don't understand this. The Adventure Show – not my field. I have no idea.
I frankly don't know any Scottish films. And I have no idea what That Sinking Feeling is or what the deal with Man Dancin' is. I'm sorry, did you say 'Running in Traffic'? I have absolutely no idea.
I know nothing about Films set in Northumberland. Sherlock Holmes Faces Death – I don't know how to begin.
And I'm completely ignorant of Films set in England. Please don't talk to me about Bring Me the Head of Mavis Davis.

I'm not hip to Goldcrest Films films. What's the deal with Escape from New York? And what is Elvis and Anabelle? Come on.

I haven't kept up on Films shot in Missouri. The Day After – never heard of it. I'm also certain that I've never heard of 16 In Webster Groves. Couldn't tell you.

Don't ask me about Films directed by Nicholas Meyer. What the fuck is Star Trek II: The Wrath of Khan?

Films set in the future are unfamiliar to me. What the shit is Circuitry Man, and what is the deal with Uma Aventura no Tempo? And I don't know how to get to Mission: Space. Damned if I know. The Airzone Solution – how should I know what that is?

I'm not familiar with American science fiction films. How am I supposed to make sense of Soylent Green, and what is Twilight Zone: The Movie supposed to be? Eyeborgs? Doesn't ring a bell. Don't ask me. Space Specks – dunno.

I don't know anything about Aviation films. Diverted – what's that supposed to mean?

And I'm not well-versed in CBC network shows. I have no clue what Adrienne At Large was or what the heck CBC News Magazine is or whether I should care. I don't have any idea what Comedy Cafe is. I don't have any idea.

I don't know the first thing about Television series produced in Montreal. And I don't know what Just for Laughs: Gags is or what in tarnation Just for Laughs is.

Concerning The Comedy Network shows, I am fully ignorant. Good Morning World – not my area of expertise. Puppets Who Kill – I don't even know where to start. Doesn't sound remotely familiar. Odd Job Jack – what does that mean? I just don't know. What, in the name of all that is holy, is The Winnipeg Comedy Festival?

And I don't know about CBC Radio One programs. Ontario Morning – I don't understand that. Trust Inc.? Come again? Never heard of it. I have no clue. I've never heard of Cross Country Checkup. I can't tell you that. 50 Tracks? How should I know? Am I supposed to be familiar with Vinyl Tap?

I couldn't tell you what Music chart shows are about. I also couldn't tell you about The TGIF Chart or what is supposed to be special about

Canada's Top 20 Countdown or if it's worth knowing. The Hot30 Countdown – I don't understand this. I haven't the faintest idea. The Weekend 22 – doesn't ring a bell.

I don't know what people mean by 'Australian radio programs'. The Matt and Jo Show – don't know. And what the hell is Merrick and the Highway Patrol, and what is Ultima Thule Ambient Music about? What the hell? What's up with The Good Oil?

I'm not conversant with Music podcasts. Coverville – what is that? And I haven't the foggiest notion what Audio podcasts are about. VGN Radio – I don't know what that is. Please don't talk to me about Judge John Hodgman. I haven't the foggiest idea. PotterCast – never heard of it. Wouldn't know. The Total Soccer Show – not my field. The Feast of Fun – I don't know how to begin.

Sports podcasts are a mystery to me. And don't ask me what Football Weekly is. What about The Joe Rogan Experience, and what is The Football Ramble again? Search me. Me1 vs Me2 Snooker with Richard Herring – what's that supposed to mean?

I also know nothing about Football media in the United Kingdom. I have no idea what Footytube is or what on earth The Big Match is. NFL Special? Doesn't ring a bell. I just don't know about that. I'm certain that I've never heard of Soccer AM.

I haven't kept up on Association football websites. And what is 'Playerhistory.com' supposed to mean, and what is Web F.C. anyway? I don't know what Football fans index is or how I'm supposed to know something about Football365 or what it is all about. How should I know? Bestiario del balón – dunno.

I'm completely ignorant of Sport Internet forums. ClutchFans – I don't even know where to start.

I don't know any Basketball media. I have no clue what The Physics of Basketball is or why people are so interested in TrueHoop. What in the world is NBA Premium TV? I just don't know.

I'm not hip to Television in the Philippines. And what is 'Myx' supposed to mean again, and what is Viva Entertainment?

Don't ask me about Television in Metro Manila. Gateway UHF Broadcasting – not my area of expertise. I couldn't tell you about Progressive Broadcasting Corporation or what the mystery about

Eagle Broadcasting Corporation is. Not a clue. What in God's name is Southern Broadcasting Network?
Philippine television networks are unfamiliar to me. Solar TV Network – I don't understand that. I'm sorry, did you say 'Net 25', and what on earth is Solar News Channel? I frankly just don't know that. Solar All Access, is that even a thing?
I don't know anything about Iglesia ni Cristo. And what is DYFX, and what is the mystery about DZCE-TV? Where is Ciudad de Victoria located? Couldn't say. Ang Tamang Daan – how should I know what that is?
I'm also not familiar with Christian radio stations in the Philippines. What the shit is DZJV, and what the heck is ZOE Broadcasting Network? What the fuck is DWSN? I'm clueless about that.
Concerning Companies based in Pasig, I am fully ignorant. How am I supposed to make sense of SEAOIL Philippines?
I also don't know the first thing about Automotive fuel brands. What's the deal with Ultramar, and what in tarnation is Imperial Oil? Nippon Oil – don't know. I haven't the slightest idea. I don't have any idea what Royal Dutch Shell is or what the current state of research is on Petronor or if it's good to know.
I'm also not well-versed in Oil companies of the Netherlands. Please don't talk to me about LukArco.
I also don't know about ARCO. The Boston and Montana Consolidated Copper and Silver Mining Company? Come again? Never heard of it.
I have no clue where Energy Plaza is. I have no idea. Who the hell is Robert Orville Anderson? Come on. Sinclair Oil Corporation – doesn't ring a bell.
I don't know what people mean by 'Skyscrapers between 150 and 199 meters'. Where is The World Trade Center Mexico City? I also have no idea where One Biscayne Tower or 191 North Wacker is. I haven't got a clue.
I obviously haven't the foggiest notion what Buildings and structures with revolving restaurants are about. The Phare de la méditerranée – I don't understand this.
I'm also not conversant with Observation towers in France. I have never been to the Grand Wintersberg. Where the hell is The

Wasenkoepfel or Eiffel Tower? I have absolutely no idea.
I know nothing about The Eiffel Tower. And I don't know who Stephen Sauvestre, Victor Lustig or Gustave Eiffel was.
I certainly couldn't tell you what People from Dijon are about. Who the shit is Jean-Pierre Leguay or Albert Marcœur?
I'm completely ignorant of Cathedral organists. I've never heard of The Camidge family. Are Richard Runciman Terry or Louis-Claude Daquin famous or something? I haven't the remotest idea.
I also don't know any Jewish classical composers. Benjamin Frankel, Julius Benedict or Hanns Eisler – who are they?
Don't ask me about People who emigrated to escape Nazism. I have no idea who Helene Thimig was. Who the fuck is Franz Kraus? No idea.
Austrian Jews are a mystery to me. Who on earth is Itzchak Tarkay, Manfred Ackermann or Alfred Hermann Fried?
I really don't know anything about Austrian emigrants to the United States. I don't have any idea who Marjorie Perloff is.
I'm not hip to American literary critics. And who is this John Hollander guy? I have no clue who Carolyn See, Marilyn Stasio, Wai Chee Dimock or Robert Appelbaum is. I don't have any idea.
I really haven't kept up on Guggenheim Fellows. Who is Richard Janko, Philip James DeVries, Julie Otsuka or Luis Enrique Sam Colop? And concerning University of Oregon faculty, I am fully ignorant. Is Geri Doran famous or something? Am I supposed to know Ehud Havazelet or Pamela Cytrynbaum? Couldn't tell you.
People from Pacifica, California are unfamiliar to me. I've also never heard of a person called Bryan Garaventa. Who the hell is Tony Cadena? Doesn't sound remotely familiar. What's up with Crash Holly, Jef Raskin or Ruth Atkinson?
And I'm not familiar with Professional wrestlers who committed suicide. I don't know who Kerry Von Erich was.
I really don't know about Suicides by firearm in Texas. Stephen Scherer – who is that? And who the shit is Joe Ball or Larry Gene Ashbrook? I can't tell you that.
I'm not well-versed in Mass shootings in the United States. I also have no idea who The Washington Navy Yard shooting was. What, in the

name of all that is holy, was The Old Salisbury Road murders, and what's The Virginia Tech massacre got to do with it? I haven't the faintest idea. The Wah Mee massacre – not my field.
I obviously don't know what people mean by 'School massacres in the United States'. Don't ask me what The Bath School disaster is. The Red Lake massacre – what's that supposed to mean? Ask someone who knows something. Are The Sandy Hook Elementary School shooting or Northern Illinois University shooting famous or something?
And I don't know the first thing about Clinton County, Michigan. Where in the world is The Stony Creek Bridge, East Ward School or Giles J. Gibbs Building?
And I'm not conversant with National Register of Historic Places in Michigan. I have no idea what USCGC Bramble WLB-392 is. The Douglas Union School, Winter Site or Palmer Park Apartment Building Historic District, is that even a real place? Don't ask me.
I also couldn't tell you what Iris-class seagoing buoy tenders are about. USCGC Spar WLB-403 – never heard of it. I'm certain that I've never heard of USCGC Woodrush WLB-407 or what USCGC Blackthorn WLB-391 was or what to think about it. What the hell?
I've never heard of Ships sunk in collisions. BAP Pacocha SS-48 – I don't know what that is. USS S-51 SS-162? How should I know? Wouldn't know. HMS H47 – dunno.
I know nothing about United States S-class submarines. USS S-15 SS-120 – what does that mean?
And I haven't the foggiest notion what World War II submarines of the United States are about. USS Quillback SS-424 – what is that? Am I supposed to be familiar with USS Moray SS-300? I just don't know. USS Ronquil SS-396 – I don't even know where to start. I have no clue. What is 'USS Sea Dog SS-401' supposed to mean, and what the hell is USS Mingo SS-261?
And I don't know any Ships built in Pennsylvania. What was 'USS Concord CL-10' supposed to mean again, and what was the deal with USS Navajo AT-52?
And don't ask me about World War II cruisers of the United States. USS Vincennes CA-44 – not my area of expertise. I don't know what USS Canberra CA-70 is or what the hell USS Atlanta CL-51 is or if the

whole concept makes sense to me. Search me.
I'm completely ignorant of Ships built in New Jersey. I have no clue what USS Huntington CL-107 is.
I also haven't kept up on United States Navy West Virginia-related ships. What about USS Herbert J. Thomas DD-833, and what is USS West Virginia BB-48 supposed to be? I'm sorry, did you say 'USNS Wheeling T-AGM-8'? Not a clue. And what was USS Stump DD-978? And concerning Colorado-class battleships, I am fully ignorant. USS Maryland BB-46 – I don't understand that. USS Colorado BB-45 – I don't know how to begin. I just don't know about that. USS Washington BB-47 – don't know.
Abandoned military projects of the United States are unfamiliar to me. And what in the world is The Special Purpose Individual Weapon, and what is The Sea Control Ship again?
And I'm not hip to Cold War aircraft carriers of the United States. USS Sicily CVE-118 – doesn't ring a bell. Please don't talk to me about USS Abraham Lincoln CVN-72. I just don't know. USS Kitty Hawk CV-63? Doesn't ring a bell. I just don't know that. I couldn't tell you about The VSTOL Support Ship.
Carrier Strike Group Nine is a mystery to me. I don't have any idea what USS Ford FFG-54 is or what USS Halsey DDG-97 is about or what it actually means. USS Rodney M. Davis FFG-60 – what's that supposed to mean? I haven't the foggiest idea.
I don't know about Active frigates of the United States. USS Samuel B. Roberts FFG-58 – not my field. USS McClusky FFG-41, is that even a thing? Damned if I know. USS Simpson FFG-56 – I don't understand this.
I don't know anything about Oliver Hazard Perry-class frigates of the United States Navy. Don't ask me what USS Lewis B. Puller FFG-23 was. I've never heard of USS Copeland FFG-25. Couldn't say.
I'm not familiar with Active frigates of Egypt. I have no idea what USS Fahrion FFG-22 is or what the deal with USS Gallery FFG-26 is or what to make of it.
I don't know the first thing about Cold War frigates and destroyer escorts of the United States. USS Bisbee PF-46 – how should I know what that is? What in God's name was USS McCoy Reynolds DE-440,

and what was the idea with USS Formoe DE-509? I have no idea. What the fuck were Garcia-class frigate, and what were Knox-class frigate about?

I'm not conversant with Tacoma-class frigates of the Colombian Navy. I'm certain that I've never heard of USS Groton PF-29 or what in tarnation USS Burlington PF-51 was or what people say about it.

And I'm not well-versed in Burlington, Iowa. What the shit is KGRS? I don't know what people mean by 'Radio stations in Iowa'. KZIA – not my area of expertise.

Don't ask me about Media in Cedar Rapids, Iowa. How am I supposed to make sense of KKSY-FM?

I surely don't know any Country radio stations in the United States. WEMB – I don't even know where to start. What's the deal with KTHK, and what is WRCY? I haven't got a clue. And what the hell is WTGE, and what on earth is KMXQ?

I'm also completely ignorant of Radio stations in Idaho. I have no clue what KSQS is or what the hell it has to do with KZJB. I don't know what KMEI-LP is. Come on.

And I haven't kept up on 3ABN radio stations. KHBR-LP – dunno. And I know nothing about Low-power FM radio stations in Arkansas. What, in the name of all that is holy, is KPWH-LP, and what is KTPV-LP anyway? What is KOZR-LP, and what is the mystery about KQIX-LP? No idea.

I haven't the foggiest notion what Christian radio stations in the United States are about. WTLI – I don't understand that. KPRZ – never heard of it. I don't have any idea.

And concerning Radio stations in San Diego, California, I am fully ignorant. What's up with KBRT, and what in tarnation is KFMB-FM? KGB-FM – what does that mean? I haven't the slightest idea.

Radio stations in Los Angeles, California are unfamiliar to me. KSCA? Come again? Never heard of it. KAHZ – don't know. I'm clueless about that. KHHT – I don't know how to begin. How should I know? KBLA – doesn't ring a bell. I couldn't tell you about KBPK.

Rhythmic oldies radio stations are a mystery to me. What is 'KTGV' supposed to mean?

I couldn't tell you what Radio stations in Tucson, Arizona are about.

KHYT – I don't know what that is.
I really don't know anything about Classic hits radio stations in the United States. WOCL – what is that? KQNK-FM – what's that supposed to mean? I haven't the faintest idea. What about WIKK, and what the hell is WRTZ? I can't tell you that. And I don't have any idea what WRQQ is.
I'm not familiar with Oldies radio stations in the United States. I'm sorry, did you say 'WTOB', and what's WTDK got to do with it?
I've never heard of Radio stations in Piedmont Triad. WFDD? How should I know? What in the world is WMKS, and what is the deal with WSIC? Don't ask me. Am I supposed to be familiar with WLXN?
I'm also not conversant with News and talk radio stations in the United States. And don't ask me what WTPL is. WWRC – how should I know what that is? Couldn't tell you. WESO? Doesn't ring a bell. I have absolutely no idea. WIUJ, is that even a thing?
I'm also not hip to Radio stations in Maryland. And I have no idea what WMVK-LP is.
I also don't know what people mean by 'Cecil County, Maryland'. What in God's name is The Cecil Whig? Can you tell me how to get to The Chesapeake City Bridge? Ask someone who knows something. And I'm certain that I've never heard of The Cecil County Sheriff's Office.
I don't know the first thing about Bridge disasters in the United States. Don't ask me where The Newhall Pass interchange or I-5 Skagit River Bridge collapse is!
And don't ask me about The Santa Susana Mountains. I don't have any idea where The Santa Susana Pass is. I certainly don't know where California's 25th congressional district or California's 38th State Assembly district is. What the hell?
And I haven't kept up on Simi Valley, California. KIRN – not my field. Where the fuck is California's 27th State Senate district? I just don't know.
I don't know about West Hills, Los Angeles. I don't know how to get to California's 30th congressional district. West Valley Christian School – not my area of expertise. Search me. And what the fuck is Los Angeles City Council District 12?

And I'm not well-versed in Woodland Hills, Los Angeles. I have no clue what Los Angeles City Council District 3 is. Do people even go to Ventura Boulevard? I just don't know about that. Where is The Westfield Promenade or Motion Picture & Television Country House and Hospital located?

I also know nothing about Shopping malls in Los Angeles, California. I have no idea where Westfield Topanga is.

I'm completely ignorant of Canoga Park, Los Angeles. And I don't know what Atomics International was.

I haven't the foggiest notion what Civilian nuclear power accidents are about. I have never been to Forsmark Nuclear Power Plant. What's the deal with KS 150? I haven't the remotest idea. I have no clue where The Mihama Nuclear Power Plant is.

Concerning Vattenfall nuclear power stations, I am fully ignorant. Where is Krümmel Nuclear Power Plant, Brunsbüttel Nuclear Power Plant or Brokdorf Nuclear Power Plant?

I don't know any Former nuclear power stations in Germany. And where the hell is The Obrigheim Nuclear Power Plant?

Buildings and structures in Neckar-Odenwald-Kreis are a mystery to me. Schloss Mosbach – dunno.

Castles in Baden-Württemberg are unfamiliar to me. I've also never heard of Sausenburg Castle. Please don't talk to me about Amlishagen Castle. Wouldn't know.

I'm not familiar with Hill castles. What the hell is Salzburg Castle? Can you tell me how to get to Frankenstein Castle or Reuland Castle? I definitely don't know that.

I definitely couldn't tell you what Rhön-Grabfeld is about. Bischofsheim an der Rhön or Nordheim vor der Rhön, is that even a real place?

I also don't know anything about The Rhön Mountains. I don't have any idea where Schleid is. What the shit is The Rhön-Rossitten Gesellschaft? I have no clue. And what is Hohe Rhön?

I don't know what people mean by 'Wartburgkreis'. Don't ask me where Gerstungen is! The Treaty of Gerstungen – never heard of it. Not a clue.

And I don't know the first thing about Peace treaties. How am I

supposed to make sense of The Treaty of Phoenice, and what the heck was The Declaratio Ferdinandei?
And I'm not hip to 16th-century treaties. What was The Treaty of Rouen?
Don't ask me about History of Rouen. What, in the name of all that is holy, is Synod of Rouen, and what was The Old Rouen tramway supposed to be? The Rouen manufactory – I don't understand that. I just don't know. The Harelle – I don't understand this. I frankly haven't got a clue. I couldn't tell you about the Siege of Rouen.
I don't know about Ceramics manufacturers of France. Chantilly porcelain – what does that mean? The Ateliers Clérissy? Come again? Never heard of it. Doesn't sound remotely familiar. Honoré Savy – I don't know what that is.
I'm not well-versed in Porcelain. What is 'Phanolith' supposed to mean again?
And I'm not conversant with Ceramic art. Brookfield Craft Center – don't know. What was 'Vernon Kilns' supposed to mean? Come on.
I know nothing about Non-profit organizations based in Connecticut. Yale University – what is that? SoldierSanta – doesn't ring a bell. No idea.
I'm completely ignorant of Visitor attractions in New Haven, Connecticut. Where in the world is The New Haven Lawn Club?
I haven't kept up on Buildings and structures on the National Register of Historic Places in Connecticut. And I don't know how to get to The Lighthouse Point Carousel. Where the fuck is Natchaug Forest Lumber Shed or Connecticut Valley Hospital? I have no idea. Concerning Historic districts in Middlesex County, Connecticut, I am fully ignorant. I don't know where the Middletown South Green Historic District was. Essex Historic District? How should I know? I frankly haven't the foggiest idea. And do people even go to Haddam Center Historic District or East Haddam Historic District?
I definitely haven't the foggiest notion what National Register of Historic Places in Connecticut are about. I have no idea where The Commodore Hull School is. I have no clue where The Orange Street Historic District is. I don't have any idea. Where is Bridgeport City Hall, Trowbridge Square Historic District or American Legion Forest

CCC Shelter?
Italianate architecture in Connecticut is a mystery to me. Where the hell was Old Bacon Academy? And I have never been to The Ninth Square Historic District. Couldn't say. Can you tell me how to get to Glenville Historic District, Bozrah Congregational Church and Parsonage or Mystic Bridge Historic District?
Historic districts in Fairfield County, Connecticut are unfamiliar to me. I've never heard of Black Rock Gardens Historic District. I don't have any idea where Mill Cove Historic District is. Damned if I know. The Norwalk Green Historic District or Kings Highway North Historic District, is that even a real place?
I couldn't tell you what Federal architecture in Connecticut is about. Don't ask me where Hebron Center Historic District is! I don't know how to get to Benjamin Bushnell Farm. Don't ask me. Where in the world is The Hadlyme Ferry Historic District or Daniel and Esther Bartlett House?
And I don't know what people mean by 'Historic districts in New London County, Connecticut'. I don't know where The Civic Institutions Historic District is.
I'm also not hip to New London, Connecticut. Kelo v. City of New London – what's that supposed to mean? What's up with The Connecticut Lyric Opera? I haven't the faintest idea.
And I don't know any United States Supreme Court cases of the Rehnquist Court. Ring v. Arizona? Doesn't ring a bell. Godinez v. Moran – I don't even know where to start. I haven't the slightest idea. I really don't know anything about Capital punishment in Arizona. I have no idea what Tison v. Arizona is or what is supposed to be special about Arizona State Prison Complex – Perryville or how to make sense of it. What in the world is Walton v. Arizona, and what is Schriro v. Summerlin again? Couldn't tell you. I don't have any idea what Arizona State Prison Complex – Eyman is.
I don't know about Women's prisons in the United States. Bayview Correctional Facility – not my field. And where the fuck is Massachusetts Correctional Institution – Framingham? How should I know? Don't ask me what The New York Women's House of Detention was. I just don't know. What about The Minnesota

Correctional Facility – Shakopee, and what is The Tennessee Prison for Women?
And I don't know the first thing about Buildings and structures in Nashville, Tennessee. Do people even go to Fort Nashborough?
Don't ask me about Visitor attractions in Nashville, Tennessee. Music City Queen – how should I know what that is? What in God's name is Nashville Children's Theatre, and what on earth is The War Memorial Auditorium? Ask someone who knows something. I have no clue where The Tennessee State Capitol or Station Inn is.
I'm also not familiar with Music venues in Tennessee. The Mercy Lounge, is that even a thing? And what the fuck is Trinity Music City? I can't tell you that. Where is Ryman Auditorium or The New Daisy Theatre?
And I'm not conversant with National Historic Landmarks in Tennessee. Where the hell is The Sycamore Shoals? I have never been to Rattle and Snap. Search me.
I'm also completely ignorant of American Revolutionary War sites. What the hell is The Cane Creek Friends Meeting, and what is The Boot Monument about? I'm sorry, did you say 'The Henry Knox Trail'? Wouldn't know. Can you tell me how to get to The Mandeville House or Revolutionary War Cemetery?
And concerning Quaker meeting houses in North Carolina, I am fully ignorant. I have no idea where Friends Spring Meeting House or Deep River Friends Meeting House and Cemetery is.
I haven't kept up on Cemeteries in North Carolina. I've never heard of Red House Presbyterian Church or Summerville Presbyterian Church and Cemetery.
I'm not well-versed in Neoclassical architecture in North Carolina. Where was Flora MacDonald College located? Memorial Reformed Church or East Avenue Tabernacle Associated Reformed Presbyterian Church, is that even a real place? I really just don't know that.
I know nothing about Presbyterian churches in North Carolina. And don't ask me where Black River Presbyterian and Ivanhoe Baptist Churches are! I don't know how to get to South River Presbyterian Church, Big Rockfish Presbyterian Church, Philadelphus Presbyterian Church or Griers Presbyterian Church and Cemetery. I'm clueless

about that.
And I haven't the foggiest notion what Properties of religious function on the National Register of Historic Places in North Carolina are about. Where in the world is St. Paul's Episcopal Church and Cemetery, Roxboro Male Academy and Methodist Parsonage, Ramah Presbyterian Church and Cemetery, St. Paul's Episcopal Church and Churchyard or Carver's Creek Methodist Church?
I couldn't tell you what Episcopal churches in North Carolina are about. I definitely don't have any idea where St. Andrew's Episcopal Church and Cemetery is.
Anglican cemeteries are a mystery to me. I obviously don't know where Christ Episcopal Church and Tashua Burial Ground is. And I don't know what Bilbao British Cemetery is. I have no clue.
I'm not hip to Basque. What the shit is Tourism in the Basque Autonomous Community, and what is the idea with Basque Radical Rock?
And I don't know about Punk rock. How am I supposed to make sense of A Skinhead, and what is the mystery about Punk rock subgenres? And I don't know any Subcultures. What's the deal with A Zine, and what is Underground culture anyway? Am I supposed to be familiar with Some Gritstone Climbs? What the hell? Psychobilly – not my area of expertise.
Fanzines are unfamiliar to me. 16 magazine – I don't know how to begin. Sleazoid Express – never heard of it. Not a clue. I have no clue what Psychotronic Video was or how I'm supposed to know something about Zine World. I just don't know about that. What, in the name of all that is holy, was Girl Germs?
I don't know the first thing about Entertainment magazines. OK! – dunno. EU Jacksonville – what does that mean? I certainly haven't the remotest idea.
Don't ask me about American magazines. What is Beyond Investigation Magazine, and what the hell is LOOK Magazine? And what is 'California Lawyer' supposed to mean, and what was the deal with Fangoria Comics? Doesn't sound remotely familiar.
I'm not conversant with Horror fiction magazines. I couldn't tell you about H. P. Lovecraft's Magazine of Horror or what on earth Terror

Australis is.

I don't know anything about H. P. Lovecraft. Tryout – I don't understand this. Thalarion? Come again? Never heard of it. Come on. And I don't know what people mean by 'Fictional islands'. What is 'Isle of the Ape' supposed to mean again, and what in tarnation is Moosylvania? Nim's Island – I don't understand that. I have absolutely no idea. What in the world is The Coral Island? I obviously haven't got a clue. And what is Tracy Island?

I also haven't kept up on Films about writers. The Waterdance – I don't know what that is. Witness 11 – doesn't ring a bell. I don't have any idea.

I'm completely ignorant of Films shot in California. What about Zoolander, and what's Criminally Insane 2 got to do with it? Beyond the Mat? How should I know? I haven't the foggiest idea. What in God's name is Frances Ha?

I'm not well-versed in Mental illness in fiction. The Language of Goldfish – how should I know what that is? Pagla Kahin Ka – what's that supposed to mean? No idea.

I've never heard of Films directed by Shakti Samanta. I'm certain that I've never heard of Alag Alag or why people are so interested in Mehbooba.

I also know nothing about Compositions by Rahul Dev Burman. Paraya Dhan? Doesn't ring a bell.

I'm not familiar with British weekly magazines. Radio Times, is that even a thing?

I surely couldn't tell you what British radio is about. And please don't talk to me about The Westerglen transmitting station. The Radio Academy Awards – not my field. I just don't know. Who on earth is Torquil Riley-Smith?

I'm not hip to Sony Radio Academy Awards. The 25th Sony Radio Academy Awards – what is that? Who is this Frank Wappat guy? Couldn't say.

I definitely haven't the foggiest notion what English radio personalities are about. And I don't have any idea who Mark Powlett was. John Kennedy O'Connor or Sarah-Jane Crawford – who are they? Don't ask me.

I definitely don't know about Writers from London. I have no clue who John Donne was. Is Israel Zangwill famous or something? Damned if I know. And who the fuck is James Caulfield or Nicholas Harpsfield?
19th-century English writers are unfamiliar to me. Do I need to know who Pierce Egan the Younger is? Who was Mary Hays? I certainly don't know.
Don't ask me about Feminism and history. I've never heard of a person called Anne Bradstreet.
I don't know any American colonial women. And who the shit is Penelope Stout, Ann Pudeator, Anne Hutchinson or Ann Hibbins?
Concerning People from Boston, Massachusetts, I am fully ignorant. Am I supposed to know Norman B. Leventhal or Joyce Ballou Gregorian?
American fantasy writers are a mystery to me. I also have no idea who Christie Golden or Elizabeth Moon is.
I don't know the first thing about American science fiction writers. Are Karl Edward Wagner or Jayge Carr famous or something?
I'm not conversant with Kenyon College alumni. What's up with Jenna Blum?
I'm also completely ignorant of People from Minnesota. I don't know who Reynold B. Johnson was. Who the hell is Aysh-ke-bah-ke-ko-zhay, Aaron Horkey, Chief Shakopee or John Schreiber? How should I know?
I'm not well-versed in IBM Fellows. What the hell is Irene Greif? Georg Bednorz, Hans Pfeiffer or Tze-Chiang Chen – doesn't ring a bell. I haven't the slightest idea.
And I don't know anything about Nobel laureates in Physics. Arno Allan Penzias – who is that? Who on earth is Abdus Salam? I have no idea. Who is this Albert Abraham Michelson, Johannes Stark or Gustaf Dalén guy?
I haven't kept up on People from Jhang District. And who the fuck is Mansoor Malangi?
I've also never heard of Pakistani singers. And I don't have any idea who Akhlaq Ahmed was. I have no clue who Junaid Jamshed, Rafiq Shinwari, Shahram Azhar or Mustafa Zahid is. Couldn't tell you.

I know nothing about Quran reciters. I've also never heard of a person called Khursheed Ahmad. Who the shit is Muhammad Farooq, Aban ibn Taghlib, Mujahid Abdul-Karim or Saad El Ghamidi? Ask someone who knows something.
And I couldn't tell you what Journalists from Karachi are about. Is Anam Tanveer famous or something?
I haven't the foggiest notion what Italianate architecture in North Carolina is about. Where the fuck is The Bright Leaf Historic District? Do people even go to Rocky River Presbyterian Church or Forestville Baptist Church? I certainly haven't the faintest idea.
I'm not familiar with National Register of Historic Places in North Carolina. Where is The Carolina Inn, Downtown Wilkesboro Historic District or Jefferson Standard Building?
I also don't know what people mean by 'University of North Carolina at Chapel Hill landmarks'. Where the hell is Morehead Planetarium and Science Center?
Planetaria in the United States are unfamiliar to me. What the fuck is The Saint Louis Science Center? I also have no clue where The Houston Museum of Natural Science is. I'm clueless about that. What the shit is The Pink Palace Museum and Planetarium?
I'm not hip to Science museums in Texas. Am I supposed to be familiar with The 20th Century Technology Museum? And I have no idea where Don Harrington Discovery Center is. Search me. I have never been to The Brazos Valley Museum of Natural History or Witte Museum.
And concerning Technology museums in the United States, I am fully ignorant. I don't have any idea what The American Airpower Heritage Museum is or what the current state of research is on The Quadrangle or whether I should care.
And I don't know any Museums in Midland County, Texas. Where is George W. Bush Childhood Home located? What, in the name of all that is holy, is The Permian Basin Petroleum Museum? What the hell? Petroleum museums are a mystery to me. The Cold Lake Museums, are that even a real place? How am I supposed to make sense of The German Oil Museum, and what the heck is The Hathaway Ranch Museum? I frankly can't tell you that. The Royce J. and Caroline B.

Watts Museum – don't know. I haven't the remotest idea. And don't ask me where The Taiwan Oil Field Exhibition Hall is!
I'm also not conversant with Industry museums in Taiwan. Where in the world is The Songshan Cultural and Creative Park?
I don't know the first thing about Museums in Taipei. I also don't have any idea where The Fire Safety Museum of Taipei City Fire Department, Museum of Zoology, National Museum of History, Lingnan Fine Arts Museum or Children's Art Museum in Taipei is.
Don't ask me about History museums. I don't know where Azerbaijan Carpet Museum is. Can you tell me how to get to Taganrog military museum? I have no clue. Where the fuck is The Prehistory Museum of Tripoli or Lopez Museum?
And I don't know about Buildings and structures in Pasig. I don't know how to get to The Ynares Sports Arena. I've never heard of Pasig Cathedral. I just don't know that.
I haven't kept up on Roman Catholic cathedrals in the Philippines. I'm sorry, did you say 'San Guillermo Parish Church'? Where the hell is Novaliches Cathedral, Masbate Cathedral or Baguio Cathedral? Wouldn't know.
I'm not well-versed in Roman Catholic churches in the Philippines. Where is The Baroque Churches of the Philippines? I have no idea what The Cagsawa Ruins is. I have absolutely no idea. Who is Our Lady of Piat? Not a clue. And I have no idea where Cainta Church or Orani Church is.
And I know nothing about Baroque churches. Do people even go to Parish Church of Saints Peter and Paul?
I'm completely ignorant of National Historical Landmarks of the Philippines. Where is Cape Melville Lighthouse located? And I don't know what The Metropolitan Cathedral of San Fernando is. Doesn't sound remotely familiar. I have no clue where The Malacañang Palace is.
I'm not familiar with Lighthouses in the Philippines. Don't ask me where Bagacay Point Lighthouse, Batag Island Lighthouse, Basco Lighthouse or Cape Engaño Lighthouse is!
I haven't the foggiest notion what Spanish colonial infrastructure in the Philippines are about. San Juan de Dios Educational Foundation –

what does that mean?

I don't know anything about Hospitals in Metro Manila. The Lung Center of the Philippines – I don't know how to begin. And I have never been to Our Lady of Lourdes Hospital. I surely haven't got a clue.

Buildings and structures in Manila are unfamiliar to me. I also don't have any idea where Harrison Plaza is. The Manila Ocean Park? Come again? Never heard of it. Come on. The Manila Hotel or Rizal Memorial Coliseum, is that even a real place?

I couldn't tell you what Art Deco architecture in the Philippines are about. And I don't know where The Quezon Memorial Circle is. Quezon family is a mystery to me. The Manuel L. Quezon University – never heard of it.

I also don't know what people mean by 'Educational institutions in Manila'. What is St. Joseph's School – Pandacan?

I also don't know any Roman Catholic elementary schools in the Philippines. What is 'The Divine Word College of Bangued' supposed to mean again, and what is Immaculate Heart of Mary College-Parañaque again? Don't ask me what The Divine Word Academy of Dagupan is. No idea.

I obviously don't know the first thing about Roman Catholic universities and colleges in the Philippines. St. Paul University Manila – dunno.

Concerning Universities and colleges in Metro Manila, I am fully ignorant. Far Eastern University – not my area of expertise. I also have no clue what Arellano University is or what the mystery about The Marikina Polytechnic College is. Couldn't say.

I'm not hip to Universities and colleges in the Philippines. University of Cebu – I don't understand this. What in the world is Guzman College of Science and Technology, and what is The Navotas Polytechnic College? Damned if I know. What's the deal with The Philippine Women's University – School of Fine Arts and Design? And I don't know about Higher education in the Philippines. I couldn't tell you about Iloilo Doctors' College or what the hell West Visayas State University, Pototan is. The University of Eastern Philippines – what's that supposed to mean? I haven't the foggiest idea.

I've never heard of Educational institutions in Iloilo City. What in God's name is The Iloilo Science and Technology University, and what is The University of San Agustin about? What is 'The University of the Philippines High School in Iloilo' supposed to mean? I don't have any idea.

I'm not conversant with State universities and colleges in Western Visayas. I'm also certain that I've never heard of The Capiz State University or what The Aklan State University is about.

And I haven't kept up on Aklan. The Governor of Aklan – I don't know what that is. Panay Technological College? Doesn't ring a bell. I just don't know. Where in the world is The Legislative district of Aklan?

I know nothing about The Legislative districts of the Philippines. Where the fuck is The Legislative district of Eastern Samar?

I'm not well-versed in Eastern Samar. The Battle of Dolores River – how should I know what that is? The Balangiga massacre – I don't understand that. I just don't know. The Balangiga bells? How should I know? Couldn't tell you. Where the hell is Guiuan Airport?

I'm completely ignorant of Battles of the Philippine–American War. The Battle of Paye – I don't even know where to start. I definitely don't have any idea what The Battle of Pulang Lupa was or what the deal with The Battle of Bud Bagsak was or what it is all about. I haven't the slightest idea. The Second Battle of Bud Dajo, is that even a thing? I just don't know about that. What the hell is The Second Battle of Caloocan?

I'm not familiar with The Moro Rebellion. Juramentado – not my field. The Hassan Uprising – doesn't ring a bell. Don't ask me.

The Philippine–American War is unfamiliar to me. The March across Samar – what is that?

I don't know anything about United States Marine Corps in the 20th century. And I have no idea what Hughes Airwest Flight 706 was or what The Multinational Force in Lebanon is. Operation Vigilant Sentinel – don't know. How should I know? What the fuck is Operation Prime Chance?

I haven't the foggiest notion what 20th-century military history of the United States are about. Can you tell me how to get to Coincy Aerodrome? Am I supposed to be familiar with The 638th Aero Squadron? Ask someone who knows something.

I also don't know what people mean by 'Aviation units and formations of the United States in World War I'. What's up with The 163d Aero Squadron, and what is the idea with The 94th Fighter Squadron? And what about The 93d Bomb Squadron, and what was The V Corps Observation Group supposed to be? Search me. The VI Corps Observation Group – I don't know how to begin.

Bombardment squadrons of the United States Air Force are a mystery to me. And I don't know the first thing about The 498th Bombardment Squadron or what in tarnation The 528th Bomb Squadron is or if it's worth knowing.

Concerning Military units and formations in Virginia, I am fully ignorant. The 222d Command and Control Squadron – never heard of it. What the shit is The Washington Air Defense Sector, and what is Carrier Air Wing Three anyway? What the hell? Carrier Air Wing Eight – not my area of expertise. I have no clue. Please don't talk to me about United States Joint Forces Command.

I couldn't tell you what Air Defense Command is about. I also have no idea where Watford City Air Force Station is. I'm sorry, did you say 'The Sioux City Air Defense Sector'? I'm clueless about that.

I also don't know any United States Air Force radar stations. Genesee Mountain Park Training Annex – dunno.

I'm not hip to Formerly Used Defense Sites. The Snark Missile Launch Complex? Come again? Never heard of it. What, in the name of all that is holy, was Gentile Air Force Station? I certainly haven't the remotest idea. Do people even go to Hawthorne Bomb Plot?

Don't ask me about Buildings and structures in Aroostook County, Maine. And where is The Fort Kent Railroad Station located? The Loring Air Force Base Double Cantilever Hangar – what does that mean? Wouldn't know. Where is Caswell Air Force Station?

I've never heard of Fort Kent, Maine. The Fort Kent - Clair Border Crossing – I don't understand this. And what in the world is The Northern Forest Canoe Trail, and what on earth is WMEF? I have absolutely no idea.

I also haven't kept up on Water trails. I don't know what Hammocks Beach State Park is or what is supposed to be special about The Bartram Canoe Trail or if it's good to know. Don't ask me what The Three Rivers Heritage Trail is. Doesn't sound remotely familiar. I don't know how to get to The Blue Earth River or French Broad River. I don't know about Protected areas of Allegheny County, Pennsylvania. What is 'The Panhandle Trail' supposed to mean again? I'm not conversant with Rail trails in Pennsylvania. I'm certain that I've never heard of The Conewago Recreation Trail or what the hell it has to do with The Perkiomen Trail or if the whole concept makes sense to me.

I also know nothing about Parks in Montgomery County, Pennsylvania. And I have no clue where Pennypacker Mills is. How am I supposed to make sense of Evansburg State Park? I have no idea. I don't have any idea where Bryn Mawr Campus Arboretum is. I haven't got a clue. I have never been to The American College Arboretum or Merion Botanical Park.

I'm not well-versed in Bryn Mawr College. Don't ask me where The M. Carey Thomas Library is! What is Years of Grace? No idea. 20th-century American novels are unfamiliar to me. The Nazi and the Barber – how should I know what that is? Once a Runner – I don't know what that is. I just don't know that. The Road Through the Wall? How should I know? I obviously haven't the faintest idea. I have no clue what Children of Light is.

And I'm not familiar with Debut novels. What's the deal with The Return of Merlin, and what is the mystery about Wideacre? What the hell is Rubicon Harvest, and what the hell is The Whaleboat House? I can't tell you that.

And I don't know anything about American science fiction novels. The Eternity Artifact? Doesn't ring a bell. Falling Free – what is that? Damned if I know. Isaac Asimov's Inferno, is that even a thing? And I don't know what people mean by 'The Vorkosigan Saga'. I also don't know who Count Piotr Vorkosigan is. What the fuck is Konstantin Bothari? Not a clue.

Fictional counts and countesses are a mystery to me. Count Paris – I don't understand that. I also have no idea who Sarah von Lahnstein is.

I just don't know.
And I'm completely ignorant of Fictional Italian people in literature. I couldn't tell you about Emilio Largo or how I'm supposed to know something about Salvo Montalbano or what to think about it. Do I need to know who The Coachman is? Couldn't say.
And concerning Fictional businesspeople, I am fully ignorant. Are Zoe Tate, Rastapopoulos, Carl Costello or Eric Northman famous or something?
I don't know any Fictional criminals. Who the hell is Artemis Fowl II? I'm not hip to Fictional socialites. Who is this Thomas Wayne, Elizabeth Collins Stoddard, Katherine Chancellor or Clare Devine guy?
And don't ask me about The Bold and the Beautiful characters. Massimo Marone – who is that?
I definitely haven't the foggiest notion what Fictional American people of Italian descent are about. Am I supposed to know Fonzie, Philip Tattaglia or Aldo Trapani?
I've never heard of The Godfather characters. And I have no clue who The Carmine Rosato Family is.
I don't know about Fictional Mafia crime families. I don't have any idea what the Soprano crime family is. And who on earth is The Corleone family? I haven't the slightest idea. What in God's name are The Magliozzi Crime Family? I certainly don't know. I don't have any idea who The Tattaglia family are.
I couldn't tell you what The Sopranos characters are about. I've never heard of a person called Adriana La Cerva. Who is Janice Soprano, Sean Gismonte or Carmela Soprano? I don't have any idea.
I definitely haven't kept up on Fictional murderers. I have no idea what Adam Monroe is. Who the fuck is Ernest Darby or Frankenstein's monster? I just don't know about that.
And I know nothing about Fictional characters with accelerated healing. Max Guevara, Sadako Yamamura, Hellboy, Quentin Collins or She-Dragon – doesn't ring a bell.
I don't know the first thing about Fictional mediums. Cassandra Craft – I don't know how to begin. Who the shit is Yoda, Madame Web, Miles Straume or Subaru Sumeragi? Couldn't tell you.

I'm also not familiar with Fictional American people of Asian descent. What's up with Lady Shiva?
Fictional characters from Detroit, Michigan are unfamiliar to me. What about Wreck-Gar, and what in tarnation is Grimlock? I don't know anything about Luther Stickell or Deathlok. Don't ask me.
I'm also not conversant with Fictional tanks. Tankor – I don't even know where to start. I don't know who Tachikoma is. What the hell? Guzzle – what's that supposed to mean? Ask someone who knows something. Landquake – not my field. What is 'A Fictional landship' supposed to mean?
I'm also not well-versed in Fictional generals. Darth Vader – not my area of expertise. Hunt Stockwell, Aleksander Lukin or Dirk Anger – who are they? How should I know?
Fictional Russian people are a mystery to me. There Lived Kozyavin – dunno. Krazy Ivan – never heard of it. I haven't the remotest idea.
And concerning Soviet films, I am fully ignorant. Am I supposed to be familiar with Robinzon Kruzo? What, in the name of all that is holy, is Family Relations? I have no clue.
I'm completely ignorant of Films directed by Nikita Mikhalkov. At Home Among Strangers – I don't understand this. Burnt by the Sun 2? Come again? Never heard of it. I haven't the foggiest idea. Burnt by the Sun – what does that mean?
I also don't know what people mean by 'Russian-language films'. What is 'The Story of Asya Klyachina' supposed to mean again, and what is the deal with Welcome, or No Trespassing?
I'm also not hip to Films directed by Andrei Konchalovsky. What the shit is Lumière and Company, and what's To Each His Own Cinema got to do with it?
Don't ask me about Films directed by Wim Wenders. How am I supposed to make sense of The Road Movie trilogy?
I couldn't tell you what A Film series is about. Jurassic Park – don't know. Don't ask me what Foolish Years is. Search me. What in the world were The Doctor film series?
I've never heard of Comedy-drama films. I'm sorry, did you say 'Kingston Paradise'?
And I haven't the foggiest notion what Unreleased films are about.

Hippie Hippie Shake – I don't know what that is. Please don't talk to me about Torpedo Squadron. Doesn't sound remotely familiar. Sabdhan Pancha Aashche – I don't understand that. I have absolutely no idea. Pesu? Doesn't ring a bell.
I also don't know about Indian comedy films. What's the deal with Malabar Wedding?
And I haven't kept up on Indian romantic comedy films. I don't have any idea what Arike is.
I don't know any Films directed by Shyamaprasad. I'm certain that I've never heard of Kallu Kondoru Pennu or what on earth Ore Kadal is.
Works about adoption are unfamiliar to me. I have no idea what Girl, Missing is.
I don't know anything about British children's novels. I also have no clue what The Scarecrows is or what the heck The Light Beyond the Forest is or what to make of it. I don't know the first thing about King Arthur and His Knights of the Round Table. Come on.
I'm not well-versed in Chatto & Windus books. I don't know what People of the Black Mountains is or what the current state of research is on The Grey King or what it actually means. The Holder of the World – what's that supposed to mean? I'm clueless about that.
Novels set in Wales are a mystery to me. The Nightmare of Black Island? How should I know? Wythnos yng Nghymru Fydd – how should I know what that is? I definitely haven't the faintest idea. The Maid of Sker – what is that? I can't tell you that. The Magician's House – not my field. The Summer of the Danes – not my area of expertise.
And I'm not conversant with Novels set on islands. The Enchanted Island of Yew – dunno. What the hell is L'isola di Arturo? I just don't know that.
I'm also completely ignorant of Italian novels. Letter to a Child Never Born – I don't know how to begin.
I'm not familiar with Sundance Film Festival award winners. What the fuck is Three Seasons?
And I know nothing about Films shot in Vietnam. What in God's name is A Yank in Viet-Nam? And what is A Story of Healing? No

idea.

Concerning Short documentary films, I am fully ignorant. What is Monument to the Dream, and what is The Blooms of Banjeli? What's up with Flamenco at 5:15, and what is In Rwanda We Say…The Family That Does Not Speak Dies about? I just don't know. The Road to the Wall – doesn't ring a bell.

Don't ask me about Films directed by Anne Aghion. What about My Neighbor, My Killer, and what is Se le movió el piso: A portrait of Managua again? Ice People, is that even a thing? I have no idea.

I also couldn't tell you what Independent films are about. Ben and Arthur – I don't even know where to start. Chopping Mall – never heard of it. Couldn't say. Amelia and Michael? Come again? Never heard of it. I haven't the slightest idea. Bela Lugosi Meets a Brooklyn Gorilla – I don't understand this.

I've also never heard of British short films. What, in the name of all that is holy, is Separate We Come, Separate We Go, and what is The Short and Curlies supposed to be?

I'm not hip to Films set in Kent. And I couldn't tell you about Chariots of Fire or what the mystery about A Canterbury Tale is. Robin Hood: Prince of Thieves – don't know. Damned if I know. What is 'Thunderbird 6' supposed to mean?

I haven't the foggiest notion what Films set in Rio de Janeiro are about. OSS 117: Lost in Rio – I don't understand that.

And I don't know any Spy comedy films. Leonard Part 6? Doesn't ring a bell. Please don't talk to me about OSS 117: Cairo, Nest of Spies. Not a clue.

And I don't know about American spy films. What the shit is Decision Before Dawn, and what is the idea with Family of Spies?

And I haven't kept up on 20th Century Fox films. I also don't have any idea what Pony Soldier is or why people are so interested in The Omen or how to make sense of it. What is 'Confirm or Deny' supposed to mean again, and what the heck is High Society Blues? Couldn't tell you. Am I supposed to be familiar with The Adventures of Ford Fairlane?

And I don't know the first thing about Films directed by Archie Mayo. I'm certain that I've never heard of Johnny Get Your Hair Cut.

I don't know anything about Metro-Goldwyn-Mayer films. And I'm sorry, did you say 'The Painted Hills', and what on earth is Copying Beethoven? What in the world is Not So Dumb? Don't ask me. Ludwig van Beethoven in popular culture is a mystery to me. 33 Variations? How should I know? A Fifth of Beethoven – I don't know what that is. I certainly don't know about that. Beethoven's Great Love – how should I know what that is?

I'm not conversant with Broadway plays. What's the deal with A Behanding in Spokane, and what is The Goodbye People anyway? I also don't know what Morning's at Seven is or what the deal with Torch Song Trilogy is. Wouldn't know. I have no clue what The Crucible is.

I'm not well-versed in Plays about McCarthyism. Angels in America: A Gay Fantasia on National Themes – not my field.

New York Drama Critics' Circle Award winners are unfamiliar to me. How am I supposed to make sense of Privates on Parade, and what is the mystery about 'Art'? Sunday in the Park with George – what does that mean? I frankly don't have any idea.

And I'm not familiar with Broadway musicals. What in God's name is Roberta, and what in tarnation is Jelly's Last Jam? Starlight Express – dunno. I just don't know. What the fuck is The Second Little Show? I also don't know what people mean by 'Musicals based on novels'. What's up with The Wiz, and what's Dracula: A Chamber Musical got to do with it? What the hell is Once on This Island? I haven't the remotest idea.

I'm completely ignorant of One-act musicals. How to Eat Like a Child, is that even a thing?

Don't ask me about Musicals based on short fiction. And I have no idea what Guys and Dolls is or what the hell Fiddler on the Roof is or whether I should care. The Apple Tree – I don't know how to begin. How should I know? One Touch of Venus – not my area of expertise.

I've also never heard of Musicals by Kurt Weill. And what is Lost in the Stars? And what is The Firebrand of Florence? Search me.

Concerning Musicals based on plays, I am fully ignorant. By Jupiter – never heard of it.

And I couldn't tell you what Education in Cavite is about. Don't ask me what The Christ the King College of Cavite Foundation is. I couldn't tell you about Good Tree International School or what in tarnation Amaya School of Home Industries is or what people say about it. I haven't the foggiest idea. What, in the name of all that is holy, is The Divine Word College Seminary?

I don't know any Divine Word Missionaries Order. Do I need to know who the Divine Word Missionaries is?

And I know nothing about Roman Catholic religious institutes established in the 19th century. Catholic sisters and nuns in Canada – what's that supposed to mean? What about The Franciscan Sisters of Mary Immaculate, and what is the deal with The Sisters of Providence of the Institute of Charity? Ask someone who knows something. What is 'Felician Sisters' supposed to mean, and what are The Canossians about?

I also haven't the foggiest notion what The Roman Catholic Archdiocese of Detroit is about. Detroit Cristo Rey High School – I don't even know where to start. Gabriel Richard Catholic High School – I don't understand that. Come on. Are Henry Edmund Donnelly or Arthur Henry Krawczak famous or something?

I don't know about Roman Catholic secondary schools in Michigan. De La Salle Collegiate High School – what is that? What is 'St. Mary Catholic Central High School' supposed to mean again, and what is The University of Detroit Jesuit High School and Academy again? I have absolutely no idea.

I also don't know the first thing about School buildings on the National Register of Historic Places in Michigan. Père Gabriel Richard Elementary School – I don't understand this. I don't know where Defer Elementary School is. I'm clueless about that. Where the fuck is Sacred Heart Major Seminary? I can't tell you that. And where the hell is The Grosse Pointe Academy or Ontonagon School?

I'm not hip to Public elementary schools in Michigan. What the shit is Canton Charter Academy, and what is Hamlin Elementary School? The Hillsdale Academy? Doesn't ring a bell. I just don't know that. What in the world is Dollar Bay High School?

I'm not conversant with Public high schools in Michigan. Am I supposed to be familiar with Berrien Springs High School? J. W.

Sexton High School – how should I know what that is? No idea. I'm certain that I've never heard of Manistee High School or what Grand Blanc Community High School is about or what it is all about. I have no clue. Holly High School? How should I know?

I haven't kept up on Schools in Ingham County, Michigan. Okemos High School – doesn't ring a bell. East Lansing High School – I don't know what that is. Doesn't sound remotely familiar. Please don't talk to me about Lansing Catholic High School.

I also don't know anything about East Lansing, Michigan. And I don't know what The Verve Pipe is. The Beaumont Tower, is that even a real place? What the hell?

Towers in Michigan are a mystery to me. Can you tell me how to get to The Ypsilanti Water Tower, Portage Lake Lift Bridge, Mackinac Bridge or Thompson Home?

Bridges on the U.S. Highway System is unfamiliar to me. And do people even go to The Intercity Viaduct, Claxton Bridge, Livermore Bridge, George Washington Bridge or Sand Hollow Wash Bridge?

I don't know what people mean by 'Buildings and structures in Bergen County, New Jersey'. And I have no idea where The Alcoa Edgewater Works was. Where in the world is Haworth Country Club, The Valley Hospital or Joe Jefferson Clubhouse? I have no idea.

I'm completely ignorant of National Register of Historic Places in Bergen County, New Jersey. And where is The Zabriskie-Christie House? Where is The Van Allen House located? I haven't the slightest idea. I definitely don't know how to get to Caspar Westervelt House, John Banta House or Abraham A. Haring House.

And I'm not well-versed in Houses in Bergen County, New Jersey. I have no clue where Thomas Demarest House or Abraham Van Gelder House is.

I've never heard of Englewood, New Jersey. Dwight Morrow High School – not my field. Don't ask me where The Englewood Public School District is! Couldn't say. What's the deal with The Moriah School? Not a clue. And I don't know where John G. Benson House is. I also couldn't tell you what Private middle schools in New Jersey are about. And I have no idea what Hackensack Christian School is or what is supposed to be special about The Hun School of Princeton.

And concerning Christian schools in the United States, I am fully ignorant. Rehoboth Christian School? Come again? Never heard of it. What in God's name is Willow Creek Learning Center? I just don't know.
I know nothing about Schools in McKinley County, New Mexico. I don't have any idea what Gallup Catholic High School was or what Miyamura High School is or if it's worth knowing. Gallup High School – not my area of expertise. Couldn't tell you.
And I haven't the foggiest notion what Public high schools in New Mexico are about. West Mesa High School – don't know.
I don't know any High schools in Albuquerque, New Mexico. I have no clue what The Public Academy for Performing Arts is or what the hell it has to do with Albuquerque Academy or if it's good to know. What the fuck is Amy Biehl High School, and what is the idea with East Mountain High School? Damned if I know.
I don't know the first thing about Private middle schools in New Mexico. How am I supposed to make sense of St. Teresa of Avila Catholic School, and what the heck is Bosque School? What's up with McCurdy High School? I haven't got a clue.
I'm not hip to Schools in Santa Fe County, New Mexico. I'm sorry, did you say 'The Academy for Technology and the Classics', and what on earth is St. Michael's High School? The New Mexico School for the Deaf – never heard of it. Don't ask me. Santa Fe Preparatory School – what does that mean? I just don't know about that. I couldn't tell you about The Santa Fe Indian School.
Don't ask me about Charter schools in New Mexico. Bataan Military Academy – what's that supposed to mean? Cottonwood Valley Charter School, is that even a thing? Wouldn't know.
I'm not familiar with Military high schools in the United States. Where the fuck was Blees Military Academy? And don't ask me what San Marcos Baptist Academy is. I haven't the faintest idea. The Honolulu Military Academy – I don't understand this. How should I know? The Marine Academy of Science and Technology – I don't know how to begin. I'm also certain that I've never heard of Fork Union Military Academy.
And I haven't kept up on Schools in Hays County, Texas. What is Jack

C. Hays High School?
I don't know about Public high schools in Texas. Seagraves High School – I don't understand that. Challenge Early College High School – I don't know what that is. I haven't the foggiest idea. Please don't talk to me about High School for Law Enforcement and Criminal Justice.
High schools in Houston, Texas are a mystery to me. The Westchester Academy for International Studies – I don't even know where to start. What, in the name of all that is holy, is The High School for the Performing and Visual Arts? Ask someone who knows something. And I don't know anything about High schools in Harris County, Texas. I've never heard of Pasadena Memorial High School.
And I don't know what people mean by 'Education in Pasadena, Texas'. I also don't know what Texas Chiropractic College is or what the heck Clear Creek Independent School District is or what to think about it. I don't have any idea where Deer Park Independent School District or Pasadena Independent School District is. Come on.
I'm not well-versed in Public education in Houston, Texas. University of Houston Charter School? Doesn't ring a bell. What the hell is Hunters Creek Elementary School? I have absolutely no idea. I also have never been to Alief Independent School District.
I'm completely ignorant of Charter schools in Texas. Transmountain Early College High School – doesn't ring a bell. UME Preparatory Academy – dunno. I haven't the remotest idea.
I couldn't tell you what Schools in Dallas County, Texas are about. What about Jackson Technology Center, and what is Classical Center at Brandenburg Middle School supposed to be? I have no idea what Lyles Middle School is or how I'm supposed to know something about Hickman Elementary School. I'm clueless about that. Montclair Elementary School – what is that?
Education in Garland, Texas is unfamiliar to me. Spring Creek Elementary School – not my field. O'Banion Middle School – not my area of expertise. Search me.
I also know nothing about Public middle schools in Texas. What the shit is IDEA Quest, and what is Benjamin High School anyway? And what in the world is Slocum High School, and what is the mystery

about Claude High School? I have no clue.

Concerning Public elementary schools in Texas, I am fully ignorant. I don't know the first thing about Gregory-Lincoln Education Center or what the current state of research is on Priddy High School.

And I'm not hip to The Houston Independent School District. Jesse H. Jones High School – don't know. Energy Institute High School – what's that supposed to mean? No idea. Am I supposed to be familiar with Kay On-Going Education Center? I don't have any idea. DeBakey High School for Health Professions – how should I know what that is? South Early College High School – never heard of it.

I also haven't the foggiest notion what Magnet schools in Texas are about. What IS 'The International School of the Americas' supposed to mean, and what's Barack Obama Male Leadership Academy got to do with it?

I really don't know any Boys' schools in Texas. Don't ask me what Young Men's College Preparatory Academy is. The St. Mark's School of Texas – I don't know how to begin. I can't tell you that. Cistercian Preparatory School? Come again? Never heard of it.

And I'm not familiar with Private elementary schools in Texas. I don't have any idea what The Carver Academy is or why people are so interested in Bay Area Christian School or what to make of it. The Emery/Weiner School? How should I know? I frankly haven't the slightest idea. Burton Adventist Academy – I don't understand that. I have no idea. The Oakridge School – I don't know what that is.

Don't ask me about Jews and Judaism in Houston, Texas. Is Hyman Judah Schachtel famous or something? What's the deal with Torah Day School of Houston? I definitely don't know.

I also don't know about American Reform rabbis. Arnold Jacob Wolf – who was that?

And I'm not conversant with Deaths from myocardial infarction. Who the hell is Leopoldo Bravo or Al Jolson?

People from Jurbarkas District Municipality are a mystery to me. Who is this Petras Cvirka guy? Am I supposed to know Jurgis Baltrušaitis, Augustinas Povilaitis or Antanas Pocius? Not a clue.

And I haven't kept up on Ambassadors of Lithuania to Russia. Who on earth is Rimantas Šidlauskas, Egidijus Bičkauskas or Antanas Vinkus?

I don't know anything about Health ministers of Lithuania. I've also never heard of a person called Juozas Olekas.
I'm completely ignorant of Lithuanian surgeons. I also have no clue who Kazys Bobelis was.
I've also never heard of Lithuanian anti-communists. I don't have any idea who Simonas Morkūnas is. Who the fuck is Vincentas Sladkevičius, Romas Kalanta, Povilas Plechavičius or Sigitas Tamkevičius? Doesn't sound remotely familiar.
Suicides in Lithuania are unfamiliar to me. And who was Saulius Mykolaitis? Who the shit is Margiris or Vytautas Vičiulis? Damned if I know.
I also don't know what people mean by 'Lithuanian Academy of Music and Theatre alumni'. I have no idea who Sigutė Stonytė, Kristina Buožytė or Audrius Rubežius is.
I'm not well-versed in Lithuanian sopranos. What's up with Violeta Urmana?
I don't know the first thing about People from Marijampolė County. And do I need to know who Antanas Gustaitis, Antanas Maceina, Juozas Adomaitis-Šernas or Algimantas Sakalauskas is?
And concerning Lithuanian writers, I am fully ignorant. I also don't know who Algis Budrys was. Ričardas Šileika, Romualdas Granauskas, Jurgis Bielinis or Laura Sintija Černiauskaitė – who are they? I just don't know that.
I'm not hip to Worldcon Guests of Honor. Bob Passovoy, Mike Resnick or Robert Silverberg – doesn't ring a bell.
I don't know any 20th-century American novelists. Who is this Nancy Hayfield, Roger MacBride Allen, Monique Raphel High, Anne Edwards or Page Stegner guy?
I definitely couldn't tell you what American women writers are about. Who the hell is Margaret Prescott Montague?
Don't ask me about Appalachian writers. May Justus – who was that? Am I supposed to know Bob Henry Baber, Denise Giardina, Pinckney Benedict or Cynthia Rylant? Don't ask me.
And I'm not familiar with American women novelists. I don't know anything about George Madden Martin. Are Elizabeth Drew Stoddard or Theresa Rebeck famous or something? Couldn't tell you.

I'm not conversant with People from Plymouth County, Massachusetts. Who on earth is William M. Straus? I've never heard of a person called Levi Reed or Francis Davis Millet. I just don't know about that.

American painters are a mystery to me. Is Rafael Vargas-Suarez famous or something? I have no clue who Carolyn Wyeth was. I haven't the faintest idea.

I know nothing about Painters from Pennsylvania. I also don't have any idea who Emily Sartain is.

I also don't know about American engravers. Who the shit is Elkanah Tisdale?

I haven't the foggiest notion what 19th-century American painters are about. Who is Benjamin Curtis Porter? I also have no idea who John Willard Raught or Frank Enders was. What the hell?

American Impressionist painters are unfamiliar to me. Do I need to know who Arlington Nelson Lindenmuth was? George Wharton Edwards or Lars Jonson Haukaness – who are they? I haven't the foggiest idea.

And I don't know what people mean by 'People from Winnipeg'. What's up with Montegu Black, Courtney-Jane White or Andrea Ratuski?

And I'm completely ignorant of Canadian television actresses. Who is this Laura Harris guy?

I also don't know the first thing about 21st-century Canadian actresses. I don't know who Jessica Parker Kennedy, Evangeline Lilly, Shannon Baker, Katharine Isabelle or Camille Sullivan is.

I've also never heard of Actresses from Vancouver. Who the fuck is Eve Harlow, Alaina Huffman or Sharon Taylor?

I'm not well-versed in Canadian film actresses. And I don't know anything about Kristin Booth, Stéphanie Lapointe, Chelsea Hobbs, Beverley Elliott or Samantha Ferris.

I'm not hip to Canadian singer-songwriters. What is 'Ember Swift' supposed to mean again? David Usher, Josh Reichmann, Ian Tanner or Greg MacPherson – doesn't ring a bell. How should I know?

I couldn't tell you what Canadian people of Jewish descent are about. Who the hell is Sandor Stern, Sylvain Abitbol or John Rosen?

I also don't know about Canadian Jewish Congress. How am I supposed to make sense of Goldie Hershon? I've never heard of a person called Sol Kanee. Couldn't say.
I'm not familiar with People from Melville, Saskatchewan. Am I supposed to know Paul Albers, Ricky Kanee Schachter or Nathon Gunn?
Concerning Canadian music video directors, I am fully ignorant. I don't have any idea who Glen Hanson, Aaron A, Mike Clattenburg, Chris Grismer or Alison Murray is.
I'm not conversant with Canadian film directors. Are Alec Butler, Léonard Forest, Nicolas Wright, James Motluk or Clark Johnson famous or something?
I also know nothing about People from Hamilton, Ontario. And who was Jim Quondamatteo or Samuel Clarke Biggs?
Don't ask me about Sportspeople from Miami, Florida. Mirtha Marrero, Glenn Sharpe, Van Winitsky or Lenny Taylor – who are they?
I don't know what people mean by 'Tennis people from Florida'. Who the shit is Carly Gullickson?
I'm also completely ignorant of Tennis people from Ohio. Barry MacKay – who was that? What's up with Tony Trabert? Come on.
I frankly haven't kept up on Tennis commentators. Do I need to know who Marcella Mesker is? And I don't know who Jim McKay or Lindsey Nelson was. Wouldn't know.
American journalists are unfamiliar to me. And who is this Linda Gradstein, Alfred Charles True, Cindy Elavsky or Peter Garrison guy?
I've never heard of American educators. I surely don't know anything about Diane Levin.
I haven't the foggiest notion what International Tennis Hall of Fame inductees are about. Lance Tingay or Gustavo Kuerten – doesn't ring a bell.
I also don't know the first thing about World No. 1 tennis players. And who the fuck is Carlos Moyá, Marcelo Ríos, Billie Jean King or Chris Evert?
And I'm not well-versed in Spanish expatriate sportspeople in Switzerland. Who the hell is Fernando Alonso?

I'm not hip to Spanish Formula One drivers. I have no idea who Adrián Campos is. I've also never heard of a person called Luis Pérez-Sala. Ask someone who knows something. I don't have any idea who Alfonso de Portago, Antonio Creus or Paco Godia was.
And I don't know any World Sportscar Championship drivers. Am I supposed to know Tony Lanfranchi or Henri Oreiller?
I'm not familiar with Sport deaths in France. Who was Marc-Vivien Foé? And who the shit is Antonio Ascari? I haven't got a clue. Pierre Maréchal, Karine Ruby or Olivier Chevallier – who are they?
Concerning 250cc World Championship riders, I am fully ignorant. Who on earth is Marco Melandri, Gyula Marsovszky or Masahiro Shimizu?
I obviously don't know about Italian racing drivers. Is Marco Zipoli famous or something? I have no clue what Ettore Bianco is. Search me.
I couldn't tell you what Italian Formula Three Championship drivers are about. And do I need to know who Stamatis Katsimis or Vittorio Zoboli is?
I know nothing about Italian Formula Renault 2.0 drivers. What's up with Edoardo Piscopo or Ianina Zanazzi?
Don't ask me about European Le Mans Series drivers. Who is this Máximo Cortés guy?
I don't know what people mean by 'European F3 Open Championship drivers'. I don't know anything about Marcos Martínez, Ma Qinghua, Carmen Jordá, César Campaniço or Zoël Amberg.
And I'm completely ignorant of German Formula Three Championship drivers. I don't know who Adderly Fong, Weiron Tan, Hamad Al Fardan, Tobias Blättler or Daniel Abt is.
Racing drivers from Bavaria are a mystery to me. I have no clue who Patrick Schranner is. Fritz Riess – who was that? I'm clueless about that.
I'm not conversant with 24 Hours of Le Mans drivers. And who the hell is Jeremy Rossiter, Chris Kneifel or Alan Rees?
I've never heard of British Touring Car Championship drivers. John Bintcliffe, Charlie Butler-Henderson, Darren Turner or Stephen Jelley – doesn't ring a bell.

I also haven't kept up on British GT Championship drivers. I have no idea who Eric De Doncker is.

I haven't the foggiest notion what FIA GT Championship drivers are about. Are Mauro Martini or Maxime Martin famous or something?

I'm not hip to International GT Open drivers. Am I supposed to know Michele Rugolo, Pedro Couceiro, Davide Rigon, Raffaele Giammaria or Stefano Gattuso?

I'm not well-versed in A1 Grand Prix Rookie drivers. Who is James Winslow, Marchy Lee or Cristiano Morgado?

French Formula Three Championship drivers are unfamiliar to me. And who the fuck is Christophe Bouchut?

Concerning People from Voiron, I am fully ignorant. Mélina Robert-Michon, Jean-Baptiste Guimet or Véronique Pecqueux-Rolland – who are they?

I also don't know any Olympic athletes of France. Who on earth is Marie-France Loval, Kévin Mayer, Louis Pauteux, Pascal Théophile or Quentin Bigot?

I also don't know the first thing about French long-distance runners. I don't have any idea who Joseph Mahmoud or Benoît Zwierzchiewski is.

And I don't know about French marathon runners. Is Georges Touquet-Daunis famous or something? What's up with Jean-Baptiste Manhès? No idea. I've also never heard of a person called Henri Teyssedou, Christelle Daunay or Albin Lermusiaux.

Don't ask me about French sport shooters. Do I need to know who Anthony Terras, Jean-Pierre Amat, Auguste Cavadini, Roger de Barbarin or Walter Lapeyre is?

I also know nothing about People from Chambéry. I don't know anything about Jean Mamy, Michel de Certeau or Jean-Claude Blanc. I'm completely ignorant of Roman Catholic writers. And I don't know who Gerard Manley Hopkins was. Who the hell is John Slotanus or Michael Novak? I frankly can't tell you that.

I obviously don't know what people mean by 'The American Enterprise Institute'. Christina Hoff Sommers – who is that?

Feminist philosophers are a mystery to me. Barrie Karp or Ann Garry – doesn't ring a bell.

I'm also not familiar with Jewish philosophers. Who is this Ibn Kammuna guy? Am I supposed to know Rose Rand? I have absolutely no idea. Are Anatol Rosenfeld or Michael J. Sandel famous or something?

I've also never heard of Iraqi Jews. Please don't talk to me about Anilai and Asinai.

I also haven't kept up on Jewish Babylonian history. I couldn't tell you about The writing on the wall or what the mystery about Exilarch is or what it actually means. The Talmudic Academies in Babylonia – what does that mean? I haven't the slightest idea. Pumbedita Academy or Sura Academy, is that even a real place?

And I'm not conversant with Jewish royalty. Can you tell me how to get to The Herodian kingdom? I have no clue who Afghana or Makhir of Narbonne was. I just don't know.

I haven't the foggiest notion what Former monarchies of Asia are about. I have no idea where The Empire of Trebizond was. And do people even go to Kingdom of Namayan or Gaochang? I have no idea. Former populated places in Xinjiang are unfamiliar to me. Sumgal? Doesn't ring a bell. And what the fuck is Xaidulla, and what the hell is Dandan Oilik? Doesn't sound remotely familiar.

And I'm not hip to Sites along the Silk Road. Where the hell is Yumen Pass?

I'm not well-versed in Mountain passes of China. Where is The Kongka Pass located? What is Yanmenguan, and what in tarnation is Hangu Pass? Damned if I know. I'm sorry, did you say 'Niangzi Pass'? I couldn't tell you what The Great Wall of China is about. Dajingmen – I don't even know where to start. What in God's name is Operation Chahar? I just don't know.

I don't know the first thing about The Second Sino-Japanese War. What about The Northeast Anti-Japanese United Army? And what is The Tanggu Truce? Not a clue. Y Force – dunno. I have no clue. The Red Spear Society – I don't understand this.

I also don't know any Anti-Japanese Volunteer Armies. I don't know what Dalforce is or what the hell Shanlin is. What the hell is the Northeast Anti-Japanese National Salvation Army, and what was the deal with The Northeast People's Anti-Japanese Volunteer Army?

Don't ask me.
Don't ask me about Disbanded armies. I'm also certain that I've never heard of Army of the Duchy of Warsaw or what on earth The Grand Han Righteous Army is. The Royal Scots Army – not my area of expertise. I haven't the remotest idea. What the shit is The Republic of Vietnam National Police Administration Service, and what is Battaglione Azad Hindoustan about?
I also don't know about Military units and formations of Italy in World War II. What, in the name of all that is holy, is Auto-Saharan Companies, and what is the idea with The XII Squadriglia MAS? Aeronautica Nazionale Repubblicana, is that even a thing? I just don't know about that.
I'm also completely ignorant of The Italian Air Force. The Italian Co-Belligerent Air Force – what is that?
And I don't know what people mean by 'Jews and Judaism in the Roman Empire'. The Boethusians – how should I know what that is? What in the world is The Enoch seminar, and what the heck is The Arch of Titus? I haven't the foggiest idea. Warren's Gate? How should I know?
And concerning Gates, I am fully ignorant. I obviously don't know how to get to The Spanish Arch. A Gate operator – what's that supposed to mean? How should I know? Bab Saadoun – not my field. I haven't the faintest idea. Where in the world is Michael's Gate or Porta Sempione?
Districts of Milan are a mystery to me. The Quadrilatero della moda – don't know. And don't ask me where Villapizzone, Porta Genova, Dergano or Affori is! What the hell?
And I don't know anything about Shopping districts and streets in Italy. Don't ask me what The Rialto is. I certainly don't have any idea what Via de' Tornabuoni is or what the deal with Corso Buenos Aires is or how to make sense of it. Couldn't say. Via Paolo Sarpi? Come again? Never heard of it. Come on. I have no clue where The Ponte Vecchio is.
And I know nothing about Streets in Milan. What is 'Via Dante' supposed to mean again, and what on earth is Via Monte Napoleone? I've never heard of Culture in Milan. The Caffè Cova – never heard of

it.

And I haven't kept up on Coffee houses in Italy. Caffè Florian – I don't know what that is. I don't know where Caffè San Marco is. Couldn't tell you.

Art Nouveau architecture in Italy is unfamiliar to me. Am I supposed to be familiar with Castello Cova? The Mackenzie Castle – I don't know how to begin. I just don't know that. Where the fuck is The Chiaia Funicular or Palazzo Montecitorio?

I'm also not conversant with Standard gauge railways in Italy. I don't have any idea where The Mondovì Funicular is.

I'm not well-versed in Railway lines in Piedmont. The Vercelli–Pavia railway, is that even a real place?

I also couldn't tell you what Railway lines in Lombardy are about. I have no clue what The Milan–Monza railway is. Where is The Como–Lecco railway, Colico–Chiavenna railway, Lecco–Brescia railway or Milan–Venice railway? Search me.

I'm also not familiar with Railway lines in Veneto. And I couldn't tell you about The Brenner Railway or what is supposed to be special about The Trento–Venice railway or if the whole concept makes sense to me.

I'm also not hip to Transport in Trentino. And I have no idea what The Trento–Malè–Marilleva railway is.

I certainly don't know the first thing about Railway companies of Italy. What is 'Rete Ferroviaria Italiana' supposed to mean, and what is Trenord again? What's up with Veolia Cargo, and what is Ferrotramviaria? I'm clueless about that.

Don't ask me about Veolia. What's the deal with Veolia Water Southeast, and what is Veolia Verkehr Sachsen-Anhalt supposed to be? What is Veolia Water East, and what's The Transports en Commun de l'Agglomération Rouennaise got to do with it? No idea.

I also haven't the foggiest notion what Transport in Rouen is about. I'm sorry, did you say 'The Rouen tramway', and what the hell is Transport Est-Ouest Rouennais? I have never been to The Pont Gustave-Flaubert. I can't tell you that. I have no idea where Rouen Airport is.

I'm completely ignorant of Buildings and structures in Rouen. And do people even go to Stade Robert Diochon? The Muséum d'Histoire Naturelle de Rouen – doesn't ring a bell. I surely haven't the slightest idea. Where the hell is The Maritime, Fluvial and Harbour Museum of Rouen? I just don't know. The Church of Saint-Maclou – what does that mean?

And I don't know any Sports venues in Seine-Maritime. Can you tell me how to get to The Stade Océane?

Buildings and structures in Le Havre are a mystery to me. The University of Le Havre – I don't even know where to start. And what the fuck is Dock Océane, and what is Le Havre Cathedral anyway? I haven't got a clue. Where is Les Bains Des Docks or Stade de la Cavée Verte located?

I also don't know what people mean by 'Cathedrals in France'. Luçon Cathedral – I don't understand that. Grenoble Cathedral – dunno. Doesn't sound remotely familiar. What the hell is Blois Cathedral, and what in tarnation is Auch Cathedral? Damned if I know. Where in the world is Rouen Cathedral?

I know nothing about History of Grenoble. Who the shit is Nicolas Chorier? I don't know how to get to The Dauphiné. Ask someone who knows something.

Concerning Geography of Hautes-Alpes, I am fully ignorant. Please don't talk to me about Oisans. I've never heard of Col du Granon or Col de l'Échelle. I have no idea.

I don't know about Valleys of France. I also have no clue where Val d'Enfer is. What about The Ubaye Valley, and what is the deal with The Val de Dagne? Not a clue. Don't ask me where The Tarentaise Valley is!

I'm also not conversant with Geography of Savoie. And where the fuck is The Leysse? The Albanais – I don't understand this. I don't have any idea. I don't know where Mont Malamot or Vanoise National Park is.

I don't know anything about Visitor attractions in Savoie. Le Corbier – what's that supposed to mean? Tremplin du Praz – not my area of expertise. Don't ask me. Paradiski? Doesn't ring a bell. Wouldn't know. Where is Tignes or Les Arcs?

And I couldn't tell you what Ski areas and resorts in France are about.

I'm certain that I've never heard of Montroc or what Hautacam is. Courchevel, Samoëns or Megève, is that even a real place? I have absolutely no idea.
I haven't kept up on Villages in Rhône-Alpes. And I don't know what Les Praz is. I also have no idea where Argentière is. I just don't know. I'm not well-versed in Tourism in Rhône-Alpes. Do people even go to Flaine? What, in the name of all that is holy, is Glacier Montanvert? I haven't the remotest idea.
Glaciers of the Alps are unfamiliar to me. The Eiger Glacier – never heard of it. The Allalin Glacier, is that even a thing? What the hell? And where the hell is The Glacier Noir or Corbassière Glacier?
I don't know the first thing about Glaciers of France. I certainly don't have any idea what The Argentière Glacier is. And I have never been to The Mer de Glace. How should I know? What the shit is The Cook Glacier, and what is the mystery about The Bossons Glacier?
I'm not familiar with Geography of Haute-Savoie. The Menoge – I don't know what that is. Where is The Thiou, Dranse d'Abondance, Aiguilles Rouges National Nature Reserve or Rhône located? I haven't the faintest idea.
I definitely haven't the foggiest notion what Geography of Drôme is about. Can you tell me how to get to The Buëch? The Baronnies – I don't know how to begin. I just don't know about that.
And I'm completely ignorant of Geography of Alpes-de-Haute-Provence. I don't know how to get to Mercantour National Park. I also don't have any idea where The Lake of Sainte-Croix or Durance is. I haven't the foggiest idea.
And I don't know any Visitor attractions in Alpes-Maritimes. The Cannes Lions International Festival of Creativity – what is that? How am I supposed to make sense of Le Suquet? I just don't know that. And what is The Promenade de la Croisette? Couldn't say. Where in the world is Fort Carré or Golfe-Juan?
I'm not hip to Buildings and structures in Antibes. Jean Bunoz Sports Hall – don't know. I've never heard of Stade du Fort Carré. I have no clue. I have no idea what Port Vauban is. I can't tell you that. I have no clue where The Villa Aujourd'hui is.
I know nothing about Indoor arenas in France. Palais des Sports de

Toulon – not my field. What in the world is Patinoire olympique de Pralognan-la-Vanoise, and what is Palais des Sports de Dijon about? Couldn't tell you.

Curling venues in France are a mystery to me. Where the fuck is Pralognan-la-Vanoise? And what in God's name is Stade Olympique de Chamonix? Come on.

I don't know what people mean by 'Olympic curling venues'. I also don't know where The Ice Sheet at Ogden is. Pinerolo Palaghiaccio – I don't even know where to start. I'm clueless about that.

I'm not conversant with Buildings and structures in Ogden, Utah. Don't ask me where Peery's Egyptian Theater is! Don't ask me what Ogden Stadium is. Search me. And where is The Ralph Bristol House? I just don't know. I also couldn't tell you about The Ott Planetarium.

I don't know anything about Theatres on the National Register of Historic Places in Utah. The Utah State Training School Amphitheater and Wall, is that even a real place?

Concerning Buildings and structures in Utah County, Utah, I am fully ignorant. And do people even go to American Fork Presbyterian Church? Where the hell is The Lehi City Hall or Beers House-Hotel? Doesn't sound remotely familiar.

Don't ask me about Italianate architecture in Utah. I have no idea where The John T. Rich House is.

And I couldn't tell you what Houses on the National Register of Historic Places in Utah are about. I have never been to The Canute Peterson House, Yard-Groesbeck House, Joseph E. and Mina W. Mickelsen House or Johnson-Hansen House.

I haven't kept up on Gothic Revival architecture in Utah. And I don't know how to get to The Lehi North Branch Meetinghouse or Payson Presbyterian Church.

I'm not well-versed in Neoclassical architecture in Utah. Where is The Samuel I. and Olena J. Goodwin House located?

I'm not familiar with Victorian architecture in Utah. Can you tell me how to get to The Pleasant Grove Historic District?

I don't know about Bungalow architecture in Utah. Where in the world is The Franklin and Amelia Walton House or Hilda Erickson House?

Houses in Davis County, Utah are unfamiliar to me. I've also never heard of The James and Hannah Atkinson House, Henry Blood House, Barnard-Garn-Barber House or John R. Barnes House.
And I don't know the first thing about Georgian architecture in Utah. I also have no clue where The Samuel P. Hoyt House was. Where the fuck is The William and Ann Bringhurst House, Richard Vaughen Morris House or Samuel Douglass House? I haven't got a clue.
I haven't the foggiest notion what Federal architecture in Utah is about. And I don't have any idea where The Gardner Mill is.
I don't know any Industrial buildings and structures on the National Register of Historic Places in Utah. Where is The Upper American Fork Hydroelectric Power Plant Historic District or Draper Poultrymen and Egg Producers' Plant?
I'm not hip to Historic districts in Utah County, Utah. The Lehi Main Street Historic District, Timpanogos Cave Historic District, American Fork Historic District, Payson Historic District or Provo East Central Historic District, is that even a real place?
I frankly don't know what people mean by 'Buildings and structures on the National Register of Historic Places in Utah'. I don't know where The Fruita Rural Historic District is.
Historic districts in Utah are a mystery to me. Please don't talk to me about Historic 25th Street. And do people even go to The Bryce Canyon Lodge Historic District? No idea.
I'm not conversant with Buildings and structures in Bryce Canyon National Park. Don't ask me where Bryce Canyon Lodge is! Where the hell is The Bryce Inn, Utah Parks Company Service Station, Rainbow Point Comfort Station and Overlook Shelter or Old National Park Service Housing Historic District? Damned if I know.
And I don't know anything about Commercial buildings on the National Register of Historic Places in Utah. I frankly don't know how to get to The McBride-Sims Garage.
Concerning Buildings designated early commercial in the National Register of Historic Places, I am fully ignorant. I have no idea where The Greenville Downtown Historic District, Hamburg Commercial Historic District or Arkansas City Commercial District is.
Don't ask me about Neoclassical architecture in Arkansas. Where is

The El Dorado Junior College Building located?
I'm completely ignorant of Art Deco architecture in Arkansas.
Can you tell me how to get to The Drew County Courthouse, Dual State Monument, Rison Texaco Service Station or Chicot County Courthouse?
I also know nothing about County courthouses in Arkansas. Where in the world is The Crittenden County Courthouse, Little River County Courthouse or Baxter County Courthouse?
I surely haven't kept up on Buildings and structures in Crittenden County, Arkansas. I have never been to West Memphis Municipal Airport.
I'm not well-versed in Airports in Arkansas. I've never heard of Marine Corps Air Facility Walnut Ridge.
And I'm not familiar with Transportation in Lawrence County, Arkansas. Where the fuck is Arkansas Highway 34, Arkansas Highway 117, Walnut Ridge Regional Airport, Arkansas Highway 25 or Cache River Bridge?
I don't know about State highways in Arkansas. And I don't have any idea where Arkansas Highway 193, Arkansas Highway 11 or Arkansas Highway 9 is.
Transportation in Prairie County, Arkansas are unfamiliar to me. I have no clue where Stuttgart Municipal Airport or Hazen Municipal Airport is.
I couldn't tell you what Buildings and structures in Prairie County, Arkansas are about. Where is American Legion Hut-Des Arc?
I haven't the foggiest notion what Clubhouses on the National Register of Historic Places in Arkansas are about. Do people even go to Hall Morgan Post 83, American Legion Hut? I really don't know where Lee's Chapel Church and Masonic Hall is. Not a clue. Where the hell is The Knob School-Masonic Lodge, Newport American Legion Community Hut or Nashville American Legion Building?
I don't know the first thing about Buildings and structures in Jackson County, Arkansas. I don't know how to get to Marine Corps Air Facility Newport.
I also don't know any Military units and formations of the United States Army Air Forces. Eaker Air Force Base, is that even a real

place?

I'm not conversant with Closed facilities of the United States Air Force. Don't ask me where North Charleston Air Force Station is! I'm also not hip to Aerospace Defense Command military installations. And I have no idea where Arlington Heights Air Force Station was. Where in the world is Finley Air Force Station, Miles City Air Force Station, Stewart Air National Guard Base or Finland Air Force Station? Don't ask me.

I don't know anything about Bases of the United States Air Force. Where is Goodfellow Air Force Base, Little Rock Air Force Base or Luke Air Force Base located?

Military facilities in Arkansas are a mystery to me. Fort Carlos – how should I know what that is? I've never heard of Walnut Ridge Air Force Station or Texarkana Air Force Station. Wouldn't know.

Concerning Pre-statehood history of Arkansas, I am fully ignorant. Where the fuck is Fort Smith National Historic Site? The Treaty of Washington City? How should I know? I have absolutely no idea. Am I supposed to be familiar with The Trail of Tears? I have no idea. Historic Washington State Park – I don't understand that. The Treaty of Fort Clark – dunno.

I don't know what people mean by 'National Register of Historic Places in Arkansas'. And I don't have any idea where The Hampton Waterworks, Star City Commercial Historic District, Rison Cities Service Station or Beely-Johnson American Legion Post 139 is.

And I'm completely ignorant of Water towers in the United States. I have never been to The Cuyuna Iron Range Municipally-Owned Elevated Metal Water Tanks. Where is The Tyronza Water Tower, Cotton Plant water tower or Fort Atkinson Water Tower? Ask someone who knows something.

I surely haven't kept up on Buildings and structures in Jefferson County, Wisconsin. What's up with Fort Koshkonong? Do people even go to Concord Generating Station? I just don't know. And what is 'The Dwight Foster Public Library' supposed to mean?

And don't ask me about Black Hawk War forts. I have no clue where Fort Crawford was. I don't know where Fort Beggs was. I haven't the slightest idea. Where the hell is Blue Mounds Fort or Apple River

Fort?

I don't know about History museums in Wisconsin. The Peshtigo Fire Museum – I don't understand this.

I know nothing about Firefighting museums in the United States. What is 'The Indiana Law Enforcement and Firefighters Memorial' supposed to mean again? Can you tell me how to get to Collyer Monument? I really haven't the faintest idea. I have no clue what The New York City Fire Museum is or what the hell it has to do with The Wisconsin State Firefighters Memorial.

I'm not familiar with Monuments and memorials in Rhode Island. I don't know how to get to Liberty Arming the Patriot. Don't ask me where The Woonsocket Civil War Monument is! I really just don't know about that. Oliver Perry Monument – doesn't ring a bell.

I'm also not well-versed in Buildings and structures in Providence County, Rhode Island. I have no idea where The Scituate Reservoir is. I'm sorry, did you say 'Hindley Manufacturing'? I haven't the remotest idea. Bridgham Farm, is that even a real place?

And I don't know the first thing about Farms on the National Register of Historic Places in Rhode Island. Where in the world is Spink Farm? I certainly couldn't tell you what Houses in Washington County, Rhode Island are about. And where the fuck is Gen. Isaac Peace Rodman House?

Houses on the National Register of Historic Places in Rhode Island are unfamiliar to me. And where is Joseph Hicks House located? I also have never been to The Nightingale–Brown House or Israel Arnold House. Couldn't say.

I don't know any Houses in Newport County, Rhode Island. I'm certain that I've never heard of The Roger Mowry Tavern. And I don't have any idea where John Tillinghast House or Wilbor House is. What the hell?

I'm not hip to Taverns in Rhode Island. Where is Waterman Tavern? I've never heard of The Smithfield Exchange Bank, Peleg Arnold Tavern or Mount Vernon Tavern. I just don't know that.

And I haven't the foggiest notion what Buildings and structures on the National Register of Historic Places in Rhode Island are about. The Pentecostal Collegiate Institute Rhode Island – what does that mean?

I'm not conversant with Properties of religious function on the National Register of Historic Places in Rhode Island. And I have no clue where The First Baptist Church in America is. Do people even go to Beneficent Congregational Church, West Greenwich Baptist Church and Cemetery or Gloria Dei Evangelical Lutheran Church? Couldn't tell you.

I also don't know what people mean by 'Baptist organizations established in the 17th century'. What is Castle Hill Baptist Church? I'm completely ignorant of Baptist churches in England. I also don't know where Carey Baptist Church is.

I also haven't kept up on Churches in Reading, Berkshire. I don't know how to get to The Church of St Mark, Reading or West Memorial Hall.

Don't ask me about Anglo-Catholicism. What the hell was Saint Martin's League, and what is the idea with the Anglo-Lutheran Catholic Church?

I also don't know anything about Lutheranism in the United States. The Church of the Lutheran Confession? Come again? Never heard of it. What, in the name of all that is holy, is The Norwegian Lutheran Church in the United States, and what was Norwegian Augustana Synod again? I haven't the foggiest idea. An Minnesota Conference – not my area of expertise. How should I know? I don't know what The American Evangelical Lutheran Church is.

Concerning Evangelical Lutheran Church in America predecessor churches, I am fully ignorant. Anti-Missourian Brotherhood? Doesn't ring a bell.

I also don't know about History of Christianity in the United States. I have no idea who William Penn or Luther Rice was.

Quaker writers are a mystery to me. I surely don't have any idea who Jacob Post was. Stephen Crisp – what's that supposed to mean? I'm clueless about that. Who the fuck is D. Elton Trueblood or Leonard Fell?

I definitely don't know the first thing about English Quakers. Is Joseph Lister, 1st Baron Lister famous or something? And who is Abraham Darby IV, Margaret Fell or Arthur Raistrick? I can't tell you that.

I'm not familiar with Presidents of the British Science Association.

Who on earth was William Henry Flower? Who the hell is Kathleen Lonsdale? Come on. I've also never heard of a person called Basil John Mason or Colin Blakemore.
People from Stratford-upon-Avon are unfamiliar to me. Do I need to know who Halliwell Hobbes was? I don't know who Hamnet Shakespeare was. Doesn't sound remotely familiar. Are Arthur Henry Shakespeare Lucas, Luella Bartley or June Goodfield famous or something?
I obviously couldn't tell you what Academics of the University of Oxford are about. Am I supposed to know Glen Newey, Valerie Beral or Antonio del Corro?
And I know nothing about Academics of Birkbeck, University of London. Who is this Jennifer Hornsby, Charlie Gere, Laura Mulvey or Delia Pemberton guy?
I don't know any Action theorists. Yujian Zheng, Harry Binswanger, Peter van Inwagen or Constantine Sandis – who are they?
I've never heard of Hunter College faculty. I have no clue who Robert Motherwell was.
I'm not conversant with People from Greenwich Village, New York. Jane Jacobs – doesn't ring a bell. Hans Hofmann – who was that? Search me. What's up with Artie Traum or Wavy Gravy?
And I'm not hip to Abstract expressionist artists. I surely don't know anything about Mark Rothko.
I'm completely ignorant of Jewish painters. And who the shit is Maurycy Trębacz? I also have no idea who Paola Levi-Montalcini or Leo Kahn is. Damned if I know.
And I don't know what people mean by 'German artists'. I don't have any idea who Beatriz da Costa was. Who on earth is Erich Klossowski, Johann Conrad Susemihl, Ellen Marx or Philipp Jordan? I just don't know.
And don't ask me about Polish art historians. Who is Beata Szymańska, Paweł Leszkowicz or Maciej Masłowski?
Concerning Art writers, I am fully ignorant. I've never heard of a person called Stephen Farthing.
I haven't kept up on Art educators. Who the fuck is Raymond Persinger, Charles Bargue or Albert Dorne?

I haven't the foggiest notion what Academic art is about. And I don't know who Don Troiani is.

I don't know the first thing about 21st-century American painters. Are Kelly L. Moran, Eva Slater, Donny Johnson or Tom Uttech famous or something?

And I don't know about Contemporary painters. Am I supposed to know Vera Hilger?

20th-century German painters are unfamiliar to me. Who the hell is Simon Dybbroe Møller, Emil Bartoschek or Bernard Lokai?

And I'm not familiar with Kunstakademie Düsseldorf alumni. Do I need to know who Georg Bergmann, Otto Piene, Thomas Ruff or Katharina Sieverding is?

I'm not well-versed in People from the Province of Westphalia. I have no clue who Paul Spiegel is. What's up with Georg Olschewski or Friedrich Lindenberg? Don't ask me.

I also know nothing about Members of the Order of Merit of North Rhine-Westphalia. Is Sönke Wortmann famous or something? Oswald Mathias Ungers – who was that? No idea.

I surely couldn't tell you what People from Marl, North Rhine-Westphalia are about. Who is this Heinz van Haaren, Christian Ahlmann or Oliver Wittke guy?

I've also never heard of Olympic medalists in equestrian. I don't know anything about Oswald Lints.

I'm not conversant with Olympic silver medalists for Belgium. And who the shit is Désiré Beaurain? I have no idea who Fernand de Montigny was. Not a clue. Who on earth is Maurice Van Damme, Pierre Dewin or Nicolaas Moerloos?

I frankly don't know any Male water polo players. And who is Geminio Ognio, Gianfranco Pandolfini, Maurizio Mannelli or Joseph De Combe?

I'm completely ignorant of Sportspeople from Florence. I also don't have any idea who Enzo Sacchi was. Who the fuck is Gianluca Berti, Pietro Linari or Giuseppe Galluzzi? Wouldn't know.

Don't ask me about A.C. Ancona players. I also don't know who Giorgio Bresciani, Emanuele Ferraro, Matteo Abbate or Antonio Montico is.

I also don't know what people mean by 'S.S. Juve Stabia players'. Are Giovanni Cervone or Leonardo Pavoletti famous or something?
I haven't the foggiest notion what People from Mexico City are about. What's up with Mario Vázquez Raña or José Luis Luege Tamargo?
I really don't know what people mean by 'Members of the Legislative Assembly of the Federal District'. Am I supposed to know David Sánchez Camacho, Ruth Zavaleta, Federico Döring, Bernardo de la Garza or Santiago Oñate Laborde?
Concerning Instituto Tecnológico Autónomo de México alumni, I am fully ignorant. Is Alejandro Poiré Romero famous or something?
And I haven't kept up on Mexican Secretaries of the Interior. I have no idea who Melchor Ocampo, Santiago Creel, Esteban Moctezuma or Eduardo Vasconcelos is.
And I'm not well-versed in Governors of Oaxaca. I have no clue who Gabino Cué Monteagudo is. I don't know anything about Víctor Bravo Ahuja. I certainly haven't the faintest idea.
People from Oaxaca are a mystery to me. Juan de Córdova, Blanca Charolet or Rosa Elia Romero Guzmán – who are they?
And I'm not hip to Missionary linguists. Who is this Jotham Meeker guy? Who the fuck is Rachel Saint? I just don't know about that.
I also don't know about Cairn University alumni. And who the shit is Duane Litfin?
I'm not familiar with Purdue University alumni. I really don't have any idea who George Casella was. Who on earth is Joel Emer, Herman H. Pevler or Herbert Newby McCoy? I have absolutely no idea.
And I don't know the first thing about Fellows of the American Statistical Association. Who is Michael A. Newton or Donald J. Wheeler?
I'm completely ignorant of American statisticians. I don't know who Otis Dudley Duncan is. I've never heard of a person called Allyn Abbott Young or Royal Meeker. Ask someone who knows something.
I've never heard of University of Wisconsin–Madison faculty. What about Florence Eliza Allen? Frank Pierrepont Graves – doesn't ring a bell. What the hell? Do I need to know who William P. Barnett, Probal Chaudhuri or Leslie Smith III is?
I also couldn't tell you what Education in New York is about. What

the shit is Machon Chana, and what on earth is Languages Other Than English? The New York State School Boards Association – don't know. Couldn't say.
Don't ask me about Hebrew words and phrases. A Piyyut – I don't know what that is.
I know nothing about Jewish liturgical poems. Zemirot – I don't know how to begin. The Ahot Ketannah – what is that? I haven't the remotest idea. What the fuck is Unetanneh Tokef, and what is Kinnot supposed to be?
I haven't the foggiest notion what Jewish music is about. Francesco Lotoro – who is that? What in the world is The Yemenite step, and what the heck is My Yiddishe Momme? Couldn't tell you.
Converts to Judaism are unfamiliar to me. Rahab – not my field. And who the hell is Daniel Olivas or Obadiah the Proselyte? I haven't the slightest idea.
I'm not conversant with Women in the Bible. How am I supposed to make sense of The Parable of the Ten Virgins, and what's Aholibamah got to do with it?
I don't know what people mean by 'Christian iconography'. I have no idea what The Bosom of Abraham Trinity is or what in tarnation The Mystical marriage of Saint Catherine is. What's the deal with Feather tights? I have no idea.
I don't know anything about Virgin Mary in art. Our Lady of Coromoto, is that even a thing? The Girdle of Thomas? How should I know? I can't tell you that. Am I supposed to be familiar with The Nursing Madonna? I just don't know that. I also have no idea who The Coronation of the Virgin or Feast of Our Lady of Snows is.
I haven't kept up on Marian shrines. And where the hell is Pontmain? What is 'Juditten Church' supposed to mean? How should I know? And I'm not hip to Brick Gothic. Don't ask me where The Cathedral Basilica of St. James the Apostle, Szczecin is! What in God's name is House of Perkūnas, and what the hell is Ebstorf Abbey? Come on. What is 'Tartu Cathedral' supposed to mean again?
I'm not well-versed in Christian monasteries established in the 12th century. I also couldn't tell you about The Abbey of San Pedro el Viejo or what Blanchland Abbey is about. Bromholm Priory, was that even a

real place? Doesn't sound remotely familiar.

I certainly don't know about Benedictine monasteries in Spain. Can you tell me how to get to The Valle de los Caídos? Please don't talk to me about Saint John of Caaveiro. Damned if I know. The Monastery of San Pelayo – I don't understand that. I'm clueless about that. Where the fuck is Sobrado Abbey?

I also don't know any Basilica churches in Spain. Where is The Basilica of Saint Mary of the Chorus located? What is The Sanctuary of Arantzazu, and what is The Santuari de Lluc anyway? I haven't the foggiest idea. I have never been to Valencia Cathedral or Sagrat Cor.

I don't know the first thing about San Sebastián. What the hell is The San Sebastian Jazz Festival, and what is María Cristina Bridge? Don't ask me what The City council of San Sebastián is. I have no clue. The Siege of Cuartel de Loyola – I don't even know where to start. Not a clue. The Funicular de Igueldo – how should I know what that is?

I'm not familiar with City and town halls in Spain. And I don't have any idea what The Casa consistorial de Sevilla is. Where in the world is The Old City Hall of Jerez de la Frontera? I don't have any idea. I'm certain that I've never heard of Algeciras Town Hall or how I'm supposed to know something about La Paeria or what people say about it.

Renaissance architecture in Spain is a mystery to me. I certainly don't have any idea where The Church of San Antón is. Where is General Archive of the Indies or Palacio de Campo Real? No idea.

I've also never heard of World Heritage Sites in Spain. I have no idea where The Serra de Tramuntana is.

And I'm completely ignorant of Comarcas of the Balearic Islands. I have no clue where Formentera is.

I know nothing about Islands of the Balearic Islands. I also don't know how to get to a Dragonera. I have no clue what Isla de sa Porrassa is. I just don't know. And do people even go to Pantaleu or Majorca?

And I couldn't tell you what Zoomorphic geographic features are about. Where the hell is The Drakensberg? I really don't know where Elephant Island or Shir Kuh is. Don't ask me.

Prehistoric Africa is unfamiliar to me. The Mousterian Pluvial – dunno. A Pluvial? Doesn't ring a bell. I just don't know about that.

Tadrart Acacus, is that even a real place? I haven't got a clue. What, in the name of all that is holy, is The Apollo 11 Cave?
Concerning Deserts of Libya, I am fully ignorant. Can you tell me how to get to The Libyan Desert? The Calanshio Sand Sea – never heard of it. Ask someone who knows something. What's up with Murzuq Desert?
I haven't the foggiest notion what Cyrenaica is about. Where the fuck is Aqfanta or Al Abraq International Airport?
I also don't know anything about Populated places in Jabal al Akhdar. And where is Wasita or Wardama located?
And I'm not conversant with Baguio. Where in the world is SM City Baguio? I also don't have any idea where The Roman Catholic Diocese of Baguio is. Wouldn't know. Mines View Park – not my area of expertise.
I don't know what people mean by 'Parks in the Philippines'. The Manila Zoological and Botanical Garden – doesn't ring a bell.
And I haven't kept up on Zoos in the Philippines. Birds International – what does that mean? What about The Ninoy Aquino Parks & Wildlife Center? Couldn't say.
I also don't know about Botanical gardens in the Philippines. Mehan Garden – I don't understand this.
And I don't know the first thing about The History of Manila. I don't know what The Manila Elks Club is.
I'm not well-versed in Museums in Metro Manila. What the shit is The Cultural Center of the Philippines, and what is the mystery about Museo Valenzuela? Where is The Mind Museum or Ayala Museum? Search me.
I'm not familiar with Visitor attractions in Metro Manila. I've also never heard of SM Mall of Asia.
Don't ask me about Shopping malls in Metro Manila. Don't ask me where SM City Bicutan, Farmers Plaza or Isetann Cinerama Recto is!
I'm not hip to Buildings and structures in Parañaque. And I have never been to the Baclaran Church. I have no idea where SM City Sucat or SM City BF Parañaque is. I haven't the faintest idea.
I don't know any SM Prime Holdings. I certainly don't know how to get to SM City Batangas, SM Aura Premier, SM Quiapo, SM City

Bacoor or Agana Shopping Center.
I obviously couldn't tell you what Bacoor is about. Bellefort Estates – don't know. Bacoor Bay – not my field. Couldn't tell you.
I'm completely ignorant of Bays of the Philippines. I have no clue where Subic Bay is.
And I know nothing about Zambales. Do people even go to Totalmed, Mount Pinatubo or Capones Island Lighthouse?
I also haven't the foggiest notion what Mountains of the Philippines are about. Mount Mantalingajan, Mount Malepunyo or Mount Panay, is that even a real place?
Volcanoes of Luzon are unfamiliar to me. And I don't know where Mount Santo Tomas or Laguna Caldera is.
I'm also not conversant with Subduction volcanoes. Where the hell is Mount Tambora?
I definitely don't know anything about Stratovolcanoes. Where the fuck is Plinth Peak or Ale Bagu?
And I don't know what people mean by 'Mountains of British Columbia'. Can you tell me how to get to Farbus Mountain or Botanie Mountain?
I haven't kept up on The Fraser Canyon. And I'm sorry, did you say 'The Skuppah Indian Band', and what is the deal with Dogwood Valley? I certainly don't have any idea where Skihist Mountain is.
I just don't know. Where is The Nahatlatch River or Churn Creek Protected Area?
Rivers of the Pacific Ranges are a mystery to me. What in the world is Alfred Creek, and what in tarnation is The Hurley River? The Cheekye River – what's that supposed to mean? I have no idea. I've never heard of The Alouette River or Birkenhead River.
Concerning South Coast of British Columbia, I am fully ignorant. And where is The Lower Mainland located? How am I supposed to make sense of Discovery Passage, and what is the idea with The Theodosia River? I have absolutely no idea.
And I don't know about The Lower Mainland. What's the deal with School District 35 Langley, and what is The Yakweakwioose First Nation about? Don't ask me where The Pitt River is! What the hell? I have never been to Chehalis Lake or Bridal Veil Falls Provincial Park.

And I don't know the first thing about Geography of Coquitlam. The Como watershed, is that even a thing?
I'm not hip to Watersheds of Canada. Please don't talk to me about The Great Lakes Basin.
Don't ask me about The Great Lakes. Mackinac Falls? Come again? Never heard of it. What the fuck is The Southern Great Lakes Seismic Zone, and what is The Great Lakes–Saint Lawrence River Basin Sustainable Water Resources Agreement again? I haven't the slightest idea. I definitely don't know how to get to The Great Lakes region.
I'm not well-versed in Seismic zones of the United States. The New Madrid Seismic Zone – I don't know how to begin. The Eastern Tennessee Seismic Zone – what is that? I can't tell you that. Am I supposed to be familiar with The Virginia Seismic Zone?
I couldn't tell you what Plate tectonics are about. What is 'The Owen Fracture Zone' supposed to mean? And what is a Platform cover? I haven't the remotest idea.
I also don't know any Fracture zones. What is the Great Lakes tectonic zone, and what on earth is The Diamantina Fracture Zone? I have no idea what The Easter Fracture Zone is or what the heck The Valdivia Fracture Zone is. I just don't know that.
I'm completely ignorant of Hotspots of North America. Where in the world is The Great Meteor hotspot track?
I know nothing about Paleogene volcanism. Do people even go to Rathlin Island or Eigg?
I'm not familiar with Protected areas of County Antrim. The Antrim Coast and Glens? How should I know? I couldn't tell you about Waterloo Bay. Doesn't sound remotely familiar. I have no clue where Lough Beg is. Damned if I know. And I don't have any idea what Slieveanorra Forest is or what the current state of research is on Portmore Lough.
I also don't know anything about Northern Ireland Environment Agency properties. What the hell is Dundrum Castle?
I don't know what people mean by 'Ruined castles in Northern Ireland'. Kinbane Castle – I don't understand that. What, in the name of all that is holy, is Moyry Castle, and what is Altinaghree Castle supposed to be? I'm clueless about that. I have no clue what

Portaferry Castle is or what the mystery about Mountjoy Castle is or whether I should care.

Castles in County Tyrone are unfamiliar to me. Roxborough Castle – I don't know what that is.

I also haven't the foggiest notion what Buildings and structures in the United Kingdom destroyed by arson are about. I don't know where Brettell Lane railway station was. What's up with The Allenton house fire? How should I know?

Filicides are a mystery to me. Am I supposed to know Assia Wevill? Who the fuck is Ernst-Robert Grawitz? No idea. Who is this Mary Ann Britland or Shirley Winters guy?

I've never heard of People from Berlin. Is Heinz Schweizer famous or something? Who the shit is Alfred Dürr, Dieter König or Ursula Hirschmann? I haven't the foggiest idea.

And I haven't kept up on Bomb disposal personnel. I have no clue who Vivian Dering Majendie is.

I don't know the first thing about British Army personnel of the Crimean War. Who on earth is Alfred Capel-Cure? I surely don't have any idea who John Granville Harkness, Edward William Derrington Bell, Thomas de Courcy Hamilton or William Bradshaw VC was. Come on.

I don't know about Queen's Own Royal West Kent Regiment officers. And who was Edmund Henry Lenon? Do I need to know who Charles Bonham-Carter was? I don't have any idea. Philip Dawson or James Frederick Lyon – who are they?

And I'm not conversant with Companions of the Order of St Michael and St George. I don't know who Edward Unwin was. Who the hell is Guy Salisbury-Jones or John Horace Ragnar Colvin? I certainly don't know about that.

And I'm not hip to British Gallipoli Campaign recipients of the Victoria Cross. William Thomas Forshaw or Edward Courtney Boyle – doesn't ring a bell.

I couldn't tell you what Royal Navy recipients of the Victoria Cross are about. Are Samuel Mitchell VC, Richard Been Stannard, George Hinckley or Richard Bell-Davies famous or something?

I also don't know any Royal Navy personnel of the New Zealand

Wars. I don't know anything about William Odgers.

I'm completely ignorant of Royal Navy sailors. I've never heard of a person called Mark Scholefield.

Don't ask me about People from London. I have no idea who Amy Ashwood Garvey, Nathan Crowley or Byron Glasgow is.

And I know nothing about Walton & Hersham F.C. players. What's up with Roger Connell, Alan Dowson, Akwasi Fobi-Edusei or Stuart Massey?

And I'm not familiar with Slough Town F.C. players. Who the shit is Micky Droy, Paul Holsgrove, Ian Hazel or Roy Gumbs?

I really don't know what people mean by 'Banstead Athletic F.C. players'. Grant Watts – who is that?

Concerning Gillingham F.C. players, I am fully ignorant. Is Albert Fairclough famous or something? Who the fuck is Franck Rolling, Charles Bunyan, Sr., Danny Cullip or David Perpetuini? I haven't got a clue.

Standard Liège managers are unfamiliar to me. Am I supposed to know Luka Peruzović?

I frankly don't know any People from Kagoshima Prefecture. I've never heard of a person called Hiroshi Moriyama.

I also don't know anything about Members of the House of Councillors. What's up with Hiroe Makiyama?

I know nothing about Female members of the House of Councillors. Who the shit is Tomoko Sasaki, Haruko Yoshikawa or Ryoko Tani?

And I'm not conversant with Olympic bronze medalists for Japan. Kosuke Fukudome – who is that? Am I supposed to know Masao Takemoto? I have no clue.

I don't know what people mean by 'National League All-Stars'. Who is this Lee Walls guy? Is Geoff Jenkins famous or something? Not a clue.

And concerning Philadelphia Phillies players, I am fully ignorant. I have no idea who Hugh Duffy was.

Milwaukee Creams players are unfamiliar to me. Joseph Herr, Fritz Clausen or Doc Adkins – who are they?

And I'm completely ignorant of New York Highlanders players. Who the fuck is Earl Moore, Guy Zinn, Monte Beville or Stubby Magner?

And I haven't kept up on Indianapolis Indians players. I don't have

any idea who Blake Doyle is.
Don't ask me about Miami Orioles players. Who the hell is Mike Willis?
And I'm not familiar with Major League Baseball pitchers. Who on earth was Lino Donoso? Who is José De La Torre, LaTroy Hawkins or Derrick Turnbow? Search me.
Columbus Jets players are a mystery to me. Al Jackson, Gene Stephens or Manny Mota – doesn't ring a bell.
I've never heard of Caribbean Series players. Are Carmelo Martínez, Charlie Hough or Jean-Pierre Roy famous or something?
And I don't know the first thing about Major League Baseball announcers. I don't know who Hector Molina or Francisco X. Rivera is.
I'm not hip to National Football League announcers. I've never heard of a person called Mitch Holthus.
I really couldn't tell you what College football announcers are about. And do I need to know who Joe Tessitore, Craig Minervini, Sharlene Wells Hawkes or Jeff Genyk is?
I haven't the foggiest notion what Women sports announcers are about. What's up with Donna Barton Brothers, Heather Cox, Michele Tafoya, Deb Matejicka or Beth Daniel?
I don't know about Winners of ladies' major amateur golf championships. I have no clue who Moira Milton was. Beverly Hanson – who was that? Wouldn't know. I don't know anything about Vicki Goetze or Edith Cummings.
I know nothing about American female golfers. Am I supposed to know Grace DeMoss, Emma Talley or Cindy LaCrosse?
I also don't know what people mean by 'LPGA Tour golfers'. And who is this Sharon Barrett guy?
I don't know any Tulsa Golden Hurricane women's golfers. Who the shit is Melissa McNamara, Lee-Anne Pace, Cathy Reynolds or Carolyn Hill?
I'm not well-versed in Golfers from Oklahoma. I don't have any idea who Blake Adams, Dwight Nevil, Robert Streb, Stacy Prammanasudh or Rocky Walcher is.
People from Altus, Oklahoma are unfamiliar to me. I have no idea who

Joseph M. Watt is.
And I'm completely ignorant of Texas Tech University alumni. Who on earth is Bud Andrews or Andrae Williams?
And I haven't kept up on Male sprinters. Who the hell is Stéphane Diagana, Yohan Blake, Rondell Sorrilo or Thomas Martinot-Lagarde?
Concerning Olympic athletes of Jamaica, I am fully ignorant. And who the fuck is Kemel Thompson, Ricardo Chambers, Dionne Rose-Henley or Merlene Frazer?
And I'm not conversant with Jamaican sprinters. Who is Lorraine Fenton, Shelly-Ann Fraser-Pryce, Warren Weir, Rosemarie Whyte or Javon Francis?
Don't ask me about Olympic gold medalists for Jamaica. Is Melaine Walker famous or something?
I've never heard of Jamaican sportswomen. Kerron Stewart, Delloreen Ennis-London or Grace Jackson – who are they?
I'm not hip to Olympic silver medalists for Jamaica. Do I need to know who Shericka Williams is?
I don't know the first thing about Olympic bronze medalists for Jamaica. I don't know who Michael Blackwood, Don Quarrie, Gillian Russell, Christine Day or Hansle Parchment is.
I also haven't the foggiest notion what World Championships in Athletics medalists are about. What's up with Silke-Beate Knoll, Roddie Haley or Kutre Dulecha?
I certainly don't know about German Athletics Champions. Melanie Kraus, Schahriar Bigdeli or Katja Demut – doesn't ring a bell.
Female triple jumpers are a mystery to me. Are Olga Vasdeki, Martina Šestáková or Tori Bowie famous or something?
I know nothing about American sprinters. I don't know anything about Esther Jones, Sheila Ingram, Charles Silmon or Lee Vernon McNeill.
I don't know what people mean by 'LSU Lady Tigers track and field athletes'. I've never heard of a person called Peta-Gaye Dowdie.
I don't know any Commonwealth Games competitors for Jamaica. Who is this Kasey Evering, Jhaniele Fowler, Romelda Aiken or Mike McCallum guy?
I'm not familiar with Recipients of the Jamaican Prime Ministers

Medal of Appreciation. The Jamaican Prime Ministers Medal of Appreciation – what does that mean? Who the shit is Trevor Berbick? Ask someone who knows something. I also have no clue who Lloyd Honeyghan is.
And I'm not well-versed in People from Florida. I have no idea who Howard M. Norton was.
I frankly haven't kept up on Place of birth missing. Am I supposed to know Félix Dockx? Thiệu Trị – who was that? I just don't know. Who on earth is Alfred Dohring or Ren-Chang Ching?
19th-century monarchs in Asia are unfamiliar to me. And who the hell is Buddha Loetla Nabhalai? Who the fuck is Prince Imperial Heung, Mozaffar ad-Din Shah Qajar, Minh Mạng or Dục Đức? I haven't the faintest idea.
I also couldn't tell you what Thai poets are about. Is Vajiravudh famous or something? And who is Vasan Sitthiket or Paiwarin Khao-Ngam? Couldn't say.
I'm completely ignorant of Knights of the Golden Fleece. Do I need to know who Ferdinand III, Grand Duke of Tuscany was? Joseph Johann Adam, Prince of Liechtenstein – doesn't ring a bell. I have no idea. I don't know who József Árpád Habsburg or Adolf of Burgundy is.
I'm also not conversant with Knights Grand Cross of the Order of Saint Ferdinand and of Merit. What's up with Count Heinrich von Bellegarde?
I've never heard of Counts of Germany. Who is this Michael Graf von Matuschka guy? Are Frederick of Isenberg, Friedrich Ferdinand Alexander zu Dohna-Schlobitten or Bernhard, Count of Bylandt famous or something? I surely don't know.
Concerning Ludwig Maximilian University of Munich alumni, I am fully ignorant. I don't know anything about Otto Hönigschmid. I don't have any idea who Albert Battel, Johann Georg Baiter or Elisheva Cohen is. I have absolutely no idea.
And I don't know the first thing about University of Breslau alumni. I have no idea who Hans Georg Dehmelt is.
I haven't the foggiest notion what Duke University faculty is about. Who the shit is Robert Pinsky or Lewis Ayres?
Don't ask me about Alumni of Merton College, Oxford. I've never

heard of a person called Sheridan Morley. Am I supposed to know Clement Barksdale, Denis MacShane or Callum McCarthy? I haven't the slightest idea.

I'm not hip to British radio DJs. Gary Davies, Don Maclean, Mike George, Kutski or Joel Ross – who are they?

BBC Radio 1 presenters are a mystery to me. Who the hell is Al Matthews or Skream?

I don't know about United States Marines. I also have no clue who Roy K. Moore is.

I don't know what people mean by 'People from Hood River, Oregon'. Who the fuck is Joseph K. Carson, Jr.? Do I need to know who Sammy Carlson, Bobby Gene Smith, Marc Alan Lee or Alex Arrowsmith is? I haven't the remotest idea.

I really don't know any Seattle Angels players. Who on earth is Clyde Wright?

I know nothing about Carson–Newman Eagles baseball players. Buddy Bolding – doesn't ring a bell.

I'm not familiar with People from Bedford County, Virginia. Is Joseph Hamilton Daveiss famous or something? Who is this Isham Talbot or Samuel Read Anderson guy? What the hell?

Kentucky lawyers are unfamiliar to me. What's up with John Calvin Mason? Daniel Breck – who is that? Doesn't sound remotely familiar. Who was Archibald Dixon, Alney McLean or Gatewood Galbraith?

I haven't kept up on Deaths from emphysema. I have no idea who Boris Karloff was.

And I'm completely ignorant of People educated at Uppingham School. I also don't know anything about Toby Spence. Who the shit is Charles Howard Hinton? Damned if I know. Are George Allan Maling, Arthur Moore Lascelles or Edward Beadon Turner famous or something?

I'm not conversant with Recipients of the Military Cross. Am I supposed to know Henry Morris-Jones? Hugh Wrigley, James Stanley Scott, Douglas Graham Cooke or Bruce Kinloch – who are they? How should I know?

And I'm not well-versed in Graduates of the Royal Military College, Sandhurst. Who the hell is Hector Lachlan Stewart MacLean?

I don't know the first thing about British recipients of the Victoria Cross. I obviously don't have any idea who Arthur Mayo or Hastings Edward Harrington was.
And I couldn't tell you what Deaths from cholera are about. I've never heard of a person called Joseph Darlinton. Do I need to know who Francisco Castellón, Nino Bixio or Louis Thuillier is? No idea.
Don't ask me about People from Romney, West Virginia. Who on earth is Catherine Pancake? I have no clue who Cornelia Peake McDonald or James Sloan Kuykendall was. I just don't know that.
And concerning People from Alexandria, Virginia, I am fully ignorant. I frankly don't know who Eric Barton is.
Oakland Raiders players are a mystery to me. What's up with James Adkisson, Darren Mickell or Shane Lechler?
I've also never heard of New Orleans Saints players. Billy Joe Hobert, Leigh Torrence, Curtis Hamilton, Derrick Lewis or Ryan Senser – doesn't ring a bell.
I'm not hip to Green Bay Packers players. Is Jim Bob Morris famous or something?
I'm not well-versed in People from Mount Holly, New Jersey. And I have no clue who Stephen Girard was.
I don't know the first thing about American bankers. And who on earth is Debbie Abono? Frederick Ferris Thompson – doesn't ring a bell. I don't have any idea. I frankly don't know who Lantz Womack, Augustus Frank or Augustus Kountze was.
Don't ask me about American businesspeople. I've never heard of a person called Frederick Kappel. I don't know anything about George Lindemann, Adam B. Resnick, Max Hoffman or Tonia Ryan. I really haven't got a clue.
Concerning United States Postal Service people, I am fully ignorant. Who was William Cooper Nell? And who the fuck is Ambrose O'Connell, Tom Hancock or Charles Henry Robb? I just don't know about that.
Deaths from stroke are a mystery to me. And who is this Millard Fillmore, Molly Bee, Anne Gwynne, James Parkinson or Charlie Drake guy?
I couldn't tell you what English geologists are about. What's up with

William Buckland? Is William Hopkins famous or something? I have no clue. Who the shit is William Samuel Symonds, Ernest St. John Burton or Osmond Fisher?
I also don't know any People educated at Winchester College. I don't have any idea who Harry Peckham was. Am I supposed to know Augustus William Hare or Sir Richard Worsley, 7th Baronet? Not a clue.
I'm not familiar with Paintings by Joseph Wright of Derby. And what is 'The Blacksmith's Shop' supposed to mean again? Where the hell was Needwood Forest? Wouldn't know. Vesuvius from Posillipo by Moonlight – I don't even know where to start.
I also haven't the foggiest notion what Collections of Derby Museum and Art Gallery are about. Who the hell is Frank Gresley? What about Derby Porcelain, and what's The British Rail Research Division got to do with it? I'm clueless about that.
I haven't kept up on British Rail research and development. I'm sorry, did you say 'The High Speed Freight Vehicle', and what the hell is The Railway Technical Centre? BREL – how should I know what that is? Ask someone who knows something. What in God's name is The Integrated Electronic Control Centre?
I don't know what people mean by 'British Rail subsidiaries and divisions'. And I'm certain that I've never heard of Travellers Fare or what on earth Trainload Freight was. How am I supposed to make sense of Sealink, and what is British Transport Hotels? Couldn't tell you. Red Star Parcels, is that even a thing?
I've never heard of British Rail brands. ScotRail, is that even a real place? Regional Railways – not my area of expertise. Don't ask me. Merseyrail – never heard of it.
And I'm not hip to Rail transport in Merseyside. Don't ask me what Merseyrail Electrics was. What the shit is Merseytram? I have no idea. I have no idea where Birkenhead Dock Branch is. I obviously don't know. I don't have any idea where The Wirral Line or West Coast Main Line is.
I'm completely ignorant of Rail transport in Hertfordshire. Can you tell me how to get to The London to Aylesbury Line? East West Rail Link? Come again? Never heard of it. Couldn't say. The Hatfield rail

crash? Doesn't ring a bell. I haven't the faintest idea. What the fuck was The Hatfield and St Albans Railway, and what is The Watford and Rickmansworth Railway anyway?
And I don't know about Rail transport in Milton Keynes. What's the deal with The Wolverton and Stony Stratford Tramway? Where the fuck was Denbigh Hall railway station? I have absolutely no idea. Where is Bow Brickhill railway station, Woburn Sands railway station or Wolverton railway station?
I frankly know nothing about Railway stations in Buckinghamshire. Where is Denham railway station, Aylesbury Vale Parkway railway station, Cheddington railway station or Monks Risborough railway station located?
I'm also not well-versed in Railway stations served by London Midland. I don't know how to get to Wolverhampton railway station, Butlers Lane railway station or Euston railway station.
I don't know the first thing about Former London and North Western Railway stations. Am I supposed to be familiar with Connah's Quay railway station? Where in the world was Longsight railway station? Search me. And do people even go to Hinckley railway station?
Railway stations in Leicestershire are unfamiliar to me. I have no clue where Market Harborough railway station, South Wigston railway station, Syston railway station or Bottesford railway station is.
I'm not conversant with Railway stations served by CrossCountry. And I have never been to Newport railway station, Inverkeithing railway station or Coleshill Parkway railway station.
Former North British Railway stations are a mystery to me. I definitely don't know where Bathgate Lower railway station was. Where the hell is Springburn railway station? Damned if I know.
Don't ask me about Listed railway stations in Scotland. I've also never heard of Possil railway station. I have no idea where Broughty Ferry railway station, Crookston railway station or St Enoch subway station is. What the hell?
I don't know anything about Railway stations served by First ScotRail. I also don't have any idea where Largs railway station or Haymarket railway station is.
And concerning Largs, I am fully ignorant. The Barrfields Pavilion –

don't know. What is The Battle of Largs? I really haven't the remotest idea.
And I haven't the foggiest notion what Norse activity in Scotland is about. Sen dollotar Ulaid … – what's that supposed to mean? The Kingdom of the Isles – I don't understand this. I just don't know. Please don't talk to me about The Lewis chessmen. I obviously don't know that. The Orkneyinga saga – not my field.
And I don't know any Chess sets. What in the world is Clamp no Kiseki?
I don't know what people mean by 'Greek sportswomen'. Are Hydna, Panagiota Tsakiri or Sofia Bekatorou famous or something?
I'm also not familiar with Women in ancient Greek warfare. I have no idea what Lamia of Athens is or what the hell Telesilla is. I have no clue who Aretaphila of Cyrene is. Doesn't sound remotely familiar. What the hell is Gynaecothoenas, and what is the deal with Lampsace?
And I haven't kept up on 1st-century BC deaths. Quintus Aponius – who was that? Who on earth was Philodemus? How should I know? Gnaeus Aufidius Orestes – I don't know how to begin. Come on. I have no idea who Laodice VII Thea or Quintus Lutatius Catulus is. And I'm not hip to Roman Republican consuls. I've never heard of a person called Publius Valerius Laevinus. I also don't know who Quintus Servilius Priscus was. I haven't the slightest idea. Who is Publius Sulpicius Galba Maximus, Lucius Licinius Crassus or Quintus Laronius?
I also know nothing about 2nd-century BC Romans. Gaius Caecilius Metellus Caprarius? How should I know? Who the fuck is Gaius Sulpicius Gallus? I just don't know about that. I couldn't tell you about Drusus Claudius Nero I or why people are so interested in Lucius Furius Philus.
And I don't know about 105 BC births. Marcus Atius or Decimus Laberius – who are they?
I'm not well-versed in Ancient Roman writers. And what was 'Scribonius Largus' supposed to mean? Alfenus Varus or Columella – doesn't ring a bell. I really haven't got a clue.
I also don't know the first thing about Ancient Roman physicians.

Who is this Antonius Musa guy?
I'm also completely ignorant of Antonii. Who the shit is Cleopatra Selene II? What's up with Antonia Major? I have no clue.
I'm also not conversant with Roman-era Egyptians. Am I supposed to know Abaskiron?
I couldn't tell you what Egyptian people executed by decapitation are about. And who the hell is Leonides of Alexandria?
Don't ask me about Ante-Nicene Christian martyrs. Do I need to know who Isidore of Chios was?
3rd-century Christian martyrs are unfamiliar to me. Is Nicasius, Quirinus, Scubiculus, and Pientia famous or something? I have no clue who Gundenis was. I really don't have any idea. And I don't know anything about Saint Otimus or Alexander of Rome.
3rd-century Romans are a mystery to me. Who on earth was Gregory of Nazianzus the Elder? I've never heard of a person called Castulus. I'm clueless about that. And I don't have any idea who Gaius Septimius Severus Aper, Gaius Vettius Gratus Atticus Sabinianus or Marcus Peducaeus Plautius Quintillus is.
I've never heard of Imperial Roman consuls. I also have no idea who Macrinus was. Who the fuck is Gaius Catius Clemens? Ask someone who knows something.
I also haven't the foggiest notion what Praetorian prefects are about. Who is Tiberius Julius Alexander?
And I'm not familiar with Roman-era Jews. Who is this James, son of Zebedee guy?
And concerning Saints from the Holy Land, I am fully ignorant. Who the shit is The Penitent thief? What's up with Epiphanius of Salamis? Not a clue. Lazarus of Bethany – doesn't ring a bell.
And I don't know any 30s deaths. Who the hell is Jesus? Tiberius Gemellus or Junia Claudilla – who are they? I certainly haven't the foggiest idea.
And I know nothing about Deified people. Am I supposed to know Hephaestion? I don't know what Julius Marinus is. Couldn't tell you. Can you tell me how to get to Sailendra? Don't ask me. Are Sugawara no Michizane or Caecilia Paulina famous or something?
And I haven't kept up on Sailendra. Don't ask me where Srivijaya is!

I'm not hip to 13th-century disestablishments. What is 'The Crovan dynasty' supposed to mean again, and what in tarnation is Mỹ Sơn? I also don't know the first thing about Visitor attractions in Vietnam. I don't have any idea what Tam Cốc-Bích Động is.

I'm also completely ignorant of Geography of Ninh Binh Province. What, in the name of all that is holy, is Cúc Phương National Park?

I also don't know what people mean by 'Geography of Thanh Hoa Province'. I have no clue what Pù Luông Nature Reserve is or what the deal with Con Moong Cave is or what it is all about. I'm certain that I've never heard of Hải Hòa Beach. No idea.

I'm not well-versed in Beaches of Vietnam. Bãi Cháy – I don't know what that is. Where the fuck is Hồ Cốc, Hồ Tràm, Đồ Sơn or Lăng Cô? Wouldn't know.

And I don't know about Geography of Thua Thien-Hue Province. What about The Thuận An estuary?

I couldn't tell you what Estuaries are about. And where is The Pearl River Delta? Salt pannes and pools – I don't even know where to start. I haven't the faintest idea. The Atlantic Estuarine Research Society – how should I know what that is? I can't tell you that. Zavratnica – what is that? How am I supposed to make sense of Sir Creek?

Water organizations in the United States are unfamiliar to me. Upper Chattahoochee Riverkeeper – dunno.

Don't ask me about The Chattahoochee River. The Chestatee River – never heard of it.

I don't know anything about Geography of Dawson County, Georgia. Where is The Etowah River located? Don't ask me what The Cartecay River is. Couldn't say.

I haven't the foggiest notion what Geography of Bartow County, Georgia is about. Leake Mounds – what does that mean? What the shit is Salacoa Creek? Damned if I know. I definitely don't know how to get to Euharlee Creek.

And I'm not conversant with Geography of Pickens County, Georgia. Mount Oglethorpe, is that even a thing?

I'm not familiar with Mountains on the Appalachian Trail. North Carter Mountain, is that even a real place?

And I don't know any Mountains of New Hampshire. I'm sorry, did you say 'Mount Success'? Do people even go to Mount Isolation? What the hell?

I've also never heard of Landforms of Coos County, New Hampshire. And I have never been to The Connecticut Lakes. Where in the world is Mount Waumbek, Mount Cabot or Umbagog Lake? I have no idea. I also know nothing about Pittsburg, New Hampshire. Halls Stream – I don't understand that. I don't know where The Republic of Indian Stream was. I have absolutely no idea. I have no clue where The Pittsburg–Clarksville Covered Bridge is.

Concerning Tributaries of the Connecticut River, I am fully ignorant. And I have no idea where The Ashuelot River is.

I'm also not hip to Rivers of New Hampshire. What's the deal with Pequawket Brook, and what the heck is The Nissitissit River? And I don't have any idea where The Millers River is. I just don't know. Am I supposed to be familiar with The Lane River? Doesn't sound remotely familiar. The Suncook River – I don't understand this.

Rivers of Worcester County, Massachusetts are a mystery to me. Can you tell me how to get to Tarbell Brook? And where the hell is The Assabet River? I frankly just don't know.

I'm completely ignorant of Rivers of Middlesex County, Massachusetts. And where the fuck is The Charles River?

I also haven't kept up on Rowing venues. The Rowing Stadium of the Lagoon? Doesn't ring a bell. Talkin Tarn – what's that supposed to mean? I haven't the remotest idea.

I'm not well-versed in Sports venues in Brazil. I have no idea what Caiçaras Club is or what The City of Rock is or if it's worth knowing. Ginásio da Portuguesa – don't know. Search me. Where is National Equestrian Center or Flamengo Park?

I also couldn't tell you what Modernist architecture in Brazil is about. What in God's name is The Edifício Copan?

Oscar Niemeyer buildings are unfamiliar to me. And what is The University of Brasília? Don't ask me where The Palácio do Planalto or Headquarters of the United Nations is! I just don't know about that. Don't ask me about Modernist architecture. Where is Eugene City Hall located?

I don't know what people mean by 'Buildings and structures in

Eugene, Oregon'. I don't know how to get to The Wallace and Glenn Potter House or A. V. Peters House.

I don't know the first thing about Tudor Revival architecture in Oregon. The Edward H. and Bertha R. Keller House or Raymond and Catherine Fisher House, is that even a real place?

I haven't the foggiest notion what Houses on the National Register of Historic Places in Portland, Oregon are about. And I have never been to The Pittock Mansion, J. G. Edwards House, Edward D. Dupont House or Joseph Kendall House.

And I'm not conversant with Reportedly haunted locations in Portland, Oregon. Where in the world is Rimsky-Korsakoffee House? What the fuck is The Shanghai tunnels? I haven't the slightest idea. I've never heard of The Bagdad Theatre or Roseland Theater.

I surely don't know about Old Town Chinatown, Portland, Oregon. What in the world is CC Slaughters, and what is the mystery about The Everett Station Lofts? The Skidmore Fountain? How should I know? I don't have any idea. Do people even go to Portland Downtown Heliport or Lan Su Chinese Garden?

And concerning LGBT in Oregon, I am fully ignorant. Darcelle XV – who is that? What's up with Hands Across Hawthorne? I'm clueless about that.

I don't know any LGBT businesspeople from the United States. Do I need to know who Bernardo Hernández González, Brent Ridge, Jon-Marc McDonald, Chris Hughes or Tim Gill is?

I'm also not hip to Comillas Pontifical University alumni. Who on earth is Pedro Segura y Sáenz or Braulio Rodríguez Plaza?

I'm not familiar with 21st-century Roman Catholics. And I have no clue who Noel Treanor or Bernard Longley is.

20th-century Roman Catholics are a mystery to me. Is Juan Soldevila y Romero famous or something?

I'm also completely ignorant of 20th-century Roman Catholic priests. I don't have any idea who Alfred Delp, Micheál Ledwith, Leo Nowak or Otto Kippes is.

I don't know anything about People from County Wexford. I've never heard of a person called Eoin Colfer, Seán Fortune, Thomas Cloney, Bagenal Harvey or Cennselach mac Brain.

And I couldn't tell you what Artemis Fowl are about. Gnommish – not my field.

I surely haven't kept up on Fictional languages. What is 'Newspeak' supposed to mean again, and what are the idea with Elvish languages? What, in the name of all that is holy, is Nadsat, and what is Chakobsa again? I haven't got a clue. And please don't talk to me about Simlish. Controlled English is unfamiliar to me. Simplified Technical English – not my area of expertise. ClearTalk – I don't know how to begin. How should I know?

I don't know what people mean by 'Controlled natural languages'. Gellish English? Come again? Never heard of it. And what about Attempto Controlled English, and what on earth is Français fondamental? I just don't know that.

Don't ask me about Simplified languages. I don't know what Basic English is or what is supposed to be special about Toki Pona or if it's good to know.

I haven't the foggiest notion what Technical communication is about. Procedural memory – what is that? I certainly don't have any idea what An Edublog is or what Technical documentation is about. Not a clue. And I couldn't tell you about TECHWR-L.

I'm also not conversant with Memory processes. What is 'Retrieval-induced forgetting' supposed to mean?

I've never heard of Cognitive psychology. Automatic and Controlled Processes ACP – how should I know what that is? And what the shit is The Psychology of reasoning, and what is Cognitive hearing science about? Come on.

I also don't know the first thing about Genetics. I have no clue what Pathogenicity island is.

Concerning Bacterial toxins, I am fully ignorant. Symplocamide A – doesn't ring a bell. And what the hell is Tolaasin? I have no clue.

I know nothing about Macrocycles. I'm sorry, did you say 'Cilengitide'? And what is Carpaine? No idea.

I'm not hip to Alkaloids. How am I supposed to make sense of Guvacine?

I don't know any Carboxylic acids. Gambogic acid – dunno.

I don't know about Xanthones. Xanthone, is that even a thing?

Insecticides are a mystery to me. Nithiazine – what does that mean? Naphthalene – never heard of it. Wouldn't know. What in God's name is N-Octyl bicycloheptene dicarboximide, and what the hell is Oxydemeton-methyl? Couldn't tell you. What's the deal with ATC code P03?

I'm not well-versed in Imides. I'm certain that I've never heard of Alnespirone or how I'm supposed to know something about Phetharbital or what to think about it. What the fuck is Lumiflavin, and what is Buspirone? I can't tell you that. Am I supposed to be familiar with Metharbital?

And I couldn't tell you what Serotonin receptor agonists are about. What in the world is Trifluoromethylphenylpiperazine, and what is CP-93,129 supposed to be?

I'm also not familiar with Pfizer. CP-532,903? How should I know? What, in the name of all that is holy, is Tolterodine, and what's PF-592,379 got to do with it? I haven't the foggiest idea. What is Quinapril?

And I haven't kept up on Purines. What about 8-Bromoadenosine 3',5'-cyclic monophosphate, and what is Queuine anyway? 8-Bromoguanosine 3',5'-cyclic monophosphate – I don't know what that is. Damned if I know. Inosine-5′-monophosphate dehydrogenase? Come again? Never heard of it.

I'm also completely ignorant of Nucleobases. Dihydrouracil – I don't understand this. Guanine – I don't understand that. I haven't the faintest idea.

I frankly don't know what people mean by 'Organic minerals'. Anthracite – what's that supposed to mean? Gilsonite – what is that? I have absolutely no idea.

And don't ask me about Coal. I have no idea what A Coal shovel is. Mechanical hand tools are unfamiliar to me. The Umnumzaan – don't know. Don't ask me what A Hex key is. Ask someone who knows something.

I don't know anything about Goods manufactured in the United States. Slinky – how should I know what that is? The Sebenza – not my field. I have no idea.

I haven't the foggiest notion what Educational toys are about. Lego

Mindstorms EV3 – I don't know how to begin. 2-XL? Doesn't ring a bell. Don't ask me. What is 'LeapPad' supposed to mean again, and what in tarnation is A Punch out book? Couldn't say. A Cartesian diver – I don't even know where to start.

I've also never heard of Paper toys. What's up with A Party horn? I know nothing about Party favors. And I'm sorry, did you say 'Confetti'?

And I'm not hip to Paper products. What the shit is A Blook, and what the heck is A Book? How am I supposed to make sense of Scotties, and what is the deal with Corrugated fiberboard? I just don't know. What is 'Paper clothing' supposed to mean?

I'm not conversant with Web fiction. And I don't have any idea what E-book is or what in tarnation Blog fiction is. Hypertext fiction, is that even a thing? What the hell? I don't know what Momo Kyun Sword is or what the current state of research is on Protagonize or what it actually means.

I don't know the first thing about Literature websites. And what in God's name is Lincoln/Net, and what is StorySouth again? Complete review – not my area of expertise. Search me.

I really don't know about History websites. What the hell is Chinaknowledge, and what is the idea with The Records of the Parliaments of Scotland? Brooklyn Visual Heritage – dunno. I just don't know about that.

I'm not well-versed in The University of St Andrews. Ever to Excel – what does that mean? And I have no clue what Dundee Royal Infirmary is or what the heck Arché is. I'm clueless about that. Am I supposed to be familiar with The Gatty Marine Laboratory? I don't have any idea. The University of St Andrews Athletic Union – never heard of it.

The University of Dundee is a mystery to me. Dundee School of Architecture? How should I know? Who the fuck is Michael Peto? How should I know?

I also don't know any Architecture schools in Scotland. I couldn't tell you about Edinburgh College of Art or what the hell it has to do with The Edinburgh School of Architecture and Landscape Architecture or how to make sense of it.

I'm also not familiar with Schools of the University of Edinburgh. And what the fuck is The University of Edinburgh Medical School?
And I haven't kept up on Schools of medicine in Scotland. What, in the name of all that is holy, is The University of St Andrews School of Medicine?
Concerning Indian Statistical Institute faculty, I am fully ignorant. I also have no idea who Anil Kumar Bhattacharya was. Who is Arup Bose or Palash Sarkar? I just don't know.
I couldn't tell you what Indian statisticians are about. Who the hell is Sharadchandra Shankar Shrikhande or Bimal Kumar Roy?
I don't know what people mean by 'People from Nagpur'. Am I supposed to know Madhukar Dattatraya Deoras? Who is this Rajkumar Hirani, Bipin Krishna Bose, Ghulam Mansoor or Kamalabai Hospet guy? I haven't the remotest idea.
I'm also completely ignorant of Filmfare Awards winners. And who the shit is Saif Ali Khan, Rajeev Ravi or Kader Khan?
I haven't the foggiest notion what Canadian male comedians are about. Jonny Harris – who is that?
Don't ask me about Memorial University of Newfoundland alumni. Are Ed Kavanagh, Bill Gillespie, Moya Greene, Siobhán Coady or Eddy Campbell famous or something?
I obviously don't know anything about Canadian war correspondents. I don't know who Suzanne Goldenberg is.
I've also never heard of The Guardian journalists. I have no clue who Richard Norton-Taylor or Victor Keegan is.
I'm not conversant with English reporters and correspondents. Do I need to know who Marie Bethell Beauclerc was? I don't have any idea who Robert Whymant, Macdonald Hastings, Seyi Rhodes or Dharshini David is. Not a clue.
People from Birmingham, West Midlands are unfamiliar to me. I've never heard of a person called Alfred De Courcy. Is Albert Toft famous or something? I just don't know that.
I'm not hip to English sculptors. What's up with Edward Grubb of Birmingham?
I'm also not well-versed in Military units and formations of the United States in World War II. What's the deal with The 900th Expeditionary

Air Refueling Squadron, and what is the mystery about The 498th Fighter-Interceptor Squadron? The 416th Flight Test Squadron – doesn't ring a bell. Doesn't sound remotely familiar. And I'm certain that I've never heard of The 847th Bombardment Squadron. Wouldn't know. I have no clue where Naval Air Station Port Lyautey is.
Military units and formations in California are a mystery to me. 148th Space Operations Squadron – I don't understand this. The 445th Flight Test Squadron? Come again? Never heard of it. Come on.
I know nothing about Space squadrons of the United States Air Force. What in the world is The 6th Space Warning Squadron?
I don't know about Military units and formations in Massachusetts. The 26th Maneuver Enhancement Brigade – I don't know what that is. I have no idea what VP-92 is or what the hell The 499th Air Refueling Wing is or if the whole concept makes sense to me. I haven't the slightest idea. The Massachusetts Wing Civil Air Patrol – what is that? No idea. What about Electronic Systems Center?
And I don't know any Air refueling wings of the United States Air Force. I'm sorry, did you say 'The 128th Air Refueling Wing'? And what is The 157th Air Refueling Wing? I have no clue. What is The 168th Air Refueling Wing?
Concerning Military units and formations of the United States Air National Guard, I am fully ignorant. The 147th Reconnaissance Wing – I don't understand that. Don't ask me what The 130th Airlift Wing is. I can't tell you that. The 166th Airlift Wing – not my field. I haven't the faintest idea. The 192d Airlift Squadron – how should I know what that is?
I haven't kept up on The Texas Military Forces. How am I supposed to make sense of The 149th Fighter Wing, and what the hell is The Texas Air National Guard? The Texas Army National Guard – I don't know how to begin. Ask someone who knows something. The 136th Airlift Wing – what's that supposed to mean? I surely haven't got a clue. What is 'The Texas State Guard' supposed to mean?
I certainly don't know what people mean by 'Airlift wings of the United States Air Force'. And what in God's name is The 103d Airlift Wing, and what is The 172d Airlift Wing about? I don't have any idea what The 19th Airlift Wing is. Damned if I know.

I don't know the first thing about Hartford County, Connecticut. The Wappinger? Doesn't ring a bell. The National Register of Historic Places listings in Hartford County, Connecticut – I don't even know where to start. I have absolutely no idea. I don't know where Connecticut's 2nd congressional district, Connecticut's 1st congressional district or Connecticut's 5th congressional district is. And I'm not familiar with Algonquian ethnonyms. The Nipmuc – not my area of expertise. Eskimo – dunno. Couldn't tell you.
I'm completely ignorant of Hunter-gatherers of Canada. I don't know what The First Nations are.
I couldn't tell you what Aboriginal peoples in Canada are about. I also have no clue what The Inuvialuit is or what the mystery about Stereotypes about indigenous peoples of North America are. R. v. Powley – don't know. I just don't know.
Don't ask me about Canadian Aboriginal case law. I've never heard of Paul v. British Columbia. What the shit is R. v. Sparrow, and what is Delgamuukw v. British Columbia? What the hell? What the hell is R. v. Drybones?
And I haven't the foggiest notion what History of human rights in Canada are about. The Komagata Maru incident – what does that mean?
I'm not hip to History of Vancouver. Alpen Club – never heard of it. Lost Lagoon – I don't understand this. I have no idea. Can you tell me how to get to The Great Marpole Midden? Couldn't say. The Great Vancouver Fire, is that even a thing? The Royal Vancouver Yacht Club? How should I know?
I'm not well-versed in German-Canadian culture. CHPD-FM – I don't know what that is. Please don't talk to me about Kitchener-Waterloo Oktoberfest. I don't have any idea. Der Bote – I don't understand that. I don't know anything about Festivals in Ontario. Am I supposed to be familiar with Canada's Largest Ribfest? And what is 'The Blyth Festival' supposed to mean again, and what on earth is The Binder Twine Festival? I'm clueless about that. What's up with The Elmira Maple Syrup Festival?
Theatre companies in Ontario are a mystery to me. And what the fuck is The Kitchener Waterloo Little Theatre, and what's The Geritol

Follies got to do with it? What in the world is Théâtre du Nouvel-Ontario? I just don't know. Where the hell is The Magnus Theatre? I'm not conversant with Culture of Waterloo Region. Tri-Pride – what is that? The Kitchener-Waterloo Symphony – doesn't ring a bell. I haven't the foggiest idea. I don't have any idea where Centre In The Square is.
I also don't know any Visitor attractions in Waterloo Region. I have no idea what The Waterloo Festival for Animated Cinema is.
I also know nothing about Animation film festivals. Cortomobile – not my field. And I'm certain that I've never heard of The Kalamazoo Animation Festival International or what on earth The Kraków Film Festival is or what people say about it. I haven't the remotest idea. Film festivals in Poland are unfamiliar to me. I don't have any idea what Camerimage is or what International Festival of Independent Cinema Off Plus Camera is or whether I should care. The Tofifest – I don't know how to begin. How should I know? I also don't know the first thing about American Film Festival or why people are so interested in New Horizons Film Festival or what it is all about.
I also don't know what people mean by 'Wrocław'. What about Wratislavia Cantans, and what is Szczytnicki Park supposed to be? Where the fuck is Wrocław exhibition ground or Wrocław County? I just don't know that.
I haven't kept up on Music festivals in Poland. Off Festival – what's that supposed to mean? Don't ask me what Chopin Festival is. Don't ask me. Przystanek Woodstock – I don't even know where to start. Come on. What, in the name of all that is holy, is Universitas Cantat? I'm completely ignorant of Mysłowice. And don't ask me where Three Emperors' Corner is! I'm sorry, did you say 'Myslovitz'? Doesn't sound remotely familiar.
I don't know about Geography of Prussia. I also couldn't tell you about Old Western Pomerania. I have no idea where The Klaipėda Region is. I haven't the slightest idea.
Don't ask me about History of Germany by location. And where was The Kingdom of Westphalia? What's the deal with Osterland? Wouldn't know.
Concerning Westphalia, I am fully ignorant. How am I supposed to

make sense of The Prussian Union of churches, and what in tarnation is The Evangelical Church of Westphalia? And where is Ostwestfalen-Lippe located? I just don't know about that. The Duchy of Westphalia, is that even a real place?

I've never heard of Religion in North Rhine-Westphalia. And what is 'The Church of Lippe' supposed to mean?

And I'm not familiar with Member churches of the Evangelical Church in Germany. What in God's name is The Evangelical Church in Central Germany?

I'm also not well-versed in United and uniting churches. The Evangelical Church of Hesse Electorate-Waldeck? Doesn't ring a bell. The Pomeranian Evangelical Church – dunno. Search me.

I don't know anything about Hesse. And what the shit is Lower Hesse, and what is The Wartberg culture anyway?

And I'm not hip to Stone Age Europe. A Causewayed enclosure – not my area of expertise. I don't know what Shillourokambos is. I can't tell you that.

Causeways are a mystery to me. I have never been to Colaba Causeway. A Causewayed ring ditch – I don't understand this. Ask someone who knows something. A Causeway – I don't know what that is. Damned if I know. Where in the world is The Makupa Causeway or Sorell Causeway?

And I don't know any Retail markets in Mumbai. I have no clue what Lohar Chawl is.

And I couldn't tell you what Neighbourhoods in Mumbai are about. Do people even go to Uran? I have no clue where The Bandra Kurla Complex is. I haven't got a clue. What the hell is Shimpoli?

Talukas in Maharashtra are unfamiliar to me. I also don't know how to get to Arjuni Morgaon, Amgaon, Umarkhed or Kagal.

I don't know the first thing about Yavatmal district. I certainly don't know where Kalamb, Yavatmal-Washim Lok Sabha constituency, Akola Bazar or Zari Jamani is.

And I know nothing about Washim district. I don't have any idea where Akola Lok Sabha constituency is.

I haven't kept up on Lok Sabha constituencies in Maharashtra. Mumbai North West Lok Sabha constituency? Come again? Never heard of it. Can you tell me how to get to Mumbai South Central Lok Sabha constituency or Mumbai North East Lok Sabha constituency? I have absolutely no idea.

I'm completely ignorant of Politics of Mumbai. Akhil Bharatiya Sena – never heard of it. Mulund Vidhan Sabha constituency – don't know. I haven't the faintest idea. Goregaon Vidhan Sabha constituency, is that even a thing? I certainly don't know. Where the hell is Vandre West Vidhan Sabha constituency or Mumbai North Lok Sabha constituency?

I don't know about The Mumbai Suburban district. What is Kandivali East Vidhan Sabha constituency, and what the heck is Chandivali Vidhan Sabha constituency? Am I supposed to be familiar with Kalina Vidhan Sabha constituency? I have no idea. I have no idea where Dahisar is. No idea. Magathane Vidhan Sabha constituency? How should I know?

I also haven't the foggiest notion what Assembly constituencies of Maharashtra are about. What is 'Jamner Vidhan Sabha constituency' supposed to mean again?

I also don't know what people mean by 'Jalgaon district'. Don't ask me where Adavad is!

And I'm not conversant with Cities and towns in Jalgaon district. Where is Jalgaon located?

Don't ask me about Jalgaon. Where is Jalgaon railway station? The Jalgaon rape case – how should I know what that is? Couldn't tell you. Government Polytechnic Jalgaon – doesn't ring a bell. Not a clue. The Jalgaon Municipal Corporation – I don't understand that.

I've never heard of Railway stations in Jalgaon district. And where the fuck is Bhusaval railway station?

Concerning Railway junction stations in India, I am fully ignorant. I have never been to Naupada railway station.

I'm not well-versed in Visakhapatnam railway division. And where in the world is The Visakhapatnam–Vijayawada section?

I'm also not familiar with Rail transport in Andhra Pradesh. Satavahana Express – what does that mean? I have no clue where The Khurda Road–Visakhapatnam section is. I don't have any idea.

I'm certain that I've never heard of The Penukonda train collision or what Chennai Central - Visakhapatnam Express is about or what to make of it. I haven't the foggiest idea. I don't have any idea what The Nagarjuna Express was.

I also don't know any Named passenger trains of India. What in the world is Simhapuri Express, and what is The Shramik express again? I couldn't tell you what Rail transport in Gujarat is about. What's up with The Udhna Varanasi Express?

Indian Railways trains are a mystery to me. What the fuck was The Assam Mail, and what is the mystery about Hazrat Nizamuddin – Indore Express? And what about The Darjeeling Mail, and what is the deal with The Patna – Kota Express? I just don't know. The Indore – Ujjain Passenger – I don't know how to begin.

Train services in India are unfamiliar to me. The Bhopal Janata Express – what's that supposed to mean? The Damoh–Kota Passenger – I don't even know where to start. I have no clue.

I don't know anything about Gorakhpur. And I have no idea what The Hindu Yuva Vahini is. I don't know how to get to Gorakhpur Airport. How should I know? Do people even go to The Syro-Malabar Catholic Diocese of Gorakhpur, Gorakhnath Math or Gorakhpur railway station?

I don't know the first thing about Roman Catholic dioceses in India. I don't know where The Roman Catholic Diocese of Mangalore, Roman Catholic Archdiocese of Visakhapatnam, Roman Catholic Diocese of Palayamkottai, Roman Catholic Diocese of Jaipur or Roman Catholic Diocese of Ootacamund is.

I know nothing about Roman Catholic dioceses and prelatures established in the 20th century. I couldn't tell you about The Roman Catholic Diocese of Mbanza Congo or what the deal with The Roman Catholic Diocese of Doba is. The Roman Catholic Diocese of Anguo, is that even a real place? Don't ask me.

I also don't know about Roman Catholic dioceses in Angola. Where the hell is The Roman Catholic Diocese of Caxito? Don't ask me what The Roman Catholic Diocese of Namibe is. What the hell? The Roman Catholic Diocese of Lwena – not my field. I haven't the remotest idea. Please don't talk to me about The Roman Catholic Diocese of Benguela.

I haven't the foggiest notion what Roman Catholic dioceses and prelatures established in the 21st century are about. I have no idea where Roman Catholic Diocese of Sultanpet is. Can you tell me how to get to The Roman Catholic Diocese of Engativá or Roman Catholic Diocese of Nongstoin? I certainly don't know that.
I don't know what people mean by 'Christianity in Kerala'. What's the deal with Christian Association for Social Action? And what is The Maramon Convention? I haven't the slightest idea.
I'm not hip to Non-governmental organisations based in India. Burning Brain Society – what is that? Dean Foundation – dunno. Wouldn't know. I'm sorry, did you say 'The Society for the Promotion of Himalayan Indigenous Activities SOPHIA'?
And I'm not conversant with Hospice. What is 'The National Hospice and Palliative Care Organization' supposed to mean, and what is the idea with Medical Orders for Life-Sustaining Treatment? A Children's hospice – not my area of expertise. Search me. Who on earth was Florence Wald?
Don't ask me about Health law. Registration, Evaluation, Authorisation and Restriction of Chemicals – I don't know what that is. I have no clue what The Family Health Care Decisions Act is or what is supposed to be special about Mandated choice or if it's worth knowing. Doesn't sound remotely familiar.
Concerning Bioethics, I am fully ignorant. Who the fuck is James Lindemann Nelson? How am I supposed to make sense of Biotic ethics? I'm clueless about that.
I definitely haven't kept up on American philosophers. Who is Alan Gewirth, Patricia Kitcher or Rod L. Evans?
I've never heard of Old Dominion University faculty. Bruce Weigl or Tony Ardizzone – who are they?
I definitely couldn't tell you what Indiana University faculty is about. I have no idea who Paul Leland Haworth or Kimon Friar is.
I'm not well-versed in Yale School of Drama alumni. Am I supposed to know Kathryn Hahn, Bruce Altman, Keith Reddin, Sigourney Weaver or Edward Cornell?
I really don't know any American people of Scottish descent. William Cumming Rose – who was that? Are George S. Eccles, Chita Rivera or

Rod McKuen famous or something? Damned if I know.
I'm completely ignorant of American people of Italian descent. Who the hell is Andy Granelli, Glenn Danzig or Andy Martin?
American heavy metal singers are unfamiliar to me. And I don't know who Peter Steele was. I also have no clue who Jerry Only or Spider One is. I can't tell you that.
I'm not familiar with American people of Polish descent. Who is this Klaus Wyrtki, Travis Tripucka or Paul Bragiel guy?
Demosceners are a mystery to me. And I don't have any idea who Misko Iho, Tor Bernhard Gausen, Arjan Brussee or Jan Robbe is.
I also know nothing about Norwegian composers. Vidar Busk, Olav Anton Thommessen, Theodora Cormontan, Øivind Elgenes or Synne Skouen – doesn't ring a bell.
I also haven't the foggiest notion what People from Kristiansund are about. Who the shit is Kjetil Bjerkestrand, Leif Georg Ferdinand Bang, Alv Jakob Fostervoll or Edvard Eilert Christie?
And I don't know what people mean by 'Norwegian non-fiction writers'. Is Evald O. Solbakken famous or something?
I don't know the first thing about Grini concentration camp survivors. I've never heard of a person called Eiliv Skard, Herman Smitt Ingebretsen, Haakon Sørbye, Ludvig Hope or Julius Hougen.
I don't know about Norwegian resistance members. And do I need to know who Olaf Gjerløw or Osmund Faremo is?
I don't know anything about Mayors of places in Aust-Agder. Who on earth is Svein Harberg, Christian Stray, Søren Hans Smith Sørensen, Nils Hjelmtveit or Jens Marcussen?
I'm not conversant with Norwegian expatriates in the United Kingdom. And who is Hans Jørgen Gundersen, Georg Kajanus, Kjell Eliassen or Ole Bjørn Sundgot?
Concerning Norwegian songwriters, I am fully ignorant. Magne Furuholmen or Kari Bremnes – who are they?
I've never heard of Norwegian artists. Am I supposed to know Hariton Pushwagner, Bendik Riis or Bjarne Melgaard?
I couldn't tell you what People from Sydney are about. And who the fuck is Stanley Frederick Utz? Who the hell is Ben Unwin or Sergio Redegalli? Couldn't say.

And I'm not well-versed in Australian people of German descent. I have no idea who Heinrich Haussler, Jona Weinhofen, Peter Hartung, Fred Lowen or Fraser Gehrig is.
I don't know any Murray Bushrangers players. I don't know who David Mundy, Jarman Impey or Brett Deledio is.
And I haven't kept up on Gippsland Power players. Are Jed Lamb, Dean Polo or Mitchell Golby famous or something?
Sydney Swans players are a mystery to me. Ben Fixter – who is that?
And I haven't the foggiest notion what Australian racehorse owners and breeders are about. What in God's name is Charles Brown Fisher? Roy Burston – doesn't ring a bell. I haven't got a clue. Do I need to know who Tan Chin Nam or Tony Šantić is?
I don't know what people mean by 'Australian medical doctors'. I also don't know anything about William Colin Mackenzie.
I'm also not conversant with Australian zoologists. And who the shit is Alistair Cameron Crombie?
Concerning Academics of University College London, I am fully ignorant. Is Carey Foster famous or something? Who on earth is Jeroen van de Weijer, Uta Frith, James Mallet or Noel Frederick Hall? I have absolutely no idea.
I don't know about Principals of Brasenose College, Oxford. Am I supposed to know Charles Buller Heberden? Who the fuck is William Cleaver, John Meare or Frodsham Hodson? I just don't know about that.
I don't know the first thing about Fellows of Brasenose College, Oxford. I have no idea who John Wordsworth or Douglas Higgs is.
I couldn't tell you what Hematologists are about. I don't know who Slobodan Obradov is.
I know nothing about University of Belgrade Faculty of Medicine alumni. Who the hell is Petar Pjesivac, Miomir Mugoša or Pasko Rakic?
Don't ask me about History of neuroscience. I also don't have any idea who Franz Nissl is. Roger Wolcott Sperry, Jakob Klaesi or Albert von Kölliker – who are they? I haven't the faintest idea.
I'm also completely ignorant of Cognitive neuroscientists. Elizabeth Bates – who was that? What's up with Jan Lauwereyns, Richard

Restak or Ursula Bellugi? Ask someone who knows something.
I'm not well-versed in English-language writers. Are Caleb Carr, Jianying Zha, Khoo Kheng-Hor or Roberta Gregory famous or something?
I don't know any Chinese-language writers. And who was Young John Allen?
I'm also not familiar with Methodist missionaries in China. I have no clue who Samuel Ross Hay is. Do I need to know who Nathan Sites, James Joseph Meadows, Moses Clark White or Erastus Wentworth was? Not a clue.
Christian missionaries in China are unfamiliar to me. What, in the name of all that is holy, was Thomas J. Arnold? And I don't know anything about David Crockett Graham or Nora Lam. Come on.
I've never heard of Smithsonian Institution Archives related. I've never heard of a person called Gerrit Smith Miller. Henry Nicholas Bolander, Solomon G. Brown or Florence Meier Chase – doesn't ring a bell. I don't have any idea.
American botanists are a mystery to me. Who the shit is John Hendley Barnhart? Am I supposed to know Charles Christian Plitt or Jane Colden? I obviously haven't the foggiest idea.
I certainly don't know what people mean by 'People from Brooklyn'. Who on earth was Bess Houdini? I don't know who Helen Engelhardt, Jacob Ostreicher, Roger L. Green or Red Café is. I have no idea.
I also haven't the foggiest notion what Burials at Gate of Heaven Cemetery are about. Is George Jean Nathan famous or something?
And I'm not conversant with People from Fort Wayne, Indiana. I have no idea who Frederick William Sievers, Hilliard Gates or Graham Richard is.
And I don't know about Mayors of Fort Wayne, Indiana. I also don't have any idea who Paul Helmke is. Who is this George W. Wood or William J. Hosey guy? Couldn't tell you.
And I don't know the first thing about People from Mount Vernon, Ohio. Who the fuck is Vaughn Wiester or Jim Stillwagon?
I haven't kept up on Sportspeople from Chattanooga, Tennessee. Who the shit is Orlando Lightfoot or Brooke Pancake?
I've never heard of American expatriate basketball people in the

Netherlands. Who on earth is Terence Stansbury?
I don't know any Temple Owls men's basketball players. I don't know who Don Shields was. Do I need to know who Mike Vreeswyk, Mark Karcher or Clarence Brookins is? I haven't the remotest idea.
I don't know what people mean by 'Small forwards'. And I don't have any idea who Roberto Bergersen or Ivan Opačak is.
Liga ACB players are a mystery to me. Am I supposed to know Jordi Villacampa, Etdrick Bohannon, Charles Judson Wallace or Hollis Price?
Alba Berlin players are unfamiliar to me. What's up with Sven Schultze, Lucca Staiger, Dragiša Drobnjak, Kenan Bajramović or Ismet Akpinar?
And I don't know about KK Krka players. Who the fuck is Domen Lorbek, Matej Rojc or Jure Balažič?
I haven't the foggiest notion what KK Union Olimpija players are about. I have no idea who Yotam Halperin, Aleksandar Radojević, Radisav Ćurčić or Marko Maravič is.
I'm also not conversant with PAOK B.C. players. Who is this Rashad Wright or Dejan Tomašević guy?
I don't know the first thing about Panathinaikos B.C. players. Are Dino Rađa or Giorgos Balogiannis famous or something?
I'm also not familiar with Olympic basketball players of Yugoslavia. Mirza Delibašić – who was that? Sabit Hadžić, Marija Tonković or Dragoslav Ražnatović – who are they? I just don't know that.
And I'm completely ignorant of Olympic medalists in basketball. I don't know anything about Modestas Paulauskas.
I know nothing about Olympic gold medalists for the Soviet Union. I have no clue who Svetlana Nikishina or Mikhail Burtsev is.
And I'm not hip to Sportspeople from Moscow. Liudmila Belavenets, Nina Vislova, Ekaterina Lopes or Maria Bulanova – doesn't ring a bell.
I'm not well-versed in Russian badminton players. And who the hell is Vladimir Vadimovich Malkov, Anastasia Russkikh, Anastasia Prokopenko, Valeria Sorokina or Aleksandr Nikolaenko?
Concerning Olympic badminton players of Russia, I am fully ignorant. Who is Andrey Antropov, Irina Ruslyakova, Ivan Sozonov or Ella Diehl?

And don't ask me about Lithuanian people executed by the Soviet Union. Who the shit is Kazys Bizauskas, Vladas Petronaitis or Kazys Skučas?
I haven't kept up on Lithuanian diplomats. Who on earth was Ignas Jonynas? I don't know who Michał Kleofas Ogiński, Dainius Kamaitis, Jonas Vileišis or Stasys Lozoraitis is. I have no clue.
And I don't know what people mean by 'Polish composers'. Do I need to know who Nicolaus Cracoviensis or Marian Sawa is?
And I don't know any 16th-century deaths. Am I supposed to know Yohanan Alemanno or Roger Dudley?
I also couldn't tell you what 15th-century philosophers are about. What's up with Peter Nigri?
People from Kadaň are unfamiliar to me. I've never heard of a person called Lucie Povova or Bohuslav Hasištejnský z Lobkovic.
I've never heard of Czech writers. I obviously don't have any idea who Vladimír Holan, Helena Lisická or Jan Čep is.
Recipients of the Order of Tomáš Garrigue Masaryk are a mystery to me. I have no idea who Josef Čapek is.
I also don't know the first thing about Czechoslovak civilians killed in World War II. Is Erwin Schulhoff famous or something?
I don't know about Jewish classical pianists. And I don't know anything about Harriet Cohen. Hilda Bor or Natasha Spender – who are they? Wouldn't know.
And I'm completely ignorant of English Jews. Who the fuck is Ian Grant? John Dunston – who is that? I certainly don't know. Are Frank Branston, Alma Cogan or Lionel Nathan de Rothschild famous or something?
I haven't the foggiest notion what Mayors of places in Bedfordshire are about. Asher Hucklesby – doesn't ring a bell. I also have no clue who Dave Hodgson is. How should I know?
I'm not familiar with English businesspeople. And who is this Ernest Bader guy? Who was Cec Thompson? Doesn't sound remotely familiar.
I know nothing about People from Hunslet. Who the shit is Harry Beverley?
Concerning English rugby league coaches, I am fully ignorant. Do I

need to know who Mark Aston, Phil Larder or Francis Stephenson is? And I'm not conversant with English rugby league players. Am I supposed to know Barry Seabourne, Danny Kirmond, Roy Hawksley, Tracey Lazenby or Niall Evalds?

I'm not hip to Bradford Bulls players. Who the hell is Toa Kohe-Love, Nathan Conroy, Steve Crossley or Lesley Vainikolo?

I'm not well-versed in New Zealand national rugby league team players. What's up with Dean Whare or Willie Talau?

I haven't kept up on Rugby league fullbacks. I don't know who Frank Mortimer was. I also don't have any idea who Walter Gowers is. I'm clueless about that.

Place of death missing is unfamiliar to me. What the hell is Christian de Bonchamps? I've never heard of a person called Lee Moorhouse, Tøger Seidenfaden or Henriette Winkler. Don't ask me.

I've never heard of Date of death missing. I have no idea who Marie Hall Ets is.

I don't know any American children's writers. Is Charlotte Zolotow famous or something? I also don't know anything about Nancy Willard or Lynne Kelly. Damned if I know.

Don't ask me about Newbery Medal winners. Who on earth is Beverly Cleary? Who the fuck is Scott O'Dell, Kate Seredy or Marguerite de Angeli? I obviously can't tell you that.

I obviously don't know the first thing about Writers from Los Angeles, California. Judy Lewis – doesn't ring a bell. Howie Klein, Kevin Lauderdale, Lizzy Weiss or Tomoyuki Hoshino – who are they? Search me.

I also don't know what people mean by 'Winners of the Yukio Mishima Prize'. Are Ōtarō Maijō, Shinji Aoyama, Genichiro Takahashi or Yoriko Shono famous or something?

I couldn't tell you what People from Mie Prefecture are about. I also have no clue who Edogawa Ranpo was. Who is this Mizuki Noguchi, Hōsuke Nojiri or Tsugio Matsuda guy? I just don't know about that.

I don't know about Edgar Allan Poe. Where is Sullivan's Island, South Carolina located? What is C. Auguste Dupin? I have absolutely no idea. Do I need to know who David Poe, Jr. or Frances Sargent Osgood was?

And I'm not familiar with Burials at Mount Auburn Cemetery. Who was Cyrus Alger?
I'm completely ignorant of American metallurgists. And who the hell is Marshall McDonald? Who the shit is Charles Washington Merrill or Howard Kent Birnbaum? I haven't got a clue.
Concerning Fisheries science, I am fully ignorant. What's up with Georg Ossian Sars? Am I supposed to know Bruno Hofer or Ed Ricketts? Not a clue.
I'm not conversant with People educated at Oslo Cathedral School. I've never heard of a person called Alexander Lange Johnson. I also don't have any idea who Caspar Wessel was. Come on.
19th-century mathematicians are a mystery to me. And I have no idea who Ioan Mire Melik or Wilhelm Wirtinger was.
I'm not hip to Members of the Chamber of Deputies of Romania. Ștefan Golescu – who was that? Is Teodor Neaga famous or something? I really don't have any idea. I don't know who Leon Sculy Logothetides or Victor Surdu is.
And I haven't kept up on People of the Romanian Revolution. I definitely don't know anything about Petre Roman.
I also haven't the foggiest notion what Candidates for President of Romania are about. And who on earth is Remus Cernea, György Frunda, Gigi Becali, Mircea Druc or Béla Markó?
Romanian Orthodox Christians are unfamiliar to me. I have no clue who Alexandru Macedonski was. And who is this Octavian Goga guy? I haven't the faintest idea. Who the fuck is Mitică Popescu, Horia Sima or Ion Nistor?
I certainly know nothing about Romanian esotericists. Who the hell is Sandu Tudor? Bogdan Petriceicu Hasdeu – doesn't ring a bell. Couldn't say.
I've never heard of Romanian magazine editors. Iosif Vulcan – don't know. Do I need to know who Ioan Slavici or Marta Petreu is? I haven't the foggiest idea.
I'm not well-versed in Eötvös Loránd University alumni. Who was Rodion Markovits? Péter Molnár, Zsolt Molnár or Alicja Sakaguchi – who are they? What the hell?
I don't know what people mean by 'Austro-Hungarian Jews'. I've

never heard of a person called Vlado Singer. Who the shit is Egon Friedell, Rudolf Charousek, Raphael Basch or Viktor Kaplan? I haven't the slightest idea.

I really don't know the first thing about Converts to Protestantism from Judaism. Am I supposed to know Eugen Rosenstock-Huessy? Are Moritz Gottlieb Saphir or Ridley Haim Herschell famous or something? I just don't know.

And don't ask me about Jewish American writers. I have no idea who Philip G. Epstein or Stuart Goldman is.

And I don't know any Undercover journalists. Is Nellie Bly famous or something? Teacher's Diary? Come again? Never heard of it. Couldn't tell you. I also don't know anything about Norah Vincent, Günter Wallraff or Mazher Mahmood.

I'm not familiar with American memoirists. Jane Addams – who was that?

Concerning 20th-century philosophers, I am fully ignorant. I obviously don't know who Herbert Marcuse was. What's up with Julius Binder? I just don't know that. I don't have any idea who Stanley Hauerwas or Radhakamal Mukerjee is.

I'm not conversant with Anglican writers. And who is this W. H. Auden guy? I have no clue who Edwin Emmanuel Bradford is. Wouldn't know.

English poets are a mystery to me. And who the hell is William Sidney Walker, Clere Parsons or Phyllis Hartnoll?

And I'm not hip to Shakespearean scholars. Who on earth was Howard Staunton? Who the fuck is Gerit Quealy, Harold Bloom, James Spedding or William Nanson Lettsom? I have no clue.

I'm completely ignorant of New York University faculty. Who is Valentine Mott, Daniel Yankelovich, Louis Capozzi, Sally Blount or Nadia Abu El Haj?

And I haven't the foggiest notion what University of Pennsylvania faculty are about. Bruce Kuklick, Yvonne Jacquette, Rafael Robb or Paul Hendrickson – doesn't ring a bell.

Members of the American Academy of Arts and Letters are unfamiliar to me. Do I need to know who David Del Tredici, Carlisle Floyd or Steven Holl is?

I haven't kept up on American composers. I've also never heard of a person called Phạm Duy. Are James Helme Sutcliffe, Gerald Oshita, Bern Herbolsheimer or Darin Gray famous or something? Ask someone who knows something.
I also couldn't tell you what Musicians from Montana are about. Graham Lindsey, Kostas or David Maslanka – who are they?
I don't know about Musicians from Wisconsin. Am I supposed to know AzMarie Livingston, Katrina Johansson or Jeff Loomis?
I've never heard of Androgyny. Futanari – never heard of it. I also don't have any idea what Metrosexual is or what in tarnation The Blitz Kids were. Doesn't sound remotely familiar. Bishōnen – I don't understand this.
I know nothing about Japanese words and phrases. Yamato-damashii – what's that supposed to mean? Am I supposed to be familiar with A Miko? I'm clueless about that. A Shuriken? How should I know? I have no idea. I'm certain that I've never heard of Genpatsu-shinsai or how I'm supposed to know something about The Shinkansen.
I'm not well-versed in Nuclear safety. Nuclear power whistleblowers – I don't know how to begin. I couldn't tell you about Normal Accidents or what the heck A Loss-of-coolant accident is or if it's good to know. How should I know? The Convention on Nuclear Safety – I don't even know where to start. I just don't know. MELCOR, is that even a thing? I don't know what people mean by 'Treaties of Denmark'. The Strasbourg Agreement Concerning the International Patent Classification – not my field. I have no idea what The Åland convention is or what the current state of research is on The Convention on Assistance in the Case of a Nuclear Accident or Radiological Emergency. I definitely haven't the remotest idea. The European Convention on Mutual Assistance in Criminal Matters – what does that mean?
I also don't know any Treaties extended to Greenland. What is 'The International Treaty on Plant Genetic Resources for Food and Agriculture' supposed to mean again, and what the hell is The Convention on the High Seas?
I really don't know the first thing about Treaties of Latvia. Please don't talk to me about The Berne Convention. What in the world

is The Patent Cooperation Treaty, and what was The Singapore Treaty on the Law of Trademarks? Search me. What the shit was The Convention on the Non-Applicability of Statutory Limitations to War Crimes and Crimes Against Humanity, and what on earth is International Convention on Oil Pollution Preparedness, Response and Co-operation?

And I'm not familiar with Treaties of the Kingdom of Romania. Don't ask me what Litvinov's Pact was. The Covenant of the League of Nations – how should I know what that is? Damned if I know. What the fuck was The Anti-Comintern Pact, and what is The Barcelona Convention and Statute on Freedom of Transit about?

I'm not conversant with Treaties extended to British Cameroons. The International Convention concerning the Use of Broadcasting in the Cause of Peace – I don't know what that is.

Treaties of the Soviet Union are a mystery to me. The Agreed Measures for the Conservation of Antarctic Fauna and Flora – I don't understand that. The Tokyo Convention – dunno. No idea. And what about The First Geneva Convention, and what in tarnation is The Outer Space Treaty? Not a clue. The Universal Copyright Convention? Doesn't ring a bell.

I don't know anything about Treaties of Mauritania. I also don't know what the Maputo Protocol is.

Don't ask me about Treaties of Mali. The International Covenant on Civil and Political Rights – not my area of expertise. I have no clue what The Vienna Convention on Consular Relations is or what the hell Hague Adoption Convention is or what to think about it. Don't ask me.

Concerning Treaties extended to Jersey, I am fully ignorant. I don't have any idea what The International Convention on Salvage is or what on earth The Customs Convention on the Temporary Importation of Commercial Road Vehicles is. And I'm sorry, did you say 'The Convention on Long-Range Transboundary Air Pollution', and what is The Energy Charter Treaty supposed to be? I really don't have any idea.

Treaties of the Polish People's Republic are unfamiliar to me. The Third Geneva Convention – I don't understand this. What's the deal with The Hague Hijacking Convention, and what the heck is The Convention on the Recognition and Enforcement of Foreign Arbitral Awards? I haven't the faintest idea. What in God's name is The International Regulations for Preventing Collisions at Sea, and what was The Convention on the Political Rights of Women again? And I'm completely ignorant of Treaties of the Byelorussian Soviet Socialist Republic. How am I supposed to make sense of Protocol I? I haven't the foggiest notion what Treaties of Burundi are about. The Paris Convention for the Protection of Industrial Property – don't know. What the hell is The United Nations Convention against Transnational Organized Crime? Come on.

And I don't know about Treaties of Togo. I'm certain that I've never heard of The Single Convention on Narcotic Drugs or what the mystery about The Convention on the Rights of Persons with Disabilities is. The International Covenant on Economic, Social and Cultural Rights – what's that supposed to mean? I haven't got a clue. The Convention on Cluster Munitions – never heard of it.

I haven't kept up on Treaties of the Philippines. What is Stockholm Convention on Persistent Organic Pollutants, and what is International Convention on Load Lines anyway? What, in the name of all that is holy, is The Convention for the Suppression of Unlawful Acts against the Safety of Civil Aviation? What the hell?

And I couldn't tell you what Treaties of Uruguay are about. What is 'The Optional Protocol to the Convention on the Rights of Persons with Disabilities' supposed to mean, and what's Metre Convention got to do with it? The Inter-American Convention Against Corruption – what is that? I haven't the slightest idea. Protocol amending the Single Convention on Narcotic Drugs – doesn't ring a bell. I have absolutely no idea. The Treaty of San Francisco – I don't know how to begin. I've never heard of Foreign relations of Postwar Japan. The U.S. and Japan Mutual Defense Assistance Agreement? How should I know? And I don't know the first thing about The Basic Treaty of Friendship and Cooperation. I can't tell you that.

I don't know what people mean by 'Treaties of the United States'. The Ramsar Convention? Come again? Never heard of it. The Sino-American Cooperative Organization – not my field. Couldn't tell you.

I also couldn't tell you about The Treaty of Amity and Cooperation in Southeast Asia.
I'm not well-versed in Treaties of the Czech Republic. The WIPO Performances and Phonograms Treaty – I don't know what that is. The Hague Convention on the Civil Aspects of International Child Abduction, is that even a thing? I just don't know about that. What's up with the Volatile Organic Compounds Protocol?
And I know nothing about Treaties extended to the Falkland Islands. The Rome Statute of the International Criminal Court – I don't even know where to start. What in the world is The Agreement for the Suppression of the Circulation of Obscene Publications? I haven't the foggiest idea. And what is Convention on the Rights of the Child? I just don't know. Convention against Discrimination in Education – dunno.
I'm not familiar with Treaties of Algeria. Please don't talk to me about The Customs Convention on Containers. The Kyoto Protocol – what does that mean? Couldn't say. And I have no idea what The International Convention on the Elimination of All Forms of Racial Discrimination is or why people are so interested in The Optional Protocol on the Sale of Children, Child Prostitution and Child Pornography.
I'm not hip to Treaties of the Pahlavi dynasty. What the shit is The Seabed Arms Control Treaty?
I don't know any Treaties of Italy. What the fuck is the Hague Evidence Convention, and what is the idea with The International Convention on the Establishment of an International Fund for Compensation for Oil Pollution Damage? Am I supposed to be familiar with The Convention on the association of the Netherlands Antilles with the European Economic Community? I surely don't know that. I don't know what The Hague-Visby Rules is.
Don't ask me about Treaties of the Netherlands. The Tampere Convention – not my area of expertise.
I'm not conversant with Treaties of Finland. The Convention on Biological Diversity? Doesn't ring a bell.
Commercialization of traditional medicines are a mystery to me. Is Conrad Gorinsky famous or something? Vincristine – how should I

know what that is? Doesn't sound remotely familiar. I don't have any idea what Bioprospecting is.

Vinca alkaloids are unfamiliar to me. And I'm sorry, did you say 'Vinpocetine'?

Concerning Vasodilators, I am fully ignorant. What about Isoxsuprine, and what is the mystery about Cinepazet? Don't ask me what Naftidrofuryl is. I have no clue.

And I don't know anything about Phenol ethers. I'm certain that I've never heard of Oxypertine.

I also haven't kept up on Indoles. Cediranib – I don't understand that. Tryptophol – don't know. I'm clueless about that. How am I supposed to make sense of Wieland-Gumlich aldehyde, and what the hell is Devazepide?

And I haven't the foggiest notion what Aldehydes are about. What's the deal with Hydroxymethylpentylcyclohexenecarboxaldehyde, and what is the deal with Glyceraldehyde?

I'm completely ignorant of Alcohols. What the hell is Moperone, and what on earth is Amibegron?

I've never heard of Piperidines. What, in the name of all that is holy, is Immepip, and what in tarnation is Pethidinic acid? N-Phenethyl-4-piperidinone – I don't understand this. Wouldn't know.

I don't know about Phenethylamines. What is 'Synephrine' supposed to mean again, and what is Normetanephrine supposed to be? And what is 'Azidamfenicol' supposed to mean, and what the heck is Oxyfedrine? I just don't know.

I definitely don't know the first thing about Diols. I have no clue what Sclareol is or what Fluvastatin is or how to make sense of it. Maslinic acid – what's that supposed to mean? Damned if I know. A Diol – never heard of it. Ask someone who knows something. What in God's name is Dithiothreitol?

I know nothing about Triterpenes. Ambrein? Come again? Never heard of it. Corosolic acid – I don't know what that is. How should I know?

I couldn't tell you what Organic acids are about. Teichoic acid – I don't even know where to start. Ascorbic acid – what is that? I certainly haven't the remotest idea.

I also don't know what people mean by 'Furones'. Galanolactone – dunno. Please don't talk to me about Losigamone. No idea. Rofecoxib – not my field. Search me. I couldn't tell you about Bullatacin.
I'm also not hip to Withdrawn drugs. Ephedra, is that even a thing? Valrubicin – doesn't ring a bell. I don't have any idea.
I'm also not familiar with Organofluorides. What is 25TFM-NBOMe? I'm not well-versed in Psychedelic phenethylamines. What in the world is an 5-APDB, and what is HOT-17 about? What's up with 25I-NBOMe, and what is Jimscaline? Not a clue.
I also don't know any Thioethers. CCK-4 – what does that mean? Am I supposed to be familiar with Enoximone? I haven't the faintest idea. And don't ask me about Ureas. Panuramine? Doesn't ring a bell. What the fuck is J-113,397, and what is Nefazodone anyway? I haven't the slightest idea. What the shit is Domperidone? I haven't got a clue. And what is 3-Ureidopropionic acid?
Benzimidazoles are a mystery to me. Rabeprazole – not my area of expertise. Tiabendazole – I don't know how to begin. Come on. I have no idea what Liarozole is or what the deal with Pantoprazole is. Don't ask me. I'm certain that I've never heard of Benzimidazole.
Fungicides are unfamiliar to me. Cycloheximide – don't know.
I don't know anything about Glutarimides. I also don't have any idea what Thalidomide is or what Bemegride is about or if the whole concept makes sense to me. I've never heard of Immunomodulatory drug. I have absolutely no idea.
Concerning Immunosuppressants, I am fully ignorant. Rilonacept? How should I know? 4-Deoxypyridoxine – I don't understand that. Couldn't tell you. I'm sorry, did you say 'Ciclosporin', and what is Anti-thymocyte globulin again?
I also haven't kept up on IARC Group 1 carcinogens. Potassium dichromate – I don't understand this. What's the deal with NickelII oxide? I haven't the foggiest idea.
I'm not conversant with Chromates. LeadII chromate – how should I know what that is? And I don't know the first thing about A Chromate ester or what the hell it has to do with Ammonium chromate. I have no idea. Don't ask me what Cadmium chromate is. I also haven't the foggiest notion what Oxidizing agents are about.

I don't know what Collins reagent is or how I'm supposed to know something about ManganeseIII acetate or what it actually means. Rubidium nitrate – I don't know what that is. I can't tell you that. Silver dichromate – never heard of it.
I obviously couldn't tell you what Pyrotechnic colorants are about. And what about Barium carbonate?
I also don't know what people mean by 'Barium compounds'. What, in the name of all that is holy, is Barium chloride, and what's Barium cyanide got to do with it?
I also don't know about Cyanides. Please don't talk to me about PalladiumII cyanide. MercuryII cyanide – I don't even know where to start. Couldn't say. How am I supposed to make sense of Zyklon B? I'm also completely ignorant of Palladium compounds. What is 'PalladiumII fluoride' supposed to mean, and what is the mystery about BistriphenylphosphinepalladiumII dichloride?
I know nothing about Metal halides. What in God's name is GoldI chloride, and what the hell is Gallium halides? What is 'UraniumIII chloride' supposed to mean again, and what on earth is ManganeseII iodide? Doesn't sound remotely familiar. What the hell is NiobiumV bromide?
I'm not hip to Manganese compounds. ManganeseII chloride – dunno. Dimanganese decacarbonyl? Come again? Never heard of it. I'm clueless about that. Manganese violet – what is that? What the hell? What is ManganeseII,III oxide, and what in tarnation is Potassium dimanganateIII?
I'm not familiar with Oxides. I also couldn't tell you about Iodine pentoxide.
I definitely don't know any Iodine compounds. I have no clue what An Iodophor is or what is supposed to be special about Hypoiodous acid. Homebrewing is unfamiliar to me. WineMaker Magazine – what's that supposed to mean? Fred Eckhardt – who is that? I just don't know that. Sodium metabisulfite – doesn't ring a bell. I just don't know. What's up with The Great American Beer Festival?
And don't ask me about Wine. In vino veritas – I don't know how to begin. The Speyer wine bottle – what does that mean? I just don't know.

Oenology is a mystery to me. What in the world is The Oechsle scale, and what is the idea with Zymology?

Concerning German wine, I am fully ignorant. I don't know who Sonja Christ is.

I haven't kept up on People from Rhineland-Palatinate. I don't have any idea who Bruce Willis, Gerhard von Malberg, Annette Schwarz, Eberhard II von der Mark or Mandy Großgarten is.

I'm not well-versed in 12th-century births. I have no idea who Roger Norreis or Josce of London was.

I don't know anything about English Medieval rabbis. Elias of London? Doesn't ring a bell. And what the shit is Hagin ben Moses? Ask someone who knows something. Who the shit is Aaron of Canterbury or Jacob of London?

And I haven't the foggiest notion what English Jews of the Medieval and Tudor period are about. Am I supposed to be familiar with Berechiah de Nicole? I'm also certain that I've never heard of Isaac of Norwich. I haven't the remotest idea. Who on earth is Aaron of York, Benedict of York or Petrus Alphonsi?

I've never heard of Medieval Spanish astronomers. Yehuda ben Moshe, is that even a thing? Who the hell is Isaac Israeli ben Joseph, Maslama al-Majriti or Jacob ben David ben Yom Tov? Damned if I know.

I also don't know the first thing about Mathematicians who worked on Islamic inheritance. And who the fuck is Ibn Muʿādh al-Jayyānī or Muḥammad ibn Mūsā al-Khwārizmī?

And I couldn't tell you what Scientists who worked on Qibla determination are about. Do I need to know who Abu Nasr Mansur was? Who is Ibn al-Saffar, Mohammed al-Rudani, Ibn Yunus or Ibn al-Shatir? No idea.

I don't know about 11th-century mathematicians. Am I supposed to know Brahmadeva? Is Vijayanandi famous or something? I have no clue.

I'm not conversant with Medieval Indian mathematicians. I have no clue who Parameshvara was. And I'm sorry, did you say 'a Virasena'? I don't have any idea. I've never heard of a person called Gangesha Upadhyaya. I frankly haven't the faintest idea. Halayudha? How should I know?

I'm also completely ignorant of 15th-century Indian people. Who is this Shahzada Barbak or Rao Bika guy?
I'm not hip to Rulers of Bengal. What about Muhammad Khan Sur? What's up with Izzuddin Yahya or Shamsuddin Ahmad Shah? I haven't the slightest idea.
And I'm not familiar with Governors of Bengal. Charles Cecil Stevens, Saifuddin Aibak or Jahangir Quli Beg – who are they?
I really don't know any Knights Commander of the Order of the Star of India. Muhammad Habibullah – who was that?
I also know nothing about Knights Bachelor. Hal Colebatch – doesn't ring a bell. I have no idea who Russell Brain, 1st Baron Brain was. I just don't know about that. I don't have any idea who John Knox Laughton, Alfred Seale Haslam or Sir Frank Forbes Adam, 1st Baronet is.
Don't ask me about Academics of the Royal Naval College, Greenwich. And I don't know who Shabtai Rosenne was. Who the shit is Eric Grove? Not a clue.
People from Bolton are unfamiliar to me. Who the hell is Frank Hardcastle, Paul Sixsmith or Franklin Thomasson?
I've never heard of People from Valletta. Is Esprit Barthet famous or something? I've never heard of a person called George Preca. I haven't got a clue. And who the fuck is Jon Courtenay Grimwood, Agostino Bonello or Girolamo Abos?
And concerning British horror writers, I am fully ignorant. I have no clue who Roald Dahl was. What's up with Christine Campbell Thomson or Elliott O'Donnell? Come on.
I don't know the first thing about Absurdist fiction. A House-Boat on the Styx – not my field. John Dimes – doesn't ring a bell. Search me. Practical Demonkeeping – how should I know what that is?
I obviously don't know about Novels by Christopher Moore. And what the fuck IS Island of the Sequined Love Nun, and what is Fluke, or, I Know Why the Winged Whale Sings supposed to be? What's the deal with Bloodsucking Fiends, and what is A Dirty Job about? Couldn't tell you.
And I haven't the foggiest notion what Vampire novels are about. The Bloody Red Baron – don't know. How am I supposed to make sense of

Sétimo, and what is the deal with Black Blood Brothers? How should I know? What is 'Those Who Hunt the Night' supposed to mean again? I haven't kept up on Tokyo Metropolitan Television shows. Mangirl! – not my area of expertise. What is 'Wizard Barristers' supposed to mean? I haven't the foggiest idea.
And I'm not conversant with Anime series based on manga. Noragami – I don't understand that. What, in the name of all that is holy, is Encouragement of Climb? Couldn't say.
I'm also not hip to Shōnen manga. I have no idea what Mashiro no Oto is or what in tarnation Hibiki's Magic is. What in God's name is The Law of Ueki, and what is The Wonderful Galaxy of Oz anyway? Doesn't sound remotely familiar. What is Ballroom e Yōkoso?
I really couldn't tell you what Supernatural anime and manga is about. Future Diary – what does that mean? Don't ask me what Tsukuyomi: Moon Phase is. Wouldn't know. Corpse Princess – I don't understand this.
I know nothing about Sharp Point Press titles. Lovers in the Night? Come again? Never heard of it. What in the world is Gaku: Minna no Yama? I certainly don't know that. And what is Sohryuden: Legend of the Dragon Kings?
Don't ask me about Romance anime and manga. Am I supposed to be familiar with A Dark Rabbit Has Seven Lives? Eerie Queerie!, is that even a thing? I have no idea.
I'm not familiar with Shōnen-ai anime and manga. What the shit is Wild Adapter, and what the heck is Marginal Prince? Gorgeous Carat – never heard of it. I'm clueless about that. Il gatto sul G? How should I know? What the hell? What the hell is Mirage of Blaze?
Mystery anime and manga is a mystery to me. And I'm sorry, did you say 'Kamen Tantei', and what is Nazotoki-hime wa Meitantei? Saber Marionette J – I don't know what that is. I haven't the remotest idea. Sexy Voice and Robo – how should I know what that is?
I don't know anything about Adventure anime and manga. Remi, Nobody's Girl – I don't even know where to start. Hero Tales – dunno. Damned if I know.
I'm not well-versed in Drama anime and manga. And I have no clue what Shirahime-Syo: Snow Goddess Tales is.

Shōjo manga is unfamiliar to me. Please don't talk to me about Strobe Edge. What's up with Skip Beat!, and what is the mystery about Otogimoyou Ayanishiki? I have absolutely no idea.
Concerning Hal Film Maker, I am fully ignorant. What's the deal with Someday's Dreamers, and what the hell is Yotsunoha?
And I don't know the first thing about J.C.Staff. I don't have any idea what I Shall Never Return is or what the current state of research is on Dream Eater Merry or whether I should care. What the fuck is Guardian of Darkness? I can't tell you that.
I certainly don't know what people mean by 'Houbunsha manga'. What is 'The Moon and the Sandals' supposed to mean again?
I surely don't know about Yaoi anime and manga. My Only King – what is that? How am I supposed to make sense of Love Mode, and what is Bondz again? Ask someone who knows something. What, in the name of all that is holy, is Hate to Love You, and what's Koi wa Ina Mono Myōna Mono got to do with it?
I've never heard of Manga anthologies. I also couldn't tell you about A Drunken Dream and Other Stories or what on earth Dash! is or what it is all about. I don't know what Truly Kindly is or what the hell Cause of My Teacher is or what people say about it. I haven't the faintest idea. Glass Wings – what's that supposed to mean?
I also haven't kept up on Moto Hagio. A Cruel God Reigns? Doesn't ring a bell. And what is Illusion of Gaia, and what is the idea with Thomas no Shinzō? I haven't the slightest idea.
I'm not hip to Josei manga. What in God's name is IC in a Sunflower, and what on earth is A Capable Man? And what is 'Vassalord' supposed to mean, and what is Happiness Recommended about? No idea.
I'm not conversant with Mag Garden manga. Ghost Hound? Come again? Never heard of it. What about Peacemaker Kurogane, and what is the deal with M3 the dark metal? I don't have any idea.
I know nothing about Funimation Entertainment. Am I supposed to be familiar with Gantz? What the shit is Aesthetica of a Rogue Hero? I certainly don't know.
I'm also completely ignorant of Arms Corporation. Queen's Blade? How should I know? Elfen Lied, is that even a thing? I just don't

know. What the hell is Wanna be the Strongest in the World, and what is Himawari! anyway?

And I couldn't tell you what Media Factory manga are about. The Severing Crime Edge – don't know. Guin Saga – not my field. I have no clue.

I'm also not familiar with Sentai Filmworks. Engaged to the Unidentified – not my area of expertise. I'm certain that I've never heard of Medaka Box or why people are so interested in One Week Friends. Search me.

I don't know anything about Yonkoma. Place to Place – I don't understand that. Bonobono – doesn't ring a bell. Don't ask me. I'm sorry, did you say '4-Koma Nano Ace'?

I'm not well-versed in Romantic comedy anime and manga. I also have no idea what Sumomomo Momomo is or what Otomen is or what to make of it. Don't ask me what Cross Game is. How should I know? Tona-Gura! – I don't know how to begin.

Don't ask me about Viz Media manga. MegaMan NT Warrior – I don't understand this. Sakura Hime: The Legend of Princess Sakura – never heard of it. I just don't know about that. Ogre Slayer – I don't even know where to start.

Superheroes by animated series are unfamiliar to me. X-Men: Evolution – what does that mean? And I don't know the first thing about Spider-Man: The New Animated Series or what the heck Spider-Man and His Amazing Friends is or if it's good to know. I obviously haven't got a clue.

YTV shows are a mystery to me. I don't have any idea what Scooby's All-Star Laff-A-Lympics was or what the deal with The Amazing Live Sea Monkeys was or what to think about it. I have no clue what Adventures of Sonic the Hedgehog is or what Rugrats is about. Couldn't tell you.

Concerning Nicktoons, I am fully ignorant. What in the world is Digimon Adventure?

I've never heard of Fox Kids. I also couldn't tell you about Johnson and Friends or what the mystery about The Adventures of Sam & Max: Freelance Police is or how to make sense of it.

I also don't know about Sam & Max. Ice Station Santa – I don't know what that is.

I obviously don't know what people mean by 'Telltale Games games'. Moai Better Blues – dunno. And what the fuck is Starved for Help? Not a clue.

I also don't know any IOS games. Battleloot Adventure? Doesn't ring a bell. Asphalt 7: Heat – don't know. Come on.

I'm not conversant with Fantasy video games. Castle of Deceit – what's that supposed to mean? Vengeance of Excalibur – not my field. I really haven't the foggiest idea. Kaeru no Tame ni Kane wa Naru – how should I know what that is? I just don't know that. What's up with Exvania?

I'm also not hip to DOS games. ABC Wide World of Sports Boxing – not my area of expertise. Moonstone: A Hard Days Knight – doesn't ring a bell. Doesn't sound remotely familiar. Wordtris – what is that? I haven't the remotest idea. I don't know what Chuck Yeager's Air Combat is or how I'm supposed to know something about Spider-Man and Captain America in Doctor Doom's Revenge.

I'm completely ignorant of Fantasy video games set in the Middle Ages. What is 'Medieval Moves: Deadmund's Quest' supposed to mean again? And what is Dragon's Earth? What the hell? How am I supposed to make sense of Chronicles of the Sword, and what in tarnation is Monstania?

I also haven't kept up on PlayStation 3 games. Ratchet & Clank Collection – I don't understand that. What's the deal with Crystal Defenders, and what the heck was Magic: The Gathering – Tactics? Wouldn't know.

I frankly couldn't tell you what IPod games are about. I have no idea what Chess and Backgammon Classics is or what in tarnation Yahtzee is. And what is Ranch Rush? I have no idea.

I also haven't the foggiest notion what Dice games are about. Three Man? Come again? Never heard of it.

I know nothing about Drinking games. Silent Football – I don't know how to begin. Please don't talk to me about A Keg stand. Ask someone who knows something. What is 'Pub Golf' supposed to mean?

I'm also not well-versed in Pub crawls. Don't ask me what The Twelve Bars of Christmas is. What in God's name is The Tokyo Pub Crawl,

and what is The King Street Run? I'm clueless about that. What about The Brides of March?
And I don't know anything about Public houses in Cambridge. I'm certain that I've never heard of The Champion of the Thames.
Don't ask me about the River Thames. Best Thames Local – I don't even know where to start. I don't have any idea where Regent's Canal or London Docklands is. Couldn't say.
London sub regions are unfamiliar to me. And where the fuck is Outer London? I have never been to Inner London. Damned if I know. Don't ask me where The London Riverside, East End of London or South Bank is!
I'm not familiar with Natural regions of England. I don't know the first thing about The Natural Areas of England. And I have no clue where the Pevensey Levels is. I don't have any idea. Where in the world are The Malvern Hills or Blackdown Hills?
Concerning Geography of England, I am fully ignorant. The Five Boroughs of the Danelaw – never heard of it. I've never heard of The National Street Gazetteer. I surely can't tell you that. The Antonine Itinerary – I don't understand this. I haven't the slightest idea. I don't have any idea what A National Character Area is or what is supposed to be special about British wildwood or if the whole concept makes sense to me.
Habitats are a mystery to me. What the shit is A Habitat, and what is the mystery about A Fossorial? And I have no clue what Mud-puddling is. No idea.
I don't know what people mean by 'Landscape ecology'. Am I supposed to be familiar with Biogeography? Ecological trap – I don't know what that is. I have no clue. Conservation biology – dunno. I just don't know. Foster's rule? Doesn't ring a bell.
I'm completely ignorant of Evolutionary biology. What the hell is a Ring species, and what is The HKA test supposed to be? I'm sorry, did you say 'The Sulcus lunatus', and what is Primordial soup again? I just don't know. Systematics – not my area of expertise.
I'm also not conversant with Biological classification. A Sister group? How should I know?
And I'm not hip to Phylogenetics. The Afroinsectiphilia – what does

that mean? A Zombie taxon, is that even a thing? I haven't the faintest idea. What in the world is Mitochondrial Eve, and what the hell is The Tree of Life Web Project?
And I haven't kept up on African diaspora. British Black music – not my field. 500 Years Later – doesn't ring a bell. I have absolutely no idea. The African Atlantis – what's that supposed to mean?
I couldn't tell you what Documentary films about slavery in the United States are about. What's up with Goodbye Uncle Tom?
I know nothing about Films about race and ethnicity. What the fuck is Catfish in Black Bean Sauce, and what is the idea with Gangs of New York? What is 'Cauchemar Blanc' supposed to mean again, and what's Halls of Anger got to do with it? I haven't got a clue. I definitely couldn't tell you about Multi-Facial.
And I'm not well-versed in United Artists films. The Admiral Was a Lady – what is that? The Second Woman – how should I know what that is? Couldn't tell you. How am I supposed to make sense of One Rainy Afternoon?
I don't know anything about Film remakes. I don't know what They Made Me a Criminal is or what on earth a Remake is. Easy to Wed – I don't know how to begin. Not a clue. What is Once Upon a Crime?
I also haven't the foggiest notion what Warner Bros. films are about. What's the deal with Mr. Troop Mom, and what on earth is Gremlins? Please don't talk to me about The Left Handed Gun. I just don't know about that. Don't ask me what The Girl He Left Behind is. Search me. What in God's name is The NeverEnding Story III?
Biographical films are unfamiliar to me. I'm certain that I've never heard of The Flying Irishman or what the hell Prairie Giant is or what it actually means.
Don't ask me about Films directed by John N. Smith. I have no idea what The Boys of St. Vincent is or what the hell it has to do with Train of Dreams or if it's worth knowing. What about The Englishman's Boy? I frankly just don't know that.
And I don't know any Governor General's Award winning novels. What, in the name of all that is holy, is The Underpainter, and what is Lives of the Saints anyway?
I also don't know about Novels by Jane Urquhart. What the shit is The

Stone Carvers?
And I'm not familiar with World War I novels. What the hell is The Good Soldier Švejk?
Concerning 20th-century Czech novels, I am fully ignorant. What is 'Too Loud a Solitude' supposed to mean, and what is The Farewell Waltz about? I Served the King of England? How should I know? Don't ask me. Am I supposed to be familiar with The Book of Laughter and Forgetting?
Czech novels are a mystery to me. Lekce tvůrčího psaní, is that even a thing?
And I don't know what people mean by 'Chunichi Dragons players'. Are Ken Kadokura, Yusuke Torigoe or Hitoshi Taneda famous or something?
I've never heard of Yomiuri Giants players. Tatsuya Ozeki, Tomoya Inzen or Lee Seung-yeop – who are they?
I'm not hip to Nippon Professional Baseball Rookie of the Year Award winners. Who is this Hiromichi Ishige or Kazuyoshi Tatsunami guy?
I'm also not conversant with Managers of baseball teams in Japan. And I don't have any idea who Yoshio Anabuki, Tsutomu Wakamatsu, Akihiko Ohya or Shingo Takatsu is.
I don't know the first thing about Sinon Bulls players. I don't know who Hsieh Chia-hsien, Wen-bin Chen, Chang Tai-shan or Chang Wen-Chung is.
I frankly couldn't tell you what People from Taitung County are about. Sung-Wei Tseng – who is that?
I'm also completely ignorant of Arizona League Indians players. I have no idea who Juan Salas or Danny Salazar is.
I'm not well-versed in Tampa Bay Devil Rays players. Who the shit is Terrell Wade? Who is Seth McClung or Travis Lee? I frankly haven't the remotest idea.
I also don't know anything about Milwaukee Brewers players. Do I need to know who Jorge Fábregas, Dave Pember, Liván Hernández, Takahito Nomura or Todd Coffey is?
And I haven't the foggiest notion what Cuban defectors are about. Who on earth is Dayán Viciedo, Yordany Álvarez or Adeiny Hechavarria?

Dunedin Blue Jays players are unfamiliar to me. Who the fuck is Corey Patterson, Casey Blake or Austin Bibens-Dirkx?
I know nothing about Nashville Sounds players. Am I supposed to know Mark Corey, Eugenio Vélez, Ray Durham or Armando Ríos? Don't ask me about Major League Baseball right fielders. Is John Peltz famous or something? I also have no clue who Chris Sexton or Lance Berkman is. Doesn't sound remotely familiar.
I haven't kept up on Miami RedHawks baseball players. I've never heard of a person called Rick Rembielak or Ty Neal.
Kent State University alumni are a mystery to me. James P. McCarthy, Wayne Alan Harold or Michael Greyeyes – doesn't ring a bell.
I'm not familiar with United States Air Force generals. Who is this Kenneth S. Wilsbach guy? Are Charles J. Adams or I. G. Brown famous or something? Wouldn't know.
I also don't know any People from Los Angeles, California. And I don't have any idea who Rick Carter, Amalia Marquez, Lawrence Tanter or Slimkid3 is.
I also don't know what people mean by 'People from San Juan, Puerto Rico'. Federico A. Cordero – who was that? I don't know who Jesús R. Castro, Kristina Brandi or Ricardo Álvarez-Rivón is. I have no idea.
Concerning Puerto Rican comics artists, I am fully ignorant. I also have no idea who Ruben Moreira was. Who the shit is John Rivas or José Vega Santana? Ask someone who knows something.
And I'm not hip to Puerto Rican comedians. What's up with Awilda Carbia? Who is Sonya Cortés, Luis Antonio Rivera, Otilio Warrington or René Monclova? I'm clueless about that.
I'm also not conversant with Puerto Rican male actors. Amaury Nolasco or Bruce Gray – who are they?
I don't know the first thing about American emigrants to Canada. And I don't know anything about Erika Brown.
I've never heard of People from Oakville, Ontario. And who on earth is Shan Virk?
I couldn't tell you what Punjabi people are about. Am I supposed to know Fazal Ilahi Chaudhry? Who the fuck is Amrik Singh Dhillon, Vivek Vaswani or Mishal Husain? Damned if I know.
And I don't know about First Pakistani Cabinet. I have no clue who

Liaquat Ali Khan was. I've also never heard of a person called Abdur Rab Nishtar. How should I know?

I'm not well-versed in People of the Balochistan conflict. And do I need to know who Balach Marri or Tikka Khan was?

I haven't the foggiest notion what Indian people of World War II are about. Yahya Khan – doesn't ring a bell. Who the hell is Karamjeet Singh Judge, Abdul Hafiz VC or Namdeo Jadav? I really haven't the foggiest idea.

Don't ask me about British military personnel of World War II. Who is this Bunny Allen guy? And I don't know who Alan Clare or John Christopher Smuts is. Come on.

I'm completely ignorant of Alumni of University College, Oxford. Are Samuel Baines, Shiva Naipaul, Geoffrey Tyler, Andrew Edis or Jacob Pleydell-Bouverie, 2nd Earl of Radnor famous or something?

Members of the Parliament of Great Britain for English constituencies are a mystery to me. I have no idea who Sir Philip Hales, 5th Baronet is. Who the shit is Thomas Lyttelton, 2nd Baron Lyttelton? I haven't the slightest idea. Thomas Pelham, 2nd Earl of Chichester, John Spencer, 1st Earl Spencer or John Campbell, 5th Duke of Argyll – who are they?

I'm not familiar with Spencer-Churchill family. Do people even go to Blenheim Palace? What's up with John Churchill, 1st Duke of Marlborough? I have no clue. Who is Lady Diana Beauclerk?

I surely know nothing about People from Old Windsor. Herne the Hunter – I don't even know where to start. And who on earth is Prince Andrew, Duke of York or Princess Eugenie of York? What the hell?

I haven't kept up on People educated at St George's School, Windsor Castle. I certainly don't have any idea who John David Morley, Michael Chance, Walford Davies, Lady Louise Windsor or Francis Grier is.

I don't know what people mean by 'People from Frimley'. Who the fuck is Suresh Guptara or Ben Clucas?

I also don't know any V8 Supercar drivers. I've never heard of a person called David Brabham or Andre Heimgartner.

I'm not hip to American Le Mans Series drivers. I have no clue who

Nick Tandy, Phil Andrews or Jamie Davies is.
I don't know the first thing about People educated at Sharnbrook Upper School. Is Sean Longden famous or something?
I definitely don't know anything about British writers. And who the hell is Gak Jonze or Mike Tomkies?
British biographers are unfamiliar to me. Who is this Jean Overton Fuller or Godfrey Elton, 1st Baron Elton guy?
I certainly couldn't tell you what Alumni of Balliol College, Oxford is about. Charles Carmichael Lacaita, Charles Savile Roundell or James William Cleland – doesn't ring a bell.
I've never heard of Members of the United Kingdom Parliament for Scottish constituencies. Do I need to know who Emrys Hughes is?
I don't know about Welsh conscientious objectors. I also don't know who Islwyn Ffowc Elis is.
Concerning Alumni of Aberystwyth University, I am fully ignorant. Am I supposed to know Siôn Aled Owen?
And I haven't the foggiest notion what Welsh politicians are about. Who the shit is Merlyn Rees? Edmund Mills Hann – who was that? Couldn't say. Are Hywel Francis or Janice Gregory famous or something?
I'm not conversant with Alumni of Swansea University. Who is Alan Cox, Alan Davison, Nicky Wire, Carol V. Robinson or Urien Wiliam?
I'm also not well-versed in Welsh songwriters. Who on earth was Ronald Cass?
Welsh dramatists and playwrights are a mystery to me. What's up with Leslie Bonnet? Mike Tucker or Alun Owen – who are they? I don't have any idea.
Don't ask me about People educated at Watford Grammar School for Boys. I don't have any idea who Gerald Moore or Simon Talbot is.
I know nothing about English classical pianists. I have no idea who Kaikhosru Shapurji Sorabji is.
I also haven't kept up on 20th-century classical composers. Is Steve Willaert famous or something?
I'm not familiar with Belgian musicians. I also don't know anything about Fabrice Lig, Jean-Marc Lederman, Danny Devos, Pascal Gabriel or Didier François.

I don't know any Belgian artists. And who the hell is Sophie Podolski? Who is this Jan Cockx, Wim Delvoye or Stephen Shank guy? I have absolutely no idea.
I'm also not hip to Belgian writers. I've never heard of a person called Marie Nizet. Do I need to know who Moïse Rahmani is? I can't tell you that. I have no clue who Jacques Danois, Edmond Picard or Robert Goffin was.
I don't know the first thing about Belgian lawyers. Am I supposed to know Paul Hoornaert?
Belgian fascists are unfamiliar to me. And who the shit is Victor Matthys? Georges Delfanne, José Streel, Reimond Tollenaere or Jef van de Wiele – doesn't ring a bell. I haven't got a clue.
I've never heard of Executed French collaborators with Nazi Germany. Who the fuck is Paul Ferdonnet?
I also couldn't tell you what People executed by France by firing squad are about. Who on earth was Joseph Darnand? Mata Hari – who was that? I just don't know. Who is Marcel Bucard or Bolo Pasha?
I don't know about French fascists. I don't have any idea who Henry Charbonneau is.
Concerning People from Deux-Sèvres, I am fully ignorant. Marie-Monique Robin or Joseph Louis Anne Avenol – who are they?
And I'm completely ignorant of University of Strasbourg alumni. I also have no idea who Charles Edward Moldenke is. Are Otto Fritz Meyerhof or Hrachia Adjarian famous or something? No idea.
I don't know what people mean by 'German Jews who emigrated to the United States to escape Nazism'. I also don't know who Emmy Noether was. What's up with Kurt Goldstein? I just don't know about that. I don't know anything about Aryeh Neier, Felix Wolfes or Paul Frankl.
I haven't the foggiest notion what Women mathematicians are about. Who the hell is Sophie Germain? Erica Flapan? Come again? Never heard of it. Couldn't tell you.
And I'm not conversant with University of Wisconsin–Madison alumni. I'm sorry, did you say 'Gordon R. Bradley'? Who is this Tony Evers guy? Search me.
I'm not well-versed in People from Winnebago County, Wisconsin.

Do I need to know who John A. Fridd, Walter G. Hollander, Harold Medberry Bemis or Pierce A. Morrissey was?
People from Oshkosh, Wisconsin are a mystery to me. Am I supposed to know Philetus Sawyer, Floyd E. Shurbert or Christian Sarau?
I haven't kept up on Members of the United States House of Representatives from Wisconsin. I've also never heard of a person called the Herman L. Humphrey. And who the shit is George Washington Blanchard, Charles Hawks, Jr., Charles Billinghurst or Ezra Wheeler? I haven't the remotest idea.
Don't ask me about New York lawyers. Steven Pagones, Anthony Brindisi, Rosalyn Richter or Godfrey P. Schmidt – doesn't ring a bell.
I'm not familiar with People from the Bronx. Who on earth was Art Donovan? I have no clue who Hell Rell, Annie Korzen, Sadat X or Robert Gossett is. I just don't know.
I'm also not hip to Notre Dame Fighting Irish football players. Who is Jonas Gray or Armando Allen?
And I don't know the first thing about Detroit Country Day School alumni. I also don't have any idea who Kenny Demens or Betsy Thomas is.
And I don't know any American writers. Who the fuck is Bryan Mark Rigg, Michelle Herman, Lorrie Moore or Mark Zaslove?
I've never heard of American women academics. I have no idea who Sue de Beer, Adriana Cavarero, Johanna Brenner, Vera Schwarcz or Linda P. Fried is.
I know nothing about University of Padua alumni. Is Jan Brożek famous or something? I don't know who Richard Mead was. I definitely just don't know that.
Concerning Rectors of the Jagiellonian University, I am fully ignorant. Who the hell is Napoleon Cybulski?
Polish biologists are unfamiliar to me. Are Ludwik Hirszfeld, Ludwik Fleck or Jędrzej Śniadecki famous or something?
I also don't know about Warsaw Ghetto inmates. Who is this Józef Celmajster, Mietek Grocher, Marian Neuteich or Ludwik Holcman guy?
I'm completely ignorant of Nazi concentration camp survivors. Do I need to know who Georg Schafer was? What's up with Ephraim

Oshry, Rudolf Sarközi, Anton Vratuša or Peter Gingold? I haven't the faintest idea.

I also don't know anything about Holocaust survivors. Am I supposed to know Yekusiel Yehudah Halberstam? Bronisław Geremek – who was that? Not a clue. Kalman Aron or Stanisław Aronson – doesn't ring a bell.

I don't know what people mean by 'Polish resistance fighters of World War II'. Who the shit is Maria Rutkiewicz?

I frankly couldn't tell you what Polish editors are about. Who on earth was Emil Zegadłowicz? And who is Alfons Mieczysław Chrostowski, Jan Koźmian or Wanda Malecka? I'm clueless about that.

I'm not conversant with 19th-century women writers. And who the fuck is Frances Burney? Elizabeth Bonhôte, Henrietta Keddie or Maria Louise Pool – who are they? Damned if I know.

I haven't kept up on English women poets. I definitely don't have any idea who Alice Oswald is.

And I'm not well-versed in 20th-century women writers. I have no idea who Margaret Caroline Anderson was. Who the hell is Livi Michael or Jody Lynn Nye? Don't ask me.

Miami University alumni are a mystery to me. Is Taylor Webster famous or something? I have no clue who John Willock Noble was. Doesn't sound remotely familiar. And who is this Catherine Murphy Urner or Bill Hemmer guy?

I'm also not hip to Fox News Channel. Are Martha MacCallum, Trace Gallagher, Shannon Bream, Carl Cameron or Dagen McDowell famous or something?

I obviously haven't the foggiest notion what Miss America delegates are about. I don't know who Judith McConnell is.

I'm not familiar with People from Pittsburgh, Pennsylvania. And I don't know anything about Andrew Carnegie. Am I supposed to know Cyril John Vogel? Come on. I've never heard of a person called Jennifer Darling, Shawntae Spencer or Murray Chass.

I don't know any J. G. Taylor Spink Award recipients. Charles Dryden – who was that?

Don't ask me about Baseball writers. And who the shit is Rob Neyer? The Baseball Writers' Association of America – I don't understand that. Wouldn't know.

I've never heard of People from Kansas City, Missouri. What's up with Goodman Ace? Do I need to know who Stephen Hunter, Shae Jones, Laura McKenzie or Charles W. Shields is? I haven't the slightest idea.

And I know nothing about United States Army soldiers. Who is Ray Zirkelbach? Edward Joseph Gardner, Cornelius Vanderbilt IV or Leon L. Van Autreve – who are they? I have no clue.

Concerning United States Army officers, I am fully ignorant. Hugh Gregg – doesn't ring a bell.

I'm completely ignorant of Harvard Law School alumni. I don't have any idea who Frederick Francis Mathers was. Who on earth is Joseph L. Rice III, Frederick Simpson Deitrick, Jim Chen or Lawrence E. Kahn? How should I know?

And I don't know what people mean by 'Fulbright Scholars'. Who the fuck is Marc Jampole, Francis J. Ricciardone, Jr. or Craig Arnold? American poets are unfamiliar to me. I have no idea who Leah Lakshmi Piepzna-Samarasinha, Alma Denny or Martha Rhodes is.

And I don't know about American people of Sri Lankan descent. Who is this Bhi Bhiman guy?

And I haven't kept up on American blues singers. I don't know who Robert Cray is. I frankly don't know anything about Chris Gaffney or T-Model Ford. I haven't the foggiest idea.

And I'm not well-versed in Musicians from Eugene, Oregon. Am I supposed to know Don Latarski, Justin Meldal-Johnsen or RJD2? I certainly don't know the first thing about American musicians. Is Harry Rosenthal famous or something? Are Ronn McFarlane or Phillip Officer famous or something? Couldn't say.

I'm also not hip to Irish Jews. Who the hell is June Levine, Ben Briscoe, David Marcus or Stella Steyn?

I'm not conversant with Irish women writers. I have no clue who Alicia LeFanu is.

I definitely haven't the foggiest notion what Irish women poets are about. I've never heard of a person called Mary Eva Kelly. And what is 'Samthann' supposed to mean again? Ask someone who knows something. Who the shit is Nora J Murray, Dora Sigerson Shorter or Ailbhe Ní Ghearbhuigh?

And I couldn't tell you what Irish Gaelic poets are about. I also don't have any idea what Aindrais MacMarcuis is. What's up with Aodh Ollbhar Ó Cárthaigh? I haven't got a clue. Tadhg Mór Ó hUiginn, Máel Íosa Ua Dálaigh or Lathóg of Tír Chonaill – doesn't ring a bell.
Don't ask me about People from County Galway. Seven Sisters of Renvyle – I don't understand this.
I'm also not familiar with Medieval Gaels. Conchobair Ó Maolalaidh – dunno. Áed Ua Ruairc – who is that? I can't tell you that.
Bishops of Clonfert are a mystery to me. Gilla Pátraic Ua hAilchinned or Tomás mac Muircheartaigh Ó Ceallaigh – who are they?
I know nothing about Medieval Irish people. I don't have any idea who William Ó Con Ceanainn is. Who the fuck is Cú Ceanain Ó Con Ceanainn? What the hell? I also have no idea who Brendan, Clement of Ireland or Sunniva was.
I don't know any Norwegian saints. And who is this Thorfinn of Hamar guy? I obviously don't know who Eysteinn Erlendsson or Hallvard Vebjørnsson was. I just don't know about that.
I'm completely ignorant of Norwegian civil wars. Who was Harald Gille or Skule Bårdsson?
Norwegian earls are unfamiliar to me. Knut Haakonsson – don't know. Who on earth was Thorfinn Torf-Einarsson? I have absolutely no idea. And do I need to know who Atli the Slender or Håkon Grjotgardsson is?
I also don't know what people mean by 'Earls of Orkney'. Is Einar Sigurdsson famous or something? Who the hell is The Earl of Orkney? I have no idea. I have no clue who George Hamilton, 1st Earl of Orkney or Jon Haraldsson was.
I've also never heard of History of Orkney. I have no clue what Orcadians are or what The History of Orkney Literature is or whether I should care.
Concerning Ethnic groups in Scotland, I am fully ignorant. Black Scottish people – never heard of it.
And I haven't kept up on Black Scottish people. Ghanaians in the United Kingdom? Doesn't ring a bell. I've also never heard of a person called Arthur Wharton. I haven't the remotest idea.
I'm not familiar with Sportspeople from Oslo. Who is this Ragnvald

Olsen guy? Who on earth is Wollert Nygren, Patrick Thoresen or Amund Skiri? Search me.

I don't know any Norwegian expatriate ice hockey people. Who the hell is Marius Trygg, Geir Hoff, Anders Fredriksen, Ørjan Løvdal or Mats Trygg?

I don't know the first thing about Norwegian ice hockey players. I've never heard of a person called Robert Hestmann, Martin Knold, Jørn Goldstein, Sondre Olden or Morten Johansen.

I definitely don't know what people mean by 'Manglerud Star Ishockey players'. I have no clue who Mats Frøshaug, Scotty Balan or Lars Haugen is.

Canadian ice hockey defencemen are unfamiliar to me. Are John Negrin, Steve Cuddie, Kevin Kimura, Philippe Boucher or Gaston Therrien famous or something?

I've never heard of Kootenay Ice players. Who is Tomáš Plíhal, Jason Jaffray, Brennan Evans or Steve DaSilva?

I'm also completely ignorant of Roanoke Express players. Am I supposed to know Derek Laxdal or Rick Kowalsky?

I'm not hip to Canadian ice hockey right wingers. I also don't know anything about Jean-Marc Routhier.

And I don't know about Quebec Nordiques draft picks. What's up with Milan Hejduk or Tommy Albelin?

Concerning Halifax Citadels players, I am fully ignorant. And who the shit is Everett Sanipass, Mike McKee, Stéphane Fiset or Greg Smyth?

I haven't the foggiest notion what Lowell Lock Monsters players are about. Tyler Moss or Garett Bembridge – who are they?

I'm also not conversant with Las Vegas Wranglers players. And I don't have any idea who Justin Bernhardt, Adam Pardy, Chris St. Croix, Nathan Barrett or Brad Cole is.

And I couldn't tell you what Greenville Road Warriors players are about. Do I need to know who Brayden Irwin, Jeff Caister, Matt Schepke, Igor Gongalsky or Drew Schiestel is?

I haven't kept up on Rochester Americans players. Trent Kaese, Andrew Peters or Jeff LoVecchio – doesn't ring a bell.

Don't ask me about Vancouver Canucks players. I have no idea who Drew MacIntyre, Magnus Arvedson or Alfie Michaud is.

I'm not well-versed in Swedish expatriate sportspeople in Canada. Is Patrik Sundström famous or something?

I also know nothing about Twin sportspeople. Who is this Alexe Gilles guy?

And I don't know any Twin people from the United States. Who the fuck is Myrl Goodwin? The Ghetto Twiinz – what is that? I haven't the faintest idea. Who the hell is Ern Westmore or The Shane Twins? I've never heard of Canadian expatriates in the United States. I also have no clue who Krista Sutton or Gail Kim is.

I'm completely ignorant of Professional wrestlers from Ontario. I don't know anything about John Tolos. I've never heard of a person called Trish Stratus, Traci Brooks or Angelo Mosca. Not a clue.

I obviously don't know the first thing about Ottawa Rough Riders players. What's up with Sean Payton or Mark Moors?

American people of Irish descent are a mystery to me. Who was John Francis Mercer? And who the shit is John Francis Daley, Edward Joseph Renehan, Sr., Dolan Ellis or Francis Rooney? Couldn't tell you.

I'm not familiar with Members of the Maryland House of Delegates. I don't have any idea who Ariana Kelly is.

I'm not hip to Jewish American politicians. Do I need to know who Nathan Straus, Jr. is?

Concerning United States Navy officers, I am fully ignorant. I have no idea who Arthur Murray Preston was.

And I couldn't tell you what American military personnel of World War II are about. Is Rudolph B. Davila famous or something? Am I supposed to know Frank Eliscu? Don't ask me.

I haven't the foggiest notion what American sculptors are about. Dudley Pratt, Arnold Zimmerman or Elbert Weinberg – who are they?

I'm not conversant with Pacific Northwest artists. Duane Pasco – doesn't ring a bell. Who is this Todd Haynes or James Koehnline guy? Damned if I know.

I haven't kept up on Artists from Oregon. I don't know who Christopher Burkett or Chris Johanson is.

I really know nothing about 20th-century American painters. Thomas Blackshear – who is that?

I'm also not well-versed in African-American artists. Who the fuck is

Gordon Parks? And who the hell is Rosie Lee Tompkins, Hughie Lee-Smith, Barbara Brandon-Croft or Daniel Minter? I just don't know. And I don't know what people mean by 'American cartoonists'. I've never heard of a person called John Cullen Murphy. Who on earth is Mark Vallen, Art Nugent, Otto Soglow or Mark Parisi? Doesn't sound remotely familiar.

I don't know any Social realist artists. What in the world is Stevan Dohanos? What's up with Moses Soyer or Byron Randall? Wouldn't know.

American illustrators are unfamiliar to me. I have no clue who Roger Tory Peterson was. Who is Boris Artzybasheff, Tommy Lee Edwards, Jack Kamen or Bascove? I just don't know that.

And I don't know about Presidential Medal of Freedom recipients. Who the shit is Mother Teresa?

I'm completely ignorant of People from West Bengal. And I have no idea who Shyamal Kumar Sen is.

I've never heard of Governors of West Bengal. I also don't know anything about Uma Shankar Dikshit. Am I supposed to know Dharma Vira? Come on. Is Padmaja Naidu famous or something? Cabinet Secretaries of India are a mystery to me. Who is this Zafar Saifullah guy? T. Swaminathan – not my field. Couldn't say. Are Naresh Chandra, B. K. Chaturvedi or Vishnu Sahay famous or something?

Don't ask me about Governors of Assam. Jairamdas Daulatram or Ajai Singh – doesn't ring a bell.

Concerning Members of Constituent Assembly of India, I am fully ignorant. Do I need to know who Purnima Banerjee was? I don't have any idea who Biswanath Das was. Ask someone who knows something. Bhagwantrao Mandloi, Raghu Vira or N. G. Ranga – who are they?

And I couldn't tell you what Bharatiya Jan Sangh politicians are about. I also don't know who Phool Chand Verma, Jagannathrao Joshi, Kidar Nath Sahani or Dinanath Tiwari is.

I certainly haven't the foggiest notion what Bharatiya Janata Party politicians are about. Debaprasad Ghosh – who was that? I've never heard of a person called Balbir Punj, Arjun Munda or Tani Loffa. I

haven't got a clue.
I'm not conversant with Members of Parliament from Odisha. And who on earth is Surendra Lath?
I don't know the first thing about Rajya Sabha members from Odisha. Who the hell is Nilamani Routray? Who is Pyarimohan Mohapatra, Chhatrapal Singh Lodha or Pramila Bohidar? How should I know?
I'm not hip to Indian politicians. Who the shit is Hiteswar Saikia? What's up with Swaran Singh? I haven't the foggiest idea. I have no clue who Kirti Vardhan Singh, Paty Ripple Kyndiah or Karne Prabhakar is.
I haven't kept up on People from Telangana. Am I supposed to know Konda Madhava Reddy? Who the fuck is Siva Reddy, Pocharam Srinivas Reddy or Nerella Venu Madhav? I have no clue.
I'm not well-versed in People from Warangal. And I don't know anything about Pothana or Kaloji Narayana Rao.
The Telangana Rebellion is unfamiliar to me. Who is this Chityala Ailamma guy?
And I know nothing about People from Nalgonda. Do I need to know who Pailla Malla Reddy, Shitab Khan, Burra Narsaiah or Mother Meera is?
I'm not familiar with German people of Indian descent. Indians in Germany – what does that mean? Suraiya Faroqhi – how should I know what that is? I have absolutely no idea. I have no idea who Gujjula Ravindra Reddy, Sujata Bhatt or Rahul Peter Das is.
I don't know what people mean by 'Indian women writers'. Kamla Bhatt, Urvashi Butalia, Aroti Dutt or Sudha Murthy – who are they?
I don't know about Indian people. I don't have any idea who M. Sasikumar is. Mrs Balbir Singh – what's that supposed to mean? What the hell? Is Syed Ahmed Quadri famous or something?
I'm completely ignorant of Hyderabad State. What's the deal with Andhra Mahasabha, and what is the deal with Wanaparthy Samsthanam? I don't know how to get to Purani Haveli, Golkonda or Vikhar Manzil. I just don't know about that.
I also don't know any Visitor attractions in Hyderabad, India. The Muse Art Gallery – I don't know how to begin. What the fuck is Telangana Martyrs Memorial? I just don't know. And I don't know

where Aza Khana-e-Zohra, Hayat Bakshi Mosque or Chowmahalla Palace is.
And don't ask me about Heritage structures in Hyderabad, India. Jubilee Hall, is that even a real place? What in God's name is The Andhra Pradesh High Court? I surely can't tell you that. And what is Armenian cemetery in Hyderabad, India? No idea. Goshamal Baradari – not my area of expertise.
I certainly couldn't tell you what Organisations based in Hyderabad, India are about. What about Andhra Pradesh Tourism Development Corporation, and what the heck is The Hyderabad Metropolitan Development Authority? Please don't talk to me about The Indian Geophysical Union. I have no idea.
I've never heard of Tourism in Andhra Pradesh. I have no idea where Maipadu is.
I'm not conversant with Coastal Andhra. What is Kammanadu? And where is Guntur district or Andhra? Search me.
Indian inscriptions are a mystery to me. Don't ask me what Ashoka's Major Rock Edicts is. Where is The Gangadhar Stone Inscription of Viśvavarman or Sanchi inscription of Candragupta II located? I surely haven't the faintest idea.
Concerning Sanskrit inscriptions, I am fully ignorant. What the hell is A Dharani pillar, and what is the mystery about Stone inscriptions in the Kathmandu Valley? I also don't have any idea where The Gwalior inscription of Mihirakula, Dhaneswar Khera Buddha image inscription or Hāsalpur inscription of Nāgavarman is. I haven't the remotest idea.
And I haven't the foggiest notion what Kathmandu is about. How am I supposed to make sense of Tundikhel, and what is Kathmandu Association of the Deaf supposed to be?
And I'm not hip to Deafness organizations. I have no idea what H.E.A.R. is or what the current state of research is on Association of Late-Deafened Adults or what it is all about. What, in the name of all that is holy, is The National Deaf Children's Society, and what is The Royal Association for Deaf people again? Couldn't tell you. What is 'The Philippine Federation of the Deaf' supposed to mean?
I'm not well-versed in Organizations based in the United States. I couldn't tell you about The National Association to Advance Fat

Acceptance or what the heck The Solid Rock Foundation is. The Institute for American Values – I don't know what that is. Not a clue. I also don't know the first thing about The Fat acceptance movement. The Fat Phobia Scale? How should I know? Headless fatty, is that even a thing? I haven't the slightest idea.
I also don't know anything about Obesity. Samsø Højskole? Come again? Never heard of it. What is 'Nicotinamide phosphoribosyltransferase' supposed to mean again? I'm clueless about that.
I haven't kept up on EC 2.4.2. Am I supposed to be familiar with an Uridine phosphorylase? And I don't have any idea what a Nicotinate phosphoribosyltransferase is or why people are so interested in Glycosyltransferase or what people say about it. I just don't know. I'm sorry, did you say 'a 1,4-beta-D-xylan synthase'?
I'm not familiar with EC 2.4. What in the world are Sialyltransferase? Transferases are unfamiliar to me. I also don't know what Acetylserotonin O-methyltransferase is.
I don't know about Biology of bipolar disorder. Serine/arginine-rich splicing factor 1 – what is that? The Tachykinin receptor 1 – what does that mean? Wouldn't know. What the shit is the DISC1?
I also don't know what people mean by 'Human proteins'. What the fuck is the NDUFV1, and what in tarnation is The 5-HT7 receptor? Sprifermin – I don't understand that. Don't ask me. And I'm certain that I've never heard of N-Myc.
I certainly know nothing about Recombinant proteins. What's up with Factor VIII, and what is the idea with An Insulin analog?
I don't know any Peptide hormones. The Melanocortin – I don't even know where to start. And what about Hepcidin? Couldn't say.
I've also never heard of Blood proteins. Hemopexin – dunno. What is The Albumin? I just don't know that.
I couldn't tell you what Single-pass transmembrane proteins are about. Lysosome-associated membrane glycoprotein – how should I know what that is? What's the deal with The Selectin, and what's Subtilase got to do with it? I don't have any idea.
Lectins are a mystery to me. What, in the name of all that is holy, is CD33, and what the hell is Myelin-associated glycoprotein? What in

God's name is Ficolin, and what on earth are Galectin? How should I know?
And concerning SIGLEC, I am fully ignorant. How am I supposed to make sense of Sialoadhesin?
And don't ask me about Clusters of differentiation. What is 'Interleukin 10 receptor, beta subunit' supposed to mean, and what is the KIR2DL4? I have no clue what RANK is or what the mystery about Basigin is or if it's good to know. I haven't the foggiest idea.
I also haven't the foggiest notion what The Immunoglobulin superfamily is about. Killer-cell immunoglobulin-like receptor – don't know.
I'm not well-versed in Receptors. What the hell is The Insulin receptor, and what is the deal with Receptor potential?
I'm completely ignorant of EC 2.7.10. LYN – I don't understand this. Non-receptor tyrosine kinase? Doesn't ring a bell. I have no clue. CD117? How should I know? Damned if I know. CD135 – doesn't ring a bell.
I'm also not conversant with Tyrosine kinases. Janus kinase? Come again? Never heard of it. C-Met, is that even a thing? What the hell?
I don't know the first thing about Signal transduction. Inositol trisphosphate receptor – what's that supposed to mean? I'm sorry, did you say 'Adenophostin', and what is STAT6 about? I have absolutely no idea. Photoreceptor protein – what is that?
I don't know anything about Proteins. Repulsive guidance molecule – not my field. Troponin – not my area of expertise. I really just don't know.
I also haven't kept up on The Muscular system. Please don't talk to me about the Interfoveolar ligament. And I have no idea what The Iris dilator muscle is or how I'm supposed to know something about Perimysium. I just don't know about that. Am I supposed to be familiar with Spastic Hemiplegia?
I don't know about Disability. Don't ask me what Shared lives is. What is 'a Social construction of schizophrenia' supposed to mean again? I can't tell you that.
I'm not hip to Ageing. And I couldn't tell you about Trying or what Metabolic age is about or what to think about it.

I'm not familiar with Off-Broadway plays. The Hot l Baltimore – I don't know how to begin. What in the world is Edward Albee's At Home at the Zoo? No idea.

I obviously know nothing about Obie Award winning plays. What the fuck is Sister Mary Ignatius Explains It All For You?

Books critical of Christianity are unfamiliar to me. The Closing of the Western Mind – I don't understand that. What about Jack Upland, and what is The World's Sixteen Crucified Saviors anyway? Ask someone who knows something. The Wittenburg Door – I don't know what that is.

I've never heard of Alternative magazines. And what is The Progressive?

And I don't know what people mean by 'Modern liberal American magazines'. I don't know what Washington Monthly is or what the deal with Sojourners is.

Christian magazines are a mystery to me. The Progressive Christian – I don't even know where to start. And what the shit was Good Words? I haven't got a clue. And what is L'Osservatore Romano? I haven't the remotest idea. What's up with Reform magazine?

I really haven't the foggiest notion what The Holy See is about. The Office for the Liturgical Celebrations of the Supreme Pontiff – how should I know what that is?

I'm not well-versed in The Roman Curia. I surely don't have any idea what Congregation of Ceremonies was. And who on earth is Raniero Cantalamessa? Couldn't tell you. I have no clue what The Pontifical Council for Justice and Peace is or what is supposed to be special about Prothonotary or how to make sense of it. Come on. I'm certain that I've never heard of Protonotary apostolic.

Don't ask me about Italian Roman Catholic priests. I don't know who Felice Leonardo is. Who was José Gottardi Cristelli or Cleto Bellucci? I have no idea.

I'm completely ignorant of People from Trentino. Who the hell is Alois Negrelli?

And concerning Italian civil engineers, I am fully ignorant. I have no clue who Taccola is. Filippo Brunelleschi – who is that? I haven't the faintest idea. Are Giorgio Ceragioli, Antonio Signorini or Luigi Giura

famous or something?
I couldn't tell you what Gandhians are about. Who the fuck is Hermann Kallenbach, Renuka Ray or Sarla Behn?
And I don't know any Members of the West Bengal Legislative Assembly. Am I supposed to know Bankim Mukherjee? Do I need to know who Arup Roy, Sukumar Hansda, Ujjal Biswas or Somen Mahapatra is? Not a clue.
I haven't kept up on State cabinet ministers of West Bengal. I also have no idea who Ram Narayan Goswami is.
I'm not conversant with Members of the Rajya Sabha. I've also never heard of a person called Tarini Kanta Roy.
I don't know about Rajya Sabha members from West Bengal. I don't have any idea who Kunal Ghosh is.
I don't know the first thing about All India Trinamool Congress politicians. Ajit Kumar Panja – doesn't ring a bell. Who the shit is Krishna Bose, Sabitri Mitra, Sovandeb Chattopadhyay or Swapan Sadhan Bose? I'm clueless about that.
I don't know anything about West Bengal politicians. Who on earth is Shankudeb Panda or Sheikh Saidul Haque?
I also know nothing about People from Bardhaman district. Maladhar Basu, Saifuddin Choudhury or Rajshekhar Basu – who are they?
I'm not hip to Indian Muslims. Who is this Iftekhar guy? What's up with Niyaz Ahmed? Don't ask me.
I've never heard of Actors in Hindi cinema. And I have no clue who Ayesha Jhulka, Vivek Oberoi or Siddhanth Kapoor is.
Indian film actresses are unfamiliar to me. Who the hell is Raadhika Sarathkumar, Komal Sharma, Vaishnavi Mahant or Padma Khanna?
I haven't the foggiest notion what Indian female models are about. Preeti Mankotia – who is that?
And I'm not familiar with Femina Miss India winners. I don't know who Manasvi Mamgai or Sonu Walia is.
I'm not well-versed in People from New Delhi. Am I supposed to know Rajesh Pratap Singh, Machendranathan, Sunil Khilnani, Vivek Kundra or Dilip Mehta?
I'm completely ignorant of Indian emigrants to Canada. Do I need to know who Rajvinder Kaur Gill was? Who the fuck is Zarin Mehta,

Arun Garg or Kim Jagtiani? Doesn't sound remotely familiar.
And I don't know what people mean by 'Canadian people of Indian descent'. Are Nilesh Patel, Jeet Aulakh, Shree Ghatage or Ashwin Sood famous or something?
People from Toronto are a mystery to me. Is Paul Chafe famous or something?
I also couldn't tell you what Canadian science fiction writers are about. Who is Marie Jakober?
And concerning Women science fiction and fantasy writers, I am fully ignorant. I've never heard of a person called Katharine Kerr. Who the shit is Diana Wynne Jones? I just don't know.
And I haven't kept up on British writers of young adult literature.
I don't have any idea who Tabitha Suzuma, Malcolm Rose or Steve Voake is.
I also don't know any English fantasy writers. And I have no idea who Anne Perry, Steven Pirie or Sam Enthoven is.
Don't ask me about Converts to Mormonism. Who is this Yanagida Toshiko guy? What's up with Reynolds Cahoon? I don't have any idea. I don't know anything about Hartman Rector, Jr. or Kenneth Hutchins.
I don't know the first thing about 20th-century Mormon missionaries. Joseph Fielding Smith, Mark Evans Austad, Paul L. Anderson, LeGrand Richards or Edward L. Clissold – who are they?
I really don't know about People from Farmington, Utah. Who the hell is Daniel Summerhays? I don't know who Robert L. Rice or Annette Richardson Dinwoodey was. I just don't know that.
I know nothing about American philanthropists. Henry Taub – who is that? Who on earth is Elihu Burritt? Search me. Am I supposed to know Jessie Ball duPont, Jack Kent Cooke or Mabel Thorp Boardman? I've never heard of The Du Pont family. Lydia Chichester du Pont – doesn't ring a bell. Who the fuck is Samuel Francis Du Pont or Lammot du Pont I? I have no clue.
I also haven't the foggiest notion what History of the Gulf of California is about. What, in the name of all that is holy, was USS Hillsborough County LST-827, and what the heck was The Third Battle of Topolobampo?

I'm not conversant with United States Navy Florida-related ships. What in God's name is USS Milton Lewis DE-772?
Cancelled ships of the United States Navy are unfamiliar to me. USNS Benjamin Isherwood T-AO-191 – what does that mean? USS Garlopa SS-358? Doesn't ring a bell. Wouldn't know. USS Turbot SS-427 – dunno.
I'm not hip to Henry J. Kaiser-class oilers. How am I supposed to make sense of USNS John Ericsson T-AO-194?
I'm completely ignorant of Cold War auxiliary ships of the United States. And what the hell was USS Vesuvius AE-15, and what was USS Vanadis AKA-49 again?
And I'm not familiar with Korean War auxiliary ships of the United States. USS Mispillion AO-105? Come again? Never heard of it.
And I'm not well-versed in Ashtabula-class oilers. USS Navasota AO-106 – not my field. USS Passumpsic AO-107 – what's that supposed to mean? I haven't the foggiest idea. USS Pawcatuck AO-108 – not my area of expertise. Couldn't say. USS Canisteo AO-99 – never heard of it. USS Caloosahatchee AO-98? How should I know?
Ships built in Sparrows Point, Maryland are a mystery to me. What's the deal with USS Palawan ARG-10, and what was USS George F. Elliott AP-105 supposed to be?
I haven't kept up on Troop ships. I have no idea what SS Haverford is or what the hell TS Pretoria was or if the whole concept makes sense to me.
I also don't know any Ships built in Hamburg. SM U-126 – I don't understand this. I'm sorry, did you say 'German submarine U-539', and what was the mystery about USS Lejeune AP-74? I haven't the slightest idea. What was 'SM UC-99' supposed to mean?
I don't know what people mean by 'World War II auxiliary ships of the United States'. Am I supposed to be familiar with USS Hamul AD-20? USS Appling APA-58 – what is that? What the hell? Please don't talk to me about USS Conasauga AOG-15.
And I don't know anything about Tenders of the United States Navy. What in the world was USS Yosemite AD-19, and what in tarnation was USS Frontier AD-25? What was 'USS Vixen PY-4' supposed to mean again? I just don't know.

Concerning Dispatch boats of the United States Navy, I am fully ignorant. What the fuck was The USS Tickler, and what's USS Lyndonia SP-734 got to do with it?

I also don't know about United States Navy Pennsylvania-related ships. And don't ask me what USS William R. Rush DE-288 was. What the shit was USS Carpellotti APD-136? I have absolutely no idea.

I couldn't tell you what Crosley-class high speed transports are about. USS Knudson APD-101, is that even a thing? USS Arthur L. Bristol APD-97 – how should I know what that is? How should I know?

And don't ask me about World War II amphibious warfare vessels of the United States. What's up with USS LST-984, and what the hell was USS Troilus AKA-46? USS Mount McKinley AGC-7 – I don't understand that. I just don't know about that. USS LST-70 – don't know. No idea. What was USS Goldcrest AMCU-24?

I haven't the foggiest notion what LST-542-class tank landing ships are about. USS LST-874 – I don't know what that is. I also don't have any idea what USS King County LST-857 was or what the hell it has to do with USS Chittenden County LST-561. I haven't the remotest idea. And I don't know what USS LST-896 was or what in tarnation USS LST-991 was.

And I know nothing about Korean War amphibious warfare vessels of the United States. USS La Moure County LST-883 – I don't even know where to start. What in God's name was The USS Hampden County LST-803, and what was the idea with USNS Harris County T-LST-822? Ask someone who knows something.

I surely don't know the first thing about Ships sunk as targets. What about USS Caron DD-970, and what on earth is ARA Bahía Buen Suceso?

Shipwrecks of the Falklands War are unfamiliar to me. I'm certain that I've never heard of ARA Isla de los Estados or what on earth ARA Narwal was. I couldn't tell you about The ARA General Belgrano. Damned if I know.

I've never heard of Falklands War naval ships of Argentina. The ARA Veinticinco de Mayo V-2 – doesn't ring a bell.

I'm also completely ignorant of Mersey-built ships. What the hell was SS San Flaviano, and what was The SS Alesia? HMS L8 – what does that mean? I haven't got a clue. HMS Spur – not my field. And I'm not familiar with Ocean liners. The MS St. Louis – what's that supposed to mean? SS Bergensfjord? Come again? Never heard of it. Come on. What's the deal with SS Duca d'Aosta, and what was SS Sardinia about? I can't tell you that. RMS Queen Mary? Doesn't ring a bell.

I'm not hip to Passenger ships of Panama. TS Leda? How should I know? SS Yarmouth Castle – I don't know how to begin. Not a clue. I'm sorry, did you say 'MV Discovery'?

I haven't kept up on Ferries of Norway. What is 'MS Thorbjørn' supposed to mean? And what is MV Queen of Chilliwack? I'm clueless about that. How am I supposed to make sense of MS Crown Seaways? Ships built in Croatia are a mystery to me. What in the world is MV Biokovo?

I don't know what people mean by 'Ferries of Croatia'. MV Ancona – what is that? I also have no clue what MF Lastovo is. I have no idea. And I don't know any Ferries of Italy. MV Moby Love – not my area of expertise.

I'm not well-versed in Ships of British Rail. PS Lincoln Castle – never heard of it. The PS Tattershall Castle – I don't understand this. Doesn't sound remotely familiar. I have no idea what PS Ryde is or what the current state of research is on TSS Caledonian Princess. Couldn't tell you. Am I supposed to be familiar with MV Princess Victoria?

And I don't know anything about Buildings and structures in the City of Westminster. Don't ask me what The Albert Memorial is. Where the fuck is The 100 Club, Methodist Central Hall Westminster or Jewel Tower? I don't have any idea.

I couldn't tell you what Music venues in London are about. Can you tell me how to get to The Jazz Café? The Crystal Palace Park Concert Platform – don't know. Search me.

I'm also not conversant with Crystal Palace, London. What, in the name of all that is holy, was Penge Common? Where the hell is Crystal Palace Park? Wouldn't know.

And concerning History of Croydon, I am fully ignorant. What the shit is House of Reeves?

I know nothing about Buildings and structures in Croydon. Shirley

Windmill – I don't know what that is. I don't have any idea what Croydon Mosque is or why people are so interested in Safari Cinema. I obviously don't know that. And I have no clue where Croydon Clocktower or Ashburton Learning Village is.
Don't ask me about Education in Croydon. Croydon College, is that even a thing? What the fuck is Spurgeon's College, and what is Cambridge Tutors College anyway? I certainly haven't the foggiest idea. What's up with John Ruskin College?
I also don't know about Baptist universities and colleges in the United Kingdom. And what in God's name is The Irish Baptist College?
I don't know the first thing about The Baptist Centre. The Association of Baptist Churches in Ireland – how should I know what that is?
I'm completely ignorant of Baptist denominations in the United Kingdom. New Connexion of General Baptists – I don't even know where to start. Please don't talk to me about The Baptist Union of Wales. I certainly haven't the slightest idea. What about The Old Baptist Union?
I've never heard of The English Reformation. What is 'John Bon and Mast Parson' supposed to mean again?
I'm also not familiar with History of Roman Catholicism in England. I don't know what The Vicar Apostolic of the London District was. Is Hugh of Lincoln famous or something? Don't ask me. And I have no clue who Thomas Godden or Humphrey Berisford is.
I haven't kept up on Bishops of Lincoln. Do I need to know who Henry Burghersh or William Wake was?
I also haven't the foggiest notion what People from Blandford Forum are about. Who the shit is Charles Brockway? Who is Henry Richard Farquharson, Kurt Jackson, Thomas Creech or Mary Gordon-Watson? I just don't know.
I'm not hip to 21st-century English painters. I've never heard of a person called Nicola Green, Graham David Smith or John LeKay.
I don't know any LGBT people from England. Who the hell is Keith Vaughan? I have no idea who Michael Dillon, Geoffrey Burridge or Steve New was. I haven't the faintest idea.
Transgender and transsexual musicians are unfamiliar to me. Are Romy Haag, Genesis P-Orridge or Wendy Carlos famous or

something?

I don't know what people mean by 'LGBT musicians from the Netherlands'. I don't have any idea who Johnny Jordaan was. Who on earth is Gordon Heuckeroth? I have no clue.

I also couldn't tell you what Bisexual musicians are about. Who is this Preta Gil guy?

I'm not conversant with Brazilian actresses. Am I supposed to know Bruna Ferraz, Lídia Mattos, Eunice Baía, Marjorie Estiano or Paula Burlamaqui?

Concerning Brazilian female pornographic film actors, I am fully ignorant. Júlia Paes – who is that?

I'm also not well-versed in Brazilian female singers. Who the fuck is Mart'nália, Céu or Lorena Simpson?

I surely don't know anything about English-language singers of Brazil. Conrado Dess, Caetano Veloso or Andrea Libardi – doesn't ring a bell. Don't ask me about Tropicalia guitarists. I have no clue who Gilberto Gil is.

I really don't know about Brazilian agnostics. And I don't know who Erico Verissimo was. Is Luís Fernando Veríssimo famous or something? How should I know?

I'm completely ignorant of English–Portuguese translators. Do I need to know who Graciliano Ramos was? I've also never heard of a person called Álvares de Azevedo. I have absolutely no idea. What's up with Cláudio Botelho, Lia Wyler or Antônio Houaiss?

I don't know the first thing about Brazilian people of Lebanese descent. Who the hell is Raimundo Fagner?

I've never heard of Brazilian songwriters. Who the shit is Itamar Assumpção? Who is Flávio José? I definitely don't know.

Sony BMG artists are a mystery to me. And I couldn't tell you about Little Mix. I don't have any idea who Perlla, Angela Aki or Emily Robison is. I haven't the remotest idea.

I know nothing about Japanese people of American descent. Denny Tamaki or Reika Hashimoto – who are they?

And I'm not familiar with People from Okinawa Prefecture. I also have no idea who Satoko Ishimine, Caroline Lufkin, Anna Makino, Yukie Nakama or Sasa Handa is.

I'm not hip to Japanese women in business. Am I supposed to know Ayumi Hamasaki or Yasuko Nagazumi?
I also haven't the foggiest notion what 21st-century Japanese actresses are about. And who the fuck is Yōko Minamida? Who on earth is Keiko Kishi, Runa Akiyama or Megumi Nakajima? No idea.
And I don't know any Japanese film actresses. Who is this Ineko Arima, Alice Hirose or Masami Nagasawa guy?
And I haven't kept up on Japanese actresses. Miyuu Sawai – doesn't ring a bell.
Japanese voice actresses are unfamiliar to me. Are Ryōko Tanaka, Yuki Kaida, Chigusa Ikeda or Yumi Sudō famous or something?
And concerning People from Shinjuku, Tokyo, I am fully ignorant. I don't know who Izumi Shima is.
I couldn't tell you what Actresses from Tokyo are about. And I don't know anything about Ai Haneda or Risa Coda.
I don't know what people mean by 'Japanese female adult models'. What's up with Yui Tatsumi, Mayu Kotono, Shoko Goto, Rui Sakuragi or Asami Sugiura?
I'm not conversant with Pink film actors. Who the hell is Reiko Ike, Junko Miyashita, Ryoko Watanabe, Jun Miho or Miki Sugimoto?
I'm not well-versed in Japanese television personalities. Do I need to know who Yasushi Akutagawa, Yoshizumi Ishihara or Atsushi Tamura is?
I also don't know the first thing about Tokyo Music School alumni. I have no clue who Rentarō Taki is.
And don't ask me about Japanese classical pianists. Duo Crommelynck – dunno. I've never heard of a person called Akiko Ebi, Minoru Nojima, Masayuki Hirahara or Hiroaki Zakōji. Damned if I know.
I've never heard of Nihon University alumni. Who the shit is Takayuki Ohira? And I don't have any idea who Keiju Kobayashi or Takchiko Bessho was. Ask someone who knows something.
And I don't know about 21st-century Japanese male actors. Who is Seishiro Kato, Tomokazu Miura, Shota Matsuda or Fumio Watanabe?
I'm also not familiar with Male actors from Tokyo. Am I supposed to know Kenichi Endō or Ryo Katsuji?
Japanese television actors are a mystery to me. Kazunari Ninomiya or

Shin Kishida – who are they?
I know nothing about Japanese stage actors. I have no idea who Keiko Aizawa, Mitsuyoshi Shinoda, Minehiro Kinomoto or Nakamura Tomijūrō V is.
I really don't know any People from Tokyo. Who on earth was Kihachirō Kawamoto? Who the fuck is Yukari Yoshihara, Nejiko Suwa, Kumiko Kashiwagi or Akiko Kamei? I can't tell you that.
I haven't the foggiest notion what Anime directors are about. Who is this Tetsurō Amino, Gorō Miyazaki or Junji Nishimura guy?
And I'm not hip to People from Chiba Prefecture. Hishikawa Moronobu – doesn't ring a bell. I certainly don't know who Tsutomu Sakai, Fumio Imamura or Akira Uchiyama is. I haven't got a clue.
I'm completely ignorant of Japanese erotic artists. Who the hell is Pinkman or Go Arisue?
Japanese writers are unfamiliar to me. What's up with Abe Akira?
Concerning People from Fujisawa, Kanagawa, I am fully ignorant. I don't know anything about Masahiko Kumagai or Motohisa Ikeda.
And I couldn't tell you what Kashiwa Reysol players are about. Do I need to know who Masakatsu Sawa is?
And I haven't kept up on People from Ibaraki Prefecture. Shirō Takasu – who was that? Is Hiroshi Yoneyama famous or something? Couldn't say. Who the shit is Masaru Kurotsu or Shun Tono?
I don't know the first thing about Kawasaki Frontale players. I have no clue who Marcus Vinicius de Morais, Satoshi Kukino or Kenji Kikawada is.
I also don't know what people mean by 'Guarani Futebol Clube players'. I've never heard of a person called Carlos César Matheus.
And I'm not conversant with Sports agents. I surely don't know who Dejan Joksimović is. Live Nation Entertainment? Come again? Never heard of it. What the hell? Who is this Kai Johansen guy?
And I'm not well-versed in Cape Town City F.C. players. John Keirs – doesn't ring a bell. Who the hell is Ian St. John or Jóhannes Eðvaldsson? Doesn't sound remotely familiar.
I'm completely ignorant of Motherwell F.C. managers. What's up with Stuart McCall or Eric Black?
I haven't the foggiest notion what Footballers from Leeds are about. I

also don't know anything about Claude Barrett. Who the fuck is David Batty or Colin Whitaker? Search me.
I don't know any Shropshire cricketers. I have no clue who Jonathan Whitney, David Brignull, Mervyn Winfield or John Maunders is.
People from Gainsborough, Lincolnshire are unfamiliar to me. Walter Lax – who was that? I've also never heard of a person called Frederick David Linley Penny, Edgar Cyril Robinson or George Gresham. I have no idea.
I couldn't tell you what English organists are about. Who is Douglas Edward Hopkins?
And I don't know about Alumni of the Royal Academy of Music. Are Adrian Bawtree, Noel Mewton-Wood, Louis Demetrius Alvanis or Roxanna Panufnik famous or something?
Concerning Fellows of the Royal College of Organists, I am fully ignorant. I have no idea who Richard John Maddern-Williams or Albert Edward Wilshire is.
I've never heard of Bards of the Cornish Gorseth. Do I need to know who Nicholas Williams, Tim Saunders, Robert Morton Nance, Donald Rawe or Margaret Steuart Pollard is?
I definitely don't know what people mean by 'Cornish-language writers'. What the hell is William Gwavas? Who the shit is Mick Paynter, Julyan Holmes, Nicholas Boson or William Scawen? Couldn't tell you.
Cornish language is a mystery to me. Am I supposed to know Edward Lhuyd? What's the deal with The Standard Written Form, and what the heck was Mundic? I certainly don't have any idea. What is Cussel an Tavas Kernuak, and what is Cornish literature supposed to be?
Don't ask me about Cornish literature. What is 'Twelveheads Press' supposed to mean? I have never been to The Morrab Library. I haven't the slightest idea. The Cornish National Library? How should I know? And I know nothing about Archives in Cornwall. The Royal Institution of Cornwall – I don't understand that. What in the world is Cornwall Record Office? I just don't know about that.
I don't know the first thing about Cornish culture. How am I supposed to make sense of Cornish cuisine? Do people even go to The Royal Cornwall Museum? Don't ask me. The Wayside Folk Museum –

what's that supposed to mean? I definitely don't know. The Poldark Novels – I don't know how to begin. And I don't know who Brenda Wootton is.

And I'm not hip to Truro. I'm sorry, did you say 'Penair School', and what is the deal with The Hall for Cornwall? Don't ask me where Kenwyn is! Come on. The River Truro? Doesn't ring a bell.

I'm not conversant with Academies in Cornwall. Am I supposed to be familiar with Wadebridge School? Camborne Science and International Academy – not my field. How should I know? I have no clue what Mounts Bay Academy is or what Newquay Tretherras is.

And I'm not well-versed in Secondary schools in Cornwall. Poltair School – not my area of expertise. What, in the name of all that is holy, is Mullion School, and what is Humphry Davy School again? I just don't know that. I have no idea what Redruth School is.

I haven't kept up on Foundation schools in Cornwall. Liskeard School and Community College – don't know.

I'm completely ignorant of Educational institutions with year of establishment missing. Instituto San Vicente de Tagua Tagua – I don't understand this.

And I don't know anything about Schools in Cachapoal Province. Colegio Ena Bellemans Montti, is that even a thing? Don't ask me what Liceo Agrícola El Tambo is. I haven't the foggiest idea. Liceo Ernesto Pinto Lagarrigue – what does that mean? Wouldn't know. What the shit is Villa María College?

Secondary schools in Chile are unfamiliar to me. Liceo San José del Carmen – I don't even know where to start. I'm certain that I've never heard of Complejo Educacional Las Araucarias or what the heck Instituto Cardenal Caro is. I just don't know. And what in God's name is Liceo Mercedes Urzúa Díaz?

I don't know any Schools in Colchagua Province. Liceo Técnico Felisa Clara Tolup Zeiman – how should I know what that is?

And I'm not familiar with Spanish expatriates in Turkey. I don't have any idea who Albert Riera, Jaime Romero or Vicente del Bosque is.

I know nothing about People from Hamburg. I don't have any idea who Heinrich Georg Stahmer is. I don't know what Adolf Philipp is. I certainly can't tell you that. And where in the world is The Anton

Wulff House?
And I'm not well-versed in German musical theatre directors. Who the hell is Rebecca Scheiner?
I've never heard of German opera directors. Who is Peter Stein?
I couldn't tell you what German theatre directors are about. I don't have any idea what Reinhard Linden is. Who is this Bertolt Brecht guy? I haven't the faintest idea. Am I supposed to know Otto Brahm or Moriz Seeler?
I don't know about German screenwriters. What's up with Werner Schroeter? I also don't know who Walter Zerlett-Olfenius or Nesrin Şamdereli is. I haven't the remotest idea.
I'm not conversant with LGBT writers from Germany. I've never heard of a person called Klaus Mann.
Concerning Writers who committed suicide, I am fully ignorant. Who on earth was Jun Sadogawa? And I have no idea who Hector-Jonathan Crémieux or Dhan Gopal Mukerji is. Couldn't say.
I'm also not familiar with University of California, Berkeley alumni. Michael Cadnum or Martin H. Williams – who are they?
I'm also not hip to San Francisco State University alumni. Are Mai Masri, Elizabeth Merrick, Robert Caruso, Michelle Paradise or Dennis Lewis famous or something?
I also haven't the foggiest notion what Actresses from San Diego, California are about. I have no clue who Raquel Welch is.
I also don't know what people mean by 'American people of Bolivian descent'. A Bolivian American – I don't know what that is. Do I need to know who Alejandro Meleán, Ben Mikaelsen or Stephanie Beatriz is? Doesn't sound remotely familiar.
I surely don't know the first thing about Hispanic and Latino American. A Nicaraguan American – what is that? Hispanic and Latino American Muslims – never heard of it. I haven't got a clue. I couldn't tell you about A Paraguayan American or how I'm supposed to know something about Argentine American. Ask someone who knows something. Brazilian American – dunno.
Argentine American is a mystery to me. And I don't know anything about Gerardo L. Munck.
And I haven't kept up on Argentine emigrants to the United States.

I don't have any idea who Pablo Kleinman, Fanne Foxe, Bernardo Huberman or Mildred Couper is.
I don't know any Alumni of the London Business School. Ted Pietka – doesn't ring a bell.
I know nothing about Polish businesspeople. And who the shit is Lew Rywin, Marek Dochnal, Adam Maciejewski or Jan Kulczyk?
Don't ask me about Polish film producers. Who is Arthur Reinhart or Andrzej Miłosz?
I've never heard of Polish cinematographers. Who the fuck is Irving Glassberg? Who the hell is Mirosław Araszewski, Piotr Lenar or Piotr Sobociński? Couldn't tell you.
I also couldn't tell you what People from Kraków are about. Kristine Vetulani-Belfoure – who was that? Am I supposed to know Orest Subtelny? I have no idea. What's up with Catherine Jagiellon?
I'm also not well-versed in The House of Vasa. I don't know who Sigismund III Vasa, Cecilia Månsdotter or John Albert Vasa was.
I'm completely ignorant of Polish monarchs. Who on earth was Stephen Báthory? Bolesław the Forgotten or Siemowit – who are they? What the hell?
I don't know about Polish people of the Livonian campaign of Stephen Báthory. I've never heard of a person called Stanisław Żółkiewski. And I have no clue who Gotthard Kettler was. I'm clueless about that. I also have no idea who Filon Kmita or Bernard Maciejowski is.
Concerning Polish nobility, I am fully ignorant. I don't know anything about Janusz Kiszka. Who is this Aleksander Ostrogski, Eustachy Erazm Sanguszko or Ignacy Krasicki guy? I don't have any idea.
I'm also not familiar with People from Radzyń Podlaski County. Do I need to know who Shmuel Shlomo Leiner, Ignacy Chrzanowski or Zofia Grabczan is?
I'm not hip to Self-Defence of the Republic of Poland politicians. I definitely don't have any idea who Małgorzata Olejnik, Bernard Ptak, Jerzy Żyszkiewicz, Waldemar Starosta or Marzena Paduch is.
I also don't know what people mean by 'Paralympic gold medalists for Poland'. Marcin Awiżeń or Andrzej Zając – doesn't ring a bell.
I obviously haven't the foggiest notion what Sportspeople from Masovian Voivodeship are about. Who the shit is Patryk Wolski?

And I'm not conversant with People from Radom. Who the fuck is Kazimierz Paździor or Saturnin Zawadzki?
Olympic medalists in boxing are a mystery to me. Are Imre Harangi, Uranchimegiin Mönkh-Erdene, Peter Hussing, Andrés Aldama or Josef Schleinkofer famous or something?
German boxers are unfamiliar to me. Who the hell is Dieter Kottysch, Vitali Boot, Manfred Zielonka, Oktay Urkal or Alexander Povernov?
And I don't know the first thing about Heavyweight boxers. Is Dereck Chisora famous or something?
And I don't know any British boxers. Esham Pickering – who is that?
And don't ask me about Super-bantamweight boxers. What's up with Jamie Arthur, Bridgett Riley, Wilfredo Vázquez, Carlos Zárate Serna or Jesus Salud?
I haven't kept up on Featherweight boxers. Am I supposed to know Fidel LaBarba? And I don't know who Harald Hervig or Josh Warrington is. I frankly just don't know about that.
I'm not well-versed in Stanford University alumni. And what is 'Mark A. Johnson' supposed to mean again? Who was Doodles Weaver? I haven't the slightest idea. Who on earth is Mustafa Barghouti, Gary B. Mesibov or Genevieve Bell?
I'm completely ignorant of Suicides by firearm in Los Angeles County, California. I have no clue who David Begelman is. I have no idea who Brian Keith or Hallie D'Amore was. Don't ask me.
I've also never heard of Businesspeople from New York City. And I don't know anything about Abiel Abbot Low. I've never heard of a person called Ralph Lauren, Ben Sprecher, Lil Mama or Mary Callahan Erdoes. Come on.
I couldn't tell you what Baruch College alumni are about. Who is this George Weissman, Jacqueline Leo, Michael J. Freeman or Larry Zicklin guy?
I'm not familiar with People from Rye, New York. I also don't have any idea who Marta Eggerth was. Richard E. Berlin, Sean Haggerty or Frank Durkan – doesn't ring a bell. How should I know?
I really don't know about Worcester IceCats players. And who the fuck is Denis Chalifoux or Daniel Guérard?
I'm not hip to People from LaSalle, Quebec. Do I need to know who

Alvaro Farinacci, Marie-Élaine Thibert, Patrick Labrecque or Patrick Carpentier is?

Concerning Rolex Sports Car Series drivers, I am fully ignorant. And who the shit is Andy Pilgrim?

I know nothing about NASCAR drivers. What the fuck is NASCAR's 50 Greatest Drivers? What's up with Brian Keselowski, Brandon Whitt or Mason Mingus? Wouldn't know.

I also haven't the foggiest notion what Top sports lists are about. The TSN Top 50 CFL Players – I don't understand that.

The Sports Network is a mystery to me. What about RDS2, and what's Canada's Olympic Broadcast Media Consortium got to do with it? What's the deal with The Hockey Theme? Search me.

I don't know the first thing about National Hockey League on television. That's Hockey – not my field. What was 'Breakaway PPV' supposed to mean, and what is the mystery about NHL 2Night? I haven't the foggiest idea.

I'm not conversant with Joint ventures. TriStar Productions? Come again? Never heard of it. What is Beijing Benz, and what is the idea with Virgin Mobile India? Damned if I know. Soueast – what's that supposed to mean? I have no clue. Huawei Symantec – not my area of expertise.

Don't ask me about Daimler AG joint-ventures. I also have no clue what The Egyptian German Automotive Company is or what Automotive Fuel Cell Cooperation is about or what to make of it. Rolls-Royce Power Systems? Doesn't ring a bell. I just don't know that. And what in the world is Denza, and what on earth is Fujian Benz?

Motor vehicle manufacturers of Egypt are unfamiliar to me. General Motors Egypt? How should I know? Please don't talk to me about Manufacturing Commercial Vehicles. I surely can't tell you that. I'm sorry, did you say 'The Ghabbour Group', and what the hell is The Bavarian Auto Group?

I'm not well-versed in Bus manufacturers. Am I supposed to be familiar with Viseon Bus? How am I supposed to make sense of Dongfeng Motor, and what is Solbus? I just don't know. What the hell is Fuji Heavy Industries?

And I don't know any Motor vehicle manufacturers of China. Huanghai Bus – I don't know how to begin. Dongfeng Liuzhou Motor Company – don't know. I just don't know. Lifan Group – I don't understand this. Couldn't say. What the shit is Roewe?

I also don't know what people mean by 'Roewe'. I don't know what The Roewe 950 is.

I don't know anything about Cars of China. The Shuanghuan Noble – what does that mean? The Roewe W5, is that even a thing? Not a clue. What, in the name of all that is holy, is The Great Wall Voleex C50, and what in tarnation is The Hafei Lobo?

I've never heard of Sport utility vehicles. The Isuzu Wizard – I don't even know where to start. And what is 'The UAZ Simbir' supposed to mean again? No idea.

And I haven't kept up on Motor vehicles manufactured in the United States. What in God's name is The Mercury S-55?

I don't know about Convertibles. The Rambler Classic – how should I know what that is? I don't have any idea what The Triumph TR8 is or what is supposed to be special about The Fiat Punto or what it actually means. I surely haven't got a clue. The Monkeemobile – what is that?

I'm not hip to Triumph vehicles. What the fuck was The Triumph 10/20? And what was The Triumph TR5? Ask someone who knows something. I'm certain that I've never heard of The Triumph Fury or what the mystery about The Triumph Renown is.

I couldn't tell you what Sports cars are about. What's up with The Alfa Romeo GTA, and what is The Rossion Q1 about? I also have no idea what AC Ace is or what the hell it has to do with The EAM Nuvolari S1. Doesn't sound remotely familiar. Don't ask me what The Lotus 23 was.

Concerning 24 Hours of Le Mans race cars, I am fully ignorant. The Ferrari F430? Come again? Never heard of it. What about The Porsche 962, and what the heck was The Toyota Celica LB Turbo? Couldn't tell you.

I'm not familiar with Grand tourer racing cars. And what in the world is The Honda HSV-010 GT, and what was the deal with The Nissan R390 GT1?

And I haven't the foggiest notion what Rear-wheel-drive vehicles are about. What is 'The Ford Transit' supposed to mean, and what is The Pontiac Grand Prix supposed to be? I'm sorry, did you say 'The Adler Standard 8', and what's The Packard One-Ten got to do with it? I'm clueless about that. The Holden Caprice – I don't know what that is. I know nothing about Vans. And what is Tata Magic Iris, and what was The RAF-977 anyway? The Mercedes-Benz Citan – I don't understand that. I have no idea. How am I supposed to make sense of Plymouth Voyager?

I'm completely ignorant of Front-wheel-drive vehicles. The Suzuki Fronte 800? How should I know? What the hell was The Panhard Dyna X? I just don't know about that.

I'm also not conversant with Subcompact cars. What the shit is The Great Wall Florid?

And don't ask me about Great Wall Motors vehicles. What's the deal with The Great Wall Haval H6?

All-wheel-drive vehicles are unfamiliar to me. The Cadillac CTS – dunno.

I don't know the first thing about Coupes. The Chevrolet Malibu – what does that mean? The BMW M3 – never heard of it. I haven't the slightest idea.

Rally cars are a mystery to me. The Volkswagen Jetta – not my area of expertise. The Nissan S30 – doesn't ring a bell. I haven't the faintest idea. And what is 'The Škoda Octavia' supposed to mean again, and what was the mystery about The Triumph Dolomite? Don't ask me. What in God's name is The Peugeot 205?

I don't know anything about Hatchbacks. And I have no clue what The Mazda MX-3 is or what in tarnation The Talbot Samba is. Please don't talk to me about The AMC Eagle. I have absolutely no idea.

I'm not well-versed in Station wagons. Am I supposed to be familiar with The Lancia Thema?

And I haven't kept up on Executive cars. What, in the name of all that is holy, is The Nissan Maxima, and what is the idea with the Audi Front?

I don't know what people mean by 'Audi vehicles'. I frankly couldn't tell you about The Audi Sportback concept or what the deal with The Audi Q3 is or whether I should care.

And I don't know about Crossover sport utility vehicles. The Saturn Vue, is that even a thing? What the fuck is The Jeep Patriot? I don't have any idea.

I couldn't tell you what Compact sport utility vehicles are about. The Dacia Duster? Doesn't ring a bell. The Land Rover Freelander – not my field. Search me. The Honda Passport? Come again? Never heard of it. How should I know? The Mazda Tribute – what is that?

I've never heard of Land Rover vehicles. The Range Rover L405 – don't know. The Land Rover DC100 – how should I know what that is? Damned if I know. What in the world is The Long Range Patrol Vehicle?

I'm not hip to Flagship vehicles. The Renault Vel Satis – I don't know how to begin. I surely don't have any idea what The Acura RLX is or what on earth The BMW 7 Series is. I have no clue. What is 'The Lancia Flaminia' supposed to mean?

Concerning Sedans, I am fully ignorant. The Kia K9 – I don't understand this. I have no idea what The Renault Clio is or what the hell The SEAT Córdoba was or what it is all about. I haven't the remotest idea.

I haven't the foggiest notion what Renault vehicles are about. I also don't know what The Renault 5 Turbo is or what the current state of research is on The Renault Captur. The Renault 6 – I don't know what that is. Come on.

I know nothing about Rear mid-engine, rear-wheel-drive vehicles. The Messerschmitt KR200 – I don't even know where to start. The Spyker C8 – what's that supposed to mean? Wouldn't know. I also don't know the first thing about The Ginetta F400 or what the heck The Matra 530 is.

I'm not familiar with Mid-engined automobiles. And what was The Jaguar XJR-17, and what the hell was The Matra Murena?

I obviously don't know any Simca vehicles. What's up with The Simca 8, and what is The Simca 5 again?

I'm not conversant with Premier League managers. Are Carlo Ancelotti, Paul Hart or Ole Gunnar Solskjær famous or something? People from Golborne are a mystery to me. Am I supposed to know Roger Hunt, Jack Rigby, Sam Reay or Fred Else?

Don't ask me about Blackburn Rovers F.C. players. Paul Comstive – who was that? I don't know who Paul McKinnon, Gaël Givet, Maurice Whittle or Edinho Júnior is. I obviously don't know that.
Oldham Athletic A.F.C. players are unfamiliar to me. Who on earth was Roy Warhurst? I have no clue who Aidan Murphy, Lee Hughes or Ronnie Clark is. I just don't know.
Concerning Muangthong United F.C. players, I am fully ignorant. Dimitri Carlos Zozimar, Ronnachai Rangsiyo, Theerawat Pinpradub or Chayanan Pombuppha – doesn't ring a bell.
I also couldn't tell you what People from Roi Et Province are about. Jutatip Maneephan, Jintara Poonlarp, Samson Dutch Boy Gym or Sumanya Purisai – who are they?
I don't know about Olympic cyclists of Thailand. Is Chanpeng Nontasin famous or something?
I'm not hip to Thai female cyclists. Am I supposed to know Supaksorn Nuntana?
I've also never heard of Polish military writers. And I don't know anything about Tadeusz Kutrzeba. I don't know who Edward Rydz-Śmigły was. Doesn't sound remotely familiar. I have no idea who Ignacy Prądzyński, Jan Tyssowski or Kazimierz Siemienowicz is.
Don't ask me about Works about Albert Einstein. I'm certain that I've never heard of Death Is the Only Answer. I have no clue where Einstein on the Beach is. I surely can't tell you that.
I'm not familiar with American biographies. What about Albert Einstein: Creator and Rebel, and what is William Wetmore Story and His Friends again? What is Murder by Family, and what the hell is Some Notes on H. P. Lovecraft? I haven't got a clue.
I'm also completely ignorant of Books about Thomas Jefferson. Don't ask me what Jefferson and His Time is. And what the shit is Thomas Jefferson: Author of America? Couldn't say.
I also couldn't tell you what American history books are about. What is 'Passion for Skiing' supposed to mean, and what is And the Band Played On supposed to be? American Sphinx – I don't understand that. Come on. Commercial Providence? Come again? Never heard of it.
I don't know the first thing about 21st-century history books. Am I

supposed to be familiar with Extra Virginity?
I'm not well-versed in Anti-Catholicism in the United States.
Bob Jones University – I don't know what that is. The New Anti-Catholicism – don't know. I just don't know that. The Know Nothing – how should I know what that is? I really haven't the foggiest idea. Who the fuck is Maria Monk?
I'm also not conversant with American secret societies. What's up with The Daughters of America, and what in tarnation is The Independent Order of Odd Fellows? The Knights and Ladies of Honor – what does that mean? I have no clue. What's the deal with The Council for National Policy?
I'm not hip to the American Revolution. The Sons of Liberty – I don't even know where to start.
I also don't know about Former regions and territories of the United States. The College Lands – what is that? The United States Military Lands – not my field. Couldn't tell you. And I have no idea what Westsylvania was.
Concerning The Vermont State Colleges, I am fully ignorant. The Babcock Nature Preserve – doesn't ring a bell. What in the world is Docendo discimus, and what is the idea with Castleton State College? I haven't the remotest idea. The King's College Tract – I don't know how to begin.
Education in Orleans County, Vermont are a mystery to me. I have no clue what The Community College of Vermont is or what the heck The North Country Supervisory Union is or if it's worth knowing. What, in the name of all that is holy, is Craftsbury Schools, and what is the mystery about The Orleans Central Supervisory Union? How should I know?
And I haven't kept up on Circus schools. Who is this Circus Smirkus guy?
I don't know any Commedia dell'arte. The Clown Conservatory – never heard of it. Who was Flaminio Scala? I have absolutely no idea. I have no idea who Charles Deburau is.
I haven't the foggiest notion what British plays are about. What the fuck is Marry the Girl, and what the heck is Harlequinade? Please don't talk to me about Mountain Language. Search me. What is

'Killing Castro' supposed to mean again?
And I know nothing about Dystopian fiction. The Tower King – not my area of expertise. Give Me Immortality or Give Me Death, is that even a thing? I don't have any idea. The Churchill Play – I don't understand this. Don't ask me. I also couldn't tell you about Cold Lazarus.
I've never heard of Postmodernism. What the hell is A Dystopia? I don't know what people mean by 'The Information Age'. Digitality – dunno. The Age of Interruption? How should I know? What is Information Overload? I don't know.

About this book

An algorithm combs through the universe of online encyclopedia Wikipedia and collects its entries. A text is generated in which a narrator denies knowing anything about any of these entries.

With thanks to Hannes Bajohr and Julia Pelta Feldman for discussions and help with translations.